WITHOUT A TRACE SERIES BOOK TWO

TRACING THE LINE

BY
ALLY BISHOP

©2015 Ally Bishop
This work is licensed under a Creative Commons Attribution Noncommercial-No Derivative Works 3.0 Unported License.

Attribution—You must attribute the work in the manner specified by the author or licensor (but not in any way that suggests that they endorse you or your use of the work).
Noncommercial—You may not use this work for commercial purposes.
No Derivative Works—You may not alter, transform, or build upon this work without written consent from the author and/or publisher.
Inquiries about additional permissions
should be directed to scarlet@scarletrivergroup.com

Cover Design by Ally Bishop

Edited by Patricia D. Eddy
Proofread by Audrey Maddox
This is a work of fiction. Names, characters, places, brands, media, and incidents are either the product of the author's imagination or are used fictitiously. Any resemblance to similarly named places or to persons living or deceased is unintentional.
Author's note: All characters depicted in sexual acts in this work of fiction are 18 years of age or older.

To Patricia D. Eddy
Many of our conversations start with, "Tell me I'm not crazy."
And she always answers with utmost conviction, "You're not crazy."
Only true friendship can be so blindly assured.
Or else we're both crazy. I'm okay with that too.
Thank you for being my friend.

Want more Without a Trace series & exclusive sneak peeks? Click here for your free novel and to sign up for the latest news, or head over to http://allybishop.com!

CHAPTER ONE

THIS KISS

Love doesn't hurt.

That's what they say. But it's a lie. I promise you, love someone long enough, and they'll destroy your soul.

I should know: with a little sister who's determined to self-destruct any day and an ex who cared more about his own needs than anyone else around him, I'm kind of over the whole "true love" bullshit perpetuated in chick flicks.

But I can't help wishing for something more, something that wouldn't require payment with a broken heart and tears. Does such a thing exist? I've no idea as I've yet to find it...and I'm not holding my breath.

"Wait—what am I doing?"

Lux shoves me through the entrance. "You're helping out a friend."

"But you said they're making a movie or something. I thought I was just here to tag along." We're in a lobby with quirky, colorful chairs and framed movie posters on the wall. I've never seen any of these films, however, and I stop our forward momentum and stare at my sister.

"Lux, what is this, exactly?"

Her gray eyes meet mine, looking entirely too innocent—and if you know my sister, she's anything but. "It's a favor for a friend. I had someone else lined up, and she got sick."

"So what am I doing then?" Lux talked me into joining her this morning because she said I'd get to see a live film set, which sounded appealing. It's not like I have many days off to spend with my sister, so I thought this would be a good time to enjoy her company.

I'm starting to have my doubts.

She grabs my shoulders. "Trust me—this will be fun."

But her amused gaze doesn't spark confidence, and I trudge beside her, suspicious. While my sister might like to pretend she's now a staid businesswoman, I know the truth: she used to be a Dominatrix, and her risk-taking side is much more developed than mine. Of course, today we're both clean-faced and in jeans and sneakers, our hair—hers black as night and mine blonde—pulled into ponytails, so no one would guess we both have our business acumen firmly planted in sexy industries. Well, sort of. Lux now runs an online dating site named Kinked, and I own what I like to call a "sensual pleasures" shop, mostly focused on lingerie and bra fittings…but the backroom offers a variety of, well, sex toys.

"Whose friend are we doing this favor for?"

She sighs and adjusts the strap of her pink tank top. "You know how Noah's friends with all these film people now? It's one of his buddy's friends."

"Hold on—we're doing a favor for someone Noah doesn't even know?" Noah is Lux's best friend, and he's an actor. And a business owner, come to think of it.

"Not exactly. I mean, he's met the guy. I think."

We're walking way too fast down a hallway towards something I have way too few details about. "Lux, what are you not telling me?"

She's saved from answering when a young couple, probably in their early twenties, exits a door just ahead of us. They're both smiling, looking at each other the way new lovers do, with flushed cheeks and sparkling eyes.

Before I can make my sister answer my question, she opens the door the two exited and ushers me inside.

It's definitely a film set. There's a screen against one wall around which cameras, poles with lights, and several people cluster. The rest of the room lies in shadow, in which Lux and I are standing.

"Answer my—"

"Lux! How are you?" A tall, thin guy pulls Lux into a hug.

She embraces him back with a huge smile. "Ger! Awesome to see you." When she pulls back, she introduces us. "Ger is the director on this film. Ger, this is my sister Zi, and she's here to fill in for Fiona."

He holds out a hand, his expression weary but cheerful. "Ah, our last victim. I mean, participant." He smiles warmly as we shake, and I'm wildly conscious of how cold my fingers are against his very warm ones. "We weren't sure if we had one more to go—the other party canceled, too."

"You don't need Zi?" Lux asks.

"No, no, we can use her. I'll get Kai to stand in. Let me sound the alarm to get ready."

"Ready for—" My question dies on my lips as he turns away, bellowing at his people to get "set up." I turn to my sister, drawing myself up to my full five-feet-eleven-inches so I can glare down at her. "What am I getting ready for here?"

My tone brooks no excuses, and she lifts a shoulder with a heavy exhale. "They're making a promotional film for a movie series they're doing. It's silly, fun, whimsical, sweet—"

"And what am I doing here, then?"

"You're one of the cast."

If the idea of being filmed wasn't terrifying enough... "Doing what, exactly?"

Lux nibbles her full bottom lip. "Making out with someone."

TRACING THE LINE

"What?" My voice drops an octave.

"It'll be fun, Zizi Baby. It's a series of strangers connecting, kissing a bit, showing who we are at our most intimate." Lux seems to rethink her words. "Hm, okay, maybe that does sound a little scary."

"No, absolutely not." I spin towards the door. "Not going to happen." But there are several people behind us now, doing God only knows what, so it's not like I can run out into the hallway. I feel a heavy hand on my shoulder, and Ger is back, a big smile on his lean face. "Zi, right? We're going to get you into hair and makeup briefly—just a few minutes—and then we'll be ready."

I glare at my sister. "Are you going to explain this to him, or am I?"

Lux takes Ger's arm. "We'll be right over."

Ger laughs and nods. "No problem. Kai's in a meeting so we've got a few minutes."

After Ger walks away, Lux doesn't even give me a second to yell at her. "Look, I know this is weird, and I know this wasn't what you expected. But you've been single for two years now. Not one date...text...anything." She grips my arms, staring into my eyes. "You need to have some fun. Let loose a little. This is safe; these are nice folks, they're doing cool things, and you get to make out with someone for a few minutes without any repercussions. Maybe you'll rediscover your sex drive."

"I have a perfectly fine sex drive, thank you very much." But I can't deny her words. I've worked so much and so hard, and if I'm honest, it's been easier than even contemplating dating. She knows why I haven't stepped toe on the field, and she's probably right: if I'm not thrown into the pool, I might never swim again. That doesn't mean I'm letting her off the hook. "Why didn't you just tell me what this was all about?"

"Because you'd never have come. And you need this, Zi. You need something. God, you're younger than me, yet you act like you're older."

I stick my tongue out at her. "Easy for you to say, Ms. Hottie-with-a-Scottie."

ALLY BISHOP

She grins, any mention of her love Fin MacKenzie turning her cheeks pink with delight. "Very true. And we need to find you your hottie, okay? But first, we have to get you in fighting condition. Today might be a good ice breaker."

I widen my eyes and blow out a breath. "I'm not sure making out with a stranger is going to fix anything."

"Maybe not." She steers me towards a door on the other side of the room. "But it can't hurt."

Here I am, makeup-ed and my hair spritzed and coiffed—the stylist insisted my long locks should be down in soft curls and used a surprisingly small amount of makeup—and I'm standing on "my mark," an "X" of black tape on the floor.

"Just do what comes naturally," Ger says, patting my shoulder. "We're looking for honest reactions."

"Don't I need another party for this?" I ask, my acidic tone a result of my nerves.

Ger chuckles. "You do. He's on his way."

I'm just hoping he's not a stunt double for a hunchback. Lux stands off-camera, chatting with a "grip," or at least, I think that's what the woman's called. A gaffer? I can barely remember my own name at this point.

In order to make me feel more comfortable, Ger introduced me to several of the people standing around in casual wear, some manning cameras and mics, others with clipboards. There aren't that many people—maybe eight, total, but it seems like a lot in this small space.

"Sorry that took so long," echoes a deep voice behind Ger.

"No worries, Kai. Zi, this is our executive producer, Kai Isaac."

I'm not a short woman, but Kai makes me feel tiny. If the man didn't play basketball, coaches somewhere must've drowned in sorrow. His dark hair, wavy, in a rumpled, not-quite-styled look begs to be touched. Like the rest of the crew, he wears jeans and a t-shirt, and he moves with an elegance that belies his casual air. But I'm captured by his gaze. Smoky green and muted amber, with flecks of gold around the center, and when those eyes meet mine, there's a softness that steals my breath.

"Good to meet you," he says with a smile.

His hand feels huge around mine as we shake, and I struggle to find my tongue. "Y-you as well."

"Now that we're all here, we can get started." Ger steps back, leaving Kai and me facing each other. "Remember: we want this to be honest, so try to relax. We're going to roll tape, and you're going to get started when you're ready. And...action."

Suddenly, the room seems too small and too big at the same time. Kai looks down at me, his full lips curved with a small grin. "Are you okay?"

"We're not supposed to talk or something first?" I lick my lips, my mouth dry, and I'm wildly aware that I didn't chew gum after eating breakfast. God, is my breath bad?

"Not really. The goal is to show what happens when strangers lose themselves in another person."

I'm pretty sure I'm already lost. I trail my hand through my hair, nerves fluttering. How am I still upright? He steps closer, reaches for my hands. His touch is gentle, and he draws my palms up to his shoulders. "Pretend we're in a club, and I've gotten up the nerve to ask the most beautiful woman in the room for a dance. You don't know me, but there's something between us." He grins, both charming and teasing. His broad shoulders are hard beneath my fingers, and as his hands rest lightly on my waist, it's impossible not to melt against him, to feel his long, muscled body against mine.

"I don't know how to dance," I whisper, then want to kick myself. With my hormones firing like loose cannons, anything's liable to come out of my mouth.

"I'll teach you." With aching slowness, he lowers his mouth to mine. His lips are soft, curious, and as we explore each other, he tightens his hold around me, his fingers slipping into my hair. He deepens the kiss, his tongue sliding against mine, and he tastes of cinnamon with a hint of coffee. I can barely take a breath as I dissolve against him. His palm grazes my hip, seeking purchase as he presses me closer, and I can feel the hard length of him against my lower stomach. Some part of me is relieved: I'm not the only one getting turned on. A small voice in the back of my mind reminds me that I'm making out with a total stranger, but that doesn't seem to make much impact. Or maybe, that's the point?

Minutes—hell, it could be hours—pass, and we break away, both breathing heavily. I catch a faint whiff of something mildly spicy—aftershave?—mixed with him, and I want more. He holds my face close, his gaze seeking. Satisfied, his lips brush against mine. An invitation, and one I'm more than happy to oblige. This time, I guide our pace, mouths hungry and wanting, my hands exploring the hard planes of his back and shoulders. He answers easily but doesn't push. Instead, I take us deeper, dropping my hand to his ass and pulling him against me. His mouth trails to my neck, searing my skin with kisses and small nips. It's all I can do not to moan. His fingers slide beneath my tank, over the bare skin of my lower back, as his lips blaze a path over my shoulder and collarbone. My knees weaken, and I hold onto him as every nerve ending sparks with pleasure.

I'm ready to explode when he gently pulls back, drawing his hands up to my shoulders. "I'd love to enjoy you even more, but I'm not sure if you'd want that on camera," he says softly. He glances over at Ger, who calls, "Cut!"

Christ, I'd forgotten where we are.

Fabulous.

My skin inflames with embarrassment. "Good point." I force a grin against my stiff cheeks, stepping out of his embrace. "That was fun."

Those unique eyes of his—both green and gold—meet mine, a hint of confusion in their depths. But he masks his bafflement quickly. "It was. Thank you." He nods his head slightly, punctuating his words. Ger sidles up to him, and I use that as an opening to escape.

Lux grabs my hands. "Oh. My. God. That was hot." She smiles. "Who knew my sister had all that sexy Dom in her? Damn."

I'm too shaken by the experience to make jokes. "Can we go?"

She cocks her head, not sure how to take my reaction, probably. "Sure. Let me just say goodbye."

"Fine. I'll wait outside." I nearly run for the door, hoping I remember which way to turn to get to the exit. The bright morning sun offers a beacon, and I leave the building as though someone's chasing me. In the intense heat of my car, the sun beating through the windows, I drop my head in my hands. What on earth did I just do? I shouldn't berate myself: if a customer came into my shop and told me of a similar experience, I'd herald her as liberated and enjoying her sexuality. But it's been so long since I experienced lust and wanting, and some part of me feels wrong for enjoying it. Especially under the circumstances—a public display like that? Even worse, I can't remember his name. Corey? No. Casey? Crap. It had a hard *c* sound. Who makes out with someone and doesn't have something as basic as the person's identity memorized?

Lux joins me minutes later, interrupting my self-flagellation. "You totally floored them in there. I think Kai is still recovering."

That's his name. Kai. His name rolls over my silent tongue, the hard *i* worth savoring. I shake myself. "Good to know. Where to next?"

"What's wrong?"

"I just...I don't want to talk about it."

"No, no. If there's one thing I've learned from Fin, you talk about shit, even when you don't want to. Spill."

I roll my eyes, inwardly cursing her red-haired love, even if he's right. "I'm uncomfortable with what happened. It's...disconcerting, I guess." I stumble through the words, not sure how to describe the heavy weight that's centered on my lungs.

"Okay. I admit, it's definitely outside of your comfort zone.

And you went over and above what they were expecting. I got to see some of the raw video while you were in makeup—most people just kissed for a bit and called it a day. You and Kai... that was something."

Given my sister's previous career and her love of sex clubs, she's seen plenty of sensual public displays. So if she thinks what happened between Kai and me was hot...

"Great. It's worse than I thought."

"Whoa. Where's this coming from?" Lux stares at me, her perfectly arched eyebrows drawn together. "There's nothing wrong with what you did. You had some fun. Blew off some steam. Enjoyed a very yummy makeout session with a delicious man—did you hear his drop-dead sexy voice? That deep timbre? Dear God. It's amazing women don't throw panties at him everywhere he goes."

Despite my angst, I can't help the grin that tugs at my mouth.

"You, dear sister, need to let your hair down more often." She fingers one of my loose curls, tossing it over my shoulder. "You spend too much time worrying about other women's sex lives, and not enough about your own."

I can't argue with her there. "Maybe. But can we talk about something else? Like what we're doing today?"

"Aren't we supposed to be shopping?"

I'm not in the mood. "I have more clothing than any one person should own, and my shoe collection might need its own closet soon. Let's go for a movie instead."

Lux shrugs. "Works for me."

We opt for *Taylor Made*, a new action/romance film starring the hunky megastar Mick Jeffries—whom Lux actually knows, no doubt courtesy of living in New York City. But the darkness of the theater serves only to insulate me with my thoughts. Lux might be right: it has been too long since I dated and had some fun. How can I, though, when something like today nearly paralyzes me with self-recrimination? Despite my confusing emotions, my mind won't stop replaying this morning's kisses...or the heat of Kai's gaze as he looked at me. When

TRACING THE LINE

was the last time I felt that desired? And he definitely wanted more—hadn't he said as much afterwards? Or maybe he was just being a flirt?

Lux drops the popcorn in my lap. "Stop thinking so hard. I can hardly hear the movie," she growls at me in a hushed tone.

I make a face but shove a handful of popcorn in my mouth, trying to re-center my attention on the romantic tension weaving between exploding Greyhounds and racing eighteen-wheelers in front of me.

But my thoughts keep drifting back to golden eyes that sought mine so deeply, I could've gotten lost for hours.

CHAPTER TWO

DEVOTED SISTERS

This morning might have been unexpected. Overwhelming. Perhaps even a bit enlightening. But tonight is hard.

Lux and I both change back at our apartment, going with slightly more elegant attire than jeans and sneakers. I opt for a skirt and decorative tank, while Lux dons skinny jeans and a blouse, finished off with espadrilles.

We're overdressed for our destination, but how do you prepare to see a relative who barely acknowledges your existence? Glancing over at Lux in the passenger seat, I don't wonder what she's feeling. Her bottom lip trapped between her teeth, she texts with intense fervor.

"Hottie Scottie?"

She finishes her message, then looks over. "Of course." She smiles briefly, her expression warming. "I hate being so far apart."

"You could move there—"

"Let's not go there again."

Fin, AKA "Hottie Scottie," attends veterinary school upstate when school's in session and teaches horse rehabilitation seminars all over the country in the summer. While I think he'd love it if she moved in with him, they've both insisted they should wait until he's graduated. While Lux's business is strictly online so she can work from anywhere, moving far away from New York City freaks her out. Currently, she stays in the city most weekends with Noah, and Fin drives down to spend the days with her. Then she lives with me during the week, determined to make up for the ten or so years we didn't see each other.

I'm not complaining—it's been great to reconnect. However, I have a sneaking suspicion she redecorated my second bedroom for herself to ensure I'm not lonely—and the truth is, without her there, I would be. I hate feeling needy, and I hate even more that I might be the reason she's not living upstate with Fin. I have to content myself with her assurances that she's not ready for that relationship milestone.

"Besides, I'll see him midweek. He's taking a few days off to spend the end of the week with me."

I nod, taking a sharp turn to our destination. "Good. You'll be slightly less neurotic when you return."

She smacks my shoulder, chuckling. "Ha, ha. Just wait until you meet Mr. Right. We'll see who's texting like a mad woman." I can feel her gaze heavy on me, though I refuse to look over at her. I tell myself it's because I'm parking the car. "Speaking of, should I get more information on Kai Isaac's availability? You two seemed to, ah, hit it off earlier."

I should have known her hours of silence on this topic wouldn't last for long. I cut the engine before meeting her gaze. "No, dear sister. I'm fine, thank you very much. Hooking up with strangers has never been on my list of fun activities."

While my pointed comment might risk offense with other people, Lux merely giggles. "Oh, Zizi Baby, the things you've missed out on. Besides, Kai's a looker. And did you see the size of his hands? You know what they say..."

I roll my eyes. "Can we not discuss him further, please? We're about to wrangle a very stubborn cat—where's your focus, woman?"

Lux sighs, her expressive gray eyes darkening. "Yeah,

yeah. I guess I'm trying to avoid thinking about it."

"Yeah, well. We're here. Might as well make our best effort."

"You're sure our grandmother won't be here?" Lux hides her nerves well, but I can hear the doubt in her voice.

"Promise. Blue says she's pretty much retired these days." Lux's mission has been to reconnect with me and our little sister Blue, but she's no desire to include our mother and grandmother in her focus. And I can't say I blame her. I'd rather not deal with them either.

Before us sits Deena's, a small diner on the outside of Bakertown that sees mostly truck drivers and country folks. It's not quaint or picturesque. The shiny metal exterior has dulled to flat gray with hints of rust and a solid coating of age. The interior hasn't fared much better. Cracked linoleum and worn booths greet us, and we have our pick at barely four in the afternoon. We choose the spot that looks the least worn and slide in across from each other.

Blue's at the far end of the restaurant, waiting on a table, her bright red hair pulled into a sloppy braid. From the back, she looks as I remember her as a child—small, narrow, breakable. When she turns around and heads for the kitchen, I'm faced with the adult she's become, and despite the knowledge, she still takes my breath away.

"She's beautiful," Lux whispers to me.

Blue is, without question, lovely. But while Lux hasn't seen our little sister since Blue was not quite fifteen, I have. Life—and choices—have created an impenetrable shell around my little sister's soul.

I'm reminded just how hard candy-coated she is when Blue returns from the kitchen and spots us. Her mossy green eyes harden though her expression barely alters. She saunters towards us, a faint, polite grin on her lips. "Just never know who's going to show up when you make Manhattan clam chowder for the soup of the day." She reneges at the last minute and leans in to give me a peck on the cheek.

"Hey, sweetie," I say, squeezing her arm.

Her gaze sweeps over Lux, and while I can't quite judge her reaction, I wouldn't call her happy. "Look what the cat dragged in."

For once, Lux doesn't have a comeback. Her eyes gloss over, and she pushes up from the booth and in surprising affection, pulls Blue into a hug.

My little sister's response is slow, but I find myself choking up a bit when I see her thin arms encircle Lux. They're both a bit teary when they finally pull apart, and Lux whispers something to Blue I can't hear.

"Let me get my other tables set—I'll see if I can sit down for a few minutes." Blue floats away quickly, as though a bit too overcome with emotion.

"That went better than I expected," I comment as Lux swipes at her eyes with a napkin. "It's been...what, almost twelve years since we've all been in the same space?"

She nods, balling up the napkin, then changing her mind and mopping under her eyes a bit more. "At least. I can't believe how grown up she is, you know? I have this image in my head of her when she was little, and I guess...well, I forgot she grew up."

"Sort of. I think she's still just barely five foot, so..."

Lux grins, but another tear escapes. "I feel like such an ass. I can't believe I waited so long to do this."

I shake my head even before she's finished speaking. "Stop. Look, there's...everyone has their time. We can't assume that everyone else's journey is just like ours. You had to work through your own shit, just like I did, and just like Blue does."

She lowers her voice. "You said she's been a little crazy, though. You're sure it's not drugs?"

I join her whispered tones. "Not anymore. But she's always been...a bit wild. Well," I correct with a wry grin, "as long as we're not comparing her to you. You were a different brand of wild." Lux snuck into sex clubs and got her "top" on when we were teenagers. If there was one person who knew who she was, at least in that respect, it was Lux. "Blue's...another story. I can't explain it."

Lux opens her mouth to say something else, but the sister in question arrives, a few plates in her hands. "Here, on the house. Today's soup and sandwich. I can get whatever you want to drink." We both ask for coffee, and Blue pours three mugs and joins us after tugging off her apron.

She slides in beside me, the booth barely making a depression under her tiny body. "What's up?"

Lux stares at her hands for a moment before answering. "I got in touch with Zi a while ago."

"I've heard." Blue says it without malice, but her point is made.

"I know. I was a coward. I wanted to see you, but I..."

I stay quiet and let them work the awkward moment out on their own. While I've never pushed Lux to meet with Blue, I was surprised she waited this long. But then, she's had her own issues to deal with.

"I'm not much of a sister, Blue. And for that, I'm sorry. I got out when I felt I had no choice, but I didn't stop and think how it would affect you and Zi. I mean, I did, sort of. But I thought you'd be okay—that I was the one that caused the problems, and if I left, things would be better."

Here we are, however, years later, still dealing with the fallout of decisions that as children, we had no part in making.

Blue eyes Lux closely, her expression unreadable. Then she lifts a shoulder. "I guess we all make mistakes, right?"

Ever feel like you are damned if you say something, and damned if you don't? That's where I'm stuck. So I take a bite of my sandwich. A long swath of silence envelops us, making me feel a bit claustrophobic.

Conversation trips over itself until Blue and Lux seem confident enough to discuss something other than the weather.

"I don't think I told you this yet, Zi. I manage this place now." Blue's expression doesn't alter, but her cheeks flush a bit.

"Congratulations." I wrap an arm around her shoulders and give her a squeeze.

"Gram's been leaving me in charge of this place, so she finally gave me the keys. It's all mine to improve on."

TRACING THE LINE

"How is Gram?" I ask, more out of concern for Blue's feelings than any real interest.

"She's okay. Her arthritis has gotten bad, so she can't do as much around here."

Deena's Diner is named after our grandmother. While Lux lumps her into the same category as our mother—irresponsible and selfish—I've gotten to know her enough to know that while Lux isn't wrong, Gram isn't quite as poorly behaved as our mother. Of course, I might be splitting hairs. Where our mother always put men and her own interests ahead of her daughters' well-being, Gram put her business ahead of everything else. But then, she'd been single all her life and completely self-reliant. Even while raising our mother, and later, on the rare occasions she had us full-time, she'd continued to have a very successful restaurant. For better or worse, I don't see her in quite the same light as Lux does, but I'm not about to give her a pass either.

"You get to make the choices, eh?" Lux asks.

Blue nods, a fiery strand pulling loose from her braid and falling over her forehead and nose. "Yep. It's a lot more hours, but it's worth it."

"Congratulations, then." Lux smiles warmly at Blue. Too many years have passed for a single meeting to smooth over the discomfort of this reunion, though, and anything involving our family isn't going to give Lux warm-fuzzies.

A bit later, as we depart, something's definitely changed. I pull Blue in for a quick hug. "I'm proud of you," I whisper.

Her gaze meets mine, and for a moment, she's a teenager again, and I've just offered my car for a night out with her friends. "Thank you."

She even gives Lux a quick embrace, and they exchange numbers.

"You know what? I'm sponsoring a fashion show next weekend. Why don't you come? In fact, if you want, you could even model with me," I tease.

Blue shakes her head. "No, that's okay. I'm not into the whole step-step-turn-hand-on-hip thing," she jokes as she imitates a model and flips her hair. "But I'll try to be there if I'm not working."

With a wave, we head to the car.

"That went..." Lux sighs as she drops into the seat.

"It went well," I assure her, plugging the key into the ignition. "Blue's not an easy egg to crack. You have to give her time to warm up."

"I know. And I screwed up. It's not like I can blame her. But that whole thing with the restaurant—she doesn't get that she's being used?"

I hold up a hand. "Hey, it's her lesson. And our grandmother is getting up there, Lux. She's got some health issues. This might be a better situation than it seems."

Lux toys with her purse strap, her fingers following its curve over and over until she finally speaks again. "What happened to her? After I left?"

I wait until we're on the short highway back to my apartment, then choose my words carefully. "You know how things were. And she won't talk about it. I headed to college the next year, and she was left behind. I mean, I saw her often, and it's not like we fell out of touch. But I think she felt...betrayed in some way. As though we moved on with our lives and abandoned her to fend for herself."

She leans back in her seat, stretching a bit. "I guess I'll have to bide my time and draw her out." She turns towards me, her lips drawn into a small smile. "Thanks for not being too hard on me when I showed up at your shop last year. I don't know if I would've had the guts to talk to you if you'd been like Blue."

"Wait, are you saying I'm the easy sister?"

With a chuckle, she answers, "That's exactly what I'm saying."

TRACING THE LINE

CHAPTER THREE

UNEXPECTED VISITORS

By the time Monday rolls around, I'm ready to go back to work. It's not often I take a whole weekend off, and while I know my assistant manager is quite capable of making the store run without me, it's still...well, this place is my baby. When I arrive this morning, I nearly skip in the front door.

White Peony Lingerie and Secrets was my brainchild three years ago when I first left my husband. I wanted something new that was solely mine, so I applied for a business loan and with one investor, opened the doors. Since then, we've been surprisingly successful given how conservative the area tends to be. While the front of my store holds sexy bras, panties, and bedroom attire, the back area offers women an opportunity to browse all sorts of sensual pleasures in a tasteful, feminine environment.

I straighten up the front tables, as while my assistant manager Amie does a great job, she doesn't have a knack for neatening. Not like I do. Of course, then I decide to redo the entire front window display. I'm knee-deep in naked mannequins and lace bustiers when the bell over the door jingles, announcing a visitor.

"I'll be right with you," I call over the partition that divides the window area from the rest of the store.

"There's no rush," a deep male voice responds.

Shit. I know that voice.

Did I mention I don't dress up for work? While I'm hardly a slob, I usually wear jeans and comfy sandals, and while most days I manage to do my makeup, today was a gym day, so I threw on some mascara and headed in.

More importantly, why is *he* in my store? Because unless there's a silhouette running around with Kai Isaac's delicious tone and topping six-foot-seven, that's exactly who's standing on the other side of this dividing screen.

Double shit.

I extricate myself from hooks and ribbons, run a hand through my hair, and straighten my tunic-style t-shirt. Why the hell do I even care? He's just a man.

That I shared a mind-shattering kiss with two days ago.

Inwardly, I groan, but I paste a polite smile on my face before emerging from my hiding place. "Kai, right?" I stick out my hand.

Dear God, he's even more delectable than he'd been on Saturday. His angular jaw has a bit of stubble, and he's wearing well-fitted jeans and a polo advertising his company, Naked Truth Films. His palm sears mine, his fingers resting the tiniest bit too long on my skin. "Good to see you."

My tongue gets lost in the back of my throat. "I...what...are you...c-can I help you?" I'm blushing like a fool. There are days I hate being so pale.

A knowing gleam shines in his eyes, but his smile remains warm and professional. "I'd like to say I was in the area, but that wouldn't be entirely true."

The faint scent of him makes my fingers itch to explore more of his sculpted shoulders, and my entire body flushes with the thought.

I have to get a hold of myself.

He continues, but something tells me he's fully aware of my discomfiture. Could it be my flaming pink skin? "When we were going over the footage from Saturday, Ger mentioned that you own a lingerie store, and I thought I'd stop in and see if you might be interested in carrying our films."

"Your films?" I don't have a clue what movies might have in common with my store, and despite my swarming hormones, something tells me I'm not going to like what he's suggesting.

"Naked Truth Films has produced an erotic series that might appeal to your customers."

A cold weight takes up residence in my stomach. "I'm sorry. I don't carry pornography of any kind." Figures I'd get all touchy-feely with a guy who exploits women. I head towards the sales counter, wanting to put some distance between the much-too-sexy porn-maker and me.

"These aren't pornography, Zi. They're erotic films." He follows me.

I wait until I'm safely behind the counter before turning to face him. "There's a difference?" I settle my gaze on his, determined not to let him affect me. As though it isn't already too late.

"There's a pretty big difference. Pornographic films objectify people, typically women—though there are plenty that do the same to men. The focus is on the sex act itself, boiling it down to pistoning limbs and genitals. Erotic films, on the other hand, encapsulate the romance and sensuality of connection and sexual energy. At least, that's what ours do." He hands me a small brochure.

I have to admit, the images *are* tasteful. At the top of the flier, "True Lust" is written. The "U" and "S" in "lust" are larger than the "L" and "T," so it reads, "True Us." "So what exactly are these films then?"

"We recruit people who are actually fond of each other, whether they are committed partners or simply those who play together. They enjoy sex and often prefer others watching them as they pleasure one another. We don't alter anything—these are real people with all their flaws and fleshy parts. We do add some soft filters and lighting, choose romantic settings, and in general, try to flatter participants. We respect those who come to us and want to take part." His passion bleeds into his descriptions of his work.

"One of my rules when I opened my store was that I will only sell things that I feel honor women and their sexuality. What you're describing sounds wonderful. And I'm sure it is." I spread my hands on the counter, pressing against them to anchor myself. Despite my retail operation, I detest sales...almost as much as turning people down. "But I don't carry any kind of film or video that contains live sex. There are plenty of outlets for people to find that, and I don't want to take any chances on something that could be...less than, I guess. I'm sorry."

He looks at me for a moment, a small smile on his lips. "You don't need to apologize. I can understand your hesitation, and I admire your commitment. What if I leave a sample here with you? Would you review a few short clips and give me your thoughts?" He holds up a hand as I open my mouth to turn him down. "Not for you to carry in your store. But you're someone who's sensitive to others, especially women—I would value your input. If you feel my films are in any way exploitative or inappropriate, I'd like to know."

I lick my lips, taken off guard. "I...um, yes, I guess that's okay."

He slides a DVD envelope across the counter. "And here's my card. Do you have a pen?"

His amber-green eyes find mine, and I swear, my heartbeat resounds in my ears. What the hell is so alluring about this guy? I hand him a pen, and our fingers graze. Sparks race up my arm, and I drop my face to hide my response.

He scrawls numbers on the back of his card. "That's my personal cell. You'll let me know your honest thoughts?"

How did I get talked into this? Oh, right. Gorgeous eyes and an incredible kisser. I scold myself even as my head nods in his direction. "Sure. I'll be in touch."

He grins, pleasure heating his gaze. "Excellent. By the way, Saturday was...something."

Oh. My. God. I may burst into flames between embarrassment and desire. Shit. I stare at my hands and manage a small nod. I don't trust what might come out of my traitorous mouth.

"I look forward to hearing from you, Zi."

I manage a quick glance at him and summon a polite smile. "Have a good day."

Have a good day? Ugh.

He's barely out of the store when I call Lux. "What have you gotten me into?"

Her gale of laughter does nothing to cheer me. "Wow. What happened now?"

With short, clipped sentences, I tell her what just transpired.

"Oo, I think the lady has an admirer."

"You jerk. You know how I feel about porn."

Lux sobers a bit. "Zizi Baby, what he makes isn't strictly porn. In fact, I would argue his work is leagues away. You don't have a problem with people taping themselves having sex, right? That's all his videos are. Exhibitionists who get the chance to spread their sexy. It's not degrading, exploitative, or offensive, I promise. Fin and I have watched a few of them... good times, let me tell you."

I roll my eyes. My sister has an exhibitionist side. You don't succeed at being a Dominatrix because you're shy about sharing sexuality with others. "Regardless, that's not the sort of thing I want in my shop."

She sighs. After a beat, she asks, "Is this really about that? Or does this have to do with the fact that a man you find irresistible might feel the same way?"

I hate it when Lux sees into me so easily. Despite years not communicating, she still reads my mind. "Shut up."

"Do I know you or what?" She cackles. "Seriously, Zi, it's not what you think it is. Give his sample a try. You'll see."

"I think I'll skip."

"But then what excuse will you use to call him?"

I groan. "Um, none. I have no interest in him anyway. Saturday was fun. And yes, he's hot. But the last thing I want is to get involved with someone who makes sex videos, even if they aren't technically 'porn.'"

The door jingles again, signaling my first bra-fitting appointment of the day. "I have to go."

"Yeah, yeah. But you should check out what this guy does before you write him off completely. I think you'll be pleasantly surprised."

"Mm. I'll let you know what I decide." I've already made up my mind, but she'll be easier to live with if she thinks I'm waffling. "Gotta go."

Kai's DVD haunts me all day, despite the fact I've dumped it into my overfilled inbox. Chances of me actually getting to it? Very low. Still, when I finally sit down after locking the front door, it's all I can do not to reach for his business card, which I've tucked into the side pocket of my purse. In fact, perhaps I do...and run my finger over his printed name.

Damn it.

Damn it.

I toss his card on my desk, face down, and check my email. Then I wish I hadn't.

"What's up, Zizi Baby?" Lux answers on the first ring. "I'm in the middle of spreadsheets and number crunching with Noah, so any interruption is a welcome distraction."

Noah guffaws in the background, bringing to mind his easy humor and smile. She's lucky she has someone who partners so closely with her business. Of course, Noah and his sister are investors in Kinked, so it makes sense. Some days, I'm very jealous of her support system. Particularly today.

"I just got an email from my landlord—the guy over at the new place. Apparently my second store expansion made headlines in the papers, and not in a good way. He's getting threatened by locals if he leases to me."

"What?" Her chair creaks loudly, and her footsteps echo across the line. "Threatened over what?"

"I guess because they see my place as a sex shop? I have no idea." I do a quick search online. I've been making plans to open a second store closer to Philadelphia, in a small suburb. While Lothington isn't exactly liberal, it's progressive enough that I hadn't thought there'd be an issue. Bakertown's handled my growing success with surprising equanimity. Sure enough, on Lothington's webpage, a forum exists for community issues, and several threads start with the subject, "White Peony Lingerie and Secrets."

"Oh my...God." I sigh over the words, unable to keep the anguish from my voice. "Lux, it's a mess. There are probably over a hundred comments on here, calling me anything from a whore to Satan's business partner." I scroll through the hateful words, astonished that my business could engender such cruelty. Tears well behind my eyes, but I fight through them. "This is..."

"Don't read them. We'll figure this out. Contact the landlord; let's see how frightened he really is. Any chance he's just warning you of their outrage? Or is he trying to get out of the lease?"

"No, he's concerned but not kicking me out."

"All right then. It's going to be fine." She takes a deep breath, the rhythm of her pacing punctuating her words. "I have no idea how anyone could get this upset over White Peony. You're Victoria's Secret with dildos, for Christ's sake. Not that it matters. Let's get a handle on this. Then we'll move." She sounds much more encouraging than I feel right now. "Don't let this get to you. No more reading. I'll take a look at the website, and we'll plan tonight when you get home. Call me? I wish I'd stayed at your place tonight instead of coming into the city. But Noah had some free time and—"

"You don't have to explain. You're allowed to have a life."

She sighs heavily. "I know. But I hate that you're alone."

I have nothing to say. It's as though I've been punched hard in the stomach, and I'm reeling from the blow. "I'll talk to you in a bit."

After we hang up, I stare at my computer screen, unable to look away from the hurtful things that are being said.

"Stores like this will only perpetuate our rape culture."

"What do we say to our children when this kind of filth is on their bus route?"

TRACING THE LINE

"Only a whore would think something like this is a good idea. We should find out if the owner's also a prostitute, since she charges for sex toys—she probably charges for sex!"

For pages, their vitriol blasts in black and white, and I consume every drop, crawling deeper and deeper inside myself. While I didn't expect a cordial welcome from Lothington—I'm one more business moving into an already tourism-driven town—I hadn't thought I'd find such resistance, either. The whole goal of my store is to give women space to explore their desires and curiosity in a welcoming environment...and instead, White Peony is being treated like a 24-hour "therapeutic massage parlor."

It's hours before I finally go home, broken and exhausted. I don't even call Lux before I fall into bed, lost in a dreamless sleep.

I conned Blue into having dinner with me Wednesday night, largely because she's broke and I cook. Though when she arrived with pecan "cuties"—mini pecan pie tarts—I might have swooned.

"Oh. My. God." Crunchy nuts and caramelized sugar assault my tongue, along with the buttery crust that could be confused with our grandmother's. "You used Gram's recipe, didn't you?"

We're enjoying dessert on my sectional couch, relaxing after a dinner of homemade Pad Thai, a dish we both love.

"Actually, I improved on Gram's recipe. Remember the huge tubs of Crisco she always had?" Blue's delicate nose wrinkles. "My neighbor introduced me to the wonder of real lard."

Her neighbor probably lives on welfare and barely makes ends meet, since Blue insists on renting amidst what we endearingly call Bakertown's "Pseudo-Hood." I've tried to get her to move in here, but she's stubborn.

"I don't want to know. But these are to-die-for. Do you make these for the diner, too?"

She grins. "Nope. Gram still insists on making most of the desserts, though she's letting me do the lemon meringue pie, finally. And I'll be damned if I'll put quality ingredients into desserts she's only charging a buck-ninety-nine for. Fuck that."

Can't blame her there. She's relaxed and open, which is an improvement over her distance on Saturday. I hate to risk breaking the comfortable moment, but I can't help asking. "So what do you think of Lux?"

She narrows those green eyes at me. "Is this why you invited me for dinner?"

"Not at all." I've learned the best way to handle Blue's intensity is to act unaffected. "I haven't had you over in months, and I know you usually bring dessert." I manage to wrangle a slight grin out of her. "But Lux wants to try again as a family, and I don't know how you feel about that."

A familiar mask drops into place, an impenetrable shield I've long wished to circumvent. Whatever harm came to Blue during our formative years—and there was plenty—she wove steel and barbed wire about herself, often creating as much damage as protection.

"She left us."

Three words—an echo to many years before, when she collapsed bleeding on my comforter. *She left us*—the words as clear then as if she'd said them. Maybe she did—her voice drowned out by her white flesh carved with razor blades, her eyes like polished peridot, as I fought to stanch the crimson rivulets leeching from her wounds. She has no memory of the day—we've talked about the evening Lux left, and in her mind, we snuggled down together in my bed and fell asleep.

I don't know why that happens, but Blue accuses her brain of being like Swiss cheese when it comes to remembering her childhood. And in some ways, I can't argue. Because I remember wrestling the metal sliver out of her fingers, nearly slicing my own in the process. Applying pressure against the seeping cuts while she stared out the darkened window as though fascinated by the midnight sky.

"She had to, Blue. You know how things were." We were

sent to a foster home at the ages of ten, eleven, and twelve. We got lucky in that we ended up in the same place together, and we stayed there, though it was more like a prison in some ways. It wasn't that Mama C was a bad person. At her core, she's got a good heart. But having foster kids was her desire, not her husband's, and as a result, the children under her care were treated like outsiders in a place that already felt like a hostile refuge.

Blue stares at her hands, her tiny fingers tipped in black and blue polish. "It never bothered you, did it? Her leaving?"

"Sure it hurt. She's our sister, and we'd never been separated. But Lux got the blame for things that weren't her fault. She couldn't call where we lived home anymore." When our foster father's brother started crashing at their house, no one paid much attention to how he treated us. Lux was the oldest of the six, and he sexually molested her—would have nearly raped her had our foster father not walked in on them. She claims she led him on, and maybe she did, but she was fifteen. She gets a pass, in my opinion. After two years of veiled accusations and a strict curfew—not that she had to return home by nine, but that she couldn't *leave her bedroom* after nine at night so she wouldn't be in the brother's path—she packed and left.

"Ten years with no contact? That's okay with you?"

I'm surprised she's willing to talk about this, so I try to answer quickly lest she change her mind. "She had to figure out what she needed. Just like you and I did. And now she's trying. That's got to count for something, doesn't it?"

A loose shrug is my answer.

"How about those Yankees, eh?" I tease when she stays silent.

Her cheeks burn with anger, and I really wish I'd kept my mouth closed. "I'm not you, Zi. I can't just move on because she's picked this moment to 'reconnect' when it's convenient for her. We needed her. We always said we were a team. And in the end, she looked out only for herself."

I may have had a similar thought in the past, so I can't criticize Blue's logic. "Can we give her a chance? See if there's a shot at maybe understanding her reasons, even if we don't entirely agree with them?"

She meets my gaze, her eyes flat. "We'll see."

Thankfully, I massage the conversation onto safer subjects, like *American Idol* and our favorite *CSI* (Las Vegas) episodes. When she leaves, she's chilly, but I can't tell if she's just being Blue, or if I've given her yet another reason to withdraw from me.

"Love you, Blue Bear."

She turns in the light of my doorway, glancing back at me with vacant eyes. "Ditto."

I can't heal her—she must choose that path. But Blue's had a tough life between addictions, suicide attempts, and learning disabilities that hurt her in school and after. Not to mention, where Lux walled off her heart and survived, and I muddled through the misery to the other side, something in Blue broke as a result of our ravaged and painful childhood. And the pieces have never quite fit back together.

TRACING THE LINE

CHAPTER FOUR

REVEALING REVELATIONS

"Why did I agree to this?" I ask Lux as she picks at the mass of curls piled on top of my head. "All I had to do was contribute some sexy underthings."

"You can't very well say you support women baring their bellies of all sizes and not do the same yourself." She plucks a lock out of my face and pins the curl back.

Honestly, even I have to admit the hairdresser did a pretty amazing job, and Lux used her dark magic with cosmetics to create a soft, sexy look. Of course, none of that makes up for the fact that I'm wearing what could be liberally called a camisole and panties...if being see-through was a social norm. Topped (bottomed?) off with five-inch stilettos that I've spent the last two days trying to walk in, and I'm an accident waiting to happen.

"Just because I encourage other women to be confident in their skin doesn't mean I have to walk around naked. Some of us prefer a bit more coverage," I grouse, my nerves expressing themselves via irritability. Even from here, I can hear the music pumping from the auditorium. We're at the "Real Woman" fashion show, which I'd agreed to sponsor in the form of a few donated outfits. Somehow, I got conned into being a participant as well.

"How do you sell lingerie with this uptight attitude?" She smacks my ass.

I nearly jump out of what little clothing I have on. "Hey! I'm not one of your clients."

She offers an evil grin. "I don't take on clients anymore, love. But you need to get laid. You're way too tight-laced." She curves her hands around my waist and leans up over my shoulder to meet my gaze in the mirror. "You are gorgeous. You have kickass curves that should be seen by the world, and you've worked damn hard to have this amazing tummy."

She's right. Two years ago, I was fifty pounds heavier. An unhappy marriage will do that to you. While I've kept the weight off, as anyone who's ever had significant weight loss will tell you, I feel as though I'm still the same size. I look in the mirror, and I *see* that I'm thinner. But the reality doesn't mesh with my mental image.

"Yeah, yeah. I'm going to do this regardless of how uncomfortable I feel. I'd rather be in sweatpants and a hoodie, however. Stop picking at me," I grumble as she dabs a wet cloth under my eye to clean up God only knows what. "No one's going to be looking at my face anyway."

She ignores my comment and keeps at me until she finally steps back with a critical eye. After several moments of observation, she nods. "Perfect. Time to get you to the stage. You go on—I want to make sure I can get a picture out front."

My stomach bounces around at her words, and I take another quick swallow of water. Why did I do this to myself? Lux kisses my cheek and disappears. Left alone, fears claw at my mind, but I focus on the steady thrum of dance beats that vibrate beneath my feet—hell, just walking in these shoes takes intense concentration. So much so that I walk right into a broad chest.

"Jesus, I'm sorry," I say as I look up...right into familiar green-gold eyes.

"Are you all right?" he asks, his hands reaching out to

steady me as I teeter.

I clutch his forearms, hoping I don't face-plant and make a total ass out of myself. "Yeah, I'm fine. Just these heels—I'm so sorry."

His hands remain on my arms, the warmth of his skin like lava. He gazes down at me, and for a moment, I swear, the world around us goes silent, as though only our heartbeats can be heard. "They do look like they might be difficult to maneuver." When I look at him blankly, he says, "Your shoes?"

"Y-yes, they are." What is it about this guy that gets me all beside myself? "I have to..." I look towards the stage entrance, which is bustling with models and last minute touch-ups.

"Right. Sorry." He steps back, reluctantly releasing my arms. "You look lovely." His gaze remains on my face—two points for that, right?—and he offers me a small smile. "Any chance I might be able to convince you to dance with me later?"

There's a huge after-event planned, complete with alcohol and a band. The idea of being that close to him again... *that* would not be good. "I can't dance," I say, irritated that the words come out like a breathy invitation instead of a firm decline.

His eyes sparkle with challenge. "Ah, that's right. I've been told I'm a pretty good teacher, so maybe we can fix that. Break a leg."

Even though my stomach wars with my esophagus for ownership of my throat, I manage to smile. "Thanks." I head towards the stage-master, hoping to God I get through this without embarrassing myself. Which is worse: passing out on stage, or vomiting on the attendees?

On cue, I step towards the ridiculously bright lights. I try to remember what Lux taught me, swaying my hips as I walk, "punching the air" with my hipbones, and thankfully, the runway blazes with spotlights, so I can't see the crowd anyway. Hell, it's all I can do not to close my eyes against the glare. And I hope Kai got caught on something backstage and isn't sitting out here. Surely I haven't done anything so awful in my life that I'm paying penance now by humiliating myself in front of some guy I *might* have the hots over?

As I tour the edge, counting in my head to the music to get all the beats and turn at the right spots, I'm amazed anew that anyone can do this for a living. After a few more pauses—turn, stare, shift direction, step—I'm finally back to the curtains, and I stumble into Lux's arms.

"You were fabulous! Oh my God—so sexy! And you'll never guess who's in the audience." Lux practically beams with her knowledge.

"Kai Isaac?"

Her smile turns to a pout. "How'd you know?"

"I practically walked on his feet backstage." I sigh and shuck my shoes off, carrying them with me back to the changing area. "He'll be easy to spot later—no doubt he'll be limping."

Lux snorts and pushes me into one of the dressing rooms. "If his inability to look away from the stage while you were sashaying is any indication, I think he'll be limping to your side for a dance."

I ignore her all-too-accurate comment as I slip into my dress for this evening. While I'd rather head home and relax with a glass of wine, as a sponsor I feel obligated to hang out and do the social thing. When I step out from behind the curtain, Lux lets out a long whistle.

"Damn. Kai will be lucky if he can keep his tongue in his mouth." She gives me a once over, then spins me by the shoulder. "You clean up fierce, Zizi Baby."

I roll my eyes, but I do feel good in this dress. It's one of those things you find on a discount rack and take a chance on, then are so glad you did. The deep plum compliments my fair skin, and the sleek material gathers and releases over my curves. Looking in the mirror, I appear sexy, which makes up for the overwhelming feelings of being an imposter—dammit, I should feel desirable, shouldn't I? "We ready?"

We head into the auditorium for the rest of the fashion show, which only lasts for a few minutes. Then Lux and I hustle to the ballroom to grab champagne and stake out our corner for people-watching. The ballroom fills up with attendees, and the mistress of ceremonies says her piece about their goals and desires for the "Real Women" campaign: to make a documentary about how to improve attitudes towards women's bodies and sexuality in our culture, both by examining our history and current trends, and then positing ideas for future change. I recognize the woman speaking, but I can't place why.

"Oh, her? That's Carice Spooning. She was a Victoria's Secret Angel for several years before quitting to start this movement," Lux answers when I ask.

I can't say I'm surprised to hear the woman worked as a model: golden skin, deep chocolate eyes set at a slant in a face that would make angels cry. Not to mention, she's at least my height with curly chestnut hair that spills like a waterfall over her shoulders. While I appreciate everything she's saying, a small part of me can't help the jealousy flaring over her lithe elegance—narrow hips, small breasts, and slim waist. I have to shove down an immediate onslaught of frumpy fear.

"And we owe many thanks to my co-creator who helped make this possible," Carice intones as she looks to the side of the stage. "Fade In Productions founder and a man who's known my heart for so long, Kai Isaac."

My gaze is glued to Kai as he joins her, his arm wrapping around her as though he does so every day. Which, given that he "knows her heart," I'm guessing he does. I can't even look at Lux—her stare weighs heavily on me, but I remain focused on Carice and Kai, who look like a power couple up there. He's saying something about believing in this cause so strongly because he sees the devastation caused by our current trends, blah, blah, blah.

All I can see is how easily Carice leans into him, smiles up at him, and is absolutely in love with him.

Shit.

They leave the stage as another speaker arrives to give a toast or something of the kind. I don't even know. I'm too busy planning my escape.

"I need to get some air," I tell Lux as I brush by her.

TRACING THE LINE

She halts me with a hand on my shoulder. "I'll come with you."

"No. I'm fine. I just need—" I hold my palm up, agitated. "Hell, I don't even know what I need. But I'll be fine."

She's torn, but she relents, and I slip out of her grasp. Thankfully, flat sandals are in fashion, so I can make decent strides to get out of the ballroom, out of this wing of the hotel. I head for the lobby, unsure of my actual destination but determined to end up anywhere but here.

"Zi!"

I startle at my name, but I recognize the voice a bit too late. I've already whipped around, caught a glimpse of Kai nearly jogging to catch up to me. I want to turn and keep walking, but strangely enough, my feet won't obey.

"You're not running out before the party gets started, are you?" he says when he finally reaches me.

"I'm not much of a party girl." I cross my arms, fighting the feelings I have whenever I'm within fifty yards of the man. It would help if he weren't so yummy. But more than that... there's something engaging about him. I can't put my finger on it. "Besides, you'll have a full dance card tonight, anyway."

He cocks his head, eyes narrowed. "I'm sorry?"

"Never mind. It doesn't matter." I glance around the room, hoping for an excuse to get away so I can center my thoughts and emotions. "I need to use the powder room. I'll see you later."

I make a beeline for the restroom and nearly collapse when I lock myself in one of the stalls. When did I turn into a teenager with a painful crush? I don't need to use the facilities, but I take a moment to catch my breath, try to envision peaceful, calm seas, and use the meditation techniques my yoga instructor taught me. Not that they work. My stomach is still doing flip-flops over thoughts of Kai.

When I finally emerge from the ladies' room, he's sitting in one of the chairs in the lobby. I steel myself and head for the ballroom.

"I get the distinct impression you're avoiding me," he says

when he manages to fall in step beside me.

"Really?"

"Zi, wait." He grips my arm lightly.

I shrug him off, but I stop walking. The music's started in the ballroom, some top-forty hit set to a dance beat. I raise my voice to be heard over the thumping. "What do you want?"

He backs up a step, surprise creasing his forehead. "I've upset you," he says after a moment. "Haven't I?"

Biting my lip, I stare at the ceiling, the wall, anything but him, trying to figure out how to respond. "No. I upset myself." I take a breath, then continue. "Last Saturday—it was...I haven't...Shit." I try one more time. "I haven't been with anyone in a while. And last weekend was fun. You're a very charismatic guy, and I enjoyed kissing you. But it's obvious from tonight, you're seeing someone. And I don't know what to make of you asking me to dance, and giving me your cell number...or any of what I feel."

"Whoa, wait. I'm not seeing anyone." His golden eyes meet mine, sincere.

"Really? Because you and Carice seem pretty chummy." Now I wish I'd stuck with heels that would raise me to the same height as him.

He blows out a breath, then gestures to the lobby. "Can we walk? At least get away from what I think is Taylor Swift's latest hit about another cheating boyfriend?"

I chuckle, despite my annoyance. "Sure."

We end up on the other side of the lobby, treading down another wing of the hotel that's deserted. At first, I thought he was waiting until we had enough quiet so we wouldn't have to shout at each other to be heard. But now, as I glance over at him, he's perhaps trying to come up with words.

"This works better if you actually speak," I tease.

He nods with a tight smile. We reach a dead end leading to an outdoor deck overlooking a lushly decorated pool. While the amenity bustles with children and adults, the deck's almost empty, save a couple on some lounges in the corner. We settle onto a soft settee surrounded by palm trees—like they're native to Philadelphia?—and exotic flowers, which offer a modicum of privacy from the outside world.

With a hard swallow, he speaks. "Carice is my wife."

CHAPTER FIVE

A LITTLE TOO MUCH

I nearly jettison off the couch, but his hand on my forearm stops me. "It's not like you think. We've known each other since college—been married for about eight years." He releases my arm but watches me closely.

"You're married."

"For now. We don't live together. Haven't in two years. We're good friends—we always have been. But the passion that brought us together died out, and while she doesn't want to admit the end, we've been over for some time."

"What do you mean, 'she doesn't want to admit the end'?"

He leans forward on his knees, his hands steepled beneath his chin. "Carice is a good woman. She's smart, beautiful, and she loves to be taken care of. I've done that for years—first when she got started in modeling, and later, when she needed a manager. I found the connections, made her get out there and follow her dream. I don't mean to make it sound as though she's not ambitious...it's how she is. And while I'll always care for her, I wanted...an equal. Someone who would be as invested in her dream as I was in mine. I got tired of constantly having to...promote her, encourage her, inspire her. She needs to be coddled. And not just on occasion, but all the time. As a friend, I can live with that—she's truly a wonderful person. But as a partner, as a husband, I..." He runs a hand through his hair, closing his eyes for a moment. "I ran out of energy, I guess. Or maybe—"

"I get it." I say the words quietly. "You got tired of being 'dad.'"

He nods. "I did. And as a result, I kept hurting her. I'd say things in frustration that were cruel. And even if they were true, they weren't things you should say to someone you love. I hated the person I was becoming, so we split up. But she depends on me for a lot, both financially and emotionally. So I've never pushed the divorce paperwork. I should have, but I didn't want to force her before she was ready. Honestly, I haven't had a reason to worry much about it. I have my career, my businesses, and it's been enough."

I raise an eyebrow. "In two years, there's never been anyone else?"

He snorts and gives me a look. "I didn't say I wore a chastity belt. But there's been nothing serious, no. Carice hasn't been ready for that, and I don't know if I have either."

A few quiet moments pass, punctuated by the shrieks of children and loud splashing. The soft conversation of the other couple on the deck reaches me, but we're too far away to hear the actual words. Kai stares down at the pool, but I don't think he's actually seeing it.

I'm not sure how I feel about his confession, but while I'm not necessarily the best judge of character, his words sound authentic.

"Why tell me all this?"

He doesn't respond right away. He leans against the cushioned couch, and after a few moments, he answers. "I like you. It's been a while since I've met someone I wanted to get to know. And there's something about you that intrigues me."

I ignore the blush that flares from my neck to my cheeks. "Oh? And what about me intrigues you so? My refusal to carry your DVDs, or my incompetence as a runway model?" I ask, a small grin forming.

His gaze doesn't waver from mine, and there's something a bit...uncomfortable. As though he's looking beyond "me" and seeing something deeper, more personal, that I rarely to show to anyone, even Lux. "You are a beautiful woman, Zi, and I find you very attractive. I don't think I was able to hide much last weekend." He chuckles as I drop my gaze, cheeks flaring. "But there's something more to you. When you give your attention to someone, you make them feel as though they matter. Even now, I can see how uncomfortable this is for you, and I hate that—but you still look at me, still give me your full focus, and you haven't once made me feel 'less than' for my awkward honesty. I'd like to get to know you better." He pauses. "If the feeling's mutual, that is."

I swallow, not sure how to answer. On one hand, this guy rocks my sex drive, and he's suggesting we...date, I guess? And my hormones are ready to leap at the chance. On the other hand, he makes sex videos, which, however well-intentioned they may be, raises a major red flag. I don't like pornography, period, and anything that could even be associated with that world crosses a very dangerous line for me. Yet I'm judging his movies, and him, without actually doing any research. Of course, I've also been down this road before, dated someone who wasn't the right fit, and my need to make things work led me into a marriage that nearly destroyed me. Fear wars with desire as I ponder his words.

"I guess that's my answer," he says quietly.

"No, it's not." I press my lips together, trying to decide what to say. "I...You scare me. It's...um...you're...different." I shake my head, frustrated that I can't seem to get the words out. "I'm sorry. I'm making a mess of this."

"I'm scary and different." He chuckles. "Not exactly a winning combination."

His humor soothes a little of my discomfiture, and I stick my tongue out at him. "Very funny. That's not what I meant."

With the surprising grace I'm starting to associate with him, he stands, hand held out to me. I stare at his long, squared fingers, his large palm open and waiting. I swallow hard, then fit my hand to his and let him draw me up to join him. His eyes look into mine, his mouth inches away. "Then why don't you show me what you mean."

My heart beats in my ears, as though the world has narrowed to the space between us. I feel like I'm on a fulcrum, unsure which way to fall. Except that only one way holds any promise.

As I brush my lips over his, his arms slide around me, pulling me against him. I sink my fingers into his hair, losing myself in the taste of cinnamon and champagne and him. With delicious slowness, I explore his mouth, enjoying his tongue against mine. He slides his hands over my hips, letting me have my way with our kiss. My palms wander over his shoulders, enjoying the play of muscles as he pulls me even closer.

When he takes over, I can only join him on the ride. Hands grasping, breaths coming in fast rhythms, he strips away every defense I have. His hands cup my ass, and when I don't object, he slips his fingers beneath the short edge of my dress, caressing my thigh. Heat explodes in my core, and all I can think is: *more*. I push him down to the settee and straddle him, uncaring who might be watching or how high my dress has hiked. His hard length cradled at the apex of my thighs, I grind against him. His mouth slides to my neck and collarbone, leaving searing kisses along my neckline. I whimper as his fingers graze my breasts, teasing the hardened tips. He pulls my dress a little lower, his mouth following course. I have to bite my lip to stop from crying out as he slips one breast free, his mouth closing around my nipple. With diligent fervor, he suckles, his teeth lightly closing over my sensitive skin. His other hand grips my shoulder, fastening me against him. Despite the layers of clothing between us, the friction sends thrills of pleasure through me as I rub against his cock.

He moves to the other breast, and I can only imagine the sight we must be, my dress half off, the panting groans, but for once, I don't care. Chills war with pleasure as my body starts to unravel. He grips my ass, then pushes aside the thin silk of my panties as his fingers seek my core. When he slips over my clit, I nearly collapse against him with the intense sensation. He strokes my slick folds, shifting my legs a bit so he has full access. With two fingers, he spreads me, feathering light pressure over my nerve endings until I'm delirious with need. He captures my mouth again, our kiss greedy and desperate. I buck against his hand, the world exploding into shiny shards. His assault on my mouth continues, swallowing my moans as I crest, then crest even higher until I don't think I can take anymore. When I finally rest my forehead against his shoulder, I'm spent; if not for his arms around me, I'm sure I'd topple over.

After a few minutes, I rouse...and become acutely aware of my state of undress. He must sense my alarm, as he tightens his arms around me. "There's no one here but you and me. The other couple must have made a run for the exit while we were distracted."

There's a smile in his voice, but my embarrassment is complete. What if they heard us...worse yet, saw us? Saw me? If there were a hole available, I'd crawl into it and never come out. And yet, some part of being so revealed turned me on.

What the hell is happening to me?

I pull my dress up, my bra tangling inelegantly at my attempt, but I manage to fully cover myself before leaping off him. As I debate making a run for the lobby, he grabs my hand. With firm pressure, he draws me against him, claiming my mouth once more. With a kiss both savage and proprietary, his hand cradles my head so I can't pull away. Not that I want to. I hang onto him, awash in desire yet again.

When he releases me, I nearly stumble, only his arms keeping me upright. His gaze locks on mine, molten.

I need to get away from him so I can think straight. Dear God. "My sister must be worried sick."

His pause tells me he's not buying my excuse, but he nods. "Of course."

We return to the ballroom, and, thankfully, he gets drawn away by someone who wants to introduce him to a friend. I look around frantically for Lux, then give up and text her.

TRACING THE LINE

I'm going to get the car. Meet me at the lobby exit.

Escaping to the parking garage, I drop into my car seat. I sit there for several minutes, trying to get a handle on my racing emotions. I've never done anything like this before. Sure, I had a few drunken makeout sessions in college. But I've never been someone to go from zero to sixty in seconds. I like speed limits and gearing up for the first kiss, the fun of little touches and innuendo before the boundaries start to blur and become fluid over who can touch where. There are small joys in the gradual build to sex, and I've always embraced them. Well, the few times I've had anything resembling a relationship.

But Kai doesn't seem interested in any rules, and he makes me want to throw all that aside and get right to riding him cowgirl style. And while I admit to enjoying the idea of making love in a public venue—a secluded park or out of the way meadow—I've never attempted to act on the desire.

Never mind that he makes sex films and is married.

I lower my head to my hands, overwhelmed by my poor judgment. What am I doing? I'd cry if I didn't feel so pathetic. I jump when my phone vibrates.

Everything okay? I'm on my way to the lobby.

With a frustrated sigh, I back out and head for the hotel exit.

"You've been silent for the entire ride. Are you going to tell me what's going on, or do I have to beat it out of you?"

We're almost home, and surprisingly, Lux has let me stew in my misery. I don't answer her, not because I want to ignore her...though perhaps I do. It's not like I want to tell her about my behavior. More because I'm not sure what to say.

"I've spent years making people beg for mercy, Zizi Baby. You wanna test me?" Lux mocks a throaty tone, á la the Godfather.

That almost makes me smile. "Give me a few minutes to

figure out how to say this."

She complies, and I wait until I've parked in my apartment's parking lot before trying to speak.

"You've always been so open and accepting of your sexuality and that of others. And I've always been jealous of that. Even when we were kids..." I stare out at the playground attached to the parking area, empty this late at night. "You always knew who you were. And you embraced it."

She doesn't speak, letting me get my thoughts out with as much stumbling as necessary.

"I wasn't like you. I was afraid. My first time—I was in college. I was drunk and with a guy I sort of knew through a friend. It wasn't memorable." I shrug. "Which, really, how many of us know what we're doing the first time anyway? But I remember thinking, shouldn't things have been...I don't know, special, I guess? Like, I should have planned more, or been in love.... Maybe it wouldn't have made a difference. But after that, I never...really enjoyed sex. It was what you did. I'd get sort of turned on, and then things would happen. I never felt like I had much control over it. It was like...I was doing it for someone else, not my own enjoyment."

Her gray eyes watch me, but she seems to think better of saying anything.

"My ex-husband was everything most women think they want. He was good-looking, built—the man worked out nearly every day—and...well-endowed, for lack of a better word." I try for a cheeky grin. "But I never wanted to have sex with him. Especially after we got married. He made it a chore—like there was something wrong with me. And I always thought maybe there was. After all, I have friends who love sex. You clearly enjoy it with abandon. Why can't I?" I'm surprised that tears are threatening, but I sniff them away and continue. "I've never felt like I was normal, I guess. And the hilarious part of all this: I'm the sex shop owner who doesn't know how to enjoy her own sexy times."

"I get the impression it's different with Kai?" She hurries to explain when my eyes go wide. "I saw him follow you out of the ballroom. And your dress is crooked, which, given the way that thing fits you, would be hard to do unless it might have been, ah, moved out of the way this evening."

I lay my forehead against the steering wheel. "Oh my God, seriously? I'm that obvious?"

She chuckles and pats my shoulder. "Only to me, sweetie. Because I care, and I saw the way he looked at you on stage. The man could have eaten you alive." Her fingers pressure me into sitting up. "You know, it's okay to not have everything figured out. And I'm sorry that you didn't feel comfortable with sex. You're right—it's supposed to be fun. We should be able to go after what we enjoy and not feel inhibited. But we live in a culture that doesn't make such pursuits easy."

"I know. And I'm not blaming my ex, exactly. But he never asked me what I wanted. And even when I tried to explore things, he'd...make little comments, or just do what he wanted to anyway. It was like I wasn't allowed to feel empowered in the bedroom. And I've never accepted that freedom for myself." I think over tonight, and the way I felt with Kai. "I came on to Kai. I mean, I guess it was more or less mutual, but he let me start things, and it felt amazing. And when he shifted the power, I didn't mind. Hell, I was even more turned on. I didn't feel manipulated or like I was losing something I wanted."

"That's because you two had a shared experience." She grins at me, her lovely face a bit jubilant. "I don't know Kai Isaac—never met him before last Saturday. But he seems like a good guy, and I've seen some of his work—the erotic films. The couples are enjoying each other the way they want to. And he captures their experience on film and allows their affection and pleasure to be beautiful and sacred. Or hell, dirty and lascivious, if that's what they want." She winks, her smile playful. "So maybe, that's who he is...a guy with whom to explore what you enjoy as a sexual being. And who knows: maybe he'll turn out to be worth dating."

I groan. "You know I'm a total traditionalist, right? Wait until the second date before even considering a first kiss. Dinner and a movie, a little mini-golf, lots of conversation before hopping into bed."

"Could be me, but I don't think Kai's all that traditional. And maybe it's time to break out of that mold. Figure out what you like, rather than what tradition dictates."

I stick my tongue out at her. But she may be right, though I don't want to admit it. Of course, she doesn't know that he's married. And if I'm being honest with myself, I'm not sure I care—assuming he was telling me the truth about his and Carice's relationship.

She checks her phone for the time. "Well, since we got back way earlier than I thought we would, you care if I take the car? I'll be back early Monday to take you to work."

Lux did me a favor by coming back to Bakertown to join me for the fashion show, especially since Fin's waiting for her in the city. "Sure. Tell Fin and Noah I said hi. And don't worry about a time on Monday. I can get Amie to pick me up."

When we unload, she rushes over to hug me, squeezing hard before letting go. "Something good might be happening here. Let it."

I nod, but as I trudge up the stairs to my apartment, doubt creeps in. Can I let go of who I've been for so long and enjoy the moment? Or am I taking risks that I'll regret later?

TRACING THE LINE

CHAPTER SIX

MEETING IN THE MIDDLE

Sunday proves to be a bit too trying for my energy. Or maybe I'm hiding from reality. Either way, I couch out with cheese curls and reruns of *90210*—the original version, thank you very much—and try not to notice the fuzzballs and dust haunting the corners of my home. My phone buzzes several times, but I refuse to look at it. It's probably Lux texting me, and while I should answer her, I'm feeling pouty.

Okay, I admit it: I wish she'd stayed here this weekend. *Not* that she should have—it's not like Fin can get into town all the time. But I'm feeling restless and alone, and having someone else around would help.

By the early evening hours, I break down and check my text messages, only to discover that the buzzing was actually my phone ringing.

I have a message. From a number I don't recognize...or maybe I saw it on the back of a business card recently?

"Zi." Kai's deep voice pauses, then he chuckles. "I'm not particularly good at leaving messages, so we'll see if I can avoid butchering this. I thought perhaps you might like to go to dinner. Together. Some night this week? This sounds as awkward as I feared it would. Well, there you have it. If you're interested, feel free to call me back. Or text me. Send a smoke signal. Whatever works." He recites his phone number. Then after another long pause, he says, "I'd really like to see you again. Okay...well, talk to you soon. I hope."

I'm giggling by the end of his rambling message. For someone who seems to have it all together, his nerves make me feel marginally better.

So dinner. With Kai. Do I or don't I? All the fears of last night come rushing back, but so do the memories of pleasure. God, I haven't dated hardly at all. I tried a few times after my divorce, but the men, the hours spent...they never felt right. And I wasn't ready—I'm not sure I am even now. But Kai's the first guy I've met that I'm wildly attracted to and, perhaps even more telling, I want to know more about.

I text Lux.

Kai asked me out. Via voicemail.

She doesn't respond for several minutes, and I'm about to text her again when her message finally pops up.

Go. Stop thinking. Stop analyzing. Say yes.

I send her an emoticon with a tongue sticking out.

You deserve some fun. Use his body! He's got a smokin' hot one. Speaking of which, I'm going back to my sexy man to finish what I started. xoxo

But I'm not Lux. I don't do casual sex. Or at least, I never have before. And nothing about being with Kai felt casual.

What are you going to do? she types minutes later when I don't answer.

I haven't decided. Don't worry about my love life—go tie down (or untie) your man!

I wander my apartment, double-checking that I took the trash out and looking for something on which to expend my nervous energy. But there's nothing besides cleaning, and I can always find an excuse not to run the vacuum.

Staring down at my phone, I make a fast decision and return his call. I almost hang up when his end rings, but he answers too quickly.

"Zi?"

I don't say anything for a moment. "Yes."

"I'm glad you called."

Am I? "I just got your message."

"And...?"

"When?" This has got to be the most uncomfortable scheduling in the history of dating.

"It's up to you. I haven't eaten yet if you want to meet tonight."

Oh. My. God. My heart pounds in my ears—way too soon. Absolutely no— "Sure," comes out of my mouth instead. Shit! I haven't even showered yet today.

"I'm still in Philly, but you're only, what, forty minutes from here? I can be there by seven, if that works. But you'll have to pick the place—I don't know much in Bakertown."

"There's an exotic pizza place downtown—really unusual. If you haven't tried it yet, I'd recommend that." Pizza. Which usually involves garlic and grease. Because that's romantic. I smack my forehead with my palm.

"Sounds great. Seven then?"

I agree and hang up. One look in my bathroom mirror informs me I've got work ahead of me, and less than an hour to make gorgeous happen. Thankfully, I went for waxing in preparation for my big walk down the runway. While I may never submit to such torture again, it's nice not worrying about shaving my legs for the next month. And yes, I went for the bikini wax option too, and *damn*. There are no words to describe the agony. But at least I get to reap the benefits.

Perhaps Kai will, too. The very thought makes my hands shake. It's a first date—that is not an excuse to sleep with the man. Or a reason to, for that matter. As though I'm convincing anyone with this argument.

After a quick shower, I rip through my clothing, determine I have nothing to wear, panic, and then settle on jeans and beaded halter that's both modest and—I hope—sexy. I have good collarbones and a graceful neck, so when given the opportunity, I love to show them off. My full hips and belly-pooch, on the other hand...let's just say that while losing weight has made me more confident in some ways, the downside no one mentions is how your skin changes when you don't have the extra pounds. Still, in clothing, I'm satisfied. I go with a heeled sandal, then futz with my hair until I get so frustrated, I leave it down. Thick and long, my hair doesn't have the gorgeous curls the stylist managed last night. So messy waves flop over my shoulders, looking more tangled than elegant.

When I manage a final swipe of mascara, I have five minutes to make it on time. Thankfully, the pizza place is within walking distance, and you should always be a couple minutes late, right? It's a BYOB establishment, so I grab a bottle of white wine out of my fridge.

I'm two minutes late. Kai waits outside, and as I turn the corner, seeing him in jeans and a fitted t-shirt, revealing his muscular biceps and broad chest...I pretend to dig in my bag for my phone so he won't see the giddiness in my expression. I don't need dinner—just him on a plate.

I can feel his gaze as I approach, and when I look up, the desire in his eyes sends my heart skittering.

"Hi."

He holds out his hand, and when I slide my fingers over his, he pulls me to him. His mouth crushes mine in a blinding kiss, and I can't focus on anything but the feel and smell of him, his heat washing over my senses. He runs his hands over my bare back, sending shockwaves down my spine, and I'm glad I went with the halter. I forget that we're standing in the middle of a small town, on a busy street, and people are probably staring at us. Instead, I revel in lust as his tongue claims mine, and I hold onto his lean waist as he explores my willing mouth and body.

His arousal stiffens between us, and I press even closer, enjoying his sharp intake of breath as he drops his forehead to mine. "If we keep this up, I might end up being very inappropriate in public."

I chuckle softly, not easing up. "There are decency laws in this town, so..."

He growls, then forces my mouth open beneath his. His urgency slows to a torturous pace, though, as his hands cup my face, teasing me with slow kisses. "Two can play at this game."

With a sass that surprises me, I nip his lip. "Yes, but only one of us can disguise her, ah, interest, Mr. Isaac. Those jeans aren't loose enough to hide much of anything."

He locates a spot on my neck, and when he uses his teeth lightly, I struggle to contain my gasp. "Hm, I don't know about that, Ms. Trace. I think we're both in trouble."

All of which is interrupted when my stomach growls loudly. My cheeks flush in embarrassment, and Kai laughs. "We'll have to call a time out and take care of that." He finishes with a chaste kiss. "Until later?"

I don't respond, but enjoy the feel of his hand in mine as we step into the restaurant. A simple design, the pizza kitchen offers unique flavors of pizza on display behind a glass partition. Pies like fig jam and arugula, pears and prosciutto, and Asian barbecue chicken line the counter, and Kai's fascinated with the choices. "I've never heard of these toppings. Carnitas and corn on a pizza?"

With a smile, I figure out my selection and order. "They claim to be the world's best taste-pairing pizza makers, and I would agree. Their pies are amazing."

He makes his decision, and with empty wine glasses in hand, we find a table. The evening crowd has dwindled, though there are still quite a few people here. Settling into our corner booth, I withdraw the wine and opener from my bag, and he immediately sets to removing the cork and pouring.

"I can't open my own wine, Sir Galahad?"

He narrows an eye at me. "Can I not be a gentleman and serve you, milady?"

While I was teasing, I'm not used to things like that. My ex never did anything for me he didn't have to—he always believed that equality between the sexes should have very stringent lines. So I could mow the lawn, take out the trash, and do all the repair work around the house. Of course, he never quite got into cooking and cleaning...

"I guess you can."

He threads his fingers between mine. "Good." He rubs his thumb against my palm, the small touch electric. "You disappeared last night."

I figured he'd ask about that, and I'd yet to concoct a good answer. So I went with the truth. "I was a little freaked out."

"I feared things went a bit too far for you."

"They weren't too far for you?" I ask, sipping my wine.

With a thoughtful look, he stares at our hands, then returns his gaze to me. "No, but I have a feeling my speed is different than yours."

"Care to expound on that?"

"I grew up in a very traditional family. We were raised with relatively open minds, though, when it came to relationships. But my parents were still...they see things as black and white. And my family is from a small town in the Midwest—being conservative in all things can seem like a statewide requirement." He winks. "They were a strange mix of political progressives and had staunch convictions about sex. I went to school at UC Berkeley—I marveled at the open attitudes about sex. Of course, I was eighteen. I thought what happened on a college campus—especially at Berkeley—was representative of the culture at large, and that my parents were simply small thinkers from a tiny town."

I snort with laughter. "Hardly."

With a sheepish smile, he continues. "Exactly. But that experience shaped how I viewed sex and sensuality. As a result, I've always been very open about sex, and I generally let partners choose their pace. You...are the exception." He shifts in his seat a bit, stretching his legs. Given the size of the booth, there's no way for him to do so without our calves touching.

I don't shrink away from the contact. "What does *that* mean?" I ask with mock suspicion.

"I knew I was pushing you yesterday, and I shouldn't have. But you are...intoxicating. I can't seem to get enough."

His words add gasoline to my fire, and I have to look away. No one's ever said anything like that to me before. While my memory of last night lingers with feelings of shame...a part of me relishes my abandon and wanton feelings as well.

"I apologize—I should have been more sensitive."

When I look up, I'm surprised to see sincerity. Why am I shocked that someone means something they say? I file that question away for later consideration. "I'm an adult, Kai. On some level, I knew what I was doing. It's not like you forced me to do anything.

"I'm jealous of your experience. My sisters and I...well, we ended up in a foster home when we were teens, and Mama C was very religious. We were expected to maintain purity until we were married. That never worked for my sisters, but I've always been a people pleaser. I tried really hard to meet her expectations, at least until college, where I fooled around a bit." Why am I telling him this? The words pour out, unbidden. "I've had limited exposure, I guess you could say."

He watches me closely. "Are you saying you've never..."

"What? No! Oh, God, please. I'm divorced. I've had plenty of sex." I could bite my tongue off and embarrass myself less, I think. "I just mean I can count my sexual partners on two... wait, three fingers."

His expression wears something between relief and curiosity. "Really?"

"Just because I own a lingerie store with some sexy extras doesn't mean I've had a wealth of, um, experience." Did I actually say that? I might as well dig out a white sundress and granny panties.

"That's fine. I didn't mean to insinuate there's anything wrong with your history, Zi. Not at all. You know what I do—and I do make films beyond the erotic, by the way. I tend to hang out with people who've explored a lot and had very active sex lives."

"Have you, um, explored a lot?" Subtle, thy name is Zi Trace. Flames engulf my neck.

His grin mimics the Cheshire cat. "You could say that, yes." He seems to be waiting to see what effect his acquiescence has on me before continuing.

TRACING THE LINE

I like to think I maintain a neutral face. But his eyes gleam with amusement, so I'm guessing, not so much.

"I would probably need more than three fingers."

"You don't need to tell me." Mortification, aisle three. Clean up requested.

He laughs, and then shakes his head. "Well, we don't need to get into details. And I have been married for the last eight years."

Ah, well, there's that. "And you haven't worn a chastity belt, if I recall correctly?" I manage to raise an eyebrow, despite my pink skin.

"True. Let's just say, fingers and toes...ah, yeah, I'd need most of them for an inventory of sexual partners."

A server interrupts us with our pizzas, and we spend a few minutes sprinkling cheese and avoiding looking at each other. Nothing quite as awkward as our conversational direction.

He takes a bite and closes his eyes. "This might be the best pizza I've ever tasted."

I cover my mouth as I chew, unable to hold back my smile. "Told you it was not to be missed."

He finishes his slice before leaning across the table to brush a crumb from my chin. I'm sure my face is beet red, but his gaze catches mine before I can drop my eyes. "You are not to be missed."

CHAPTER SEVEN

FIRST BASE

"Any chance you watched the sample I left with you?" Kai asks after we've gorged on pizza and desserts that the pizza joint is known for—you'd never know their peanut butter and chocolate-covered sponge cake is gluten-free.

"I didn't." The wine has coated my brain in a warm haze. "I'm sorry—I have...a bad history with pornography, so I'm resistant to even viewing what you gave me."

Concern draws his brows together. "I'm so sorry. May I ask what happened? Or is it too private?"

I consider his question, then shrug. Might as well get the icky parts out now while my inhibitions are low enough... and I haven't gotten involved with him. "My ex had a thing with porn. I never really minded as lots of people like to watch it, and in college, my roommate would pick up a few films sometimes, and we'd all make fun of the silly lines and fake orgasms." He's holding my hand, but I withdraw my fingers, needing to bolster myself to get the words out. "My ex started trying to get me to watch porn movies with him, sort of as a prelude, and I always found the sex degrading. Not that all of it is, I guess. But what he liked...the women were always plastic surgery Frankensteins, and they were being used hard and called names. I guess if they're being paid and they don't mind, it's fine. I don't want to be treated like that, though.

"After the first few years of marriage, he started trying to get me into acting out some of his favorite scenes, even talked about getting 'a third.'" I bite the inside of my lip, trying to stem the hurt that still surges when I remember our conversations. "I'm not a prude. What people do in their private moments is their business. But *I* don't want that. I'm not built that way. And when I resisted some of his ideas, he got irate. It went from being a suggestion to a requirement, and when I wouldn't do the things he wanted, I was 'punishing' him or 'not woman enough.' I...it just got worse from there. And around that time, I got pregnant. I'd always dreamed of having a family, and while things were definitely not ideal, I thought maybe...well, it was a stupid thought. Kids don't repair relationships. If anything, they make them harder."

He stays silent, his eyes never leaving me as I speak. I rush through the rest, desperate to get it all out. "I miscarried at three-and-a-half months. It...broke me. I had an ultrasound photo of this tiny being—I'd heard his heartbeat. At that point, I'd made plans, picked out nursery colors, told friends. And it hurt my ex-husband too, of course. I don't mean to diminish his suffering. He didn't handle the loss well either, but where I retreat when I'm upset, he comes out swinging. After...well, we already had problems, obviously. And I knew that I didn't want to have a child with someone who had control issues." I lift a shoulder. "So that was the end of everything, in some ways."

I inhale deeply, trying to wipe away the image of my baby that always intertwines with the pain and humiliation around the end of my marriage. "I'm not saying that the films you make are the same thing, Kai. Lux assures me they aren't. But I...I swore I wouldn't carry any movies or films like that in my store, both because I don't want to have to watch them to find out if I'm willing to endorse them, but also because so rarely are they done with a respect to women. My sister was—well, I guess she still *is*, just privately—a Dominatrix. She fulfilled the fantasies of submissives for a living. There's nothing wrong with humiliating play if that's what both partners want, but that's not something I find sexy or appealing—"

"You don't have to defend your preferences, Zi. You're allowed to not like things." He reaches out, but then draws back, as though not sure what to do with his hands. "I would never ask you to do something you don't want to. That's part of having a 'partner' and not just an outlet for sex. Both people should be engaged in pleasure they each enjoy." He shakes his head, his voice hardening. "That should never have happened to you, and I'm so sorry that you were hurt."

I don't think I've told Lux the whole story about my divorce. Not because I wouldn't, but she's never pushed me for details. And afterwards, many of our friends drifted away, especially once I opened my store. Most people I used to hang out with were having children or preferred to engage with other couples. When I lost my marriage, I ended up losing more than just the man I thought was my soulmate. And being that alone changed me, made me a lot tougher.

I say as much to Kai. "I don't think it ever occurred to me how far-reaching that impact was." While I've barely known this man a week, I feel a need to tell him everything, and strangely enough, he seems, while sympathetic, unfazed by it. "I don't know why I told you all of that. But thank you for allowing me the space to do so."

"Of course. I wish there was a way to ease the pain of that experience for you."

I shake my head. "I'm over most of it. Seriously. Opening White Peony forced me to get out of my funk, and when I did, I discovered that while getting divorced—and all the trauma that went with it—was awful, I also got my freedom back. I always felt cowed and like I couldn't be honest about who I was, and in fairness, I felt that way long before I met my ex. When I was on my own again, I discovered more about who I am and what makes me tick than I ever understood before. So in some ways, getting divorced was the single most liberating thing that could have happened to me."

A server starts putting chairs up on the tables around us

with a not-so-subtle glare, and I check my phone, surprised to see that it's after nine. "Wow. I had no idea it was so late."

We dispose of our trash and exit the restaurant. On the street, the humid evening air brushes over us. Kai reaches for my hand, and fitting my palm to his feels like the most natural thing in the world. We walk slowly down the block, neither willing to broach the heavy topic between us. But telling Kai about my past lifted a weight I hadn't realized I'd been carrying, and I feel a bit daring as a result. "I live around the corner."

"Shall I walk you home then?"

"I'd like that."

"You're an amazing decorator," he calls from somewhere in the living room.

"Not really. I just pay attention to Pier One Imports sales and hope for the best," I retort as I pour milk and sugar into our mugs. It occurs to me too late that I don't know how he takes his coffee. And I realize: I don't know if I've ever done this before. I mean, sure, I've invited guys back to my place... but never with so little known about them. "I hope you like sweet coffee." Damn.

"I'll drink it any way it's offered, to be honest."

He's examining my bookshelf when I come back into the room, and he smiles as he turns to me. "And your reading collection is impressive."

My cheeks flame as my shelves have an extensive collection of erotic fiction and how-to sex books. "Don't assume I've read all those. People think when you own a shop like mine, you want all the material you sell. Most of those were gifts that I've yet to read."

His eyes sparkle with mirth. "Hm-hmm. That's what they all say."

I set the coffee on the end table, and when I stand up, he's beside me, too close, too irresistible. Leaning forward, I place my mouth on his, letting him decide the next step. His hands hold my face, his lips gently slanting over mine. Torture seems his goal, and he does so brilliantly. I whimper when he finally steps back.

"We can either talk and have coffee," he says with lust darkening his gaze. "Or we can let it get cold."

"I can always brew more."

That's all the encouragement he needs. Throwing artistry aside, he devours me, his hands exploring, teeth nipping my jaw and neck between kisses. I barely catch a breath, unable to do anything more than hold onto him as he sets fire to every nerve ending in my body.

"Come here," he says with a rasping whisper, then sits on my couch, drawing me down so I straddle his lap. Rather than pull me in for another kiss, he leans back and slides his hands under my halter and eases down my bandeau-style bra. With achingly light touches, his thumbs feather across my nipples. I try to hold his gaze, but the sensation forces my eyes closed. He continues to tease the hardened nubs, pinching with gentle pressure. When he slides my halter over my head, I comply willingly, then gasp as he takes my nipple into his mouth, the over-sensitive tip shooting electricity down my center. I hold onto his shoulders, thankful for his hands supporting my back as he feasts on my breasts.

When he finally returns to my mouth, I'm languid with desire. I collapse onto his chest as he drives our kisses even deeper, tongues discovering an erotic dance.

"Stand up for me for a moment."

His whispered words take a moment to penetrate my haze. "Why?"

He draws a finger down my cheek. "I want to see you. Is that okay?"

Nerves zing back into focus. I've never had much confidence about my body, despite my determination to help other women find theirs. But then again, he saw most of me last night at the fashion show, right? I obey his request, wanting nothing more than to cross my arms over my chest to hide myself. But I manage to stand straight before him, and when I have enough courage to look at him, his gaze holds only admiration and desire.

For me.

"You are beautiful, Zi." He runs his hands over my thighs, up to my waist. "May I?"

His fingers grasp the button, but he waits for my nod before he peels my jeans off my hips. I wore one of my favorite string bikinis, and with my clothing and sandals now discarded on the floor, only small triangles of fuchsia lace cover me.

Kai presses a kiss against my hip, then moves to my stomach to do the same. I'm wildly aware of my pooch, the loose skin of my abdominals that won't ever be flat, despite my best efforts. But he's oblivious to my concern as his hands trace my hips, then slip between my thighs. He eases me closer so his knees separate my legs. There's no mystery left—I can feel the wetness pooling in my panties. He takes his time, fingers sliding along the silk edge.

"I don't know if I can stay standing," I manage to say on a breath, eyelids sliding shut. I can feel his gaze on me, watching my expressions, and for the first time in my life, I don't mind. It's actually quite erotic, having this much attention paid to me, and I keep my eyes closed and allow myself to be enveloped in the feeling.

"I'll catch you." He slides one finger beneath the material, my slick folds offering no resistance. Adding another finger, he widens them along my inner lips, teasing the side of my clit with only the barest of contact.

I bite my lip to contain a whimper, but I can't stop the moan as he fills me, his fingers sliding deep inside. My hips follow his slow rhythm, unable to resist. His thumb finds my clit as the delicious tension starts to rise.

Then he stops. I nearly stumble forward, but he stabilizes me as his mouth replaces his fingers. Stars shoot across the backs of my eyelids as I struggle to maintain my balance. His hands steady my hips as his tongue makes a fiery path over my skin. I don't object—I barely know what I'm doing—when he eases me down to the couch, taking his place. He slips off my panties and spreads my thighs. Then his mouth descends, and I'm gone, lost in a blaze of blinding, euphoric, unending light.

TRACING THE LINE

CHAPTER EIGHT

HOME RUN

I'm curled against him when the world makes sense again. He's sitting beside me on the couch, his arm draped around me. After a few hazy moments, I notice that I'm naked—and he's not.

"What just happened?" I ask, my voice a bit hoarse.

"I believe you had at least two, possibly three orgasms." He kisses the top of my head. "And I'm pretty sure the last one knocked you out."

I cover my face with my hands. "I'm so sorry."

He chuckles and pulls my hands away. "Don't be. You were enthralling. I've been told I'm good before, but I don't know if I've ever made anyone come so hard, they ended up unconscious."

I can't help it—I giggle. Almost uncontrollably. Probably because, well, I haven't been with anyone in entirely too long. And I couldn't tell you the last time I orgasmed with such ferocity. "I can't believe I passed out like that."

"Did it feel good?"

I nod. "Very."

"Then that's what matters." He tilts my chin so he can kiss

me, and when I pursue his mouth further, he allows me free reign.

My sleepiness gives way to arousal, my hormones purring happily as I move to straddle him once more. "You have entirely too much clothing on," I say against his mouth.

"You are welcome to remove it if it pleases you." His smile interferes with our kiss, so I take advantage of the interruption and pull his t-shirt off.

His broad, muscled shoulders make my fingers itch to explore. A light dusting of hair coats his chest, narrowing to a fine line at the waist of his pants. There's something desperately sexy about his jeans against my bare thighs, and I want nothing more than to grind down against him and feel his hard length, but I don't want to rush this, either. My palms sculpt the hard planes of his abs, find the hollows of his collarbones and neck.

"Lift up for a moment." He helps me balance on my knees, then digs in the pocket of his jeans before sliding them off. I barely register the square of foil he drops on the couch before he pulls my hips down against him. Only the thin cotton of his underwear separates us, and I embrace my desire as I rub against his cock. It only serves to stoke my fire, and I revel in the friction as he leans forward to worship my breasts.

Soon he reaches between us, his fingers purposeful, but I stop him. "I want you inside me before I come again."

He raises an eyebrow. "Sweetheart, that's definitely going to happen before the night's over, but you are so wet, I can't resist." When he reaches for me again, I let him.

The skin of his fingers is both soft and rough, and the contrast creates exquisite sensations. I lean back, bracing myself on his knees. I can't believe I'm getting turned on *again*, but I am. I hear a snick of foil, and then a very different texture glides against me. He works his cock over my skin, the silken head teasing my entrance. When I can't handle any more, I slide down, taking him inside me.

I groan and fall forward against him, unprepared for his girth and length as my body stretches around him. I can't move for several minutes, both too aroused by the intense connection and too full to imagine moving an inch. He holds me patiently, massaging my back and rear.

"You okay?"

When I can bear to move, I brace my hands on his shoulders. "It's been a *really* long time." I sigh. "And I'm not used to, um, your size."

His grin is only slightly smug. "Then I hope I please you."

I bite his full bottom lip lightly, then kiss him for a moment before meeting his gaze. "Try not to let it go to your head. Pun intended."

But the humor evaporates when he lifts me up so he can slide back inside. I'm caught between pleasure and some overwhelming feeling I can't put into words. He guides me into a slow cadence, letting me ease down over him again and again. Building pressure begins to explode across my body, sparking every nerve. Soon I'm dependent on his direction as my climax breaks over me. He drags my mouth to his, swallowing my cries. I'm shaking as I recover from my release.

"Give me a minute," I say, stunned I'm even capable of speech...and that I could orgasm *again*. But I'm determined not to be the only person enjoying this evening, so I force myself upright. "You aren't even close, are you?"

He cups my jaw, his thumb caressing my cheek. "I'm having a wonderful time. Don't worry about it."

I narrow my eyes at him. "Not good enough." With careful movements as my legs are a bit wobbly, I stand. He's truly stunning—and I'm not just referring to his, erm, *parts*. He's a big man, with long, lean limbs and a narrow waist, and I pull him to his feet, enjoying the height difference. It's rare I get to feel short. "What do you enjoy?"

After a long moment, those lovely eyes thoughtful, he presses his mouth to mine. "I'll show you if you'd like."

A thrill echoes in my stomach, but I nod anyway. "Very much so."

He looks around the room, then guides me over to the far wall. He adjusts my direction so I'm facing the wall. His chest curves to my back. "You know how some guys are breast-men and some are ass-men?" His mouth wanders my neck and shoulders, leaving a hot trail that curls my toes. "I'm definitely an ass-man. And yours is gorgeous." He places my hands against the wall, shoulder-width apart and eases me forward with gentle pressure.

I've never cared for being taken from behind one way or another—it's just one more position to try. But as he eases himself into me, I can't stop moaning. There's something about being wanted this way as his hands cup my ass, spreading me...but he's too cautious. "I won't break, Kai. Fuck me."

He surges into me, and I have to brace myself for his assault. His hands squeeze my ass, my hips, driving me crazy with need. He lightly smacks my rear, and when I groan, he does so again. The slight pain wars with the incredible high. He murmurs dirty phrases in my ear, and I get even wetter. As he nears his climax, his cock grows harder, thicker, and he holds himself deep inside me, my hips pulled firmly against his. Then he slips his fingers between my legs, and I shudder, my pussy tightening around him until he joins me. With a guttural groan, he explodes inside me. He wraps his arms tightly around me, as much holding onto me as supporting me as I vibrate against him.

Standing no longer an option, we collapse onto the floor. I snag the folded blanket I store under my end table and drape the soft fleece over us. Lifting up on an elbow, he tucks me against him, then traces the outline of my jaw with one finger.

"You're a sight to behold. I've never seen a woman quite so...engaged." I try to look away, but his hand halts me. "You're beautiful—like a wild creature, untamed and without care for expectations."

There's nothing but sincerity in his eyes, so I try to relax into his words. "Thanks, I guess. I'm not usually like that—I mean, with the multiple orgasms and such."

"Either I'm *that* good, or you haven't been with the right people."

I snicker softly. "Hm. Well, there've only been three."

"Four."

"Erm, yes. Well, either way, it was…I've never experienced anything like that before. I'm not sure what happened."

His dark hair falls over his forehead, the wavy locks lending even more roguish charm, damn him. I'm sure my frizzy hair has both flattened and widened as a result of our lovemaking. I can't resist reaching up to smooth the soft curls from his face, and he kisses my wrist. "What are you thinking?"

Nibbling at the inside of my mouth, I'm not sure how to answer. Do I tell the truth and risk scaring him off? Or do I wait to speak until I know him better? They say truth is always the best strategy, but I'm convinced "they" have never tried dating in our modern world. Since everything else about tonight has been honest, I dive in. "I'm wondering what happens next? I'm not used to this. I have sort of a…dating guide that I created in college after a drunken mistake that I never repeated again."

"Hm. I'm intrigued. Tell me about this dating guide."

I prop my head on my arm so I can maintain his gaze. "First date, something simple. Coffee, or a weeknight dinner. Chat, get to know each other. See how it feels. If there's a second date, then something more traditional. Mini-golf, a weekend dinner, maybe a hike."

"No dinner and a movie? Isn't that a dating requirement?"

I wrinkle my nose. "No. You can't talk during movies, and how can you possibly know if you want to kiss someone if you barely know them?"

"Ah, so the goal of the second date is the first kiss." His hand curves around my waist, stroking gently and without intent. The contact calms my nervous stomach.

With a shake of my head, I continue. "No, not necessarily. Second date is really getting into the person—who are they now that the first date jitters have worn off? And could this be more?" I slip my leg between his, his warmth beckoning in the chilly air-conditioned room. "But the first kiss may or may not happen that date."

"Don't you think it should? I mean, a first kiss can tell you a lot about a person."

"Like what?"

"Hm. Well, let's take our first kiss for example." He grins as my face flushes. "I knew immediately that you were giving. You offered as much in that kiss as you took, probably even more so. And I knew you were nervous, so you're someone who gives of herself even when her instincts might tell her otherwise...that's a generous person."

"Or a fool."

He ignores my interjection. "I sensed your fear—that you'd been hurt badly before. But when you opened up to me, you were willing to try again. And then you grabbed my ass—"

I cover his mouth with my hand. "You were not supposed to mention that." He lightly nips the fleshy skin of my palm, eyes laughing. When I snatch my hand back, he dives beneath my jaw, tickling my neck with kisses. I shriek and try to wriggle away, but he holds me in place easily.

"And," he says over my laughter, "then I knew you'd be a lusty bed partner."

I shove against him, pushing him onto his back and following him with my body so I lie on top. "You inferred a hell of a lot from a kiss, Mr. Isaac."

Adjusting the blanket so we're covered, he rests his hands on my back. "And I was right."

Honestly, his inferences from that kiss offer both insightful logic and embarrassing truth. Could he really tell I was damaged? Did I indicate that I wanted to give love another shot? "Hm. Well. That's neither here nor there because we're discussing *my* dating guide, not yours."

"True. But you might need to tweak yours a bit. I mean, after all, this is technically our first date..."

I drop my forehead to his chest with a dramatic wail. "Don't remind me."

With fingers combing through my hair, he chuckles. "I think it went quite well. Are you complaining?"

I rest my chin on my knuckles. "I'm not. This was...amazing."

"Then we might have to do it again. Have a second date. What do you say?"

"I could be convinced," I say coyly.

"Is that a challenge?" He tilts his hips, reminding me that he's going to be ready for round two in the near future.

"Maybe."

"There's still the matter of our"—he glances at the coffee mugs on the end table—"coffee."

I snort. "They're no doubt iced coffee, now."

"Ah, well. No point in worrying about them, then." He tips me onto the floor, so I end up on my back. Then he gathers my hands and draws them over my head. "I'm sure we can find other amusements."

We do.

TRACING THE LINE

CHAPTER NINE

LUNCHTIME CONFESSIONS

Lux doesn't return from NYC until Tuesday morning, and I surprise her with lunch plans.

"Blue asked to get together."

Her mouth pops open. "Seriously?"

"Seriously. And if we don't leave in" I consult my phone for the time, "three minutes, we're going to be late."

We manage to get there a few minutes early—Blue suggested a new sushi joint in nearby Doylestown. A quaint-if-touristy historical landmark in Pennsylvania, Doylestown doesn't lack in restaurants or shopping. It's all I can do to propel Lux past several shops on our way.

Blue's early, which is a rarity. I offered to let her ride with us; after all, we live in the same town. But she insisted on meeting us here. She probably didn't want to deal with awkward car conversation.

We find her in the back of the restaurant. She wears a skimpy camisole and jean shorts that could double as bikini bottoms, and her fiery hair flows loose over her shoulders.

Lux takes the lead, and Blue responds with surprising energy, hugging Lux back. My heart nearly overflows with joy—I've wanted to see us together for so long. And it seems like that might be happening. I embrace Blue, her waifish build delicate in my arms. I kiss her forehead like I used to when we were younger, and rather than being annoyed, she smiles.

"So what's good?" Lux asks as we take our seats.

Blue doesn't look at the menu. "The sashimi here is the best I've had, but if you don't like raw—"

"Oh, I do." Lux smiles. "I'm pretty sure you get thrown out of the city if you don't like raw fish."

"Then definitely the sashimi, and they have a dragon roll that's weird, but really good."

We settle on a group meal, and when the waitress leaves, Blue fiddles with her napkin. "I have news."

Those three words are enough to strike fear into my gut. "Oh?" *Please don't let it be about family shit. Please, oh, please.*

"I enrolled in college."

That's enough to get both Lux and me staring.

"You don't need to look so shocked," she grumbles. "It's not like I'm not smart."

Lux stammers, "N-no, that's not it."

"I thought you were dead-set against it." I narrow my gaze at her. "Last time I mentioned school, I thought you were going to shove your fist down my throat."

Blue sticks her tongue out at me, then tucks her hair behind her ear, a nervous gesture. "Yeah, well. If I'm going to manage Gram's place, I should know what I'm doing. And I can go around my schedule, which will make running the diner easier."

"When do you start?" Lux asks.

I can feel her doubt. While I'm not willing to totally throw away Gram's interest in having Blue run her diner as a possible win-win situation, Lux has good reason to be suspicious. Gram *is* a selfish woman. Plus, I know how Blue can be. Flaky's not the right word...but it's not the wrong one, either.

"In the fall. I picked out my classes yesterday." Blue digs into her small leather bag, a knockoff designer label across the garish bright pink and blue faux leather. "Here's my schedule."

She presents the itinerary proudly, as though it's a diploma.

I take the sheet from her and share it with Lux. "Sketching and sculpture? I didn't think you drew anymore—didn't you give that up when you were in high school?"

Blue shrugs, her expression closing. "I had to pick electives. I figured it would be easier than horseback riding."

Damn me for being a sister. "No, it's great. I just didn't know you had any interest."

"Maybe I don't." Her mouth tightens into a flat line.

Fuck.

"Five courses—that's intense." Lux hands the course list back to her. "I loved my economics class, but I almost flamed out on my lit-one course."

"Why'd you almost fail?" Blue's careful not to look at me, and I feel even worse.

"I couldn't get into the classics. Don't get me wrong—there's plenty to be said for Shakespeare and Dickens. But we jumped right into Yeats and Byron." Lux shakes her head with distaste. "I couldn't understand why everyone thought they were so profound. 'Ode to My Plant' and a 'Poem for the Weakling.'" She shivers. "I basically prayed that when the final arrived, it would involve some sort of blood sacrifice. I was more likely to manage that than understand poetry."

Blue chuckles and takes a sip of her soda. "Hm. Good to know."

"You might love it. I didn't, though." Lux eyes our little sister with pride. "So you're going to be a college graduate."

With a self-conscious shrug, Blue looks away. "Let's not get carried away. I'll be lucky if I can finish my first two years of community college."

"You'll do great. You've always done anything you set your mind to," I remind her.

Her gaze meets mine, those mossy eyes hard with meaning. "What were my choices?"

I'm lost in a haze of "what the fuck just happened?", but then her mood lifts, and I think I'm forgiven. I'm not sure why, but I'll take it.

"What's up with you, Zi? You're a bit glow-y today. New guy? Or a new vibrator?"

"Very funny," I retort, but I smile at Blue's joke.

"I'm betting new guy." Lux winks at Blue. "There's definitely been someone sniffing around."

I groan, dropping my chin into my hand. "Really? 'Sniffing around' like I'm a dog in heat?"

"Well, are you?" Blue asks, her smirk joined by a raised eyebrow.

"There's definitely been a lot of heat going on, I'll put it that way."

"Details!" Lux scoots her chair closer. "All of 'em. Right now. I *knew* something happened while I was away. I could practically smell sex in the air."

"Oh. My. God. Would you stop? Right now." I mock-glare at Lux, unable to deny anything since my face is engulfed in flames.

Lux whoops. "I knew it. You can't hide squat from me. I was barely home five minutes, and I knew." She does some sort of hip-hop dance in her chair, and Blue joins her.

Since I'm the only person at this table who didn't get the rhythm gene, I stew in embarrassed silence. "Are you two done yet?"

They both grin at me, heads nodding. "Spill!" they nearly say in unison.

So I do. The barest details, as I'm not one to kiss and tell. Well, that's what I try to do. Lux manages to pressure more out of me than I intend to say.

"So Kai Isaac is hung, eh?" Lux chortles in merriment. "Can't say I'm surprised. What is he, six-foot-four? Five?"

"Six? I'm not sure—but really tall," I agree.

"Pictures? I've never seen the guy." Blue pouts from her side of the table.

Our sushi boat arrives, a massive wooden ship with all manner of raw fish piled on its planks and decks. Given that there are only three of us, I have no idea how we'll finish it all. Lux taps away on her phone while Blue and I dispense soy sauce and wasabi into little bowls. When we finally dig in, Lux hands Blue her phone. "Sir Isaac, or perhaps, Sir Fucks-A-Lot."

I nearly spit out my sushi roll. When I manage to swallow, I object. "You *cannot* start calling him that."

Blue admires the image on the phone. "Damn. He's hot. Oh, wait, here's his IMDB—he's six-foot-seven. Wow. No wonder his dick is huge."

I shove another piece of sushi in my mouth and ignore them. Or try to, at least.

Lux dips a roll in soy sauce. "Is he a real prospect, or just your boy toy?"

With my mouth full, all I can do is give a withering glare to Lux.

"Hm. So definitely more. Interesting. First guy on the horizon in, what, two years, right?"

"First guy since my ex." I sip my drink.

"Wait, first sex since the ex?" Blue asks, then grins at her rhyme. "First sexin' since the ex-in'?"

I roll my eyes. "Yes, if you must know. I figured battery-operated was safer."

"So you're okay with his movies, then?" Lux asks as she debates her next flavor excursion from the array of colorful choices. "No issues with them?"

"What movies? What are we talking about?" Blue looks between Lux and me.

I glare at my chopsticks while Lux answers. "Kai's a film producer. And one of his projects is True Lust films, where he films real people having sex—very tasteful, very sexy. But they're not remade with plastic surgery or focused on only genitalia. And his movies look at the couple, not just the woman's parts."

Blue turns her gaze to me. "You have a problem with that?"

Since neither of them knows the issues in my first marriage—and I'm limiting myself to one full confession per month—I try to shrug it off. "I'm not a fan of pornography. But his movies are fine."

While Lux isn't buying my brush-off, Blue doesn't seem phased. "Sounds like he's a good time, if nothing else."

The rest of our meal passes pleasantly enough, with Lux updating us on Fin's horse training, which is going well, and her company's expansion—they're considering offering a wider inclusion offer, for those who aren't hardcore into kink but are still more sexually open—as well as updates on Noah and his sister Ella.

"We're invited for July fourth, if you two are up for it."

"Sure, I'm in," I say easily. I'm not as close to Noah and Ella as Lux is, but I like them. And since we don't have much family, Lux and I have been doing holidays with them.

"I don't know. I might have to work that day." Blue's discomfort radiates, and I signal Lux to let it go.

Not that she ever listens.

"It's up to you. But I'd love to introduce you to them. They've become like family to me—and I know they'll love you."

Her words carry more edges than she probably realizes, and I wait for Blue to snap back at her. Instead, something flashes in Blue's eyes I've never seen there before—longing, perhaps. And she nods. "Okay. I'll see if I can get the day off. I can't make any guarantees though."

Lux nods, pleasure in her smile. "Cool. Just let me know."

We navigate the rest of our time together with surprising ease. And when we get up to leave, the hugs are easier, last a touch longer, and when Lux and I pile into the car to head home—after she indulged in a few stores—she glances over at me. "Today was a good day, wasn't it?"

"It was. I'm glad to see Blue starting to open up a bit."

"I hope I can make things up to her."

I lay a hand on Lux's arm. "Don't try. We can't change the past. But we can forge something new—and we are. Let that be enough for now."

"God, you sound like my therapist." She gives me a half-grin. Then her expression sobers. "I need to ask you something."

I can guess where this conversation is going—I've felt the weight over my head since our conversation in the restaurant. I turn the engine over and make a big deal out of pulling into traffic. She waits until I have nothing but highway in front of me, then asks, "Have you really watched Kai's movies yet?"

Blue, I can fool. Lux knows me too well. "No, I haven't. I've been too afraid."

"You need to. They're harmless in my view—I think they're sort of wonderful in a way. But whatever your issue is with porn...you need to make sure you're okay with what he does."

I tighten my hands on the steering wheel, my stomach turning sour with the conversation. She's right. I know she is. "What if I'm not?" I take a breath. "I *like* him, Lux. For the first time in a long time, I'm having a good time. He's texted me three times today, and I don't even remember how many times yesterday. Just flirty, sweet comments. And it's fun. I haven't had anything like this in so long."

"And the sex sounds amazing."

"It was. I mean, we've only been together one time so far, but...yeah, it was pretty incredible."

She doesn't say anything. She doesn't need to.

"The DVD's at the store. It's not like I have a good excuse." I groan at my trepidation. "How does someone who hates porn get involved with someone who makes it?"

Lux's chuckle is wry, but not pointed. "The same way someone like me ends up with a guy who doesn't know squat about BDSM."

"Yeah, but Fin likes it."

"Thank God." Lux nods. "That's definitely a plus. And Kai's stuff isn't porn," she reminds me yet again, "but they are sex tapes, and you have a no sex-tape rule. There's no point in getting involved with someone if all you'll end up wanting is for him to change."

I exhale heavily and nod. "I know. I'll watch them this week."

TRACING THE LINE

CHAPTER TEN

ASSUMPTIONS CHALLENGED

"I love your place."

I look up to meet the friendly gaze of a customer who's been in the shop for about an hour. Between examining nearly every bra I stock and exploring the sex toy room in the back, she's been demanding, and I escaped behind the sales counter for a break. She's actually very sweet, but also one of the more intense customers I've experienced.

"Glad we can help you find what you're looking for," I say as she piles her purchases on the counter. "Anything gift wrapped?"

When she shakes her head, I ring her up.

She's eyeing a few of the last-minute purchase items—lip balm that offers a pleasant burn against the skin and vibrating cock rings in bright colors—when she takes another look around. "Do you have naughty videos?" She whispers the words as though someone might hear her, though we're the only ones in the store at the moment.

I paste a smile on my face. "No, I'm sorry. I don't carry porn."

"Aw, damn. I always feel skeevy looking for things online,

and there are no decent porn shops around here—they're all sketchy without windows." She tucks a long strand of heavily bleached hair back in her braid.

And there you have it, Zi. Your own issues are standing in the way of a customer's needs. "Let me give you a website that might have something fun for you. And you won't have to feel weird about checking it out." I wink at her. I hope Lux is right when she says Kai's films are female-friendly. I jot down True Lust's website on her receipt and add it to the bag. "See if there's something there you like."

"Thanks so much. Yeah, if you had videos, that would be awesome."

Yeah.

I have plans to meet up with Kai again tonight. He offered to make me dinner, and I could hardly turn that down, could I? Of course, my insides turn to jelly the minute I think of what may happen after dinner...or before. With my thoughts firmly distracted, I manage to get through the rest of the day, and as I close up the shop, I remember my promise to Lux.

With a fair amount of resistance, I force myself to dig out the DVD Kai left. The sleeve offers no indication of the content, and the disc itself is plain. I lock myself in the office and pop the sampler in the computer's drive. Here goes nothing.

Romantic—not sleazy—music plays against relatively innocuous introduction credits. A woman, attractive, in her mid-thirties if I had to guess, dressed in a slim-fitting dress, walks across a tropical landscape, towards a man sitting on a patio. When she reaches him, her smile expands, the look in her eyes warms, and the way that he reaches for her...they're clearly familiar with each other. Their movements are natural, the lighting soft. The two make love on the patio, both on the furniture and on a blanket that's been spread artfully over the ground. While it's without question an erotic scene and special attention is paid to all the, erm, involved parts, the focus remains on their pleasure. And there's tenderness and sweetness as well. The video is short, followed by two more in similar taste, though one involves mild bondage, and the other, a threesome.

Lux was accurate. These are tasteful, sensual, engaging explorations of sex by lovers, and there's nothing disrespectful or demeaning present.

I'd be lying if I said that I wasn't aroused. The videos were longer than I expected, so I'm glad I dressed up today in a sundress, rather than my usual casual clothing.

With conflicted emotions coursing through me, I head to my car and put Kai's address into the GPS app on my phone. He's rented a house here while his company is working on a series of videos with locals. It's not too far, about twenty minutes, and try as I might, I can't get what I just watched out of my mind. By the time I pull into the small, private driveway of Kai's home, I'm nearly soaked with need. The small villa is half of a California-style duplex with arched doorways and tiled roofs.

Kai's waiting on the elegant brick patio, and I barely notice what he's wearing when he stands to greet me. I pull him to me, kissing him with all the ferocity the last hour has built. He doesn't object, his arms holding me tightly.

"Fuck me," I insert between pants as his lips travel my neck and shoulder.

He leans back. "We should go inside?" He finishes on a question, hesitant.

The patio faces a somewhat secluded cul-de-sac, but nothing prevents someone from walking into the back yard or the short distance between this house and the next. And something about the possibility of being seen drives my arousal even higher. "Here. Now."

With a brief smile, he returns to my mouth briefly before turning me away from him. He draws me against his chest as his hand reaches beneath my dress. "I see you came prepared." He chuckles in my ear.

I removed my panties in the car at the last stoplight before his development. A good call, apparently. My amusement turns to a deep moan as his fingers slip inside me. I push my ass against him, enjoying the feel of his length trapped in his jeans.

He rewards me with another finger, fucking me with his hand. Pinned against him, I drop my head back, sensation taking over.

"Bend over, Zi."

He motions to the small metal and glass table before me, and I comply. He lifts my dress over my back, then explores my ass with his palms. I can't believe how this affects me—and how little my nakedness bothers me. As he teases my wet center, I bite my lip to stay silent. When his fingers fall away, I want to scream in frustration, but I hear his pants' zipper, then the head of his cock slides against me. He feels even larger than he did on Sunday, and when he spreads me and eases inside, I bite my lip as I'm split in two.

Careful not to move, he strokes my back and rear. "Is this what you had in mind?"

"God, yes," I say softly, shifting ever so slightly against him, enjoying the intense feeling of fullness. "It's all I could think about on the way over."

He holds my hips and rocks back just a little. "I like your idea of a greeting."

I'd laugh if I weren't so overwhelmed by cascading sparks over my skin. When he pushes forward, I moan. He does so again with aching slowness as I shudder under the exquisite pressure.

"I...I can't take much more." I barely expel the words between breaths as he continues his subtle torture.

"You can. Trust me." He withdraws from me completely, leaving me gasping. "I haven't even started yet."

When his tongue touches my clit, I nearly leap off the table. But his hands anchor me in place, his mouth focused on my tiny bundle of nerves. There's no stopping the noises I make as I erupt in shards of light. He continues his assault, not stopping until I'm spent. I drop my face to the table, the cool glass welcome against my overheated cheek.

Then he guides himself back into me. "See? Not even close to finished."

Ready for him, I tighten my muscles around his cock, causing him to grip my hips tighter. "Me neither," I retort.

This time, he finds an intense rhythm, and I join him. My earlier orgasms have done nothing to sate my fervor. His hands caress my breasts, pinching my nipples, following the curve of my waist, and every touch stokes my fire. There's nothing but deep pulsing need radiating out from our joining. Whimpers and moans echo in my ears, and I know I should silence myself—someone could overhear us. But there's no logical thought present. The sharp sting of a smack against my ass melds into the symphony of pleasure, and I want to beg him not to stop.

When he finally pours himself into me, I shake with my own release, though I've no idea when it started or when it will stop. He strokes my sides and hips as I quake, allowing me time to come down from the incredible high. Limp and sweaty, I weakly object when he gathers me into him. "I'm a mess."

"So am I." He massages my back and neck gently. "I don't think I've ever seen anyone have an orgasm the way you do."

I snort and bury my head in his neck. "God, it's so embarrassing."

Gripping my shoulders, he holds me away from him. "Why?"

Wrinkling my nose, I slip out of his hands and reach for the wine bottle I discarded when I leapt on him. "Because I'm noisy. And I take forever to...you know."

"Orgasm?" He holds the door for me as I step into the house. Sweet, cool air greets me, drying the perspiration on my skin. The small home has an eclectic charm with grungy antiques remade into modern art and muted colors peppered with bright swaths of red and orange.

"Yes. Orgasm." I stick my tongue out at him as I place the bottle on the kitchen table.

"You don't take long—at least, not in my experience. And it doesn't matter—that's part of who you are. Why is it a problem?"

This conversation feels strange to have while not touching, so I slip my arm around him, enjoying the solid feel of his body, the way he immediately turns towards me. "If it's not a problem for you, I guess it's okay."

"Definitely not a problem for me. I'm more enthralled with how you seem to get taken over by one ongoing orgasm. It doesn't stop for you, does it?"

I resist hiding behind my hands. "I'm not always like that, but yeah, if I'm really turned on...I can't seem to turn things off."

"Fascinating." He drops a kiss on my mouth, then releases me. "Let me go freshen up, and I'll put the finishing touches on the roast. I should have asked—do you eat meat? I can whip us up some roasted vegetables and couscous if not."

"I'm a carnivore," I assure him. He disappears into the back of the house, and I wander the small living room and dining area, admiring whoever decorated. They have a good eye for turning rusted, ugly things into beauty with some modern upholstery and bits of lace. I'm nothing like that: I look for layouts in the Target or IKEA shopping catalogues, then try to recreate them. The less effort designing my comfort takes, the better.

Minutes later, Kai emerges in a bright orange polo and long shorts. One sniff confirms he showered. "That's not fair. You get to smell fresh as a daisy, and I'm skankified."

He laughs as he pulls me close, his lips finding the spot on my neck that always drives me wild. "I like you dirty, though. And salty." He runs his tongue over my skin. "But if you insist, you are welcome to use the shower while I get dinner ready."

I nearly run into the bathroom, desperate to shower off. The scent of his soap lingers in the damp air, and I don't take long. The high point: no underwear means I'm not stuck wearing a sweat-soaked pair. There's nothing I can do about my dress, and thankfully, I have some deodorant in my car, so when I return to the kitchen, I feel moderately refreshed.

Dinner is delicious—a roast cooked perfectly in a red wine and herb marinade, and a Caesar salad tossed from scratch. I nearly swoon over the dressing, which has always been my favorite part, anyway. A crusty loaf of bread from a local baker, spread with chipotle butter, rounds out the meal, and we have fresh berries for dessert.

"My God, I may never eat again. That was wonderful."

He smiles at my appreciation. "I'm glad you enjoyed it."

"You are quite the chef."

"You didn't grow up in my home and not learn how to cook. Thankfully, I liked it, so I was an apt pupil." He stays my hand when I start to collect my dishes and utensils. "I'll get them later. Come. Sit with me in the living room?"

He lights several candles around the room, and after refilling our wine glasses, we snuggle into the couch. My legs automatically drape over his, and I lean back against the soft cushions.

"We should probably talk about earlier."

I look away, but he's right. "Yeah."

"You were pretty insistent, and let's be honest: I was not about to turn you down. But we didn't use anything."

"I'm on the pill. I have been for years to regulate my cycle. So no worries about me getting pregnant."

His fingers interlock with mine. "I'm clean. I was tested not that long ago, and I've never had anything."

"Me neither."

Awkward, anyone? He squeezes my hand. "So we're okay with that? Going forward?"

"I think so. But...what is this, exactly? Not that I'm complaining—I'm the one that attacked you." I grin at him. "But how do you see...what we're doing here?"

His gaze moves over my face, stopping at my mouth, then returning to meet my eyes. "Right now, you're driving me crazy. However, if you mean where things might lead, I don't know. I'd like to find out though, if that's what you're asking."

In the dim light, his eyes are golden, only the edges tinged in dark green, and I'm captivated. "I watched the sample." The words surprise me, as I'd meant to say something in response to his comment.

He chuckles, picking up on my astonishment. "Ah, so... any chance that had something to do with your determination earlier?"

I try to mold my expression into denial, but give up when I can't help laughing. "Maybe a little."

"How do you feel about them? I know you were worried."

"I was." I reach for my glass, if nothing else to have something to do with my hands. After a sip, I offer him a small smile. "They're not what I expected. You're right. They're not porn. They were respectful, sexy, and...fun, honestly. They were very tasteful, as well."

"I take that as high praise." He holds up a hand when I make a face. "I'm not kidding. You have reason to be sensitive about the content, and that you weren't bothered tells me we're doing something right. Your response is exactly what I want these films to create."

"Why did you decide to make these in the first place? I'm not judging—I'm just curious."

He relaxes back against the couch, giving his response some thought. "Porn gets a bad rap, in the sense that there's nothing wrong, in my view, with watching others enjoy sex. I've never seen the big deal about putting intimate encounters on tape. Some people love to record themselves, and others love to watch it. But where porn fails is that it's not done in a way that respects both parties, or that revels in the beauty of the moment. I figured: why not create a healthy environment where both parties can enjoy what turns them on? So I guess that's why I made these. To show that you could create something of beauty, not degradation and exploitation."

"So...should I take that to mean you like taping yourself?" I ask, one brow arched.

He flashes me a daring smile. "Let's just say I appreciate both sides: taping and watching."

I chuckle at his response, but then I shake my head. "I understand the appeal, but I'd never let anyone record me."

"You don't have to."

"That's not going to disappoint you?"

His brows draw together. "Not at all. You have your preferences, and they don't have to match mine every time. I may enjoy elements of what I do, but there's no requirement for those in our relationship."

My insides thrill at his words. "Is that what this is? A relationship?"

He leans in and brushes his mouth over mine. "I hope it's the start of one."

TRACING THE LINE

CHAPTER ELEVEN

EMOTIONAL YOGA

Last night was unbelievable.
Kai's text nearly has me swooning.

"Aren't you the one who yells at me for being tied to my phone all the time?" Amie chides as we hunch over our inventory lists.

I avoid looking at her; then I recount the panties in my hand for the third time.

"Oh, wow. This is serious. Who's Mr. Sexy-Texts?"

"How on earth would you know if it's got anything to do with sex?"

Amie rolls her eyes the way only a twenty-one-year-old can. "Let's see. In the entire time I've worked with you, you've never kept your phone on you," she ticks off her points with her fingers, "gotten so many texts that I could base a rap rhythm around their arrival," another finger, "and jumped to answer them like your ass is on fire. Not to mention, your skin turns beet red every time you read them. Guessing that they're sexy-texts doesn't require the skills of a space engineer."

Sadly, she's right. Kai and I have seen each other every night for the last week. At first, we each came up with an excuse to stop by—I left my lip gloss at his place. A friend had given him some movie tickets. But after a couple of days, we gave up the pretense and admitted we couldn't stay away. During the day, my phone chime rings at regular intervals. Sometimes, it's just random stuff—like a picture of his to-go lunch not living up to his gourmand tastes. Or my humor over a customer asking if we sell white cotton granny-panties.

But more often, it's a bit more, *ahem*, racy.

Your cock felt incredible. I can't wait to have you inside me tonight. I can't decide: should I do you, or dinner, first?

TRACING THE LINE

I chuck my phone away from me and pretend I don't hear Amie's chortle.

"Girl, you have it bad."

I try really hard to ignore my cell's persistent dings, but after a half hour, I can't resist any longer. In addition to Kai's response—*Definitely me—I'm already hard*—several new emails fill my business inbox.

"I'm saved by work messages." I stick my tongue out at Amie and navigate to my email app. Then I wish I hadn't.

Re: Repent of your sins, whore

Desist in your attempts to bring your vile "business" to our neighborhood. It will not be tolerated. Such evil will NOT influence our children and young people to sin. Go before God and beg his forgiveness. Pray that he'll cleanse your soul from such depravity. Otherwise, you'll burn in hell for your transgressions.

If you continue your plan to open your store here, there will be retribution.

Citizens of Lothington

Anyone arrogant enough to reject the verdict of the judge or of the priest who represents the LORD your God must be put to death. Such evil must be purged from Israel. Deuteronomy 17:12

There are two more emails with similar threats, but my hands are shaking so hard, I can't make sense of their messages. Why would someone send this?

"What's wrong? What happened?" Amie reaches for my phone, and I let her take it. Her face hardens as she reads. "Fucking Goddamn prick asswipes."

Amie's known for her colorful phrasing.

"I need to call my sister."

She hands me the phone, then grips my shoulders. "Don't let these assholes get to you. They're just trying to scare you."

"I know. But it's working."

"Don't let it. They're shitheads with nothing better to do with their time than twist Bible verses to do their bidding."

I know she's right, but an email from the landlord was one thing. This...is something else altogether. Lux left for NYC this morning; when I call her, traffic roars in the background.

"Hello, my gorgeous sister. It's barely sub-ninety here in the city, and I'm sweating like a pig. But I'm determined to get serious about exercising. I just ran half a mile—aren't you proud of me?"

She sounds so cheerful, I feel guilty for having called. I hate to rain on her sunny mood. "I am. Good for you."

"Uh-oh, something's wrong—I recognize that tone. What happened? Do I need to rough Kai up?"

"No, it's nothing like that." I forward the emails to her and explain. "I'm not sure what to do, Lux. Should I withdraw my application for the space? I mean, I know the landlord was freaked out and some folks were upset, but I didn't expect this."

"Fuck no. This is total bullshit. You can't go around threatening people to get your way. And whoever this pathetic cretin is, we're going to call down the law on them." Her fury breathes fire through the speaker. "I cannot believe some zealot asswipe would be so stupid."

She and Amie get along well, in case you couldn't guess.

"Call the cops and file a report. Sadly, they probably won't move all that quickly on this, but I know a private investigator. We'll see if she can shake any spiders from these webs. In the meantime—can you stay with Kai? Make sure you aren't alone? I'd come home now, but Noah and I are due at a meeting with an investor in two hours. By the time Fin gets here, it'll be too late to get my usual train."

My brain hadn't gotten to the realization that this threat might, in fact, be more than virtual. And while I know she's right, my anxiety revs into high gear. "No, stay where you are. But now I have to hide?"

"Not hide, just be smart. Kai's a big guy who's probably got a scary side if anyone gets near his woman. I'll come back as soon as I can—probably tomorrow."

"No, no." I scrub a hand over my face, trying to get a grip on all of this. "I'm sure Kai won't mind if I stay at his place tonight, and I'll figure shit out. You need to focus on your business and your time with Fin, and I'm an adult. You stay in the city."

"Fuck that. Fin would totally agree with me—I'm coming home."

Despite my stress, my heart warms when she calls my place "home." "Let's see what your P.I. friend says first, okay?"

"I'll call Fiona as soon as I get off the line." She pauses, then adds, "Please be careful. Whoever sent this email is a coward. But until we know more, be careful."

I leave Amie in charge of the store—and unfortunately for her, inventory counts—and head to the police station. While the cop on duty is sympathetic and takes down my details, she's unsure how soon they'll get back to me, though she assures me they take threats like this seriously.

I've never felt so unsafe in my life. As I walk out of the precinct, I find myself rushing to get to my car and slamming the locks as soon as I'm inside. How in the hell do people live when they feel threatened? I'm tempted to call Kai, but honestly, I need to see him. I key in his office's location on my GPS and try not to break too many driving laws on my way there. When I walk into the lobby, a young guy with a half-spiked, half-shaved head sits at the desk, a headset curved over one ear. He smiles brightly at me. "Can I help you?"

"I'm here to see Kai."

He reviews his computer monitor. "Do you have an appointment?"

"No, I...I'm...ah..." We've not discussed our official status as of yet. Saying I'm his "girlfriend" feels a bit too forward. "Just tell him it's Zi. He'll know who I am."

"Zi Trace?"

I nod cautiously. "How do you know—"

"You're on his list of regular visitors. Go on back."

Despite my emotions, I'm oddly pleased to know Kai put me on his "list." At least one thing is going right today.

Of course, I don't know where Kai's office is. "Which way?"

He leaves his desk and walks me down the hall. "I shouldn't have assumed you knew," he apologizes.

"No, that's fine. Since you know my name, what's yours?"

My question induces another one of this kid's brilliant smiles. "Cyrus. But everyone calls me Russ. Pleased to meet you."

Russ's easy manner and genuine handshake tamp down my nerves a bit. He's also dressed in some of the funkiest clothing I've ever seen—a sleeveless leather bomber-style vest over a crimson and cobalt striped t-shirt, with banana yellow military-type pants and leopard print Chucks. I'm torn between laughing and desperately wishing I could pull off such a look with his aplomb.

When he delivers me to Kai's door, I offer him a genuine smile, both for his guidance and for distracting me. "Thanks, Russ. Good to know you."

After another wide grin, Russ heads back to the front. Kai's on the phone, but when he sees me, his face lights up. He jots down "conference call" on his desk pad. "Ten minutes."

I nod and mouth, "Going to grab some water."

The small kitchenette has a fully stocked refrigerator, and Russ's microwaving something when I walk in.

"Conference call," I say when he raises his pierced eyebrow.

"Ah, yeah. That's going way over. Drink?" He offers me a soda from the refrigerator.

I'm not much of a sugary drink person, but my stomach warns me I haven't eaten since this morning, so I accept the can and join Russ at the single table.

"What's your position here?"

Russ laughs. "Just about anything they need. Currently, I'm assistant to the chief—well, technically, chiefs, since Ger and Kai both run the place." He shrugs, retrieving his lunch from the microwave. "Since there aren't a lot of jobs in my field out there, I'll clean toilets as long as they keep me on."

"Your field being film?"

He nods, eyeing the steaming pocket of goo before him, then splashing hot sauce all over it. "Graduated three years ago, ready to make my mark. Headed to L.A., thinking I'd

103

show them how it should be done." He winks, his pale blue eyes full of mirth. "Needless to say, I was hungry and nearly homeless a year later. Thank God for Kai, or I'd probably still be dumpster-diving in Beverlywood."

"You're here with Kai?"

"Yep. Well, not exactly. I mean, I am, but he sent me here to work for Ger when he was looking for a personal assistant. When they put Naked Truth Films together, I practically begged them to hire me. Offered my body and everything." He sighs dramatically. "Sadly, they only wanted my professional skills."

I can't help laughing at him. "You are too much."

"Sweetheart, you have *no* idea. And I bat for both teams, if you ever really want to find out." He flutters his lashes as he turns his charm on me. "So tell me: is he as good as he looks? Because I've seen that man naked, and let me tell you: I might have cried that he's so determined to be straight."

I'm not sure which surprises me more: that he's seen Kai naked, or his question. My shock must show on my face.

"Oh, honey, I lived with him—I might have purposely walked into the bathroom at an inopportune time." Russ looks heavenward with innocence. "Can you blame me?"

"No, I can't. And just between you and me," I lean in, "he's even better than he looks."

"I will now honor my ancestors and become an alcoholic, wherein I can drown my sorrows."

When Kai finds me almost a half hour later, his apologetic look quickly turns to amusement when, upon seeing him, Russ and I burst into laughter. "I can never leave you two together again. I won't have any secrets left."

Russ stuffs the remnants of his lunch into the trashcan and pats Kai's shoulder as he leaves. "I fully approve of this one, boss-man." With another wink at me, Russ disappears into the hallway.

"Do I even want to know?"

"Probably not," I answer as I slip into his arms. The whole reason I came here still weighs on me, but Russ's diversion helped. I take a moment to enjoy Kai's warmth, the gentle pressure of his hands as he rubs my back.

When I can't avoid it any longer, I step back and take Kai's hands. "I need to tell you something. And ask for a favor."

"You don't even need to ask."

Kai's answer to my request to spend the night is a relief, even though I was pretty sure I knew his answer. He stayed quiet while I explained what happened this morning and showed him the emails. So quiet, in fact, I couldn't sense his reaction. Even now, he's distant.

"I don't mean to inconvenience you with this," I say hesitantly.

It takes him several moments to look at me, and when he does, he shakes himself. "I'm sorry." He reaches for me. "I...try to take in information before reacting."

"I'm not sure what that means." I accept his hand, but I don't move any closer.

He inhales deeply and then expels his breath in a sigh. "Let's figure your situation out first. I'll explain in a little bit, I promise." He coaxes me closer, and this time, I let him. He smells fresh, safe, like him, and it's reassuring. But I can't ignore the hard cords of muscle pushing the veins in his forearms to the surface. Is he angry that I dumped my problems on him?

Calm and precise, he uses his professional voice when he speaks. "Let me contact my attorney. We'll find out what can be done. You said your sister is calling her P.I. friend? Good." He presses his mouth to my forehead. "You don't have a security system at your apartment, do you?"

I shake my head. "No, I've never had anything like this happen before."

"Are you hungry?"

His sudden change of subject throws me. "Um, yes?"

We're quiet on the walk to a deli down the block. Kai holds

my hand, placing me on his left, away from traffic. I can feel the pressure of his thoughts, but he doesn't seem to want conversation. Not until after we've ordered and taken our seats does he let his guard down.

"I'm sorry. My initial response to what you told me was rage. And that wouldn't help you. So I needed to turn inward to get it under control."

"Oh." I finger the edge of a pickle hanging off of my sub. "Did that work?"

"It did." He offers a hint of a smile. "When I was younger, I had an anger problem. I've never attacked or hit anyone—well, not since I was a teenager," he amends with a wry tone. "But when Carice and I were first married...when she would get hurt or something would upset her, I'd want to destroy anything and anyone in her path. She never fought for herself—she let people take advantage of her. And I'd get livid. While I never physically went after anyone, I said and did things I'm not proud of."

"We've all done that when we're angry."

"This was more than 'angry,' Zi. I would go into rages, shut down outside influences, and I'd stew on things for days. Weeks, even. Afterwards, I'd be ashamed, and I'd swear to never let my emotions get out of hand again. But the cycle would restart when something else happened to tick me off."

My stomach gurgles, so I satisfy the demand with a few bites of my sandwich while he talks.

"One time, I got so furious, I busted a door in our home. Carice was terrified." He hasn't touched his food. His hands lie flat on the table, and he stares at them as though reliving the moment. "I feared I'd become a monster. I would never have hurt her—never. But that she didn't know I wouldn't...I realized just how far I'd gone." His eyes close, and when he reopens them, he meets my gaze. "I went for anger management therapy, which helped. But it wasn't enough. I needed to deal with things that I hadn't."

He doesn't speak for a few minutes, and I'm not sure if I'm supposed to say something. Anger management therapy equals a good thing, right? Or is this the wildly waving red flag I'm warned to look for, but tend to ignore?

When he continues, his voice has an unaffected quality, as though he's learned how to keep emotion at bay as he tells his story. "My younger brother was bullied when we were kids. And not the you'll-grow-out-of-it kind. He was mocked and tortured because he was the 'different' kid—the odd kid." Kai looks over my shoulder as though trying to find some anchor to tether himself to while he dips into painful waters. "When he was fourteen, he killed himself. I was sixteen at the time, and I've never felt so helpless or so useless as I did in that moment. I was the older brother—I should have protected him, right?"

I open my mouth to object, but he shakes his head. "I know. It wasn't my fault. But that's how I felt at the time. I lived with that guilt for years, and as a family, we didn't talk about things. My parents were destroyed, and they blamed themselves, the same way I did. So you can imagine, living that way, it...takes a toll. When I scared Carice so badly, I knew I had to fix whatever was off balance inside me. I got counseling and figured out why I felt the ways I did. As a result, I've learned how to channel that energy into a different path, but sometimes, it takes a few minutes for me to do so. I hope I haven't just freaked you out." His expression, moments ago a mask, turns to concern and perhaps a bit of fear.

"Maybe a little." I give him half a smile as I digest his words. "When I was younger, I had a lot of emotions concerning how I was raised...or lack of raising, really. And I struggled with depression. So I can understand your feelings more than you might think. How long have you been able to moderate yourself like this?"

"I was twenty-five when I sought help, so about eight years? You can talk to anyone who works with me—Ger's known me the longest, of course. I know how to handle myself when I get angry—it's like second nature. But that's not to say the response has disappeared."

"Your body was strung tight when we were in your office." I remember how hard his muscles felt beneath my fingers.

TRACING THE LINE

He bows his head. "Someone threatened you. You matter to me. I'm not going to take that lightly."

Neither of us eats very much, but we're not inclined to leave, either, as we sit there for several minutes, not speaking. My ex was immature, a bit of a jerk at times, but he'd never been a hothead. Not really. Of course, he was never very protective of me, either. Everything I've seen of Kai has been passionate and focused, but with a levity and logic I admire. Even his ambitions seem to be tempered in a version of morality he's created based on his own life experience and conclusions.

"Is this why you and Carice don't work? The anger thing? Wait, I phrased that wrong." I hold up a hand, trying to rework the words in my brain before trying again. "I mean, the fact that she doesn't stand up for herself and needs a lot of support? You mentioned that at the fashion show."

With a nod, he answers, "In a way. Carice loves feeling small and delicate while someone bigger takes the load." He shakes his head in frustration. "That makes her sound awful, and she's not. It's just her...thing. She's the perfect woman for a big alpha-male who wants to be looked up to and worshipped. That's not me." He stops. "That's not exactly right either." He bites his cheek, then tries again. "I learned how to work with my emotional response because I started identifying triggers. Once I understood the things that bother me and recognized my physiological signs, I could address them consistently. Problem more or less solved. I've been doing it for a while now, but when you constantly feel like the front-man for someone else... She's a good person, but she likes being catered to, being protected, and I take on that role naturally. I fix problems, given the chance. She needs someone who can handle that all the time, who wants to constantly support and encourage her. God, that makes me sound like an ass, too." He rubs his forehead, looking embarrassed.

"No, it doesn't. It makes sense, actually. I have a sister for whom I've never been enough. I want to be, and I've always tried to be there for her. But she needs something I can't give her, and I've never been able to figure out what that is." Blue's enigmatic gaze comes to mind. "You can love someone a lot and not be the right fit for them."

His relief is almost palpable. "That's the way Carice and I are. I care for her—I always will. I stand behind her brand and her causes. But she needs someone who has...I don't really know what. More than I can offer, certainly."

We wrap our sandwiches and take them back to his office. The walk back offers little conversation, but our linked hands swing comfortably between us. We're careful, though, even as he kisses me and promises to meet me back at his place. I insisted I could go home and pack a bag on my own. I know he'd rather go with me, but I refuse to be coddled.

His honesty shifted our balance, and we're both stepping a bit high. As I drive home, I ponder what he told me. While the idea of "anger issues" concerns me, they don't for the reasons I initially feared. After all, my ex had control problems and could pop off quickly. However, I don't worry about that from Kai, which may be as telling as it is foolish to give much weight.

No one's perfect. I hide from things I don't want to deal with and avoid addressing conflict straight on. I haven't yet laid out a coping mechanism that enables me to stop a behavior that causes me more harm than good.

Kai's dealt with his issues. He's found a way to work within his shortcomings, and that's the work of a conscious, evolving person. So while I admire him greatly for it—and for being willing to share something that could paint him in a poor light—I wonder if he's way out of *my* comfort zone. Because if he's got a handle on his crap, that means I owe him the same responsibility on my end.

And that makes me really nervous.

ALLY BISHOP

TRACING THE LINE

CHAPTER TWELVE

SLEEPOVERS

Despite the rather passionate evenings Kai and I have spent together, we've yet to actually "sleep" together. In fact, I'm not sure we've even had sex in a bed. When I mention my thoughts to Kai as we eat our leftovers from lunch, a small grin curves his mouth.

"You might be right. Didn't we sort-of end up in your bedroom last night?"

I drop my hand to my hip. "Not unless you count having sex in the hallway. We might have briefly fallen on my bed between rounds." For some reason, most of our sex has been either on his patio, in his living room, or, when Lux is away, on my couch or floor. What's our objection to a bed? I've no clue.

"This is also the first time we've eaten before sex," he points out.

Also true.

Neither of us seems inclined to change that immediately, and we go through the ritual of cleaning up, tiptoeing around each other in an awkward dance. When there are no surfaces left to wipe down and we've washed *and* dried the dishes, we're both left staring at the floor.

"Wine on the patio?" he asks without quite meeting my gaze.

"Sure."

When we're situated in our respective chairs, I finally speak. "Maybe I'm more freaked out by your admission earlier than I'm willing to admit."

With a nod, he leans back, his long body almost too big for the chair. "I can understand that. But I'm not sure how to fix it."

"You don't have to. You told the truth—that's what we always say we want people to do. You shared a part of you that's...real. You had something tragic happen as a teen, and you didn't know how to deal with it. I know how that can eat you up inside."

"I'm not perfect, Zi, not by a long stretch, but I've never hurt anyone, and I've never been physically aggressive towards anyone. I can't say I've never run off at the mouth because, well, I was a young man once." He flashes a disarming smile. "And I was a dick on occasion. But I've never been arrested, never—"

"Remember how you told me the other day that I didn't need to justify myself to you? Same advice to you, buddy." I nudge his foot with mine. "I believe you. We all have demons, Kai. You've learned how to deal with yours...that's more than many of us can say."

He's quiet for several minutes. "I don't want you to be afraid of me."

"I'm not. I promise. I put up with a lot of shit with my ex, but I'll be damned if I'll ever do that again. So no worries." I run a finger over the rim of my glass, then take a sip so I can formulate my thoughts. "But you also said something that...I don't know. It made me both a little scared and a little...happy, I guess."

Kai leans forward, resting his elbows on his knees. "What's that?"

"You said that I 'mattered' to you."

His brows nearly hit his hairline. "Was that in question?"

"Maybe?" His surprise makes me feel foolish for doubting. "I was hoping this was more than just a good time, but we've both been a bit absorbed in, well, the sex part, so I wasn't sure if..."

He stands, then pulls me out of my chair and into his arms. "Do you really doubt that I care for you?"

I look up into his golden eyes, the desire there consuming. "We haven't talked about it."

His mouth crushes mine, his tongue sweeping in, claiming me. I swear I can feel his heart beat against my breast, and he holds me so tightly, I can only give into his kiss.

Breathless, he pulls back, his gaze piercing. "Yes, I care for you. Very much. Please don't ever question that. And I'm sorry I didn't make my feelings clear enough for you. I'll make sure that doesn't happen again." His lips curve in a slow smile.

I slide my hands into his hair, enjoying the warmth and softness. "I care for you, too. Thank you for sharing your story with me, even though I'm sorry you went through all of that."

"It's made me who I am, in many ways." His fingers find the edge of my tank top, sliding underneath to brush over my bare skin. "To assure you that you mean more than just sex, should I refrain from making any moves on you tonight? Make a wall of pillows between us on the bed?"

"Don't you dare," I whisper as his palm skims my waist, then moves upwards. "I don't think either of us could manage vows of celibacy right now." He cups my breast, his thumb rubbing over the nipple.

"True." Nudging my tank and light bra out of the way, he frees my breast. Soon his mouth replaces his fingers, suckling me hard, then softly laving the tip. He takes his time, and the setting sun warms my shoulders as he moves to my other breast. Eventually, he tugs at the waistband of my shorts, wriggling them over my hips, my panties going with them. I strip off my shirt, standing naked before him, enjoying the desire in his eyes.

"You like the risk of being seen, don't you?" He nudges me back towards the table.

My stomach wobbles at his words. "Maybe. I don't know." But he's right. I never knew I was much of an exhibitionist, but even though the likelihood of being seen here on the patio is low, it's still present. And the very idea of being watched is... turning me on.

He guides me onto my back against the cool glass of the table. "Dessert never looked so good," he teases as he nudges my knees apart. He pulls his chair close so he can sit and then drapes my legs over his shoulders.

Spread and open to him, I feel wanton and euphoric. When he teases my wet center with his fingers, exploring the delicate folds, I whimper, every touch like delicious flames. He makes me submit until I'm vibrating beneath him, desperate for more. Even then, his tongue opens me with exquisite slowness. His fingers crest my center, then withdraw, and I buck my hips in frustration.

"Jesus, Kai, don't make me wait any longer."

In return, I get a smug chuckle. "I wondered how long it would take."

"You—Ah!"

He quells my outrage by stroking his tongue over my clit. I arch my back, widening for him, and he sinks his fingers into me. With hungry moans, I writhe beneath his attention, the table squeaking in protest. His patient strokes drive me higher until I'm standing at the edge, a white-hot plummet before me. When I leap, my body explodes with sensation. His hands grip my thighs, holding me in place so I can't twist away as pleasure rolls over me in magnificent waves.

When I finally return to earth, he eases me onto his lap, his erection rock hard and pressing against my entrance. I wiggle my hips a bit, enjoying his length as I settle against him, taking him in as my body adjusts to the welcome intrusion.

"I could watch you come for hours." His teeth find a tender spot on my neck.

I moan as he adds pressure. "Hm. Keep that up, and I'll let you." I suck in air as his hands grip my ass. "It's as though you know all my...weaknesses," I say on a breath as he shifts beneath me.

"You've got a few more I want to enjoy," he whispers as he moves me ever so slightly, giving him even deeper purchase. "In time."

He guides us in a gentle rhythm as he lights fires across my skin. I fight my orgasm, largely because I want him to reach his pleasure first. But his mouth demands my acquiescence, and he captures my cries as I buck against him. When I collapse against his chest, he presses a soft kiss to my shoulder.

"Maybe I'll watch you for a while longer." His cock twitches against my hyper-aroused nerves.

I manage to raise my head, a bit woozy from my climax. "We'll see about that."

"That was impressive," he teases as we lie in bed, both a bit weary.

I extend a hand over his chest, enjoying the texture of his smooth skin and wiry hair. "Hm. Give me a little time to recover, and I'll try for a repeat performance."

He turns on his side, gazing down at me. "I'll leave that up to you. You may have outdone yourself." He kisses me lightly.

"Mm-hmm." I return the kiss, drawing his tongue into my mouth and sucking lightly, as I just did to his cock.

He falls onto his back, his smile relaxed. "You are too much."

I move so I'm lying on top of him and trace a finger over his slanted cheekbone, then down over the sharp angle of his jaw. "You said you'd like to watch me for hours. Is that sort of what people get out of your films, do you think? The enjoyment of watching someone else's pleasure?"

"I hope so. I mean, that's the goal. Traditional pornography only focuses on what you as a viewer can get out of it for yourself. The orgasms aren't real, the setups are absurd, and the focus is strictly on the mashing of genitals." He curls his arm behind his head. "I like to think in our films, you get to see the sexual experience from the perspective both as a viewer, and also as a participant. Our actors—they aren't professionals. And while they may make some money off their film, they aren't doing it for that reason. They truly enjoy being watched, and therefore, the audience gets to take part. To me, it's a much more involved sexual experience and eliminates the objectification and degradation we see in porn. Don't get me wrong—we have films that involve humiliation—but only because the parties involved *enjoy* that kind of play."

"Do you?"

His eyes widen. "Do I what?"

"Do you enjoy...well, not just humiliation, but do you like more, um, kinky kinds of play?"

"Such as?"

"Any of it? We've not really had that 'talk' yet," I say, making quote marks with my fingers.

He brushes my hair from my face, tucking a lock behind my ear, his gaze on mine. "I'm open to exploring things, if that's what you mean, but I don't have any specific 'must haves' that would fall too far into the kinky world. Well, I do like taking you from behind," he winks, "seeing as which you have the most luscious ass I've ever seen on a woman. And you seem to enjoy being spanked."

I drop my face behind my hands, my whole body heating to a flashpoint.

He chuckles, then holds me in place with one hand when I try to scoot off him. "No, you wanted to talk about it, and we should. There's no point in being embarrassed."

When I dare to look at him again, his mouth is curved in a half-smile.

"Ugh. It sounds so...weird when you say it out loud."

"Why? Have you never been spanked before?"

I make a face. "Not since I was a child. And I've never been hit ever while having sex. And I don't like anything kinky." Except having sex in possible public venues, apparently.

His expression says he read my mind. "Can it be that the sex shop owner is uncomfortable with some of her own sexual preferences?"

The directness of his question blows past my objections and hits home. It takes me a few moments to respond. "I guess I do." This time when I slide off him, he lets me. "I've never thought about it. I've always been...well, the most open-minded person people said they knew. I mean, kinky sex, weird sex, pansexual preferences...I've never cared what anyone did in their own bedroom."

He props himself on his elbow, watching me.

"But I don't think I've ever thought much about my own

likes. I've always had pretty vanilla sex—tab A, slot B stuff. Lux has been the wild one with her love of BDSM and the lifestyle. Blue, on the other hand, she never had any qualms sleeping with anything that moved. But I was 'normal,' I guess. Or that was my perception...probably everyone else's too." This conversation has taken me by surprise, and I can't stop talking. "Maybe because I was the middle child in a less-than-normal living situation? I swear, Lux had the middle-child syndrome more than I did. It's almost like I decided to be the older child, in some ways. Get the college degree, have a normal job, marry the average guy..." I'm talking fast, my fingers ticking off my points.

Kai traps one of my hands, pressing my knuckles to his mouth. "It's okay to be you, Zi. You know that, right?"

To my surprise, tears prick at my eyes, and when I turn to him, one slips over my cheek. "What if I don't know who I am?"

He traces the moist path with a finger, then tips my chin up. The green of his eyes darkens around the gold, and he speaks slowly, as though trying to make sure I hear every syllable. "Then you take time to find out." He draws me in, tucking my body around his, my face buried in his neck. "And you do know who you are. You're a successful business owner; you're a confidante to clients who come into your store looking for answers that go beyond sexy underwear. And you're an incredibly sexy, beautiful, sensual woman whom I admire greatly. Start there."

I nod, the salty remnants of my tears tangy against my tongue. "Thank you for saying that."

He pulls back, staring down at me with intensity, his hand holding my face. "Hey, I'm not doing you a favor—you don't have to thank me. I'm being honest with you. You are all of those things. Don't doubt that."

"I know. I do. I just...I haven't felt this confused in a long time, and today, with the emails and such..."

"Emotions are high. That's normal. But you'll figure things out. And I'll help you any way I can."

Looking into his eyes, seeing his conviction...it gives me a new appreciation for what he shared with me earlier. While I wouldn't accuse Kai of being a pushover, I can see his willingness to put my needs over his own. We can all be pushed and prodded into doing things we don't want to, but he doesn't require that. He simply needs to care.

"Thank you."

"Since we're on the topic, how are you feeling about everything?"

"Anxious? I've never had anything like this blow up in my face, and I'm not particularly religious, despite my foster mother's best attempts. So while I'm trying to understand the town's worry, I'm not sure how to frame this to make sense of it all."

"There's no sense in people who terrorize others. Please don't try." He presses his lips to my forehead. "Tell you what: why don't I draw you a bath so you can relax a little?"

"Hm, does that mean you're going to share it with me?"

"That might not be all that relaxing."

I wrinkle my nose at him. "Spoil sport."

He tips me off of him and steps into a pair of shorts. "I have an idea, if you insist. Might both relax you and help you release that anxious energy."

If this place ever goes on the market, I might cash in my retirement to buy it. The bathroom houses the biggest tub I've seen in a residential home—complete with claw feet and a padded rim.

"What man has bubble bath just lying around?"

"This man." He snatches the bottle out of my hands, adding a generous amount to the running water.

"Please tell me you're going to fuck me thoroughly before I get in?"

He gives my ass a firm tap. "You are a difficult woman to be a gentleman around. Would you let me do something nice for you, dammit?"

"That would be nice. Very—" I slide my hand over the noticeable bulge in his shorts, "—nice."

He closes his eyes as my fingers squeeze and massage his

erection. Then, with effort, he removes my hand. "Do I need to tie you up to get you in the tub?"

I laugh, then wink. "I've never been much for bondage, but you might convince me."

He hugs me hard before he steers me to the prepared bath. Bubbles teem over the surface, and despite my mounting desire, the froth looks very inviting. He holds my hand as I settle into the almost too-hot water.

I release a sigh. "This does feel pretty good."

He gives me a withering glance, but he's unable to resist grinning. "Gee, really? I wouldn't have guessed."

"It would feel even more relaxing if you joined me."

Leaning against the double sink, he regards me with amusement and frustration. "You know, I'm trying to do the right thing, be the good guy, let my girlfriend take it easy after a stressful, downright scary day full of whack jobs and confessions. You don't make this easy."

I prop a leg over the side of the tub in what I hope is a sexy pose. "I'm making this extremely easy." I consider what he said. "Girlfriend now, is it?"

"Are you objecting?" His smirk suggests he's not concerned with my response.

I lift a shoulder, giving him a coy grin. "I didn't say I was." I rub my toe along the edge of the tub. "You sure you don't want to join me?"

He shakes his head but gives in with a heavy sigh. He removes his shorts without looking at me, but I'm pleased to see my effect on him when he finally turns around. I lean forward so he can sink down behind me.

"Think you can manage to just lie here for a few minutes?" He draws me back, tucking his legs beneath me so my full length covers him.

I ignore his question. "This is an impressive tub—I've never fit comfortably in these things."

"If I remember correctly, they had it custom-made, just for that reason. The owners are both tall—the guy's nearly as tall as me."

"I haven't met too many men your height. It's a nice change. I'm used to dating shorter guys." His hard cock throbs beneath my ass, and I tighten my gluteus muscles, teasing him.

"Amateur." He bends his legs, separating mine easily so I'm splayed open. "You will take it easy, if I have to hold you down to do it."

"Promises, promises." I have no idea what's made me so feisty tonight, outside of the fact that I do feel safe with this man. Something in his eyes, both earlier as he offered me his dark secret, and later, when he confirmed his affection...I can't forget the warmth in his eyes. And it makes me want to do all sorts of nasty things to him.

He gathers my hands and locks them against my stomach, secure under his tight hold. He growls when I try to slide my ass against his cock. Then he bites my shoulder, a bit harder than usual, and I'm so turned on, I stretch my neck to give him better access.

Ignoring my attempts to wriggle free, he uses his free hand to trace the outline of my pussy, making wide circles around the outside, punctuated with a few teasing dips towards my center. I arch against him when he gets closer to where I want him, but he continues his ridiculously slow torture.

"Lie back on me and breathe deeply." He draws my hands up my body, resting them between my breasts, still confined by his grip.

Since I can't move my upper body, I have to behave. I do as he suggests, largely because his fingers continue to ply my delicate skin with light touches, never going quite high enough, but my growing need burns hotter still.

He never increases his pace, and my head lolls on his shoulder, eyes closed. Eventually, his fingertips slip inside, but they don't linger. Instead, he continues teasing and tempting, never giving me enough stimulation to draw out an orgasm, but just enough to keep me aroused.

"Are you ready to get out?" he asks as I tip my hips up, wanting more.

I nod, languid. "Mm."

He chuckles as he helps me up. "Relaxation achieved." He dries me, then himself.

Whatever that was, I'm now deliciously numb, my body still thrumming from his touch but my mind blissfully empty.

When he tucks me in bed, I frown. "Are you seriously not going to let me come?"

"I never said that." Kai slides in beside me, his body warm against my already chilled limbs. "But you aren't lifting a finger, either."

My legs fall open as his hand returns to its earlier task. I can't keep my eyes open, but I can feel him watching me. This drawn-out, slow burn leaves me both hungry for more and ready to fall asleep.

"Please," I whisper as he pushes a strengthening wave higher and higher inside me.

"Relax, baby. I've got you."

His fingers stroke inside me, and I moan with their increased pace. When my orgasm finally crests, the gentle, rolling waves shift over me for several minutes. He doesn't retreat, letting the soft, encompassing blanket of sensation cover me completely.

I don't even remember falling asleep.

/ **TRACING THE LINE**

CHAPTER THIRTEEN

STARS, STRIPES, AND HIGHLANDERS

"Ye Americans and yer messy concoctions of meat," Fin declares in his deep Scottish brogue as he digs into a hot dog heaped with chili, onions, relish, and mustard. "God bless ye," he finishes before taking a massive bite. Chili drips down his chin, and Lux busts out laughing.

Kai and I are late to the July Fourth cookout hosted by Ella and Ian Crane. Their home—a gorgeous two-story in Long Island, New York—is several hours away, after all. But, well, we also pulled over to the side of the road as Kai couldn't drive with my mouth around his cock. Then we ended up outside of the car and taking full advantage of my short dress.

Ahem.

When we arrive, everyone's already at the table with full plates in front of them. I felt bad enough about being late, so I'm glad they didn't wait. Blue bowed out last week, much to Lux's disappointment. I can't say I was surprised, as I keep reminding my older sister: Blue requires baby steps. There's a hard-candy shell around that girl that's tough to crack.

Lux hops up from the table and leaps on me with a hug. "Finally! I was almost ready to call you." When she steps back, her gaze takes in every detail. "But I see I needn't have worried." She gives me a smirk, then turns to Kai. "And I'm glad to see you taking such good care of my sister."

Kai looks like he's trying to figure out the joke, but then he smiles and leans down to buss her cheek. "Good to see you again."

We introduce him—well, Lux does—to everyone. Ella and Noah are siblings, and longtime friends of Lux—I think they met in college, if I remember the story correctly. It doesn't take much to see the resemblance between Ella and Noah—they both have thick, dark brown hair that falls in curls and stunning blue eyes with irises ringed silver. While Noah's still single, there's a pretty raven-haired woman beside him, and I nod when Lux introduces her as "Viv." Ian's an attorney in New York City, and he used to be considered one of the city's most eligible bachelors—alongside his best friend and mega movie star Mick Jeffries, who's also here today—until he met Ella. Ella and Ian's little girl Mia is three, an adorable bundle of chestnut ringlets and brilliant blue eyes, and she uses our interruption as an excuse to run in circles around the table, gifting everyone with a potato chip or baby carrot, depending on what she deems fit for them.

Lux settles back beside Fin, and it's good to see them together again. Fin, his auburn hair a bit longer than the last time I saw him, smiles warmly and stands to give me a hug. "Aye, good to see ye, Zi. You look lovely as always." He and Kai shake hands. They're of similar height, though Kai's taller by a few inches. Mick positions a few chairs between him and Fin, then leans in to shake Kai's hand.

Kai looks a bit dumbfounded. "Mick Jeffries?"

"You didn't warn him?" Ella teases after cajoling Mia back into her chair and coming over to greet me. "You cruel woman."

She squeezes me tight, and I return the gesture. Noah, Ella, and Ian have tried hard to become as close to me as they are to Lux. If not for the geographical distance between us, perhaps we would be. I admit: sometimes I feel a bit like an outsider when they're all together, which can make me a little cranky. Lux is *my* sister, after all. Despite our ten-year estrangement, she and I have become really close again...but perhaps I'm still working through a few issues?

Ella's warmth makes it impossible for me not to try, and as her pleased gaze meets mine, I discover I'm happier to see her than I expected.

"I like—this is the one Lux was telling me about?" she leans in to whisper.

I give her a slight nod, and she winks. "Cute," she mouths

before turning to greet Kai.

We get plates and fill them with standard American holiday fare: burgers and hotdogs, potato salad, coleslaw, cubes of expensive cheeses and bits of olive mixes. I've never had holidays the way Noah and Ella do, and they always go out of their way to make it fun. Mick and Kai immediately fall into conversation about movies, and Fin and Noah join in while Ian mans another round of burgers on the grill. Lux and I catch up—she's been in the city for the last week since I've been staying with Kai.

"Any more nasty emails from the ass...inine jerks?" Lux corrects her language as Ella tucks in beside us, Mia on her lap.

"Yeah, what's going on with that? Lux brought me up to speed." Ella's concern forms a frown on her pretty face.

"Nothing so far. The police said the message came from a public ISP, so I'm screwed. Anything more from Fiona?"

Lux shrugs. "Her guy got the same info. She's been checking into some of the online comments on the township's website, and there's a ton of vitriol there." She hands me Fiona's number. "Call her tomorrow—oh, wait, she's out of town. Call her on Friday. I think she's back then, as she had a few ideas about tracking the sh—craphead down."

"I'm not even sure if it's worth it. The landlord's still on the fence. I have a request to appear at a township meeting later this month and plead my case, basically. Kai's attorney said that if they apply enough pressure, short of trying to sue the township, I won't have much traction. And I'm not going to make a legal mess out of this."

Ella squeezes my arm. "I'm sorry, Zi. This is so stupid. Do you want Ian to look into it? That's not his field, but..."

"No, it's fine. Kai's attorney has been great, and Kai refuses to let me pay for it. But thank you. That's very kind."

Lux shakes her head. "Okay, enough crappy talk for one afternoon. Let's talk about the dreaminess that is Kai. Mia, Uncle Fin would love to take you inside to play with Tag, wouldn't you, Uncle Fin?"

Fin's lost in the guys' conversation, but when Lux's hand

strokes his back, he immediately withdraws—it's kind of cute, actually. Even after a year, he's as besotted with her as ever, and she seems to feel the same way.

"Of course, ye wee nipper. Come here, firecracker!" He lifts Mia high over his head, making her squeal and raise her hands like she's flying. She laughs hysterically when he pretends he's going to drop her, then cuddles her against his chest, her small body curled in one arm. She looks like a tiny rag doll against his broad chest. "Let's go find the pooch, eh?"

"I'll join you," Noah calls, standing. "I should take Tag out anyway." Viv follows him, and I feel mildly guilty for not including her in our girl-talk. But knowing how Noah goes through women...let's just say, the boy can't seem to decide on a flavor of the week, much less of the month. I think the dog was supposed to help him get women...but I've no idea why he thought he needed any help. The man's gorgeous, but despite his humor and generally good heart, something's broken in him. Hell, I can relate to that, for sure.

Ella's gaze doesn't leave her daughter until they disappear into the house. "I swear, you and Fin can never move away—I'll never find a babysitter as good as Fin. Not even Noah, and I'd trust him with Mia's life. Fin has such a way with kids."

"And animals. He's some kind of horse whisperer." Lux sighs.

"Oh, speaking of which, don't let me forget to talk to him about getting riding lessons for Mia. I want to get his advice." Ella trails off as though she's making a list of questions for him in her mind.

"Since he's so good with children..." I tease Lux, knowing what her answer's going to be.

She holds up a hand, as per her usual. "Don't even. I swear, Mia's given the man procreation tendencies. He's been dropping hints."

I chuckle, admiring Fin's bravery. "I'm amazed his balls are still intact."

"Well, he wouldn't serve me very well without them," she says with an arched brow. The Dominatrix is never too far beneath the surface with my sister.

"It's still a pretty firm no, then?" Ella asks gently.

When I ask Lux such questions, I annoy the crap out of her. But something about Ella's spirit seems to soothe Lux's beast.

"Right now, it's no." Lux tugs her dark hair loose and draws her fingers through the shiny, coiling strands. She wears a red-white-and-blue striped camisole and shorts that use only slightly more material than you might require for bikini bottoms, but on her, they serve only to point out how beautiful she truly is. "But who knows? He wants to, you know, finish school...get situated with his practice."

Fin already has a horse-training portfolio, and when he can swing it, he travels across the country with his mentor working with troubled animals.

"He might have proposed."

"What?" Ella and I say at the same time.

Lux's full lips pull into a frown. "I know. Don't get me started."

What was just a small resistance to getting married has turned into legendary refusal on Lux's part. Fin wants nothing more than to whisk her off to Vegas—or even have a full event with a white dress and three hundred guests—whenever she's ready, but Lux has been dead set against even contemplating a date.

"What did you say?" I'm shocked she didn't tell me.

"Don't get upset—he just did it last night."

Something flashes in the sun, and I nearly do a double-take as I realize there's a ring on her finger. And not just any ring.

"Dear God, he must've spent a fortune," Ella breathes after grabbing Lux's hand so she and I can gape at the lustrous sparkle. Blue-tinged metal I can only assume is platinum shines in a stark, modern design. An emerald cut diamond sits suspended in the center, and to my inexperienced eye, the rock is huge.

Lux looks miserable. "He did. Way too much. I knew he was taking on more clients than he should, but Jesus. Then he does something like this."

I shake my head in wonder. "I assume this means you said

yes?"

She sighs, her gray eyes softening despite her irritation... which makes me think someone is protesting a bit much. "It wasn't a traditional proposal. He said he wanted to give me something to show how much he loves me, and that he's in this with me for, well, you know, ever." She can't look at either Ella or me. "And he wanted to have something on my finger that, um, means that I belong to him since he wears a ring for me."

"Oo, sneaky. He did a whole BDSM claiming thing on you." While there's no question who Doms in their relationship, I have a sneaky suspicion that on occasion, my very strong-willed sister enjoys turning the tables—not that she'd ever admit it. Doms often want to leave something on their subs as a marker of ownership, and the ring Fin wears was her gift to him not long ago. A sign both of her love...and her mark on him. Fin was smart enough to demand equality with a diamond—not even Lux can turn that down.

She narrows her eyes at me, then gives in. "Arsehole," she says, mimicking his accent. "Yeah, yeah. And it was sweet and romantic and adorable."

"So you didn't actually have to say yes or no, then? To anything?" Ella asks, confused.

"No—I mean, yes, I had to answer him. He wanted to know if I wished to be with him long-term." Lux stumbles over her words, which tells me more than anything else she says. She might not have said "yes" to marriage, but she agreed to a lifetime commitment with Fin.

Anyone who knows my sister is well aware of her fear that she'd never find the right guy. I nearly explode with happiness. "Oh my God, Lux. This is so great." I pull her into a hug, and after some mock resistance, she gives in. She's shaking a little, and when I try to pull back to check on her, she won't let me. So I hold her while she pulls herself together, thankful for once that she clings to me, instead of the other way around.

Ella kisses her cheek, in typical genteel-Ella fashion. "I'm very happy for you. Whatever this is." She winks.

"Okay, enough about my no-marriage-engagement."

Lux swipes a finger beneath her eyes, then turns to me. "Your turn—tell us all about Kai."

I barely get five minutes to myself the whole day, which is actually more glorious than it sounds. I excuse myself to use the restroom, really as a way to get a few minutes of quiet. We're playing a card game now—Cards Against Humanity—and my sides ache from laughter. The day holds true to typical northeastern weather—high humidity, high temperature, no wind. But the sticky atmosphere does nothing to stop our holiday celebration.

When I step inside the cool house, I wander to the kitchen and nearly walk right into Noah.

"Hey, Zi." He smiles broadly, and I'm struck by what a good-looking guy he is. It's easy to get used to him as Ella's not-so-serious brother, but he's quite a looker.

"Hey yourself. How are you? I haven't had a chance to talk to you yet."

He gestures to Tag's leash. "I just put Mia down for her nap, and I'm taking Mr. Poops-A-Lot for a walk. You want to join me?"

I nod, and we head out the door. We enjoy a few moments of silence as Tag sniffs industriously along our path. Noah got Tag from the shelter as a puppy, believing him a mutt. But now, at over a year old, it's clear that Tag is an American Staffordshire—also known as a pit bull. He lives up to every bit of his breed: funny, charming, and deliriously happy with people. He lets Mia pull him around by his collar, and then stares at her adoringly while she plays with his ears.

"So how are things? Lux said you're bowing out of Elementary?"

"What?" He looks over at me, surprise widening his eyes. "No, not bowing out. Just letting some of our staff handle more of the day-to-day stuff. Mick asked me to help him open a film and theater school in the city for kids, so I've been assisting with the planning and footwork."

"Really? That sounds wonderful, Noah."

He grins, a small dimple punctuating his expression. "It is. I've been wanting to get into the acting world for so long, and I took a small part last year in one of Mick's movies—did I tell you that?"

"Um, no," I say and punch his shoulder lightly. "How could you not email me at least? Text? And why haven't I seen this movie yet?" While I may not be super close to him and his sister, Noah and I sometimes fall into texting each other quips and silly pictures. Not often—just a couple times a month.

"Well, it's not a big deal, and the movie doesn't release until later this year. But yeah, we had a lot of fun on the set the couple of days I was there, and Mick and I started talking about his ideas. I'd had something similar sketched out a few years ago—one of those things you save on your hard drive in a 'wishful thinking' folder—and it clicked. We just found the right space—it's not far from my apartment, actually—and we're going to open the end of summer, I think. So I'm taking less of a role in Elementary, but I'm not leaving or anything. Jesus, Ella would have my head."

"That's amazing. I remember the conversation we had last Christmas, and you were looking for something that really excited you to be part of—it sounds like you found it. I'm so happy for you."

"Thanks." His pleasure over my excitement is evident, and it occurs to me that perhaps it's not the amount of time spent together that determines the depth of friendship. Maybe it's simply caring.

We wait for Tag to find the perfect spot for his needs—my God, you'd think the grass had to be of exotic seed and perfectly fluffed before the dog finally settled on a location—and then we head back.

"So you and Kai—it's serious?"

My cheeks flame at his question. "Oh, I don't know. I guess? It's been two weeks? Three maybe? Hard to say we're super serious. But I got some threatening emails—"

"Lux told me about those. You okay?"

"Yeah, I'm fine. I mean, it's going to be fine. But because of that, I've been staying at Kai's place when Lux isn't in town."

"He seems like a great guy. I know Ger, his buddy, and Ger can't say enough good things about Kai. I'm glad I finally got to meet him."

His words are like a salve to any doubts our conversation might have stirred up. "That's good to know. How about you? Viv seems nice." In truth, Viv seems...quiet. Like a pretty vase you keep dusted and on a shelf for viewing only. But perhaps that's because she's the stranger in a group who all, more or less, know each other.

"Yeah, this was a bad call today. We've been out a few times, and I thought she'd have fun, but she's...well, let's face it. We're all entrepreneurs with a lot of passion and focus, and Viv's an admin assistant to an accountant. Nothing wrong with that," he hurries to explain as though I might judge his words, "but I think she's more into me for—"

"Sex?"

Now it's Noah's turn for pink cheeks. "I wouldn't have said it quite that way, but perhaps." He chortles, his embarrassment short-lived. "Wouldn't be the first time."

I shake my head, complete with eye roll, at his comment. "Yeah, yeah, lover boy. But no sparks with this one? Lux said you were testing out the dating-for-more-than-one-night experience."

"Online dating sucks." He shrugs, as though his words say

it all. And they probably do.

"So maybe you'll meet someone in your new foray. Perhaps some hot, single mom will enroll her kid in your program," I tease.

"Oh, yes, that'd be brilliant. I can barely manage to keep up with Mia—can you imagine me with a kid of my own?"

"Mia likes you well enough."

His expression brightens at the mention of his niece. "Well, that's because Mia is brilliant and perfect. Minus the poopy diapers, mind you." He shivers. "Bleck. I'm not cut out for kids, I don't think. Nieces and nephews, bring 'em on. But my own...nah, I'm good with a dog. Tag's happy as an only-dog, anyway."

I grin, wondering if he might be right. Noah's not big on romantic commitment, obviously. Until he conquers that fear, it's better not to bring any children into the mix.

"Hey, next time you're in the city with Lux, don't be a stranger. I'll show you the school plans and stuff."

"Sounds good." On impulse, I give him a quick hug. "I'm proud of you, Noah. You're doing something really good here, and it's going to be awesome. I know it."

His pleased smile is my reward. I leave him at the front door and follow the side of the house around to the back.

The sun's just setting, allowing the coolness of night to seep in. Kai's getting another bottle of water by the ice bucket near the fence gate. When he sees me, he glances behind him at the table where everyone's chatting and laughing, then slips out the gate and grabs my hand.

We end up in Ella and Ian's open garage, and with a little searching, find the button to lower the garage door. Then he pulls me into him, the dark, windowless space leaving us blind. His mouth finds mine, hungry and demanding, and I give in with abandon. The faint scent of gasoline and cut grass dissipates as I get lost in the feel of Kai's mouth, his hands roaming my body, the cinnamon and spice of his scent.

"Your friends are wonderful," he whispers, both of us breathless.

"I'm glad you like them. It's mutual." His lips capture mine again.

I reach for his shorts, tugging at the button.

"You want to do something here? In the garage?"

His surprised questions make me chuckle, and I manage to dislodge his waistband and slide the zipper southward. I'm not sure if he's more shocked that I have every intention of fucking him in a less-than-romantic garage, or because we're in Ella and Ian's house, technically, but I don't care. I've never felt this alive around anyone.

Any objections he might have are quelled when I lean over the car beside us, pressing my ass against his very ready erection. "Unless you would prefer the driveway? The neighbors might notice, though."

My answer comes in the form of his cock sheathed to the hilt inside me. He presses my thighs apart with his, ensuring that I have no leverage with which to respond, and then, with a ferocity I crave, he pounds into me. We're careful to stay quiet, his hand covering my mouth when I accidentally whimper. He fucks me hard, without mercy, and I come apart at the seams as the friction sends me flying. My orgasm rolls into the next, and then the next.

He's nearing his own crescendo when he stops suddenly, turns me so I'm facing him. Setting me on the hood of the car, he enters me as though he belongs inside me, and his mouth takes mine with such gentleness, I'm not sure how to respond. I wrap my legs around his hips, and as I feel him implode, I press my mouth over his, containing his groan.

For minutes after, he holds me without speaking, his breath rasping in my ear. His heart beats strong against my hand, and whatever we were before this moment has been shaped into something else completely...and will never be the same.

TRACING THE LINE

CHAPTER FOURTEEN

DYING WISHES

It's almost nine at night when my phone rings. Noah left to take Viv home, but the rest of us are still here. Ian made a fire in their outdoor fire pit, and we're all seated—or lying down, in Kai's case—on blankets in the grass. Kai's warm shoulder leans against my thigh, and when my ringtone sounds, I'm tempted to ignore the interruption. But something tells me I need to answer.

Blue's sob greets me.

My stomach lands somewhere in my toes. "Blue? Where are you, baby? What's wrong?"

I can't make out her words, and after a few moments listening to her incoherent shrieks, I realize she's not only crying, she's drunk. Or high.

"Shit," I say softly. Kai's watching me, and when I look up, Lux's gaze meets mine.

"We have to go," she says to Fin.

Whatever conversation was occurring has shushed, and Ella looks from Lux to me, then back at Lux. "What's wrong?"

"It's our sister," Lux says.

Blue's still freaking out, and I can't get her to slow down. I keep the phone to my ear as Kai helps me to my feet, and I look apologetically to Ella and Ian. "I'm so sorry," I whisper.

Ella waves off my apology and gives me a quick hug. "Call me later?" she mouths, her hand in the shape of a phone beside her cheek.

I nod to Ella, then to Ian and Mick to say good-bye. Fin and Lux follow Kai and me to the street.

"Blue, honey, tell me where you are. Are you home?" She's fallen into long wails, and I'm not even sure she can hear me. "Blue, I can't help if you don't tell me where you are." I shrug to Lux and Fin, unsure what to do. "Blue?"

Then Blue screams so loud, I rip the phone away from my ear. Mid-shriek, she hangs up. I try to call her back, but she doesn't answer.

"Now what?" Lux looks at me, her face a mask.

"I...don't know. She might be at her apartment. Or she could be anywhere."

"Is she seeing anyone? Does she have any friends we can call?" Fin asks, concern and confusion in his gaze.

"No idea. Blue's never mentioned anyone serious, and I don't know whom she hangs out with anymore. Who knows? Let's go home." I turn to Kai. "Can you take me to Blue's? I can at least check to see if she's there, and I'll try to call her again on the way."

"Would she harm herself?"

His question doesn't surprise me, and I realize belatedly that he must be thinking of his little brother, and the nightmare of that experience. "I don't think so. Years ago, maybe. But I don't think she'd do that now."

With an affirmative glance, he unlocks the car and tucks me inside. "Do you want to go with us?" He looks at Lux and Fin.

Fin doesn't even bother to glance at my sister before reaching for the door handle. Lux climbs in, and when I look over my shoulder, her expressionless gaze is painful to see. If there's one thing Lux does well, she controls a situation.

Blue's not one to be controlled, though. She doesn't let anyone get too comfortable. I don't know if I've ever dealt with her quite like this, but I remember the wild emotional fits she had when she was younger. Whether tonight is driven by emotion or substance abuse, I'm not sure. One thing I do know: my little sister has never made life easy on herself...or anyone around her.

Blue lives in a rundown apartment complex on the other side of Bakertown. In an area known to have drug issues, low-income housing fences the perimeter of her street. When she first moved here, I wanted her to stay with me, but my ex forbade the suggestion. Honestly, he might have been right. Our marriage may have broken up even faster with my tempestuous little sister around. Still, I hate that she lives somewhere that doesn't feel safe from the moment you pull onto the block.

She keeps a spare key in a filthy planter at the end of her sidewalk, and I dig through the broken plastic in the dark. Once I have it in hand, all four of us troop to the door. Lux remained silent for most of the ride, and Fin and Kai made a bit of small talk. Kai didn't let go of my hand, and even now, he hovers close to me. On one hand, I want to snap at him that I'm fine, I can handle this; I'm used to my sister's antics. But the other side of me is so thankful I'm not alone and for his calming presence beside me. I bite my lip and unlock the door.

Her place is a jumble of colorful decor and…well…stuff. Piled on every flat surface. Blue's not dirty—the old carpeting and vinyl prove she regularly vacuums and mops. But she tends to collect things. Nothing seems untoward, and I call her name softly, then louder.

I leave Lux and the guys in the living area and trail into the kitchen. Dirty dishes line the sink, but the space is well kept, the counters wiped clean. When I venture into her bedroom, I see her telltale bright red hair streaking across the floor at the end of the bed.

"Back here!" I call as I drop to Blue's side and shift her to her back. Her breaths come in soft whispers, dragging a sigh of relief from me as I check her pulse. She smells like a bar, but all her vital signs are fine. An empty bottle of scotch lies on its side not far from her hand. Who knows how much she drank, but that explains her condition. Kai nudges me out of the way so he can lift her onto the bed. She looks so small and fragile in his arms, her bare feet tiny—she's always looked like a doll, almost too petite to be human.

TRACING THE LINE

As I search the floor and bathroom, Lux asks, "What are you doing?"

"Checking for pill bottles. She overdosed when she was nineteen. I think she's just passed out from too much booze, but I want to make sure."

"We should call an ambulance, then." Lux's voice is stony.

When I meet her gaze, though, I spy the fear behind her walls. "I don't think she did—I don't see anything suspicious." In fact, the only pills she has in her bathroom are aspirin. "She's been clean for several years, but I always worry."

I sink down beside Blue, checking her pulse again.

Fin lays a warm hand on my shoulder. "I checked her out—humans aren't that much different from animals, aye? And I have some basic EMT training. I think she's just knackered from drinking."

I nod, offering him an attempt at a grateful smile. He and Kai bow out to the kitchen, leaving Lux and I alone with Blue. The light overhead casts a harsh glow, so I flip the switch. Brightness from the kitchen threads through the doorway, and we're awash in shadows—and not only the ones we can see.

Lux sits at the end of the bed. "It's easy to forget how small she is."

"She looks like a child when she's not all made up and full of attitude." I guide a few strands of hair behind Blue's ear, her heavy breathing a relief to hear.

"And you ignore the amount of ink this girl has amassed. I thought I was hardcore when I got my shoulder done." Lux brushes the edge of Blue's tank above her shorts. "Holy shit."

Since Blue's lost to the world, I turn her gently so Lux can see at least a bit of her tattoo. Blue has a full back piece that extends across her abdomen—a wild collection of hearts and flowers, skulls and bones, koi and Asian characters. The colors are vibrant and intense, with patches of black and white, all against a deep blue background that looks like the sea in places. A massive dragon sits at the bottom of the design, and his tail circles her waist.

"Damn. That's some of the finest work I've seen."

I nod. "I remember when she got it done. The last time she got out of rehab—when she was finally sober and seemed to be putting things together in her life."

"I can only imagine how expensive it was."

"You have no idea. She was friends with the artist, probably sleeping with him, come to think of it, and I gave her money towards it for her birthday. She'd never admit how much she paid." I ease her against the mattress, stroking her hair back from her face.

"What are these?" Lux points to the scars inside Blue's thigh. They're faint, thin white lines at odd intervals along the inside of her legs.

"She's a cutter. Ever since we moved to Mama C's. Maybe even before. I don't think she does it anymore, but I used to find her a bloody mess when we were kids. Getting the stains out of her clothes was always a trial."

"Why didn't I know about this?"

I meet her gaze and say my next words carefully. "You had your own issues, sweetie. Blue begged me not to tell you—she didn't want you to think less of her."

Her mask slips a little, revealing the sadness I've always known is there. "I shouldn't have left."

"You didn't know what would happen."

"I didn't know what *was* happening," she retorts, her full lips pressing into an angry line. "Jesus, how could all this go on? Was I that oblivious?"

I let her harsh tone echo in the silence, having wondered that myself in my low moments. How could she leave us, when she had personal experience with how unprotected we were at Mama C's? But we were children, and worse yet, children for who abuse was normal. So I don't blame her for running, not now. But Blue did. And some days, even my scars feel a bit tender.

"I thought you didn't need me anymore," Lux says quietly. "You were only a year younger, and Blue...I thought she was doing okay. She'd finally found her art, her grades were decent...I thought..."

I reach for her hand, but she turns away. "Lux, we all had to survive the best way we knew how, and we did. Sure, it wasn't ideal. But whether or not you were there wouldn't have changed the outcome—and that's probably just as painful to hear, in some ways," I say in apology. "No one should have to go through what you did."

I lie down beside my little sister, amazed at the differences between us despite our shared DNA. After a few quiet minutes, I ask, "Do you remember when we'd all crawl into your bed at night so we could read your *Seventeen* magazine?"

Lux nods. "And this little shit would steal all the blankets so you and I would freeze." She runs a slim finger over the top of Blue's foot. "Jesus, her skin's paler than mine. You can see every vein."

"Well, in fairness, she was probably colder than both of us with no meat on her bones. And you never let her turn the pages." Blue would melt down over her lack of control, and Lux lorded it over her. "We were monsters."

That makes Lux chortle. "Yeah, we were."

Blue stirs beside me, and I nearly sigh with relief. "Blue? Baby, can you hear me? Open your eyes, honey." I stroke her hair as her lashes flutter. Red veins color the whites of her eyes, the irises pale. She brushes my hand away, a sure sign she's returning to herself.

"What happened?" Her words are slurred but understandable.

"I have no idea. You called me freaking out. You were unconscious when I got here."

She rubs her face but doesn't try to sit up. "I had a few drinks."

"I think you had a whole bottle." I try to keep my tone pleasant, but annoyance seeps in. "Why the hell did you get so drunk?"

Her expression turns hostile, as though she's about to raise her voice, but then she curls onto her side, her sobs soft whimpers.

"Blue, sweetie, what happened?" I lay a tentative hand on

her back, and when she doesn't push me away, I rub her trembling shoulders. "What's wrong?"

She's inconsolable, and when she lunges into my arms, hanging around my neck, I gather her slight frame to me, giving Lux a baffled look. When her emotion turns to hiccups and sniffles, Lux grabs a roll of toilet paper in lieu of tissues—there's none to be found—and I push Blue's hair out of her face. Cupping her cheek, I force her to look at me. "What's wrong? Tell me."

"It's Mommy. She's dying."

We're at an all-night diner in town. Blue didn't last long—she passed out again, and there wasn't much more we could do.

The four of us look worse for the wear, though Fin and Kai put on brave faces despite their exhaustion. Apparently, Lux hasn't told Fin much about our family issues; at least, any more than he needed to know. "So yer mum gave all three of ye up when ye were teens, if I remember?"

Lux snorts, the sound bitter and ugly. "No, we were taken from her for neglect and endangerment." She closes her eyes and takes a deep breath. "And here I thought I got all my anger out in therapy." Her wry joke falls a bit flat, and Fin pulls her close and kisses the top of her head.

"What about yer father? Why did he not take ye?"

Before Lux can answer—and largely to save her from even more acidic energy—I respond. "Who knows if they even knew about us?" When his ginger eyebrows shoot up, I explain. "We each have a different father—if you couldn't tell by how little we look related." In truth, the only common traits among the three of us are possibly our noses, and we have more or less heart-shaped faces.

Kai lays his palm on my knee without suggestion, and his comfort keeps me from falling apart. "Our mother was—is—a drug addict. Always has been. And she looked for something new and shiny every time she got bored. Sadly for us, that usually meant new men."

"Or women," Lux inserts.

I nod in agreement. "True. She was an equal opportunity train wreck."

"So your fathers were different ethnicities then? Is that where your names come from?" Kai asks politely.

Lux snorts. "Do I look Latin to you? No, she picked whatever came to mind. God only knows where she got my name. She named Zi for what—some fantasy character she liked as a kid?"

"I'm not even sure it exists. My full name is Ziamora," I explain to Kai. "No middle name because she couldn't think of anything at the time."

"And what mother names her kid 'Blue'? She got that out of a fucking crayon box, I guess."

Sadly, I think Lux might be right. We've never understood our names or why our mother chose them, and when we asked her, she gave us a different story every time—if she answered us at all. "I named you for my favorite cartoon characters when I was a kid." "Your father asked me to name you that before he died." "I just liked the sound of it."

"If she's dying...do ye want to see her?" Fin gazes down at Lux, concern deepening the lines around his mouth.

She doesn't look up at him, but offers a quick shake of her head. "No."

He looks over to me, his eyebrows quirked in question.

"I don't know. If she's really dying, this may be our last chance to find out what went wrong...maybe get some answers."

"We're not going to find out shit. She's a selfish bitch who never gave a damn about anything but her own fucked-up problems."

There's no point in arguing with Lux, and I'm not sure she's wrong. I check my phone to see if Blue texted, but the screen remains blank. She'd fallen asleep before we left, and just as she was ready to pass out, I made her promise to text me when she got up. She probably won't, but I can hope.

The four of us make a half-hearted try at food. At three in the morning, it's a bit early for breakfast. Fin puts away a huge stack of pancakes, though, plus eggs and bacon, and Lux and I tease him in an attempt to lighten the mood. He tells Kai stories about his parents and growing up in Scotland—he was a semi-pro baller for a time, and when Lux met him, he even did some modeling. Fin's a born storyteller and a bit of an entertainer, so we end up laughing several times. The cheer eases the tightness in my chest, and when we trudge out into the still-dark morning, I give him a hard hug.

"Thank you."

He squeezes me back. "Aye, well, I'm glad I could do something. Lux and ye will figure this out—I've never met more capable, kind women than the two of ye. And yer sister must have a bit of that too, somewhere."

"She does, I think."

Lux slips her arms around me as we part. "I love you. I know I don't say it very often. But I do. And Blue, too."

I pull away so I can look at her. "None of this is our fault. Blue would have been a mess regardless of the choices you made—please don't blame yourself for any of this."

She nods, but her tired eyes are hooded with sorrow. I wrap my arms around her, uncaring that I probably smell less than pleasant after a long day in the sun. We hold on to each other for a few minutes, and she kisses my cheek before climbing into the car.

TRACING THE LINE

We drop Fin and Lux off at my apartment, and I go home with Kai.

"Is Blue close to your mother?" he asks as we get ready for bed.

I slide under the covers, thankful for a comfortable bed, a shower, and air conditioning. "I don't think so. She's close with our grandmother—well, as close as you can be to a woman who's harder than granite. The diner she works at is owned by Gram. But Gram washed her hands of our mother a long time ago—probably when she got pregnant for the third time with a different guy. She wasn't much of a grandmother—God knows she didn't take care of us. And Blue...she tries to find her place in all the wrong ways, I guess."

"Do you believe her when she says your mother wants to see all three of you?"

Blue told us our mother's dying wish: to have all three of us in the same space again. Of course, we've no idea what she's dying of or if she really is near death. Blue was fuzzy on details—apparently all of this came from a "friend" of our mother who called Blue. It sounded like the "friend" was her last lover—or one of them—and based on Blue's few details, not someone who was likely to stick around. I guess kudos to him for at least contacting her family. "Who knows? I'll worry about it...some other time. The last thing I want to do is deal with this, period."

He climbs in and automatically reaches for me. I snuggle into his side—this has become our nightly ritual over the last week or so. I inhale deeply, soothed by his scent and solid presence.

I'm tired, but sleep doesn't come right away. Kai's deep breaths keep me company for an hour while my mind rolls over the events of the day. I don't want to give my mother any more thought than I have to—she's certainly given us as little presence in her life as possible. But there's a part of me—the child on the inside—that wants her mother and probably always will. How much credit do I give her needs, versus the adult in me that knows I'm destined to be disappointed?

ALLY BISHOP

TRACING THE LINE

CHAPTER FIFTEEN

WITNESSING THE TRUTH

Two days later, I've yet to hear from Blue. I've called her each day to check in, but she's not returned my messages. I got a short text this morning assuring me she's fine and will be in touch when she's done working, but unless she's pulling forty-eight hour shifts at the diner, she's avoiding me.

Since Amie's at the Bakertown store, I head to Lothington to meet with a carpenter and a painter. If Kai knew I was going without him, he'd probably not be happy, but I can't live my life afraid. There have been no further emails, and since Lux and Fin have been at my place, I spent last night at home. I refuse to admit how much I missed having Kai beside me in bed.

I'm early when I arrive at the empty retail space, so I park down the street. Sitting in my car, I dial the number that Lux gave me for the private investigator.

"Hamilton Investigations." A thick southern twang swaggers over the words.

"Fiona?"

"You got that right, sugarplum. With whom do I have the pleasure of speaking?"

Who talks like this? I don't think Lux would play a joke on me over something so serious. "I'm Lux Trace's sister, Zi," I say cautiously.

"Oh, heavens, sweetpea, you're on my list of people to call today—well, I would have called Lux, so it's just as good that you dialed me." She shuffles some paper, then taps on a keyboard. "I just closed your file, so let me just...ah, there it is. You got yourself into a hornet's nest worth of trouble, darlin'. There are none so committed as those that believe the Good Lord and baby Jesus are on their side, and sweetie, these folks believe you're the next antichrist. Mm-mm."

I massage the bridge of my nose. "I'm starting to think I should just give up this plan. I had no idea there would be this kind of backlash."

"Oh, sweetpea, don't you dare. There's a group of folks who've got their granny panties in a twist over this, but there are quite a few in the community who've defended your store. Don't lose hope. While the righteous are mighty vocal about their objections, I'm exaggerating a tiny bit about your candidacy as the next beast of the three-sixes." Her amusement carries across the phone line. "Besides, I doubt God cares much for their yammering, beyond wondering what in hell they claim to be doing in his name. Besides, aren't you opening soon?"

"No, I won't open until the fall." This has gone from a complicated adventure to an intense, unpleasant one.

"Best I can tell, this is a small religious group who's done things like this before. The leader is probably this Zachariah Lemke—you can see him all over the community boards. I can't prove he sent you that email, but the diction fits." Her southern drawl lessens as she turns serious, making me wonder how much of it is put on for show. She's definitely got an accent, but nowhere near as intense as earlier. "He's riling up some other folks, and it looks like he's got his own group of loyal followers, but they're outliers—crazy-ass folks like those Westboro Church people that act like cretins at funerals. No one takes them seriously, but they're heinous nonetheless."

"Is he dangerous?" If he's just a mouthpiece and nothing more, I'll feel slightly less frazzled.

"My gut says no, but I'll be damned if I trust that—you haven't met my ex-husbands. You'd have thought my instincts would have protected me from making that mistake more than once." Her chuckle rides a hard edge. "But looking at his past antics, it seems as though he's more interested in being a blowhard than anything of substance. Don't let him get to you—you open your store and show that two-bit hustler why he's no better than a billy goat yanking his chain."

I sigh, unsure what to do. Well, there's nothing I can do until the township meeting anyway. "All right. Thanks, Fiona.

What do I owe you?"

"Don't worry about it, sweetpea. I didn't do that much, and I owe Lux a few favors anyway. Do me a solid and stay safe, now, y'hear? She's worried about you."

Why on earth my sister is owed a few favors by a P.I., I've no clue. But I thank Fiona and hang up. Fuck. This Zachariah Lemke doesn't sound all that pleasant—who has a name like that outside of serial killers? I shiver.

Fabulous.

My storefront sits at the end of the block, and as I approach, something doesn't look right—there's something painted on the front glass. When I'm finally close enough to figure out details, I discover a spray-painted message scrawled across the window. "Whore Store, Deuteronomy 17:12."

The same Bible verse from the email.

I immediately spin around, terrified I'm being watched. But when my logical mind subdues my panic long enough to think through the situation, I touch the paint—it's dry, which means this must have been done long before I got here. Perhaps overnight? Days ago?

I call the landlord. He assures me that a neighbor would have told him about the vandalism, so it must have happened within the last twelve or so hours. I call the police next. Amid the painter and carpenter consultations, I intercept cops and my landlord, fill out police reports, and spend the next several hours on autopilot. I give them the name of the guy Fiona suspects—Zachariah Lemke—and they assure me they'll look into the situation, but the cop's sympathetic gaze suggests there's not much chance they'll find anything or that they'll spend many resources. Maybe I'm reading too much into things, though.

By late afternoon, I'm barely coherent. I haven't responded to any of Kai's texts, which have gone from sexy (*I missed waking you up this morning, my mouth between your legs, and hearing your moans*) to concerned (*Zi, I'm worried. Amie said she can't reach you, either. Are you okay?*). I heard my phone, but with everything going on, I didn't have the wherewithal to answer.

I call Amie first, only because it's store-related—she can't find a special order for a customer—and then I call Kai.

"Thank God. I was ready to come search for you myself. Are you okay?"

"I'm sorry. I just..." I steel myself against the emotions that threaten. "It's been a long day." The words tumble out of me in a flood, and several minutes later, I've told him all the details of the day.

"What are the police going to do?" His voice is measured but warm, though I can sense his worry.

"This is illegal, so they're going to look into it. They're also going to get in touch with the private investigator and see if they can figure out where it all leads."

"You sound exhausted."

"I am. Of course, I'm wired from all the intensity. I need a break, and I feel like all I find are new problems."

His deep voice caresses my ear. "I'm so sorry, Zi. I wish I didn't have to work tonight—I'd take your mind off of everything. And no, I don't mean with sex."

I chuckle, relieved at his distraction. "Oh, really? What else would you do?"

"Well, not *just* sex. How does a full body massage—appropriate body parts only—and homemade double-chocolate cupcakes with vanilla ice cream sound?"

"Sure, torture me when I can't have them—or you."

"I'm sorry, babe. Hey, you know what?" He pauses as though thinking about his next words. "Let me call you right back. Give me five minutes. I have an idea."

I use the time to grab a coffee at a small coffee shop on the next block and return to my car. My cell rings just as I close the door.

"Why don't you join me? I'm on location not far from Bakertown, and you can see what I do."

"Is this a True Lust filming?" My insides thrill with curiosity.

"Yes, and the actors would be happy to have you on set—they love to be watched, so the more, the merrier."

"Did my boyfriend just ask me to a live sex show?"

His smile warms the phone line. "He did."

Kai gives me the address, and I key it into my GPS. I'm caught between nerves and arousal during the drive. For all my open-minded attitudes, I've never been to a strip club. The craziest things I've ever attended are those in-home sex toy parties. So the whole idea of watching another couple during their most intimate behavior...but I'm curious. I'm also worried I'll be uncomfortable, though clearly they won't be if they don't mind strangers watching them.

I end up on the outskirts of Bakertown, where agricultural scenery makes green and brown swaths over the rolling hills interspersed with flat plains. The late afternoon sun slants warm rays over the picturesque view, and despite today's mounting stresses, I find my tension easing.

Kai's car is parked beside an old farmhouse, behind which sits an ancient barn that's been well maintained. The whitewashed clapboard sports a beautiful Amish hex design in contrasting colors of blue and salmon. When I pull in, Kai exits the barn, almost as if he's been waiting for me to arrive.

"Hey." I can't stop smiling as I meet him halfway.

He embraces me tightly, and I can barely take a breath. "I'm so glad you're okay."

When he releases me, I can see the crease of worry between his brows. "I'm sorry I frightened you. I didn't mean to—"

He presses a finger to my lips. "You're an adult. You don't have to apologize—life happens. But when I couldn't reach you...after that email, I got concerned." He kisses me gently, almost chastely, then takes my hand. "Let me introduce you. We have to get started, or we're going to lose the light."

The barn has been remodeled into a fashion designer's palace. Fabrics drape every available hook and surface, along with easels balancing sketchbooks and torso dummies. Antique sewing machines add to the decor, as well as vintage shoes, purses, and coats displayed in cubbies and corners. Creative passion oozes from every angle, and I can't stop looking around.

"What is this place?" I ask with awe.

Kai smiles. "It belongs to a friend of our actors. That she agreed to let us use this space is incredible." He introduces me to the actors—all *four* of them—three men and one woman. I nearly swallow my tongue in surprise, and Kai's grin suggests he's enjoying my reaction.

Ger bypasses greetings and slings an arm around my shoulders. "Good to see you again. You're soon going to be a pro." He winks before returning to...whatever it is camera guys do.

Russ smiles in greeting, unable to leave his spot—he's applying makeup on one of the male actors. "Zizi Baby is back!" he hollers with a wolf call.

I stare at him. "My sister calls me that—how did you know?"

He surprises me by looking immediately bashful. "Oops. I swear I don't know your sister. Wait, there was that girl last week, never did get her name, but she looked sort of looked like you...Oh, never mind, she was formerly a he, so she couldn't be your sister, or could she?" He glances up from his work to wink at me. "I'm *kidding*. You just look like a 'Zizi Baby' to me."

I shake my head at him and laugh. "Good to see you too, Russ."

Kai and Ger are eyeing something in the barn, then they adjust the lavish leather couch in the center of the space. A huge animal pelt spreads out in front of the large sofa, and Ger and Kai move about the room, nudging and tweaking materials and furniture, until they seem satisfied.

Kai joins me as I lean against a wall, trying to stay out of the way.

"So these four know each other, right?"

He nods. "Three of them are in a relationship together—the fourth is a mutual friend of theirs."

"Wow. I can't imagine—I think it's hard enough to figure out the dynamics living with one other person. Trying to do so for two other people...yikes."

"They make it work. Carla, Ben, and Samson have been together for almost five years now, I think. Taye's an occasional player, if I remember correctly. So," he slides his arm around my waist, "you don't think you want to bring Ger in for some fun on occasion?"

My eyes widen. "What? I—"

He kisses me while trying to contain his mirth. "I'm teasing. I promise." He strokes a finger over my chin. "But the look on your face—"

I skim my hand over his sides, where he's ticklish, making him shrink away with a laugh. "Mm-hmm. Two can play at that game."

He winks at me as he draws me close again. "No, believe me. I admire their determination to make it work, but I don't share well with the other kids." His mouth finds mine, his fervor echoing his words.

I'm breathless when he leaves me to return to the job. Ger's manning the camera, and they have a boom mic suspended over the rug—I'm trying *not* to figure out what kind of animal the fur belonged to. Kai explains the focus, the pacing he thinks will work, and how to position themselves during taping. The sun's sepia rays turn the barn's interior to a soft pinkish brown, and I can see why they chose this time of day: romance lives in this lighting.

Kai returns to me. "We're starting—is your phone turned down?"

"I left it in the car."

"Perfect." He drops a kiss on my mouth. "Just like you."

TRACING THE LINE

He returns to his place beside Ger, though Ger already has the camera to his face, his fingers pressing buttons and turning dials. The four players strip out of their robes. The men wear black briefs, and while they may not do this for a living, they probably could. While there's not a six-pack among the three, their bodies are smooth and muscled, a testament to either gym-time or fortunate genetics. Carla, on the other hand, is not quite as tall as me, and lithe, wearing a simple pink bra and panty set. A twisting tattoo of Mexican skulls, lush flowers, and dark, sinuous demons runs from her left ear to her ankle, covering one arm in an elegant ink sleeve, as well as the side of one thigh. I've never seen anything quite like it.

One man remains on the couch—Taye, I assume—while the other three converge, touching and kissing. As they ease into their play, I feel self-conscious, as Carla is very thin, her build that of a dancer with narrow hips and small, pert breasts. But as her lovers pass her between them, a scar beside her navel winks in the soft light. She has a bit of cellulite on the back of her thighs, and I chide myself for noticing—and for my envy. As the three men worship her, slowly delving into her secrets, I'm able to see her as she is: a real woman whose beauty doesn't need perfection. Their affection for each other is obvious, and as fingers seek and lips find, the romance of the scene heightens. When the actual sex begins and Taye joins them, it's like a slow, erotic dance. The men do not shrink from touching each other, but Carla is their focus. When her lusty cries betray her orgasm, her lovers cover her with their bodies, and she greedily accepts their offerings.

In any other environment, this would be a "gangbang," degrading and viewed only as a means to a selfish end. But watching the four lovers interact, taking and giving pleasure as though such acts are second nature, I wonder how small our views of sexuality have become—or perhaps always have been. And I see why Kai admires Carla and her lovers' ability to make it work—they display their commitment as though it's a thing to nurture and grow, rather than to possess and hold dormant.

CHAPTER SIXTEEN

AFTERGLOW

Russ offers to drive my car back to the Naked Truth office so I can ride with Kai.

When I object to inconveniencing him, Russ assures me it's not a hardship.

"Zizi Baby, I can't buy a car on what that lout of yours pays me. Let me pretend I'm in the lap of luxury and have wheels."

Kai glares at him. "I offered to buy you a car."

With an injured expression, Russ props a hand on one hip. "I've told you before: I'm not sleeping with you no matter how much you beg—not even for a car. I can't handle this kind of workplace harassment." He can only manage to keep up the act for a few seconds before dissolving into a smile. "No worries, boss-man. When else would we have our man-to-man convos if you didn't pick me up for work?" Then he snags my keys and skips towards my Mazda.

"He really can't afford a car?"

Kai unlocks his car, then opens my door. "He could, but he's eyeballs-deep in student loans. I told him to work on those, and I'd drive him where he needs to go. I've threatened to get him a car several times—a cheap used car just to get back and forth to work—but Russ..." He rounds the car to his side. Once the engine turns over, he continues. "He's a good kid—I'm seriously amazed he followed me all the way here. And he doesn't want a handout, even though I've argued it would be easier on both of us."

"Can't fault him for wanting to do it on his own, then."

"No, I can't." He sighs, annoyance warring with amusement. "But there are days...not that I'm complaining. He can do almost anything we ask for, and he puts up with some strange hours and even stranger requests."

The sun begins its deep descent, bruising the clouds and bleeding pink and orange across the sky. The drive isn't long—maybe a half hour—but I'm lost in thought, considering the day and this evening's revelations.

"You're awfully quiet. I can't decide if you're horrified by what I do and you're trying to figure out a nice way to break up with me, or if you're wild on hormones and want to fuck me senseless when we get home." Kai aims for a joking tone, but there's a bit of fear behind his words.

I lay my hand on his knee. "I've never seen anything like tonight. I mean, I've seen sex, and I've seen group sex before—not live, but in porn movies." I chew my lip in thought. "But I've never seen love expressed—true love—through intimacy. Not like that. And I don't mean because there were more than just two people."

"I understand."

The blue glow of his car's lighting holds his profile in relief, and my gaze follows the line of his forehead down his aquiline nose, the curve of his full lips and strong chin. "That's why you do this, isn't it? To show that?"

He nods slowly, his eyes focused on the road. "I don't think I had any such grand notions when I put the idea into action. At some point, I needed to make a consistent paycheck, and the porn industry is huge. Why not tap into what's already there, but find a niche no one is really addressing? But the more I do this, the more people I meet who volunteer to take part—and let me tell you, you'd be surprised how many people offer to be in our films and would do so even if they weren't getting paid—the more I see love in all its facets, and I'm astonished how we try to package such intangible beauty in greeting cards and cheesy holiday traditions."

My lips curve at his words, echoing my thoughts so clearly. "I can see that. Thank you for inviting me to join you today. This was...enlightening."

"You sound more conflicted than enlightened, though." He takes my hand, pressing my fingertips to his lips.

"I am, but not in a bad way. It's making me rethink my prejudices, I guess. Do you think it matters if Carla, Ben, and Samson break up next year? Does it make what they expressed today less because it wasn't forever?"

"Quite the opposite. I want to believe that love can last forever—I want the happily ever after just as much as the next person. But I don't believe that what those three people feel today, in this moment in time, is less real or valuable because they couldn't make it work for life. Things change quickly, and we grow as people." He lays my palm on his thigh so he can grip the steering wheel. "When I married Carice, I didn't question that we were right for each other. Not then. And you know, we probably were. It's not like either of us are horrible people. But as I started to see my flaws and work on them, I began to see that as much as I cared for her—and I still do—she's not the right person for me anymore. Not because there's something wrong with her, but because I've changed. I understand my own needs for a partner more now, better than I could have in my twenties."

"That makes sense." Of course, I've forgotten that they're still married. Convenient, the things our brains choose to overlook, eh?

Silence carries us back to his place.

"I should have asked if you wanted me to take you to your place. I didn't even think—"

"It's fine. I can sleep either place." My words fall like rocks to the bottom of a lake, and I'm not sure how to fix things. I haven't been able to stop thinking both about today...and the fact that Kai's legally bound to another woman.

The last few weeks, I could overlook his matrimonial status with everything else going on, but our conversation tonight brings the fact into stark reality once again. I head for the bathroom when we get in the door, desperate to shower off some of the dirt from the day; besides, the time gives me separation from Kai to formulate my thoughts.

My hair's still wet when I find Kai with a glass of whiskey on the patio.

"Can I get you a drink?" he asks, his voice polite and cautious.

I shake my head and sit down across from him. A large candle flickers on the table, casting a golden haze over us. In the dim glow, he could be a model for a modern Michelangelo seeking to capture the beauty of a man: rumpled hair, bare-chested but still in jeans, his broad shoulders thick with muscle. The gold of his eyes glimmers against the shadows, and I can't stop looking at him.

Perhaps he feels the same, as his gaze doesn't stray from mine.

"I've upset you, but I'm not sure how." His voice, quiet and low, shatters the stillness.

"You haven't. Well, you have, but it's not new. I mean—" I break away from his spell, shaking my head to clear it. "It's nothing I don't already know."

"Can you be a bit more specific?"

I can't help snorting. "That would help, wouldn't it?" I inhale the heavy night air, humidity thick and pungent with fresh cut grass and summer blooms. "You're married. I conveniently forgot that part the last few weeks. Well, I guess I chose to overlook it, really. I know you'd said it wasn't serious between you and Carice anymore—that it was over. But legally, you're still bound to her."

He nods, running a finger over the mouth of his glass before taking a drink. "I am. And I haven't lied to you about that."

"No, you haven't."

Crickets fill the awkward space, their roughened song more chafing than soothing. "When I contacted my attorney for you, I also asked him to prepare paperwork for me. I asked Carice for a divorce this morning."

The heavy rock in my gut hovers, unsure whether to thunk or vanish. "What?"

"It's hardly a relationship milestone you deserve to celebrate—I'm sorry you have to deal with it at all. I was going to tell you—preferably when things with your family weren't so stressful."

"With Blue, things are always intense. It's part of her genetic makeup." I'm not sure how to react. Do you say "congratulations" when someone files for a long overdue divorce? "Why did you decide to do it now?"

"It's time." He eyes the diminishing liquor in his glass. "I've not had a reason to worry much about it, to be honest. She may be in denial over our inevitable end, but I'm not. And I've no wish to hurt her—she's a good person."

"But?" I prod when he hesitates.

He narrows his gaze at me. "God, this isn't how I want to do this."

And the boulder in my stomach plummets. "Do what?" The sadness in his voice sends my imagination careening down unpleasant roads to outcomes that will only lead to pain. After all, he did tell me he wants someone who's an equal, able to handle the drama in her life. And lately, I've been anything but. Did he figure out that we're not the right fit? Does he think I'm just like Carice?

He stands and reaches for my hands, pulling me to my feet. "God, your hands are freezing."

My teeth are chattering, too. "What don't you want to do 'like this'?" I demand again, though my voice comes out as a whisper.

With a grace I've come to expect from him, he places my hand over his heart, his fingers like a brand against my cold skin. "I wanted to do something special, not tack it on to discussions of my legal status." His palm curves around my neck, anchoring me as he dips down to brush his lips over mine. He tastes like whiskey and warm cinnamon, and I can't help responding when his tongue slides over mine. My mind's pinwheeling with confusion, and when he pulls back, his expression mirrors my thoughts. "What is it?"

"I don't know what's going on. Two seconds ago you sounded like you were going to tell me you needed space or break up with me." I sound so small, I want to kick myself.

"What? No." Disbelief wrinkles his brow. "Why would

you...? Jesus. No." His laugh comes out with a hoarse edge. "Oh my God, Zi. Do you think I would have invited you today if I intended to end things?"

He has a point. "I'm sorry. It's just...with all the crap with my family, I thought maybe it freaked you out. I know you want someone who's able to handle her shit, and lately, I feel like I'm coming apart at the seams. I've never been so weak in my entire life."

His hands cup my face, and he kisses me before speaking again. "Zi, you...your whole family has been through hell. Don't get me wrong, it's not like my childhood was a paragon of happiness and joy—you know that. But I had my parents. I had friends who were there and got me through. Compared to you and your sisters, I feel ridiculous for having emotional issues that I needed to get help for." He holds up a hand when I open my mouth. "I know, we all have our own journeys and all that. But weak? You? You're one of the strongest people I know. Watching you and Lux try to come to terms with things the other night...I admire you beyond what I can express. Can't you see that?"

I don't know what to say. I had no idea he felt this way, or maybe I was so caught up in my own insecurities that I couldn't see it?

"I suck at expressing myself apparently, and for that, I'm sorry." He grips my hands again. "I might have gotten a bit carried away with how easily you and I fall into bed together...and I should have been more forthright." He kisses my knuckles, then places my hands on his shoulders.

I lean against him, thoughts awhirl as I seek his eyes for grounding, anything, that will help me navigate the onslaught of emotions his words have created.

"I love you. That's what I wanted to say, but not like this, not here when I'm still a mess from the day and we're discussing my soon-to-be-over marriage."

His declaration takes me off-guard. "Really?"

He drops his forehead to mine. "Really. I love you. I've wanted to say that for days now—I wanted to tell you at Ella and Ian's when we were sitting on the blanket. You looked so beautiful in the firelight," he brushes a strand of hair from my face as a humid breeze blows over us, "and I wanted to capture that moment on film so I could revisit it a thousand times. Then your sister called, and I watched you battle not only your demons, but Blue's and Lux's, and you were...steadfast."

"That's what every woman wants to hear from a man," I tease, feeling a bit giddy.

With a grin, he lifts a shoulder. "You were brave and audacious. How's that?" When I nod approval, he continues. "You know what amazed me the most?"

I shake my head, unsure I can speak without giving away the emotions building in my throat.

"You love even when it doesn't make much sense to. Lux pulled me aside at the picnic and gave me the lowdown about your ex—and about how I better behave if I'm going to be with you."

My embarrassment now complete, I drop my head to his chest, hoping to hide my flush.

He squeezes my shoulders. "It's fine. She was right—you don't deserve to be hurt again. Ever. And after everything you've been through, you still love with as much passion and ferocity as though you were never destroyed by it."

Destroyed. The word stings, but I can't think of a better one to describe the ending of my marriage...when Lux left when I was sixteen...when I lost Blue to drugs, then got her back in nearly as bad a shape as before.

"God, you're one of the strongest people I know. And I love you. If you'll have me, I'd like to 'make it official' between us. If you want that."

Now it's his turn to look at me with questions in his eyes.

I press my lips to his, hoping to convey the words I cannot string together. Moments later, when I'm finally able to draw a breath, I rest my cheek against his.

"I love you too."

Despite our confessions of love, we both fall into bed...and sleep.

The sun pokes through the blinds the next morning, the golden rays teasing my eyelids open at about the same time hands spread my thighs. I barely have time to register what's happening when Kai's lips close around my clit. With a gasp, I arch my back, pressing myself against his expert tongue. His fingers delve deep inside me, curving along my inner walls until I'm bucking against his mouth.

"That's got to be a record somewhere," he teases as he peers up at me from between my legs. "I don't think I've ever known a woman who can come as quickly as you do."

"That's me—Fast-Fuck-Flo."

"Wait, what?"

I cover my face with my hands, hysterical at my own corny comment. "Ignore me. I'm barely awake."

"Mm. Best time to take advantage of you, then." He rises to his knees, naked and obviously ready for more as he guides me to my stomach. "You have the most delicious ass I've ever seen."

Given that I've always thought I have a bit too much in the caboose, I'll take the compliment. "Glad you enjoy it."

His hands cup my rear, massaging gently. His touch feels wonderful, and I relax under his ministrations. He lifts my hips so my ass is in the air, then continues his reverence of my posterior. When he taps my cheek lightly with a hint of a sting, I don't mind. "Is that okay?"

I've wanted him to spank me again, even though I'd never be able to ask. I bury my face in the crook of my arm. "Yes."

Then his fingers find me again, separating my folds until he's rubbing the bundle of nerves with the faintest pressure. Then he pauses and smacks my rear with a bit more force.

The sharp zing makes me start but quickly melds into pure sensation as his fingers resume their stroking. With slow progress, he delivers a few more solid spanks, and I groan as the instant pain blends into even more intense pleasure. When he nudges his cock against my pussy, I'm so aroused he slides in with no resistance.

I push up so I'm on all fours. He tries to pace us, using slow thrusts occasionally punctuated with his palm striking my ass cheek, but I need more. "Harder, Kai. Please don't go easy on me."

He grips my waist with one hand and slams into me, and I surge back against him. With savage energy, we come together, again and again, my ass stinging with his slaps. My wordless moans urge him on, and every time I think I'm about to fall over the edge, the magnificent fury drives me even higher. When I can't hold myself up anymore, I fall to my shoulders, bracing my head on my arms. I can feel him thicken even more, his climax mounting. Kai leans over me, kissing my shoulder as he fucks me with slow purpose. He presses my hips to the bed so he can lie on top of me, his cock still plunging deep, and slides his hand beneath my stomach. His fingers find my tiny nub, and as he anchors himself inside me, I can't help tightening around him. He drives my climax without mercy, even as I shudder and buck beneath him. I'm hoarse as I cry out yet again, unable to stop the sensations crashing into me.

When he reaches his own release, he curls over me, around me, burying his face in my shoulder. Instead of rolling apart, he shifts so we face each other, holding me tight as we both struggle to catch our breaths.

"Every time I think it's as good as we can get, it gets better."

I can't stop the smile spreading over my face. "I don't even know how to put it into words. I've never felt like this...ever."

"You're good for my ego." He grins, his hand easing over my hip. "Did I hurt you? We probably should have talked about that before I jumped in."

My face burns at his question. "Yes, you hurt me, but I also wanted it. God, I can't believe I'm saying that."

He rolls to his back. "You're bothered by the fact that you might, in fact, be a bit kinky yourself."

"I'm starting to think I haven't a clue what 'open-minded' even means."

Kai chuckles and rubs my back as I flop my head on his shoulder. "You're very accepting when it comes to others. But I think you've kept yourself and your desires hidden to make others happy. Maybe it's time to explore your sexual identity a bit more."

I trace a finger over his chest and collarbones, pondering his words. "I've never liked pain, though."

"I'm not suggesting we invest in nipple clamps and caning lessons." My look of horror broadens his smile. "I wouldn't be up for that either; don't worry. From what I've seen, quite a few women enjoy being spanked during sex—I don't know if that's necessarily enjoying pain so much as the conflicting sensations heighten arousal. And while I've never done much more than the occasional ass smack, I enjoyed this. With you."

"That makes sense, actually." I feel somewhat mollified with his explanation. "I wish I could see it from your perspective."

"What do you mean?"

"You get to see everything when you take me from behind. I get to stare at the bed." I stick my tongue out at him. "While I have to admit, you've definitely made me a convert to that position, I'm jealous that I don't get to enjoy the whole picture, I guess."

He doesn't say anything right away; instead, he draws a circle over my palm. "I could tape us, if you'd like. Privately.

And you can have the recording."

My eyes nearly pop out of my head. "Um, no."

"You'd own the recording—I wouldn't even have a copy."

While my immediate response is overwhelmingly N.O., my hormones thrill at the thought. What the hell has happened to me? Who is this crazed sex fiend? "Let me think about it."

"No pressure. It's just a suggestion."

But as I get my shower and dress for our day—I've got to stop in at the store to check in, and then we're spending the day wandering a nearby town—I can't stop thinking about his offer. I've never wanted to be taped. Hell, I've never even allowed lovers to take pictures. But watching Carla and her partners yesterday has made me rethink a lot of my assumptions. About love. About what's sexy and erotic. About who I am as an "open-minded person." I'm still working my way through a lot of those conflicts and ideas.

Being with Kai, the sensual way I feel, I want to see that—the whole picture. I'd love to witness what he sees, and more than that, I like the idea of being seen—even just via the eye of a camera.

He's at the table, a cup of coffee before him and one at my spot, as well. I take my seat, then look at him. "I'd be the only person with a copy of our...movie?" What the hell do you even call these things?

He doesn't try to hide his surprise. "Of course. If that's what you want, that's the way it will be."

"And we could do something like what you did for your other movies—a romantic location, soft lighting, all that jazz?"

"If you want."

"Who all would be there to film us?"

He straightens his coffee mug and speaks carefully, as though I might spook. "You saw who was there yesterday. It can just be you and me, and we'll use a tripod, or if you want it to be a bit more professional and slick, we could have Ger record us."

My stomach flip-flops at the idea of having someone watching us so closely. Then I realize that's exactly what I want.

TRACING THE LINE

"Okay. Let's do it."

CHAPTER SEVENTEEN

FAMILY FEUD

"No." The stubborn set of Lux's jaw informs me this line of questioning is pointless.

But never let anyone call me less stubborn than my sister. "Lux, she's dying. It's not a farce. It's not some sort of ploy to get us to see her."

"And you know this how?"

We're having lunch in the backroom of my store, so we're both talking softly—albeit intensely—so no one overhears. "I went to the hospital myself with Blue. I talked to the doctor."

"Then you already saw her—you don't need me there."

"No, I didn't. She was sleeping, and I wasn't there for that. I wanted to make sure it was the truth." Normally, you can't pry a burrito out of my hands, but right now, our Mexican fare is barely touched and getting cold. "Look, I know how you feel. I do. And I don't disagree with you. But she's got little time left—she can barely even speak." Years of smoking cigarettes have finally caught up to our mother. "I'm not asking you to do this for her. I'm asking you to do this for you...because you may regret not seeing her after she's gone."

"No, I won't. I've made my peace with the shit she did, but I'm not going to pretend like it never happened. I don't love this woman, Zi. I'm not bound to her like Blue is—or at least, like Blue is always trying to be. I don't need her approval or her final words. Nothing about her or her life interests me, and while anyone dying of disease has my compassion, I'm not going to shed a tear when she takes her last breath." Lux crosses her arms, her gray stare never flinching. "The destruction that woman wrought on helpless children is unforgivable, Zi. And I've worked really hard to let go and move on with my life."

I take a deep breath. I'm not sure I should push any harder.

TRACING THE LINE

Our mother doesn't deserve her final wish, if I'm being honest. The damage she did to us may not be evident to outsiders, but you only have to spend a few hours with Blue to see the effects. Why Lux and I ended up less dependent, I'm not sure. Our personalities are built that way, I guess. "I understand all of that, Lux. And I admire it." My office computer's fan whirs softly beside me as I struggle to find the words I want to say. "Maybe I'm not asking for you. Maybe this is about me. I don't want to face her alone, and as much as I love Blue, I can't count on her to understand and respect my feelings. She's too lost in her own."

Lux contemplates her meal for several moments. Then the stiffness in her cheeks eases, and her gaze softens. "I'm sorry." She wraps a coil of raven hair around her pale finger. "You've always put on such a strong front; I didn't think about how this might affect you." She pauses, then closes her eyes. "For you, I'll go."

I didn't realize how much I needed her to say that until after the words hit me. "Thank you."

We pick at our food, neither of us in much of a mood to eat. I text Blue, make arrangements to meet her at the hospital tonight before our mother gets another round of pain killers, so she should be awake.

The rest of the day goes by in a blur: bra-fittings, two product exchanges, and one woman tries to return a used dildo (yes, this actually happens, and no, you can't return sex toys, period). By the time I close the store and get in my car, I'm numb. But after I pick up Lux, my stomach crawls up my throat the closer we get to the hospital.

I don't want to do this.

I haven't seen our mother since I was eighteen. Gram forced her to come to my graduation, despite the fact I didn't want her there. Gram, for all her uselessness as a grandmother, does believe in proper behavior in public and family loyalty. So she marched our hungover mother into the high school's gymnasium with the gumption of a four-star general. Of course, she couldn't stop our mother from getting high in the bathroom, so afterwards, when all of my friends and I were taking pictures and being silly, my mother acted like an ass, screaming about how her children hated her and how we never gave her credit for giving everything she had to us. The police finally removed her, and she ended up in prison for thirty days and then in rehab for the fourth or fifth time. It's hard to keep track. After that, I never tried to contact her again, and Gram's insistence that I make an effort with my mother destroyed any relationship we might have cultivated. I get it: she's Gram's kid. You don't give up on your children. But I'd had enough, and putting up with Gram's harsh judgments of my life and my decisions got old quickly. For all our mother is a wreck, you don't have to look far to see who helped make her that way.

Lux and I are silent as we ride the elevator to the cancer ward. Signs point us to oncology, and soon we're only a few feet away from our mother's room. Blue texts me that she's almost here, and it gives us an excuse to stay in the hallway, to wait a few more precious moments before we have to face the woman who engenders so many conflicting emotions in us... well, in me, at least.

"Your fingers are freezing," Lux comments as she takes my hand.

So are hers, but I don't say anything. Hands tightly held, we play on our phones—anything to distract us from what we're about to do.

When Blue arrives, her bright hair is pulled back in a french braid, her face clean of makeup, revealing her freckles and clear skin. She appears fourteen instead of almost twenty-seven. Part of me aches to hold her when I see the fear and confusion in her eyes. But her hug is perfunctory, her stress tightening her frame, and she barely speaks to us before stepping towards the door. She has a canvas bag in her hand, filled with what appear to be boxes.

"Wait." Lux grabs her shoulder.

Blue turns, her eyes hard. "I know you don't want to be here."

Lux narrows her gaze and drops a hand to her hip. "Blue,

TRACING THE LINE

I get that you're mad at me. I don't blame you—had you waited so long to reach out to me, I'd be pissed too. That's fine. But today's not the time. I'm here for you and Zi because we're sisters. Like it or not, we share this mangled history, and the woman behind that door—she crafted it. She's the reason we ate macaroni and cheese for one month straight. It was her fault that we were left to fend for ourselves when I was only eight and I had you two to take care of for nearly a week. She's why we ended up in foster care. I know you have issues around all this, and that you've tried to have a relationship with our mother. I don't understand why—I'm not going to pretend to. But I respect your journey, just as I've had to take my own. And I'll be damned if we're going in there as anything other than sisters. You can hate me later all you want. But for today, I'm asking you to put it aside and remember that we all lived these memories, however they may have affected us differently. Can we do that for the next hour? Please?"

My jaw nearly drops at Lux's words, but I manage to keep a banal look on my face. Blue stares at Lux for several moments, the tension thickening with each second. "Fine. She shouldn't see us at odds anyway. Not when she's dying." With surprising meekness, she lets Lux step in front of her and open the door.

Nothing prepares you for seeing the near-dead. There's no amount of visualizing or preparing yourself that enables you to imagine the smell of over-sanitization and plastic tubing, tinged with the heavy ammonia of waste. Machines tick and *whoosh*, along with a steady bleeping that distracts me momentarily from having to observe what's left of our mother.

When we were children, she was beautiful. I guess we all see our mothers as the most beautiful beings ever, particularly when we're little. But even as a teenager, I was jealous of her flawless skin, the way her flaxen hair fell in lax curls down her back, the way her waist was always tiny. One of her boyfriends once said she had the perkiest "tits and ass" he'd ever seen, and I couldn't disagree with him. Her blue eyes deepened to almost violet around the pupil, and without makeup, she looked like a sensual wood nymph denied her delicate wings. With makeup, she became a sexual vixen, ensnaring many an unsuspecting lover in her trap.

She's forty-nine years old—barely middle-aged. And she looks like she's seventy. Her lush body has dwindled to bones, barely enough to tent the blankets piled on top of her. Her lovely face wears harsh lines sunken into valleys and troughs around her skull. Her thick hair is gone, replaced by uneven, white shag, probably a result of her radiation treatments.

I wouldn't recognize her as related to me, much less my mother.

"Mommy, look who's here." Blue sits on the bed, beside this stranger. "You wanted to see us all together."

Lux doesn't move from her place beside me, and a quick glance confirms she's in the same state of shock I am. I tuck my arm around her waist, pulling her with me as I step forward. "Hi, Mom."

Her voice has always been deep and smoky. I can still remember listening to her sing when she'd have her friends over. One of them always had a guitar, and he'd play while she sang covers.

"Ziamora, look at you." The words gurgle out of her throat, barely taking shape, but a trace of her spark still lights her gaze. "And Lux. You always were the prettiest, weren't you?"

Lux draws herself taut beside me. "We're all beautiful, Mother. Just like you were."

Those strangely clear eyes, set in a decaying body, turn

knowing, but perhaps she realizes there's no more energy to waste trading barbs with her eldest daughter. "Thank you for coming." Knobby fingers clutch Blue's hand. "You remembered what I asked you to bring?"

Blue nods, her face locked into submissive patience as though our mother isn't a skeleton and we're all here for a picnic. "Of course. I can remember things, you know," she chides with a grin that draws out her dimple. She withdraws three boxes from the bag she brought with her.

"I made these..." Our mother closes her eyes, swallowing hard. She takes the straw as Blue holds a cup of water close. After a small sip, she waves the glass away. "I made these before I got too sick." Her voice strengthens, her determination to get the phrases out tightening her shoulders. "It's not enough, I know. But I wanted you to have them."

We each receive a shoebox-sized package with metal protectors on the corners and decorative aluminum edges. They're hand-painted as well. Mine is covered in lilacs and peonies, Lux's in peacocks, and Blue's in art supplies. Blue nods to me, coaxing me to open the box. When I do, I discover it's filled nearly to the brim with detritus from my childhood. A My Little Pony I'd treasured—one of the babies that you only got in a McDonald's Happy Meal—that our mother had discovered in a thrift store and bought for me. Pictures from the only birthday party I'd ever had, complete with a piñata and custom cupcakes for each guest. A small, spiral-bound notebook—inside is my mother's handwriting, detailing my first few weeks of life. There's a small pile of pictures, most from when I was under five years old, though a few from when I was older, before we went to foster care.

Lux holds hers with stiff hands, but when I give her a questioning gaze, she relents and peers inside. Hers also has an assortment of sparkly, wispy items from our childhood. She withdraws a pencil molded into the shape of a treble clef—I was horribly jealous of her when she won that in her grade school choir for perfect attendance. A small leather-bound book, the contents of which likely mirror my wire-bound one.

More photos, tiny erasers in funny shapes that she'd hoarded when we were little, and a Barbie doll in a rich green cloak, complete with white furry hood, cuffs, and stole. When she looks at me, her eyes are glassy with unshed emotion, but the hard line of her lips betrays nothing.

Blue squeals when she investigates her own cache. "Mommy, how did you find all of these?" She holds miniature animals in her palm from a farm set she'd treasured.

"I've kept all of these things...for years," our mother whispers. "I wanted to make sure...you...had them." She closes her eyes, as though the simple act of talking exhausts her. And it probably does.

Blue delves deeper, looking through all the pictures and other bits that are in her box. She withdraws a paintbrush with a bright pink handle. "You remembered," she says with awe in her voice. Then she bends down to brush a kiss against our mother's forehead.

"You took these from us," Lux says, her voice hard. "I remember looking all over the place for that pencil—I couldn't find it anywhere. You told me someone at school probably stole it to teach me a lesson for being so haughty. These aren't gifts—this is your guilt. Nothing more."

Blue's eyes widen with shock, and sadly, I know Lux is right. I'd had the same thought just before she spoke, as I remember my pony going missing when I got home from a friend's house one day. Our mother accused me of being careless and losing the toy, and I'd been grounded for days. And Blue's paintbrush was a gift from one of our mother's boyfriends. When it went missing, our mother smacked her face, then punished her for losing an "expensive" gift. Looking at Blue's surprise, I don't think she remembers that...but then, she doesn't remember a lot of things from when we were children. Truth, however, sinks in, and her thrill over the boxes dissipates quickly.

Our mother locks gazes with Lux, and I think she's going to snap back—or at least, as much as she can. But then she closes her eyes, and a single tear trickles down the concave surface of her cheek. The machines keeping our mother alive seem to grow louder, the inverse of a cavern's echo, until I want to cover my ears, run out of the room—anything to get away from the yawning void of the moment.

"Mommy?" Blue's voice, childlike when she's not angry, sounds even younger as emotions threaten the edges.

"The truth will always get you in the end, Grace. How many times have I told you that?" Our grandmother steps beside me. I didn't hear her arrive, nor do I know how long she's been standing there. Long enough, I suppose, to hear everything. "Your girls aren't that big of fools."

Gram wears plain jeans and a plaid, button-down shirt, looking more like a man than a woman. Traces of our mother's beauty peek through her aged face, but hardness sweeps away any comparison. Where our mother was soft and lovely in appearance, our grandmother was harsh and blunt. When our mother was sober, she'd been more like her mother—she's one person where drugs and alcohol actually made her kinder, more fun to be around. The whys behind our mother's brokenness have never been clear—nor has her relationship with her own mother. But there's little love lost, at least from what I can tell. The tall, tough woman beside me resembles no one in this room, neither in features nor presence, and for that, I'm thankful.

"Well, isn't this fun?" Lux rolls her eyes at me, then centers on our grandmother. "You're looking well, Grandmother. Better than I expected, based on Blue's description."

Blue stares at her hands, the tiny animals still clutched in one fist, while the other droops in the box of stolen treasure. She doesn't look up as pain cracks over her facade.

"I appreciate your concern, Lux. I have rheumatoid arthritis—not pleasant, but it's not killing me yet. You girls look like life's treating you well. Wouldn't you say, Grace?" She seems unaffected by her dying daughter.

Silence weaves a suffocating web over the room. Blue finally shoves her box aside, right into our mother's hip, and tears out of the room, her pounding footfalls reverberating down the hallway.

Lux turns to our mother, her expression surprisingly calm. "I'm sorry you're dying. You did this to yourself—all of it. The drugs, the lies, the abuse, the neglect. But you are still my mother. And I'm sorry to see you like this. I hope you find what you always seemed to be looking for when you get to the other side, because I know you never found it here." With a sharp nod of her head, she brushes by me on her way out the door.

My mother's eyes find mine, pain mixed with longing, truth mixed with whatever lies justified her actions all these years. I war with compassion and rage, all soaked thick with desperate love for a woman who never knew how to protect herself, much less her children. "I loved you, Mom. Back before all of this happened, you were the most amazing woman in the world to me. Beautiful, funny, smart. Always the life of every party. I'm going to remember you like that."

Another tear escapes, and she nods. "Thank you."

"I don't know why you couldn't love us. I'm not sure I'll ever understand." I turn to my grandmother, her coldness practically chilling the room. "But I'm going to guess that it started with you. Whatever you did to her, you did to us, too. Mock your dying daughter when she can't fight back—ridicule her now. But remember this: someday, you'll be lying this close to death. And there'll be no one there, no one to mock, no one to remember the good times, no one to even try to care. I hope that's enough for you, Gram. Because it's all you'll have left."

Her eyes are so light blue, they appear almost white. Nothing fazes them, not now, not in the past. When I turn on my heel, I know it's the last time I'll ever see either of these women again, and my heart breaks in two.

I find Lux asking about Blue at the nurses' station, but they haven't seen her.

"I know where she is."

Her gray eyes, so different from mine, so different from

our little sister's, lock on me. "Where?"

We thread our way through the hospital's patchy crowds, descend floors, and jog for the exit.

"We grew up in this town, Lux. This is all Blue knows." Behind the hospital, several acres lie fallow, with a small playground that's long been let go. An old train track runs the length of the space, and when we were kids, we'd walk here. "We lived just over that ridge—well, for as long as we lived anywhere."

Lux looks back at the hospital, then at the landscape. "Oh my God. The hospital wasn't here then."

"Nope. That was built about ten years ago. Maybe a little longer."

Even from the distance, I can see Blue sitting on one of the old swings. The humid breeze blows strands of her hair towards the sky, the sun glinting off the copper. "This was her favorite spot when we were growing up, and it's walkable from Mama C's." She looks much as she did the last time I found her here, only that time crimson stained her pale skin as she chewed pills as though they were candy. When she tumbled from the swing into my arms, sticky blood coated my shaking fingers, making dialing my small flip phone almost impossible. My shrieks resonated in my ears as I struggled through CPR, fighting to remember the stupid acronym for the steps. A-B-C? C-B-A? C-A-B? Tears fell like raindrops as I fought to keep my sister alive.

I really wish Blue would find a new spot to hide from the world since I always seem to be the one who has to find her. A place with fewer bad memories for both of us.

When we approach, surprisingly clear green eyes find mine. "I'm sorry. I didn't know." Her tears left shiny tracks on her cheeks and her nose reddened. But her voice is steady, if congested. "I thought she was trying to do something to make up for...well, you know what I mean."

I drop to a crouch before her, my hands on her knees. "I know, baby. I'm sorry. I wish things were different."

"Me too." She falls forward into my arms once again, her

legs circling my waist as I tumble onto my ass. Her strength deteriorates into sobs—silent, shaking, desperate wails that can't find a voice. I hold her tightly, wishing there were something I could say to ease the pain of an unrealized reality.

I feel Lux's arms circle my shoulders as her head drops between mine and Blue's, and we crumble into pieces never meant to be glued together.

TRACING THE LINE

CHAPTER EIGHTEEN

THE BELLE OF THE BALL

Can you meet me at the office, beautiful?

I stare at the text message from Kai. We're supposed to get together for a late dinner at his place, and all I really want to do is curl in a corner and bawl my eyes out. I sort of hoped that tonight would be low-key with a homemade meal and plenty of wine, but it appears that's not meant to be. Hopefully whatever he has planned will work with my jeans and tank top, smeared makeup, and ratty ponytail.

I drop Lux at our apartment. Both of us were silent on the ride home; what more is there to say?

The summer sun hedges along the horizon, as though refusing to give up the day. I turn on some gentle music for the ride, but that does little to soothe my spirit. When I pull into Kai's office, the parking lot is empty. I sit there for a moment, debating if I misread his message. But a quick review proves I didn't. I glance around again, wondering if I'm too early.

Then I spot it: an envelope taped to the office door. I slip out and grab it, then hop back in my car. Inside the packet is a single sheet of paper. A shortened web address and a passcode are printed in neat handwriting, very masculine.

I don't think I've seen Kai's handwriting. Ever.

I really hope this is his handwriting.

With nervous fingers, I enter the address into my phone's browser, along with the code, and I see my face, close to Kai's.

"I don't know how to dance," the me on the screen says.

"I'll teach you." And then Kai does just that, his mouth lowering to mine. The video plays, and as self-conscious as I am about watching myself, I can't look away. Kai looks delicious as always...and even I don't look half bad. When the short film ends, the credits tell me to scroll down. In the description area of the video, there's a message.

"Meet me at Crandall's Lake, south side." There's another link, and when I activate the URL, I'm rerouted to directions from my current location. Despite my weary soul, I'm smiling as I head towards the rendezvous spot.

Crandall's Lake is a staple of Bakertown. The small lake—probably man-made, but hey, it's still really pretty—is surrounded by quaint, Victorian houses, many painted in bright, cheery colors. One is an old bank, renovated into a beautiful lakeside villa. When we were children, Lux, Blue, and I spent many days feeding ducks stale bread and playing hide-and-seek around the water. Of course, that's because our mother left us here so she didn't have to bother with us for the day, but still...Crandall's Lake holds some good memories of time with my sisters.

The sky has turned molten with the setting sun, and while several people still wander the lakeside, the south side is empty. I spy Kai's car parked in a small lot. I pocket my car keys and take the stairs down to the trail that runs the length of the water. The evening's reflection appears like a painting across the still lake, brilliant colors smudging into deep shadows. The contrast mirrors my feelings tonight, and I find myself drifting along the path, lost in thought.

"Are you meeting anyone?"

Kai's voice doesn't register immediately, so when it does, I startle. "I didn't know where you were." I try to smile, but emotion slams into me like a tidal wave, and suddenly I'm crying. He slides his arms around me, and I fall into him, sobbing against his shirt. He rubs my back, murmuring words I can't make out over my muffled whimpers. I've no idea how long we stand there, me lost in a river of regret and shame while Kai soothes my shaking shoulders.

I finally wind down to unattractive snuffling, and he lifts my face to his. With a gentle kiss, he says, "Come with me."

When he takes my hand and leads me back the way I came, I apologize. "It's been such a long day—I didn't realize how much it affected me." We climb the stairs as though we're returning to the street, but then he turns. We cross a small bridge to the back of one of the lovely Victorians I've always admired.

"Where are we going?"

A sparsely decorated slate patio spreads out before us. The few bits of furniture—a couple of chairs, a dining set, and a chaise—are sumptuous. The small table has been set with wine glasses and plates, several candles guttering—more pillar candles flicker and snap at regular intervals around the space.

I realize he's dressed to kill in fitted black pants and a white dress shirt that he's left unbuttoned at the top and rolled the sleeves—he looks both elegant and relaxed when he pulls out a chair. "For you."

I take the seat, unable to keep the surprise off my face as he sits across from me. We look out onto the lake, where a few small dinghies float, the passengers only shadows as the day fades. "This is like a fairytale setting. Whose house is this?"

He smiles, clearly pleased over my response. "A friend of Ger's. They go to Maine for the summer, and he keeps an eye on the place."

"I wish I'd dressed for the occasion." I stare down at my jeans and stale t-shirt in horror. He looks like he's ready for a modeling shoot, and I'm fit for Walmart.

"You look beautiful." His cheer dissipates. "Though I wish I'd planned this for another night; I feel terrible to drag you all the way out here when you're already exhausted. Tell me what's wrong. What happened?"

His thoughtfulness makes me feel even worse. "I don't want to spoil our night with that."

"You won't. If you don't want to talk about it yet, that's fine. But I'd like to hear, when you're ready."

The waterworks threaten again, and I snag my napkin. "My mascara's done for anyway," I joke, my voice shaking. Between tears and sniffles, I relate my time at the hospital. He listens quietly, only interrupting if he has a question, but otherwise, he lets me unload all the angst from the day. When I'm finished, I look across the table at him, my hand tucked in his.

"Now you know all my dark secrets. Still think dating me is a good idea?"

He rises and leans in to kiss me. "That has never been in doubt. Keep talking while I grab the appetizers." He slips inside the house and returns with a plate of fruit and cheese.

I nibble half-heartedly, wishing I could forget today's drama and focus on the lovely evening he's planned.

Kai eyes me for a moment, then nods his head. "Let's do dessert first." He grabs my hand and draws me to my feet. Along the edge of the patio, he's setup a small speaker system. He taps something into his smartphone, and soft music—likely a soundtrack from a movie—fills the air.

"When we were children, my mother forced my brother and me into dance lessons. Well, she had to sit on me to do it. TJ practically leapt at the chance. We took them for two years, but eventually, I was too big to wrestle into the car." He winks, his face drawn into soft lines as though lost in thought. "But my brother loved dancing—and he was quite good. If there was a beat, he could move to it and create his own routines."

"I'm jealous. I always wanted to learn, but by the time I was old enough to actually make choices for myself, we lived with Mama C, and she believed dancing was 'of the devil,' so the three of us didn't even attend our proms."

His brows draw together in concern. "I'm sorry. That's—"

"Don't be. I'm not sorry I missed that. I was awkward, and the only guy I would have gone with was nearly as much an outcast as me. Not to mention, the dresses that year were hideous." I mock-shudder.

He grins, his hand curving over my hip. "I'm sure you would have looked amazing, regardless." He laughs when I roll my eyes. "You watched the video? Where we first met each other?"

My skin heats, no doubt turning my cheeks pink. "Of course. How else would I have gotten here?"

"Good point." He chuckles. "You said you didn't know how to dance, and I said I'd teach you. So…" He steps back, my hand still in his, and performs a deep bow. "Milady, may I have this dance?"

Pleasure and embarrassment surge within me. My mouth drops open for a few seconds before I actually get the words out. "But I'm a mess. And you look magnificent. I—"

"You are stunning, in or out of clothing." He presses his lips to mine, effectively silencing any further argument. "We can do this naked, if you'd prefer?"

I laugh at the image, and shake my head. "No, no, clothed is fine."

"It's not every day I get to ask a beautiful woman to dance with me. So, I ask again, milady, may I have this dance?"

When I nod, he draws me against him, his arm strong behind my back. He curls his hand under mine, and walks me through a basic waltz step. Kai moves with the grace of a seasoned dancer, and I can only imagine what his brother must have looked like. When I'm somewhat competent in the steps, I ask him.

"TJ and I were like night and day...but some people asked if we were twins." He shrugs lightly, his lips curving up. "He was always thinner, more...defined, I guess. Did you ever watch old movies?"

"With Mama C. She loved old musicals."

"Ever see Fred Astaire dance? That was TJ. He loved tap, but give the guy some hip-hop, and he'd immediately transform into a master of rhythm. He adored the art of movement—had he lived, he wanted to move to New York City and train with the masters."

Another song begins, and he shows me a few variations on the steps. I giggle my way through a tango, wherein we both nearly end up on our asses in laughter. When a romantic ballad finally plays, he guides me into a simple slow dance.

"Why did your brother..." I start my question before I think through how sharp the words might sound.

"Kill himself? It's okay. It was a long time ago," he says with a deep breath. "While I miss him daily, I can talk about it."

I lay my head on his shoulder, listening to the slow, steady beat of his heart as we sway to the music.

"TJ was always sensitive—injured animals, hurt feelings. He experienced others' emotions as his own. It drove my parents crazy, as he would get lost in sorrow when the neighbor's cat died, or a friend got turned down for the softball team. I don't think any of us understood how intensely he felt things." He trails his lips along my hairline, almost absently, before speaking again. "When we were in middle school, the bullying started, but it was...well, kids are cruel. But TJ had his dance friends, and he lived at the studio. He volunteered for every fundraiser, traveled to every event even if he wasn't performing. He'd beg friends' parents to take him if our parents couldn't. When we got into high school, however, things changed. If you haven't adhered to a peer group, they decide where you belong. And he was always...I don't know if he was gay, to be honest. I often wondered if he was bisexual, as he didn't seem particularly drawn to people based on gender. He had a huge crush on a girl when we were in eighth grade, but in his freshman year, there was a boy in his class that he seemed interested in.

"We lived in a rural area of Illinois, despite being so close to Chicago. And boys liking boys did not go over well. As a dancer, he already had the deck stacked against him—he wore tights on stage, for Christ's sake. That ruined him for in-crowd consumption right there. But when it got out that he liked this other kid..."

I let him speak, unsure what to say. I know what it's like to be on the outside looking in, never quite fitting the mold, but I never had to deal with people outright hating me.

"What made things worse was that he started school early, as his birthday was in November. So he was always the youngest kid in the room. He insisted the other kids hated him. Our parents felt that he was just being TJ—overly sensitive and dramatic—as we all knew him to be. Deep down, I knew it was more than that. He had the shit beat out of him one day, right before summer break. But the months off seemed to make a difference. He traveled with the dance team—they went to Orlando to perform at Disney, which was a huge coup for them. And I was pretty sure he'd had his first sexual experience while he was away. I can't be sure—it's not like we talked about it, but he came home calmer, happier, and I guess I sort of forgot about the end of the school year and how distraught he'd been."

"Your parents didn't say anything about the beating?"

"He hid it from them—begged me not to tell them. He said it would make it worse if they insisted on talking to the school about it...which they would have done, of course." He sighs. "We were teens—we slept late, avoided hanging out with Mom and Dad, disappeared all day to a friend's house. They never knew, and like I said, I think it became 'you know TJ...' He was a nice kid, good-looking, got decent grades. There wasn't much reason to worry, at least from their perspective."

The end of the song leads to a haunting melody, one not made for dancing. We end up in the chaise lounge with our wine glasses refilled, sitting side-by-side.

"Anyway, by the start of his sophomore year, things got worse. His locker was broken into, pictures of mutilated genitals and homosexual slurs taped inside. They lured him to an empty playground and jumped him. That put him in the hospital. Our parents couldn't ignore those signs. And I don't mean that they ignored earlier ones...they were good parents. It's just..." He stares out at the lake, now a deep, murky purple, a charcoal vision of the sky etched in its waters. "I explained to you my emotional issues—take those, and multiply them, and that's TJ. But without the bitterness that drives my temper. He..." Kai presses his lips together. After a few breaths, he tries again. "He was an emotional kid, and it was hard to tell when things were really wrong, or when it was just TJ being TJ. When things were amazing, he was over the moon with joy. But when things were bad, he was barely functional."

"It almost sounds as if he might have been bipolar."

Kai nods with a sad smile. "When I sought out a therapist, that was her guess, too, and he may have been. It doesn't seem that long ago, but back then, you didn't get shrinks for your kids, you know? You gave 'em more Wheaties and swept issues under the carpet. Our parents went to the school and demanded the kids answer for what they did, but it happened off school property, so little could be done short of police intervention. And as TJ predicted, it only made things worse. They had to pull him out of school for his own safety."

"Oh, God. I'm so sorry."

He squeezes my knee, then continues in an even tone. "Days after, right before he was to start at a private school, we found—" He breaks off, shakes his head. "I found him. In our bathroom tub. He'd overdosed. He'd made sure everything was neat and tidy, so no one would have to clean up after him, which was so TJ. God forbid anyone have to do anything kind for him."

I want to reach out, pull Kai against me and offer some sort of comfort. But strength informs his body language and tells me I'd get more from the action than he would. Instead, I reach for his hand. "Thank you for sharing your brother with me."

Appreciation lightens his expression. "I often wonder what he'd be doing right now, and I have to think he'd have made it in New York. Maybe not to Broadway, or anything so grand—although, he was amazing. But perhaps he'd have found a troupe. Or maybe doing something like your friend Noah—he loved to teach dance to others. He believed so strongly that any involvement in the arts could change people for the better." Kai shakes his head with a wry grin. "Jesus, he had more conviction at fourteen than I had at twenty-four."

We sit in companionable quiet, listening to the music,

watching the sky for falling stars—we catch sight of two, pointing them out to each other like children. A few runners circle the lake, along with a young woman and a puppy, presumably out for an evening potty-training lesson. Whatever broken edges left jagged between the two of us, results of our childhoods and missteps of adulthoods, they soften in the glow of this perfect night, the half moon reigning contentedly above the clouds.

A sexy beat shifts my mood, and with a bravery that is most likely the result of exhaustion and wine, I stand and point a finger at Kai. "You don't get to move."

"I'm going to have to if you want dinner."

I shake my head, leaning down for a kiss, then pulling away at the last moment. "Dinner can wait." I have no ability to move to music—rhythm has never been my forte. But with as much swaying and hopefully provocative hip grinding as I can manage, I strip out of my clothing, down to my bra and panties. The one benefit of owning a lingerie shop—your underwear always matches. Fortunately, I went with a hot pink satin and lace set today. Only candles and a few strategically placed fixtures light the patio, but it's enough that anyone could see me if they were looking. Which...I apparently like.

Kai's gaze never leaves my body, and his admiration quickly turns to lust. "So when do I get to put my hands on you?" he asks when I slap him away as I wiggle my ass in his face.

"Hm. When I say so." I press him back into the chaise, then kneel between his knees. I take my time, running my fingers over the material, his erection pulsing. When I finally unbutton his pants and slip my hand inside, he exhales heavily.

"I envisioned this night going much differently," he says before groaning as I twirl my fingers over the head of his cock. "*You* were supposed to be on your back."

"Are you complaining?" I ask, squeezing his shaft firmly.

He drops his head back, eyes shut tightly. "No, no. Just—"

I enjoy his caught breath as I cup his balls with my other hand, nudging his pants and briefs lower. When I take him into my mouth, he closes his fist around the chaise's cushion, fighting for control. I take him deeper, opening my throat to his thickness. His palm rests against the back of my head, a gentle pressure that causes moisture to pool between my legs. I want to finish him this way, listen to the sounds of his pleasure, but he reaches for me.

"I need you—I need to be inside you."

There's an emotion in his eyes I can't identify, but I can't deny his request. He nearly rips his shirt as he discards it, shucking off his shoes and pants. Naked, he holds my arms as I straddle him, but then he guides my legs so they circle his waist. His cock trapped between us, he kisses me, need and desperation building. He rocks against me, using my wetness to glide over my tense nerves.

When I try to capture his cock, draw him inside me, he stills my movement. "Let me." He holds me close, continuing his slow, sweet torture. I hold onto him, tightening my legs around him. When he finally tilts my hips and slips inside, I cry out as an orgasm overtakes me. The sharp, heavy explosion leaves me clutching his shoulders as my body falls apart around him.

He grins when I meet his gaze. "God, I love watching you come. It's like the shatter of lightning during a spring rain—unexpected and immediate, with rolling thunder in its wake."

"You are way too poetic," I grumble half-heartedly, my body still quaking.

"My minor in college was writing." He nips my neck. When I yelp, he takes full advantage and runs a finger over my side.

I smack his hand away with a shriek of laughter. "You will pay for that." I wriggle off him, then turn and lower myself onto him. He feels like heaven as he fills me, the intensity rousing my hyper-aware skin.

His hands wander my back, and I lean forward, balancing on his knees, and control our rhythm. My own breath loses pace, coming out in pants, and he tips me back against his chest, using his legs as a brace against the chaise so I can't fight him. "Come for me, Zi." His fingers find me, exploring the tight junction of our coupling. I buck against his hand, my pussy like a vise around his cock, but I don't give up easily. The intensity increases until he can't resist any longer. One arm tightens around me as he loses himself, while his other hand pushes me over the edge alongside him.

Unable to move, we both start laughing. Whether from emotions or the intense pleasure, I don't know. But we both shake with amusement so hard, I tumble off him, falling against the soft cushions. When we settle enough to speak, he maneuvers himself beside me.

"You are something very unexpected." He kisses the inside of my wrist, then my palm. "And very, very precious."

I lay my hand against his cheek. "As are you. Thank you for tonight. Today was hard, and I wasn't sure I was up for this when I first saw your note. But this was exactly what I needed."

"And we haven't even eaten dinner yet."

I grin. "I don't think either of us noticed."

We eschew clothing and enjoy a meal of homemade lasagna, steamed asparagus, and double-chocolate brownies—"my mother's recipe, which she still doesn't think I have." We stay up as late as we can manage before falling asleep on a couch in the sunroom beside the patio, wrapped in each other and a blanket. I vaguely hear his whispered "I love you" as I drift off.

TRACING THE LINE

CHAPTER NINETEEN

MAKING AMENDS

I call the police the following day to see what's happened on the investigation into the vandalism of my Lothington storefront. Of course, I get a voicemail. As the bizarre religious messages have started again; all I can do is forward them to the police, for all the good it does. I avoid checking my email unless absolutely necessary.

After our evening at the hospital, Lux is distant. We all deal with grief different ways, but I'd be lying if I said her chilly silence doesn't hurt. She disappears to the city for a week, and I try not to let her absence bother me. Blue's in the same space, it seems, as my text messages go unanswered again. Kai's the only shining light, and I find myself at his house more often than my own.

It's Friday morning, early, and I can't sleep. I try not to wake him, but when he turns over with a bleary eye in my direction, I give him a sheepish smile. "Sorry."

He drapes a lazy arm around me. "S'okay." He tries to hide his yawn, and then smiles at his failure. "You can't sleep?"

I shake my head against his shoulder.

"Your sisters?" When I nod, he hugs me tighter. "Why don't you go talk to Lux? Blue might be a lost cause right now until she can get a hold of herself—at least, based on what you've told me about her—but Lux is probably feeling the same way you are. She's not one to get all sappy with emotion, I'm guessing?"

"No, she's not. I wish she'd turn to me for once, you know? Be sensitive to what I need sometimes." I hate feeling petty, but there are days when our relationship feels unfair, and I take it personally. She's always been able to contain her emotions and ignore them. She's the one that walked away from

Blue and me for almost ten years—and most days, I totally understand why she did. I don't even think she was wrong. But moments like this, when I'm hurting, I really wish she'd be a bit more sensitive to my needs. When I mention my bitterness to Kai, my voice barely a whisper, he slides up on his elbow so he can look down at me.

"I'm not making excuses for her, Zi. You are my priority, and I hate that you're hurting. But Lux isn't like you. She holds everything inside. It's not that she doesn't care—but probably because she cares too much. And I'm betting—not knowing her that well, of course—that she doesn't want to dump her emotions on you." He traces the curve of my cheek down to my chin. "You put off this persona that you can handle anything, and by God, you pretty much do. You never seem to need anyone."

"But it's just an act. Or at least, that's how it feels lately."

"Hey," he lays his finger over my lips, "stop. You've had a hell of a couple of weeks. Anyone would crack under the strain. And it hasn't stopped you for a second. Your strength and determination is one of the things I love about you—among many others. Lux probably feels weak right now, and she's not going to be comfortable feeling like that beside you, her younger sister. That's not how she operates."

I ponder his words. "So you think she's convinced I'm handling all of this without her and I don't need her?"

"Something like that."

"So what do I do?"

"She's probably not going to come to you."

I roll my eyes. "So that means I have to chase after her."

He stays quiet for several minutes, and I can almost feel his thoughts. I refuse to speak them, so he finally does. "She's the one who found you."

I glare at him, even though I know he's right. I'd told him the story of how Lux tracked me down a little over a year ago when she'd finally worked up the gumption. And fair or not, I probably wouldn't have gone looking for her. Well, maybe I would have...but not yet. I wasn't angry at her, per se. But the sixteen-year-old me, the one that watched her pack a small duffle and begged her not to leave...that me hadn't quite gotten over her betrayal. Maybe that part of me still hasn't.

"I hate you when you're right."

"Hm." He moves so he's on top of me, his thighs spreading mine. His mouth finds my breast, teeth closing over the soft tip until the nipple hardens beneath his attention. "I'm about to be right about something else, too. You can hate me later."

My laughter turns into a sigh of pleasure as he proves his point.

Afterwards, though, I turn to him as we're brushing our teeth. "Ah should go tahk ta heh."

He chuckles at my toothbrush-interrupted words. Finishing his ablutions, he dries his face with a towel. "Try that again."

I spit in the sink, then wipe my mouth. "I should go after her. Talk to her."

After a quiet gaze in the mirror, he leaves to get dressed. Damn him. His silence is as much agreement as I'm going to get—he won't talk me into doing something I'm not sure about. But the longer it takes me to get dressed—I only have two outfits at his place, and I'm pretty sure I've worn all the pieces in different variations during the last week—the more sure I am. I pull on my jeans, sneakers, and, when my tank top is suspect after a thorough sniff test, one of his clean t-shirts. Later, I'll change into one of the pretty tanks I carry in the store during summer months.

Then I check my calendar—I have two appointments this morning, and one in the afternoon. Amie can handle closing the store. Kai and I eat a quick, mostly silent breakfast, but when he leaves, he kisses me until I'm whimpering against him. "You'll figure this out," he says against my hair as he hugs me.

"I know. I just wish it didn't hurt so much."

TRACING THE LINE

With a half-grin, he grazes his knuckles over my cheek. "The things that matter usually do." He's about to open the door when he turns back to me. "Not to change the subject, but our conversation last week, about filming you and me..."

The shift in subjects has me stumbling for mental ground. "What? Oh, *that.*" My cheeks flare with fire. "Yes?"

"I booked some time with Ger this weekend, but with everything going on, I'm going to ask him to reschedule—"

"No." Gee, I sound so sure of myself even as my stomach shivers with nerves. "If he has time, let's do it."

"I found a location I thought you might like, but I wanted you to see it first."

I pull his mouth to mine, returning a bit of his earlier passion. "I'm sure it's perfect. And I could use the distraction. Terrifying distraction it may be, though." I make a face.

He kisses my forehead. "You are going to lie back and enjoy—I'll do all the work." With a wink, he's gone. I grab my bag, stuff my dirty clothes into the side pocket, and head to work just long enough to take care of my appointments. Then I point my car to the city early enough to beat the bulk of rush hour traffic—as long as I hop a commuter train and not attempt to drive in—and hope for the best.

Lux shares an apartment with Noah in a pretty Brooklyn neighborhood with old brownstones jammed cheek-to-jowl amid attempts at greenery and gardens, mom-and-pop stores, and tiny playgrounds. Early evening casts long shadows by the time I knock on the door of their apartment, the echo of the sound not giving me much hope that anyone's home. But then Tag's barking greets me, soon followed by his wiggling joy as Noah opens the door.

"Tag, down!" Noah's voice hardens with command as Tag jumps up on my thighs.

I'm stunned when Tag immediately drops to his haunches, his tongue falling out of his mouth. "Wow. Impressive." Of course, Tag's hind end vibrates with his barely contained energy.

Noah sighs a long-suffering breath. "We've been working on his manners. Haven't quite gotten the 'sit until released' thing down yet." He tosses Tag a treat, then Tag leaps up on my knees. Noah groans and reaches for Tag's collar. I push his hand away.

"No, it's fine. Let me say 'hi.'" I smooch Tag between the eyes, his silky fur too tempting to resist. He slurps me across the face, and I giggle, careful to keep my face away from his tongue as I scrub his back and sides with my fingernails. After a moment, he flops on his back, belly revealed for rubbing. I acquiesce and am rewarded with his sparkling brown eyes gazing at me with adoration. "Besides, where else do I get such excitement over my greeting?"

"I don't know. Kai seemed pretty enthralled on July fourth," Noah teases.

My cheeks turn pink, and I focus on Tag's velvet belly.

"I assume you're not here to see Tag—or me, for that matter. I'm not sure where Lux is, though, truthfully. She left this morning and hasn't been back since."

"Shit." I pause in my ministrations, and Tag lifts his head in confusion. "Oh, fine, you little mooch." I continue stroking his soft tummy as I think. "Any ideas where she might have gone?"

Noah leans against the doorframe. "No clue. She's been

'off' since she got here. I tried getting her to go out for a night, but all she'll do is work. Hell, Fin threatened to leave his horse training seminar early, but she's been adamant that she's fine, which we all know is a lie."

"Did she tell you what happened?"

"Nope. Can't get a peep out of her. And while Lux may not tell everyone her life issues, she'll usually confide in me. The most I got out of her was last night, after a few drinks, she admitted she's dealing with something, but the minute I suggested talking about it, she clammed up."

I lift a shoulder in frustration. "I'm not sure what to do. She's barely responding to my text messages."

Noah invites me in, and I end up giving him a brief overview of what happened.

"Shit." He echoes my earlier declaration. We both sit there, Tag wandering between our hands for constant affection. Noah checks his watch. "Damn. I've got to get down to the acting school—we have some rehabbing going on and I promised to lock up before I'm due at a late dinner for Elementary."

I wave him away. "You go. I'll figure this out."

"Stay as long as you need to. You know where the spare sheets and pillows are if you need to sleep over. Fin's due in sometime tonight, so I assume she'll be back before too long." He gives me a warm hug, letting me rest against him for a few moments. "She needs you, Zi. She just doesn't know how to ask. And if there's one thing we all know about Lux, she doesn't ask for anything. Ever." He shakes his head in amused frustration.

After he's gone, I wander their apartment, trying not to pry but also looking for any clues where she might have disappeared for the day. I peek in her room, but outside of the usual array of clothing everywhere and an unmade bed, there's nothing to help. I nibble on a nail, trying to think. Then I shake my head at my own foolishness. I know exactly where my sister is—or at least, where she will be if she doesn't return to the apartment soon.

When she's still absent around eight, I head out. Paddled

is one of the few sex clubs in New York City. Mind you, there aren't many in the country to begin with, according to Lux. So the fact that Paddled exists at all, and has for almost thirty years, is saying something. According to her, while there's an erotic mystique to the idea of a sex club, the reality is...well, they're everyday people who enjoy kink, may take part in public nudity and acts, and quite honestly...look like you and me. Once you realize that, the shine fades, and Paddled becomes like any other social environment. Okay, maybe not, but you get the idea.

Just after eight, I enter the underground club—they opened only minutes before. A tall, exotic woman mans the drink bar—Paddled is strictly non-alcoholic—and I suspect she's probably a "he" during her off-hours—no woman looks that perfect. Still, her makeup is better than mine even when I put in some effort. Figuring she probably knows most people who walk in the door, I head over to the counter.

"I'm looking for Lux Trace—she's a regular, I believe," I say by way of greeting.

Dark chocolate eyes narrow, eyeliner enhancing the sharp tilt at the corners and making the look venomous. "Who's asking?"

"I'm her sister, Zi." I hand her a business card.

Her large hands, bedecked in long nails with wild designs, angle the card so she can read the print. "Mm-hmm. What do you want with Lux?" Her suspicion hasn't faded, but I think we've moved out of the "destroy first, ask questions later" territory.

"We've got...family issues. I need to talk to her about... stuff." I'm not sure if I should be pleased she looks out so intensely for my sister...or annoyed that I apparently appear that threatening. Aside from my height, I don't think I've got samurai written all over me.

The bartender puckers her lips, gives me another once-over, then holds out her hand. "Tice, baby." She has a firm shake, but not harsh. "Good to meet you. I can see the resemblance around the eyes, but other than that, you two didn't come from the same combo, I'm guessing."

"Different fathers." Why am I admitting such personal information to a complete stranger? Oh, right, because she still looks like she could snap my neck while pouring a non-alcoholic mojito. "Good call."

Tice smirks, then releases a huge smile. "It's not like you two would be confused for related, that's for sure. Lux is on the balcony, up in her favorite spot. Let me get you a refill for her—she's not been much for chitchat today." She mixes a cranberry drink of some kind, creates another juice concoction, and hands me the two glasses. "Here you go, baby. On the house. Lux is good people—I'm assuming you are too." While her cheer doesn't alter, there's a subtle threat behind those words.

I snicker to myself—first I go to a sex club to find my sister, then I'm threatened by a drag queen. My life is certainly never boring.

This early, little is going on. A few "dungeon rooms" are in use—small spaces with barred doors—and the occasional grunt of pain or pleasure reaches my ears as I climb the stairs. Otherwise, the main floor is barren, though I spy a table being set up in the far alcove—perhaps for a caning or whipping? While this isn't my world, getting to know Lux and her reasons for taking part has obliterated any preconceived prejudices I may have had. I appreciate others' needs to find acceptance of their fetishes, and to honor their kinky desires, as long as they follow the BDSMer's code, "safe, sane, and consensual."

Lux slouches in a corner, fingering the straw in her empty glass. She's off in another world, her usually sharp, mildly amused gaze distracted. If I didn't already suspect her mood, her clothing would give her away: leather pants, simple black boots, and a sleeveless gray sweater. My sister never shows up in her element with less than her favorite corset and five-inch-heel thigh-boots.

"Tice sent this up for you." I slide the fresh drink across the cocktail table, then pull a stool over for myself.

She startles at the sight of me, then deepens her frown. "What are you doing here?"

Whatever Tice made me, it's delicious—a cross between pineapple and orange juice, with a frothy, creamy finish. I sip my drink before answering her. "Looking for you. You've got a damn bodyguard down there. I thought I might have to rough her up to get information on you."

That manages to wrangle half a grin from her. "Tice's got my back." Her mirth is fleeting, and she gets lost again, staring at her deep red drink.

My goal to find her fulfilled, now I don't know what to say. Perhaps there's no need. I sit quietly across from her, watching the occasional arrival as people trickle into the club. The alcove's entertainment starts in earnest, punctuated with slaps of a leather flogger, followed by increasingly strained and euphoric gasps.

"I shouldn't have left."

I'm so engrossed in the activity that it takes a moment for me to register Lux's words. "Why do you say that?"

"Look at Blue. She's a fucking mess. And last week at the hospital—what the fuck was that? A mother and a grandmother so removed from...God, Zi, we were children. Babies." She sighs, staring out at the club but likely not even seeing it. "We deserved better. I look at Mia and how much Ella loves her. She'd never let anything happen to her if she could prevent it. You should have heard her conversation with Fin over horseback riding lessons. The kid's barely three, and Ella's trying to plan for her desires and her safety, to make sure whatever she needs or wants, she'll have available. Isn't that what parents do? I mean, not everyone has the money Ella and Ian have, but don't even poor parents look out for the physical and emotional well-being of their kids?"

She continues to rail against the unfairness of our childhoods, all of which I've said myself. I listen, letting her get all the bitterness out.

"And I left you. And Blue. As though I had some right... as though turning a certain age made abandoning your family okay." Her eyes turn glossy, but she won't let the tears fall. "I left you, and I feel terrible about it. And there's not a damn thing I can do. Now our mother's dying, our grandmother's a piece of shit, and Blue's going to be torn in two again. Will she survive this? I don't even know. How would I? I barely know her."

"Stop." I cover her hand with mine, and when she tries to yank away, I hold on. "*Stop.*" I can't tell if she's going to rip away from me and walk off or not, but after a tense few seconds, she relaxes a fraction, her fingers limp beneath mine. "None of this your fault. Any more than it's mine, or Blue's. Hell, I'm not even sure it's our mother's fault. Entirely," I'm quick to add as she opens her mouth to argue. "Our grandmother isn't exactly a paragon of motherhood. And our mother...I don't know. I wonder now if she's got some sort of mental illness."

"Like, say, too many drugs in her system 24/7?"

"At this point, it's semantics. Look, shit happened. We got a raw deal when it comes to our crappy family, and nothing can change that. You left because you were a prisoner in a place that was supposed to be a refuge. It's not your fault that asshole tried to rape you; neither are you to blame for how Mama C's ex-husband tried to make it your fault his brother's a sexual predator. You were fifteen, Lux. A child. I don't care if you did wear tight t-shirts—some forty-year-old guy trying to force you to do anything is wrong."

She closes her eyes, fighting emotion. "And then I left you and Blue to deal with the mess."

"We were safe. As safe as we could be, and we weren't your kids. I'm not condemning you."

"Blue does."

"Well, that's Blue. She's got issues." I shake my head, dismissing her determination to find blame. "I'm not mad at you. I mean, maybe I was at some point. But if anything, you showed us how to stand up for ourselves, and you made yourself successful. You could have been a statistic, gotten pregnant too soon, had multiple kids to unknown fathers, just like our mother. But you didn't."

She pulls her hand away to cover her face, her fingers

checking under her eyes for smears. "I'm a fucking mess."

When she looks up, I lick my finger and wipe at a black smudge by her eye.

"Ew!" She jerks away, but she's laughing. "Jesus, that's gross!"

"Some days, I wonder who's the older sister here."

She sticks her tongue out, crossing her eyes, and we both dissolve into giggles. Hysterics tinge the edges perhaps a bit more than actual humor, but right now, I'll take it.

"Can we get out of here?" I ask after we've sobered. "I'm way underdressed for this place."

She snorts. "You and me both. Let's go."

We sneak out the back entrance, then head for the subway. We're quiet on the way back to Brooklyn, but when we approach her and Noah's apartment, she nearly knocks me over with the force of her hug. I rest my chin on the top of her head, gathering her close.

"I wish I'd have stayed. At least until you both were able to leave, too."

I rub her back, pressing a kiss to her scalp. "I'm glad you didn't. We needed someone to prove that wasn't any way to live. And too much longer might have broken you. Blue and I might not have had things easy after you left, but Lux, they weren't that tough on us, not like her asshole ex was to you."

That seems to be enough, for now at least. When we burst through the doors, Tag and Fin greet us. I settle for stroking Tag's wiggling body while Lux takes strength in Fin's arms. They remind me that for once, I have someone waiting for me back home, and I can't wait to get back to him.

TRACING THE LINE

CHAPTER TWENTY

FOR THE RECORD

I leave the city the next morning. Lux and Fin walk with me to the subway, the first leg of my trip back home. She hugs me tightly. "Love you, Zizi Baby."

"I love you, too." I give Fin a squeeze, enjoying the scent of freshly washed male. While Fin's not my type—redheads have never done anything for me—he's definitely a hottie, and you couldn't find a nicer guy. Except for Kai, of course. "Keep her out of trouble."

His grin flashes with amusement. "As if I have any sway over her wild ways? Ye do know yer sister, right?" He winks and pulls Lux to his side. I leave them kissing at the subway entrance and wind my way through the labyrinthine tunnels to my track. Headphones offer a tiny bit of solace against the loud transportation system, but by the time I reach my train platform about a half hour or so later, I can't ignore the nervous energy that courses through me.

Kai texted me early this morning, giving me instructions for our "taping" this afternoon. Well, if you can call them instructions.

I'll pick you up around three. Wear whatever you like, whatever makes you feel sexy. I can't wait to peel every stitch off and taste you until you scream. Preferably my name. ;)

Oh, and I love you.

I hadn't had a chance to message him back between getting breakfast with Fin and Lux—Noah wouldn't be caught dead at that time in the morning, much less awake—and getting to my subway stop on time. Now, on a train above ground with plenty of cell phone signal, my fingers shake as I key in a response.

So I guess my question is, who'll be spending the most time on their knees this afternoon?

I love you, too.

Unlike me, Kai doesn't have any excuses for not responding immediately.

That depends. I'm happy to kneel at your feet for hours, my love, as long as your legs are spread.

I nearly shove my phone into my bag, as though everyone on the train can read his words by looking at my face. I bite my lip, struggling to keep the ridiculous grin from cracking my cheeks.

I don't mind taking turns. Besides, doesn't your favorite position involve me on all fours?

We continue like this for several minutes, until my cheeks are in danger of spontaneously combusting.

I'm not going to get through this train ride with my dignity intact if we keep this up. So behave. But I'll keep in mind your earlier suggestion—I do like you rock hard.

I can almost hear his chuckle when he replies.

Then I'll leave you with this: I can't wait to take full advantage of your wet pussy later. I intend to use every part of my body to make you a very, very satisfied woman.

I shuffle through my bag for my e-reader, but you can imagine how successful I was at trying to focus on anything for the rest of the ride.

Kai's at my apartment on time. When I answer the door, his mouth opens, but he offers no words as his gaze takes me in.

I ordered this dress when we'd first talked about making a video. I'd been eyeing it for some time, but given the price tag and nature of the outfit, I couldn't imagine getting my money's worth out of the purchase. The modest neckline dips in the slightest "V" and is held in place with stitching at the shoulders, the sleeveless design leaving my arms bare. The pinkish red material falls in loose folds to a high, fitted waist. Completed with a flowing skirt, this could be a very simple, very tasteful cocktail dress.

Except for the part where the length falls barely past my rear and you can see right through it.

I chose dark, almost eggplant colored lingerie—a g-string and matching bra. I debated thigh-high nylons, but given that the temperature is in the nineties, I nixed that idea and wore simple, flat sandals.

I save Kai from commenting by pressing my lips to his. His hands circle my waist, then slide lower to pull me in, ensuring I don't miss how my appearance has affected him.

"You better pace yourself, Mr. Isaac. You have to perform again later," I say against his mouth.

He kisses me thoroughly, his palms traveling my body. "Don't remind me."

I lean back so I can meet his gaze. "Are you nervous?"

"I am about to make love to the most beautiful woman alive, on camera no less. And I want this to be perfect for her. So yes, I'm a little...anxious."

His admitted vulnerability eases my strain. "That makes two of us. But we're in it now, right? No backing out." I wink, relieved to be the supporter instead of constantly supported. I leave him at the door to grab my bag and don a longer, terry cloth cover-up typically used for the beach. "An afternoon of debauchery awaits us. Shall we?"

Despite my bravado, as we drive through farmland, I start jittering inside. We're well into the city, heading towards a destination I've yet to extract from him, when he reaches for my hand.

"You're freezing."

"Just starting to feel the pressure, that's all. I'll be fine."

He glances at me thoughtfully. "I can take your mind off your nerves, if you'd like."

"Oh?" I turn my gaze to him, catching the sexy curve of his lips. "And how would you do that?"

"Give me two minutes."

I look at him with amusement, momentarily distracted. He navigates the narrow roads leading off the main highways as though he's an expert of the city, then opts for a dead-end lane on a narrowly divided block. He puts the car in park, but keeps it running so the air conditioning can keep us cool.

"First, let's get this out of the way." He reaches for the hem of my cover-up.

"Like this?" I bunch the material of both garments around my waist, exposing my legs and hips.

"Much better." His hand slides over my knee, nudging my thighs apart. "Relax your legs."

I've never played games like this, much less in the car. Well, unless you count the blowjob I attempted on the Fourth of July, where we ended up having to pull over.

Okay, so maybe I've just never had sex acts performed on me in a car.

"Close your eyes and recline your seat back." His voice soothes, his commands gentle.

I follow instructions, and as I lie back, he trails his fingers over the lower half of my torso. He seems directionless, as though he wants nothing more than to stroke my bare skin. I find myself drifting, enjoying his touch and the steady sound of the car's quiet engine. When he finds his way between my legs, I remain loose-limbed. He tucks my panties out of the way, using two fingers to explore my core. His contact is light, almost purposeless, slowly drawing my body into arousal. He dips inside me, his finger—then fingers—finding a lazy rhythm. When heat starts to wash over me, I barely recognize my orgasm—as though feeling this high were a natural state of being. He never rushes, even when I arch against his hand, moan filling the car.

"Hm. Now you look ready for your close-up," he whispers, the words winding through my delicious haze.

My arms and legs feel boneless, and I vaguely register his leisurely pressure between my legs still sending small shockwaves over my skin. "I...ah..." I'm trying to string words together, but while another orgasm doesn't feel imminent, energy builds inside me again. "Don't we...have to...?"

He kisses my fingers as I reach blindly for him, then takes my hand. "Ger can wait. I've paid him for the night."

I moan as sensation peaks, sending my thoughts spiraling. Time has no meaning—hours could have passed, for all I can tell, as the endless pleasure rising through my core captures my focus.

When he finally withdraws his hand, I could fade into sleep. "You are better than Xanax."

"I'll keep this in mind the next time you get nervous."

I open my eyes to find his gaze, fiery gold with desire, and I stroke his cheek. "Thank you. That was...unbelievable. Where did you...learn that?" I ask uncertainly as I force myself to sit up and adjust my clothes.

"In college, I had a friend who could get any woman into bed—and more than that, they'd beg for him to sleep with them again. They were sober, mind you. He wasn't even all that good-looking, at least from my point of view." When I arch an eyebrow, he holds his hands up. "I wouldn't believe it if I hadn't seen it. One night, we were out getting some drinks, and I asked him his secret."

"*That* was it?" I straighten my seat.

"No, not exactly." He grins. "But he did say that his only real gift in the bedroom was taking his time with a woman. And since women can have multiple orgasms, he made sure his partners did."

"You give him too much credit. I've never had anyone even attempt something like that. It was like one rolling, stretching feeling that felt like it could go on forever."

"That part I figured out on my own. But it was good advice. Prior to that, I was probably the worst lover ever—well, maybe just a typical guy, in that respect. I had fun, but I'm not sure I did much for my partners."

I breathe in easily. "I can't remember the last time I felt this peaceful."

He leans over to give me a kiss. "Good."

We glide back onto the road, but soon we're deep in the city. Turning off a main street, we reach a narrow passage, barely wide enough for the two cars already parked here. On either side, well-preserved brick buildings face-off, their small windows inlaid, all or in part, with stained glass. We park just outside a small gallery, and he guides me to the far end, where a side entrance is propped open. Before we walk in, he pulls me to the side.

"I wanted to give you a few options, as I've noticed some things that you seem to enjoy, but I'm not sure how you want to proceed. Ger has the camera, and he's the only person who's going to be in the room with us if that's what you want. Since you like the risk of being seen…Carla's a professional makeup artist, and I asked her to stop by for you. I also put her, Ben, and Samson on notice in case you wanted them to watch. They live nearby, so it was easy to arrange. But this can just be you and me. Whatever you are most comfortable with."

He's gauging my reaction carefully, and I feel a bit drunk after our earlier play. But his thoughtfulness—and recognition—towards my desires offsets any surprise.

"There's no rush to make a decision—you can think about it for a few minutes."

I shake my head. "No, I watched them. And it was beautiful." I suck in a breath. "I'd love to be able to give them the same gift." I hesitate. "Are you okay with them being here? You haven't said what you want."

"I'm with you. And I've never been all that shy." He kisses the tip of my nose. "Shall we?"

The building houses a small fine arts store, with refinished wood floors and ancient exposed beams. Kitschy and elegant, tiny framed canvases dot the walls, artfully displayed without being overshadowed by larger masterpieces tilted against the walls. The lighting offers a soft yet plentiful brightness, with a few extra lamps placed inconspicuously around the room. A single leather lounge occupies the center of the space, covered in decorative throws.

Ger acts as though he does this all the time, but then, I suppose he does. He and Kai discuss camera angles and locations, looking to me for approval. Kai explains what they're asking, but I don't understand much of the lingo. So I nod, figuring at this point, does it really matter?

Carla arrives, and she greets me with a hug. "It's good to actually talk to you. Kai asked me to bring some makeup. May I?" She's as pretty as I remember, with a cute pixie haircut that gives her a mischievous, sexy look.

Whatever I manage with some brushes and drug store palettes is nothing compared to the art form Carla practices. When she directs me to a mirror on the wall, I nearly do a double-take. It's me if I wore no makeup...but had perfect natural coloring to highlight my best features.

"You're a miracle worker." I cock my head for another view, fascinated by my reflection.

She laughs and shakes her head. "I had the perfect canvas to work with." She stands behind me, her hands lightly touching my waist. "I'm so jealous of your curves. I can work out for hours a day and do yoga until I'm a wet noodle, and I never manage to even have hips."

I meet her gaze in the mirror. "I've always thought I had a bit too much curve. And I think you are stunning."

"Aw." She blows me a kiss. "We're both hot and sexy, right?"

I'm thankful for her easy manner. While my nerves have returned, they're in the background.

"You'll do great. And these guys are so easy to work with. Well, I guess you already know that about one of them, right?" She grins and packs up her makeup case. "I'll be back in a bit—

me and the boys will sneak in so you won't even know we're here unless you look for us."

I touch her shoulder as she turns to leave. "Can I ask you something?"

She smirks, amusement lighting her dark gaze. "Let me guess: how do you make it work with three of you?"

My face gets hot, but I shake my head. "No, actually. I can't imagine that boils down to a simple formula—it's doesn't for two people, that's for sure." I bite the inside of my lip, not sure how to phrase my question. Then I give up and ask, "I'm curious how you felt so comfortable the other day? You seemed completely at ease, and I'm not sure how to do that."

"That's simple. You and Kai are here to enjoy each other. And the only way to make him happy is for you to be happy. That's your only focus tonight. The rest of us, what we think or don't think—none of that matters. When you remember tonight—or watch the video," she winks, "what you'll remember is whether you enjoyed the moment."

She captures my fingers in a quick squeeze before leaving, and I'm left to my own devices while Ger and Kai murmur over details.

At least, until Kai crooks his finger at me with a small grin. He's changed into a robe, which means that, well, the time is nigh. I meet him in the middle of the store, and he buries his face in my hair, letting me sag against him. "Nervous?"

"A little. But I'm ready." I step back, and he nods to Ger. After confirmation, I remove my covering, my gaze focused on Kai's. He doesn't break our connection as he unwraps his robe, and Ger takes them from us.

Kai wears only black bikini briefs, his muscled body on display in the soft lights. If I weren't so distracted by nerves, I'd probably be star-struck.

"On your mark," Ger says quietly.

Kai positions me behind the lounge. "I'll be right back," he says against my ear. "Don't look at the camera—fantasize about what I'm going to do to you in just a few minutes."

He wrings a stuttered laugh from me before walking away.

I swallow hard as I stand alone, facing Ger's camera lens. I try not to shake, though my fingers vibrate against the couch.

"Action." Kai's voice calls out somewhere behind me. I do as he suggested, staring down at the couch. I wonder if this is how Carla felt, moments before her lovers approached. The risk of being seen on Kai's patio or by the lake felt daring. The reality that someone *is* watching, much more filming us...I have a momentary urge to call the whole thing off, but as I suck in air, convinced I'm about to meltdown, Kai's warmth caresses my back. When his lips find my neck, I can't help leaning against him. I'm still wildly aware of Ger in front of us, of the heavy glare of the camera, but as Kai's hands travel up my sides, my head falls back against his shoulder. Eventually, he turns me, easing me up onto the back of the couch.

His mouth devours mine as I wrap my legs around his waist. I forget about the filming, about whether anyone's watching, and breathe in Kai and his confidence. We kiss for minutes on end, the relaxed pace soon eclipsed by raw need. He peels my dress off, then teases my breasts before removing my bra. For a moment, I remember that somewhere beyond us, people are watching, but then his teeth close over my nipple, and all thought slips away. His strong arms hold me as I arch beneath his mouth, desperate for more.

"I need to feel you," I groan softly as I grind against him.

His tongue tangles with mine before he pulls back with a grin. "Are you in that much of a hurry?"

"Yes." I nip his bottom lip lightly. "We aren't going for feature length, are we?" I arch an eyebrow, enjoying the unintentional double entendre.

Amusement sparkles in his gaze, though I imagine we look like we're exchanging sexy nothings. "I was hoping for a bit longer than a commercial." He drops his mouth to my neck, returning my bite. "But I aim to please."

He spins me roughly, forcing me over the lounge. I gasp when his palm lands over the curve of my ass. The sharp sting serves only to arouse me further as he massages my backside. He slips my g-string to the side and dips his fingers inside me, first two, then three. With alternating purpose, he spanks me, then caresses my burning skin before teasing my center. I can barely take all the sensations as they swirl into bright shards of pleasure.

When he frees his erection, pressing the hard length between my ass cheeks, I urge my hips against him. He spreads me, nudging the head slowly inside. My jaw drops as the aching progress splits me apart, an orgasm quaking deep in my core. Noises I don't recognize as my own fill the air. With measured effort, he repeats the slow torture until I'm begging for more.

Then he surges into me, pressing my legs wide with his thighs. His thrusts are punishing, his hands gripping my hips so hard, I can't do anything but let him take me. And I'm breathless, nonsensical as I whimper each time he sinks into me.

I'm unable to form thoughts when he finally lifts me, drawing me against him. His cock pulsates inside me, and I collapse, letting him guide my arm up, placing my hand on his neck. Then his lips brush mine, echoing our first kiss.

"I love you." He mouths the words against my lips, his hand cupping my breast, and despite the setting, the erotic tension, the presence of others, it's only him and me.

I return his kiss, hoping my actions convey more than I can put into words.

"Come with me." We separate, and he takes my hand. We hike the stairs to the loft where more paintings and etchings hang from the walls, interspersed with handmade trinkets and pottery. Carla, Ben, and Samson have likely been up here the entire time, curled around each other, and when we pass them, they are kissing softly, hands seeking lazily over each other.

Carla averts her eyes from her lover, meeting my gaze with a small smile. I nod, still too aroused to focus but appreciating her gentle acknowledgement.

Kai grips my waist, setting me on a small window seat. I vaguely register Ger behind us, but then Kai's mouth covers mine. He gives me no break as he anchors his hands behind my knees, holding my legs apart. He sheaths himself with one motion, drawing a moan from me. I brace myself against the small, deep-set window frame as he gains even deeper reach.

His gaze locks onto mine, the dark green warring with gold. Intensity builds as the friction sends me over one edge, then back up to another. When I finally tip over the high precipice, waves buffet me, my cries turning into hoarse groans. He covers my mouth with his, shuddering as his climax takes him. I reach for him as he sinks to his knees. I slide down to the floor, and we clutch each other, both shaking in the aftermath.

I've never believed we need another to make us whole—not after my childhood. I've always had myself, and no one else seemed to care enough to prove otherwise. But in Kai's arms, I wonder if I missed a nuance. Maybe we are whole on our own...but perhaps the expression of our truth requires another.

TRACING THE LINE

CHAPTER TWENTY-ONE

WHEN ALL LEVELS OF HELL BREAK LOOSE

"You can do this." Lux grabs the 3x5 cards out of my hands. "Start again."

I glare at her and cross my arms. "No. I'm not going. I sound ridiculous." I drop heavily onto my couch, as though she's going to physically force me up.

If there's one thing Trace sisters excel at, it's stubbornness. Lux raises a perfectly shaped eyebrow at me. "If you're going to give up and let some zealous nut-job turn you into a pussy, far be it from me to convince you otherwise." She tosses the cards on the couch and stalks to the kitchen.

We've been practicing my speech for the Lothington township meeting all day. Or at least, it feels that way. In reality, it's probably only been a couple of hours. The meeting's this Wednesday, and I'm beside myself with nerves.

I double-check my email, rereading the recent message from the cop I've been working with over the vandalism. They found Zachariah Lemke, traced his online behavior, and easily connected the spray painting to him. While there's no obvious connection to that and the emails, the officer feels pretty confident they can bring charges against him based on the evidence.

So I'll have to show up for a hearing in a few weeks.

Great.

Either way, Lothington's citizens have been riled up against me, and unlike Lux, I don't have any faith in my orating talents. I'm a putz with this kind of stuff—I nearly failed speech class in college. Give me a woman with the wrong bra size and a complex about her midriff, and I can make her feel like a million bucks in under an hour. Stick me behind a podium with notes and a hostile audience, and go figure—I'm useless.

I give her a few minutes before peeking in the kitchen. Lux made a bowl of popcorn and appears to be focused on a fashion magazine. The strained set of her shoulders gives her away, though.

"That might be easier to read if you turned the magazine right side up." I risk taking a seat at the small bar set that barely fits in my kitchen.

She lays a withering stare on me, then shuts the glossy journal. She shoves popcorn in her mouth, probably to avoid saying her next words.

"You're right. I know I have to do this. But can you understand why I'm terrified?"

She pushes the bowl towards me. "Of course I can. I'm not heartless, Zi. I wish I could do this for you, as I'd have no problem making the fuckers smile while I shoved their balls down their throats."

I chuckle at her description and reach for the snack. "I love how genteel you are in debates."

"Debating is fine. You want to be a dick, though, and I'm going to point it out." With a heavy sigh, she props her chin on her hand. "I totally understand, Zi. I do. But you have to do this. You can't chicken out. People are only bullies when they think they can get away with it, and especially in this case, they're wrong. They don't even know what they're fighting against except that it involves sex, so therefore, it must be bad."

"Particularly hilarious because I have no intention of having the same stock there—hell, I may only do lingerie in the beginning. We'll have to see."

"Exactly. Some asshole got people brandishing pitchforks, and now they're out for blood on the basis of someone else's beliefs—most likely not even their own."

"I'm glad he's at least been picked up, though I admit to being afraid of retribution."

Lux pats my hand before grabbing the bowl back. "Don't be. Remember what Fiona said: the guy's a closet activist with internet bravado. He's done this shit before, but he's never been violent."

That may comfort her, but I'm still worried. Regardless, Wednesday looms large. My phone rings with a text message, and I grab it from the living room.

Have I told you how deliciously hot you are today?

I grin at the phone, and Lux makes kissing noises. "How is your prince of the silver screen today?"

Are you editing a certain movie? And no, not today, but I think you proved it yesterday.

"He's fine." I can't look at her for fear I'll burst into embarrassed flames. I told her about the filming—it's not like I could hide such a thing from her. She'd spied my inability to stop smiling as soon as she arrived this evening.

"Mm-hmm. Sounds like he's more than fine." She snatches my phone, then runs into her room and closes the door.

"Hey! Give me that back!" I squeal in outrage as I take off after her.

"Oo, oo, another message!" she yells from the other side of her door.

I shove against the cheap plywood as the knob's lock clicks. "You bitch. Give me my phone." My insult doesn't have much bite when I can't stop laughing.

"Kai, you naughty, naughty boy. 'I've almost come three times, and I'm barely finished with the first five minutes.' Hm, what should I reply?"

"Don't you dare! Lux, I will....I don't know what. But you will not like it if you say *anything* to him."

"How's this? 'Baby, I'm on my way over. You can edit

while I ride you cowgirl style.'"

I chew my nail, both amused and irritated. "I'm going to kill you."

She turns the lock and opens the door. "Nah. You love me." She tosses me the phone, and I catch it on the edge of my fingertips.

I double-check to make sure she didn't type anything in the text box. "Some days..." But when she falls back on her bed, I join her, lying in the opposite direction. "I should paint your toes."

She lifts her head, flexing her feet so she can examine them. "God, they're awful. I'm usually so good about getting mani-pedis. Lately, though." She drops back down, relaxing her body.

"I know." Between all the emotions we've been dealing—or not dealing—with, there hasn't been time for much beyond holding on and trying to breathe through the drama. I haven't heard from Blue, though I've texted her every day, several times a day. I've started sending her brief thoughts, odd photos from my day. Anything so she knows she's loved, but doesn't feel like I'm pestering her.

I key in a quick response to Kai: *I can't wait to help you out with that problem. Tomorrow night?* He has a late Skype conference tonight with a possible investor in a new film for his "other" company, and I need to actually clean my house before it starts to resemble Blue's.

I don't know if I can wait that long. I might have to kidnap you and take you away for a hedonistic getaway for a few days. ;)

My near-giggle has Lux nudging me with her calf. "What'd you say?"

I open my mouth to read the text to her when another text comes in, this one from Blue. "Hold on."

She's dead. Funeral's Wednesday.

I swallow hard, unable to reconcile her message against my good mood. Numbness shadows my mirth, picking apart my joy, piece by piece. Who sends that kind of news in a text message? Why?

"What's up?" Lux sits up, her hand on my back.

I nearly show her the message, but I refuse to succumb to Blue's cruelty. "Our mom. She's..."

"Oh." Her hand lays heavy on my back, both a welcome comfort and impossible weight. After a few minutes of silence, interrupted only by the pernicious bird outside her window and the dull roar of nearby traffic, she slides down beside me, pulling me against her.

I'm so much bigger than both of my sisters—I always have been. Bigger boned, bigger hips, bigger everything. I've even thought that, in some ways, I have a bigger heart, more prone to caring and getting hurt. That might have just been my ego speaking as right now, it's the smallest, dwindling into an empty void. As Lux holds me close, her fingers trailing through my hair, her voice murmuring soft words, I disintegrate into nothingness.

"How's she doing?" Kai's voice echoes down our small hallway.

Lux answers quietly, and I can't make out the words. I've moved to my bed, at least, so I'm not in the way, but the blankness remains. When Kai crawls in beside me, I don't move. Even when he fits himself around my inelegant sprawl.

Thankfully, he doesn't go for pat phrases or trite sayings. His breath lingers beside mine, calming the anxiety that creeps around the edges. We remain this way for some time—still, quiet. He lets me interrupt the solace, choose the moment of breaking.

I don't even realize I'm sobbing until he gathers me closer, pulling my head onto his shoulder. He envelops me, as though knowing at any point, I may fall to pieces. Lost in confused sorrow, I shake and heave, unable to even pull in air.

"You've got this, baby. Take a breath. You're going to be okay." He massages my neck as I fight to gasp. "Focus on my hand." He interlaces our fingers and pulls back so they're in my face. "Stare hard and find the breath. You can do this."

As stupid as his words sound to me in my panic, they work. As I train my eyes on the fine coating of hair on the back of his hand, the struggle eases, and I suck in hard. After a few more minutes, I'm able to breathe without effort. And I realize his knuckles have turned white from my death grip.

"Sorry," I whisper, yanking my hand away.

He stretches his fingers, then brushes the cold tips over my cheek. "I'm okay."

"I'm a mess." I duck down, hiding my face against his chest.

"You're normal, actually. I'm more worried about Lux than I am about you."

"She'll be fine. She's dealt with all our shit. Well, most of it."

"And you haven't?" He tries to look down at me.

I give in and look up. In the soft pink light from my bedside lamp, he looks like a fallen angel with his mussed curls and strong jaw in shadow. I can only imagine what I look like with my frizzy hair and blotchy face. "I thought I had. I just..." I trail off, then fumble for my phone on the bed. I have to get up to find it, pushed deep beneath my pillow. I unlock the screen and hand the cell to him without looking.

He lifts up on his elbow as he takes my phone. He stares at Blue's message for a few seconds. "Wow. That's...harsh."

"Thank you." I manage another deep breath, thankful that inhaling is getting easier. "That's what I thought. I mean, the message is tough enough, but the way she did it...why wouldn't she tell me in person? Or at the very least, call me? Is there some new protocol that we deliver bad news via texts?"

"Not that I'm aware of." He widens his eyes and blows out a breath. "Is that typical of her?"

"Who the fuck knows? Blue's such a...mystery. I never know what to expect." I cross my legs so I can balance my elbows on my knees. I drop my chin into my hands.

He joins me, nearly knee to knee. "It's not my place to make assumptions about your sister—I barely know her. But based on what you've told me, and what I've seen, I'm not sure you should place too much weight on this. You said she's emotionally unstable, and this might be the only way she *could* deliver this. Not that I'm making excuses for her," he's quick to add when my gaze flattens. "I'm not saying any of this is right. But you know she's a loose cannon, right?"

I hate his logic, and I hate even more that he's probably right. "So I'm expecting too much, basically?"

With the look of a man scared to step into a minefield, he nods slowly. "Your expectations of Blue might be more than she's capable of living up to. At least right now. In a situation like this."

Despite the empty hole in my chest, his careful wording brings a small grin to my mouth. "You don't have to tiptoe around things, Kai. I'm not going to go off on you."

My assurance doesn't assuage his conviction, but he presents his hands to me, palms up. I lay mine over his, thankful that he's so much bigger than I am—it's rare I feel petite. His thumbs rub against the side of my pinky fingers as we both stare down at the simple touch.

Earlier, my stomach had curled into such emotion, I was nearly dry heaving. But now, it gurgles, a reminder that a few handfuls of popcorn do not make a meal.

"I can whip up something if you'd like."

"You don't have to—"

He stops me with a gentle kiss. "I don't mind. Since I'm not leaving you tonight and I still haven't had dinner, why don't you join me in the kitchen so I can get started?"

Lux sits at the table, staring blankly at her magazine. Even though the pages are turned the right way, she's not seeing the celebrity gossip. I join her, and beneath the table, she grips my hand. With Kai, we talk about inane things—stupid pop culture, weird YouTube videos on our Facebook feeds, and funny movie moments that have little to do with our topic of conversation. None of it makes sense, but Kai weaves the distraction, never letting silence enter the meal as we opt for the living room floor and coffee table. He made a masterpiece of what was left in our cupboards: grilled cheese sandwiches, fried potatoes, and frozen broccoli.

And with his easy way of soothing people, we get accustomed to the heavy, confusing grief of losing our mother, one minute, one second, one pained heartbeat at a time.

CHAPTER TWENTY-TWO

SORROW'S EMBRACE

Wednesday offers sunshine and a clear sky, as only Mother Nature can be so cruel. Perhaps it's a blessing—there's nothing worse than standing in a cold, wet rain with nothing left to combat the empty chill. There's no viewing, only a service for the interment. I've no idea who paid for anything—Blue? Gram?—and it's not like we all hug and share our sorrow when we arrive.

Blue's there with Gram, probably the only reason she's on time. I chide myself for the thought, but I'm hiding behind anger to get through the day. After I bury the mother who's left more questions and angst behind than answers, I have to go defend my right to do business at the Lothington township meeting. This day just keeps getting better.

Kai offered to come with me—insisted—but I refused. While having him beside me would be a blessed support, some part of me wanted to do this alone. Losing my mother has the odd side benefit of not having to fight for reasons why I should love her—not anymore. And I do—I can't help caring because she gave me life, and for what it's worth, probably did the best she could with what she had. At least, that's what I'm telling myself. The truth is probably a lot more complicated.

And maybe that's what I want to face alone.

Fin tried the same thing with Lux, but she and I were determined to keep this in the family. Noah and Ella were both a bit more staid—prepared to attend, but accepting when we asked them not to.

Therefore, only a few people stand around the small, simple casket—a few of Gram's friends that I might recognize if not for the heavy jowls and crinkling skin of age. If our mother kept in touch with anyone from her wild days, they aren't here. A nondescript priest from a local Episcopal church offers the eulogy, and we bow our heads. Lux stands to my right, her long hair tucked into a modest bun, her usual sexy style encased in a surprisingly chaste black suit. Blue stands off to my left, several feet away, in dark pants and a black tank top. Her wild hair blows in a humid breeze. She's barely looked at me since we arrived.

Sweat trickles down my back, sticking to my navy blouse. My mind's blank as the cleric performs the holy rituals and surprisingly short-winded blessings. Then it's over.

Gram turns to her friends, as though purposely not looking at her three granddaughters, and walks out into the cemetery with them. Lux threads her arm around my waist, leaning her head against my shoulder. I hold her tightly, pressing a kiss against her hair.

I look over at Blue, desperate to get some sort of sign from her, anything, that she's in there. She doesn't move, doesn't seem to be breathing. Her arms cross her torso in an impossibly tight embrace, her hair hiding her face.

The funeral director comes to me—God only knows why since I've done nothing for this funeral so far—and nods. "Just let me know when you're ready."

I look at him, questioning. "I'm sorry?" And then I see the gravediggers, standing off to the side, muddied tools beside them. The casket rests on a lowering system, ready to descend into the neatly dug grave. *I have to give the word to bury my mother?* Jesus.

"We have to tip the gravediggers," Lux whispers to me, drawing some money out of her small black bag.

"Are you serious?" I'm lost, having never participated in any of this before, and things move around me too quickly, too slowly.

"Go ahead," I say to the funeral director, manufactured sympathy hanging over his long face.

"No!" Blue launches herself on top of the casket, arms wide. "Get back, you fuckers! Leave her alone!" She glares at the funeral director and diggers with venom, screeching the words.

Lux looks at me, eyes wide. "Shit."

"Give us a minute," I say to the slightly less sympathetic director, and he gestures to take our time.

I rush to Blue's side. She's shaking, gripping the casket with desperate fervor. "No..." Her sorrow-worn moans scratch over her throat, a testament to how much emotion she's been through the past few days. "Th-they can't h-have her-er." She wails through her hiccups, and Lux shrugs at me. Short of manhandling her, I don't know how to remove her.

We stand beside her for probably a half hour, Lux and I both staring out beyond the graveyard. Awkward doesn't begin to describe my feelings. Every time we attempt to gently extract Blue, she screams as though we're clawing into her. The gravediggers have taken two smoke breaks, I think, and the director is making phone calls on his cell.

"This is ridiculous," Gram snaps as she marches up beside me. "Blue, get off of there immediately. You're making a scene."

For once, our sister doesn't respond to our grandmother. A slow trickle of tears course over Blue's face, but otherwise, she's still.

"Leave her be." Lux's voice reaches barely a whisper, but the command in her voice leaves no room for argument.

I watch our grandmother, idly curious what her response will be. I'm aware how detached I feel, recognize it as a coping mechanism to deal with the disaster today is. I wish I could do more—be more for Blue, for Lux. For now, I'm hoping to get through.

Gram stares at Lux, her lips twitching as though she's working through a response. Finally, she raises her hands in defeat. "Fine. She's your sister. You deal with her." And with that, she leaves. No final comment for her daughter, no words of comfort or shared sorrow with her only living relatives.

And we wonder why our mother was fucked up.

After a few minutes, I tug gently at Blue's shoulder, and she doesn't respond. But neither does she wail in protest. With gentle hands, we pull her off the casket, supporting her limp body between us as we take her to the car.

"I'll sit in back," Lux says as we fasten the seatbelt around Blue. I nod, thankful she's doing so. The ride may be silent, but our thoughts fill the quiet louder than any words.

We tuck Blue in on the couch, covering her with blankets, and she falls asleep. Lux retreats to her room, the door closed. I change, preparing for the next mess I'm going to face.

I sit beside Blue for a while before I have to leave for the meeting. I brush her hair back from her face, admiring the way her nose turns up just slightly at the end. How her rosebud lips, naturally bright pink, purse like a small heart as she sleeps. Amazed at how blue her veins are, showing just beneath her pale skin. She's always reminded me of a doll, delicate and easy to break. How does any mother look down at such perfection, such innocence unspoiled, and destroy it so completely? I kiss her forehead, smelling the strawberries of her shampoo.

"I'm so sorry, Blue." A tear drops from my cheek to hers, finding the dried path of my baby sister's grief. That's how we've always been—thrown together, willing or not, and shoved into what others wanted.

Dark thoughts follow me to the meeting, and I push them down, focus my mind on the images of my notecards, the words I want to say to convince people who hate what I supposedly stand for, not to. An exercise in futility, in my opinion. But I'm in this now. I will finish it.

Good luck, Zi. I'm thinking of you.

I run a finger over the screen of my phone, as though

doing so brings Kai's warmth closer. I'll text him when I finish. Hell, I'll probably call him and beg him to meet me at the house.

The meeting's at the township community center, a large warehouse-style building on the city proper limits. I'm barely on time, but I don't care. I want to get this over with so I can go home and lick my seeping wounds.

"Ms. Trace, I'm Mayor Green. So good to finally meet face to face." A tall, tanned man with the look of a soccer-dad and car salesman combined greets me. "I hope tonight will give us some answers and make things easier for everyone."

How bad is it that I'm not remotely interested in whatever that's supposed to mean? But I paste what I hope is a smile on my face and shake hands with whomever is presented to me before the meeting comes to order. I'm handed a roster of tonight's issues, with mine near the very end. Why am I not surprised? The room fills up fast, and I find a seat towards the back.

While they debate zoning changes and playground funding, I let my mind go blank. After an hour and a half of endless droning, I hear my name called. "Ms. Trace, are you coming up here?"

Clearly, they've called me more than once. I scramble to my feet, dropping my 3x5 cards on the floor. "Sorry. I'm nervous," I say with a hopeful grin, but I can't find a single friendly gaze. I toss the cards into my bag, straighten my suit jacket, and make my way to the podium. A simple wood structure, the front panel is carved with a dove and cross, suggesting it probably did time as church furnishing. I find myself giggling at the absurdity of everything: my mother's death, my destroyed little sister, the people sitting before me who make assumptions based on fear and misguided notions. It's all hilarious, and I brace my hands against the podium while I shake, holding in peals of laughter.

Several throats clear, and seats squeak with uncomfortable shifting.

"Ms. Trace, are you okay?" Someone—I think it's the

board's secretary—asks with caution.

I hold up a hand, staring hard at the wood grain finish beneath my fingers. *Pull it together, Zi.* "Sorry. It's...been a long day." I look out at the relatively small band of people—maybe a hundred or so—that has turned out, probably to get some free coffee and homemade brownies. "I buried my mother this morning." If they looked uncomfortable before, they're even more so now. Hushed gasps echo in the large hall, but I wave them off. "Really, it's okay. She wasn't a great mom. Not like the wonderful women who brought these baked goods for us here today. She didn't even know how to make macaroni and cheese—I learned how to when I was six. And between my older sister and me, we took care of our younger sibling. We did wash, used a vacuum cleaner, and took care of ourselves for most our childhood. We ended up in foster care, and even then, we looked out for each other.

"I'm telling you this because...well, first, so you understand that if I seem a little shaken tonight, it's been a really long day. I'm sure many of you can understand that. But I'm also saying these things because I want to share with you who I am. I'm someone who understands what it's like to be scared for your children, to want the best for the people you love. I get that many of you want to make sure your neighborhoods are safe and that your town doesn't become one that's scary at night. I understand because when I was much too little to have to worry about such things for me and my sisters, I did." The words pour out, nothing like what I rehearsed, which involved something about improving tourist numbers and adding to the aesthetic of the shopping district.

"My business isn't selling porn or sex—it's making women feel good about themselves. I sell lingerie that makes your partners feel sexy and embrace their femininity. I offer a safe place for your daughters and granddaughters to ask questions. Do you know that there are things they won't even say to their best friends or doctors, but they'll ask me when I do their custom fitting? Things like, should I take birth control if I'm having unprotected sex? Am I still pretty even though I had to have my breasts removed because of cancer? Will anyone ever love me again?

"I fitted a woman last month who had severe bruising across her abdomen and legs. You and I both know what that means, right? Only because she knows me, because she's been shopping in my store for over a year, was I able to suggest she go to the women's shelter rather than go home and face another beating.

"This is my work, ladies and gentlemen. Helping women find what makes them feel like beautiful beings, to express their sexuality in a way that is right and healthy. Yes, I sell some fun, battery-operated items in the back of my store. But are we really so out of touch that we think offering such harmless things threatens our culture or contributes something evil? Most of the women that come into my store are partnered, the bulk of them married, and they buy underwear. That's it. Occasionally, they pick up a fun toy to enjoy at home. Is that any more harmful than buying a sexy dress for dinner tonight or picking up condoms at the local drug store?

"I am not here to hurt your town or encourage bad behavior. Some of you have seen the vandalism on my storefront. That's someone's fear, and it's ugly. But no one here did that. We're all just trying to do what's right. I promise you, my window dressings are pretty, tasteful, nothing even as risqué as your local Victoria's Secret.

"My business is no different than the carpet seller down the street, or the insurance office next door. And I'm very good at what I do because I care about making people feel their best. Can you honestly say that's something you don't want here in Lothington? I hope not because I chose this town for my second store because I love what you have here—a gorgeous, progressive town full of arts and culture that draws tourists and locals to join in and take part. I want to be one of the members here that encourages that kind of attitude and gives back to the community. And I hope you'll see that as something you can support."

I don't know how to finish. The verbal spigot has run dry, and I stand there, unsure what happens next.

TRACING THE LINE

"Any questions for Ms. Trace?" The secretary nods to the audience.

An older woman, seated towards the back, raises her hand. "Do you offer sizes for larger women?"

Her question throws me off—I'd expected some sort of digging, pointed question. "Um, y-yes, I do. I offer sizes for all women—if I don't have it, I can order it, and then I'll stock it for you."

Satisfied, she nods with a small smile.

Another hand raises, and a man, probably in his mid-thirties, speaks. "I think what you're doing is great, Ms. Trace. My wife and I have been to your store in Bakertown, and it's very nice. We're totally behind you coming to Lothington. I think anyone here that has an issue should go visit your store before they judge it. It's just like Victoria's Secret at the mall on the east side, but like you said...um, nicer."

His praise nearly buckles me. I'd been prepared for viciousness. His kindness would likely bring tears to my eyes if I weren't cried out. "Thank you. I remember you—your wife... she's a blonde, right? She wore blue Chucks that I admired?" They also bought a very impressive vibrator that uses Wi-Fi.

Don't ask.

He nods, blushing. "That was us. We'll be back in soon."

After that, no one else raises their hands, so I nod to the board members and step away from the podium.

"Isn't it true that the man you're seeing makes pornography that you sell in your store?"

The shouted question comes from the back of the room, and I search the faces, trying to figure out who spoke. When I find her, I've no idea who she is. She's narrow-framed, with limp, dark hair and a drawn face. Her bright blue eyes blaze with determination.

"I'm sorry. I have no idea what you're talking about."

"Kai Isaac." She pronounces his name incorrectly with a hard *a* as she holds up a black and white printed page. "'He owns Fade In Productions, which started out as a production company for pornography.'" She reads off the page as though it's a Wikipedia listing. "Fade In Productions transitions to independent films with *real world* focus, and Isaac created Naked Truth Films, which has become a leading name in erotic film. Isaac himself starred in several pornographic titles, including *Inside Her* and *The Woman Beneath*, considered two of the most unique pornographic films because of their thematic content.'"

I barely remember to inhale, much less swallow over the hard lump in my throat.

"I seen you with him online—some fashion show where you danced around nearly naked. You date a pornography producer—so how can anyone here believe your nonsense when you say you won't bring that kind of filth to our town?"

"Th-there is no pornography sold in my store. Anyone who shops there can verify that. If you don't believe me, come in tomorrow and look. We open at ten in the morning—I wouldn't have time to 'hide' anything." My mind's reeling, and I have to get out of here. But I refuse to look guilty, so I aim for the back of the room.

Her shining eyes follow me as I nearly stumble towards my seat. "You peddle Satan's merchandise, Ms. Trace. And we won't have that here, exposed to our children when we take them to Murdock's to get ice cream."

"Mrs. Lemke, that's enough. Take your seat." The secretary speaks firmly over the woman when she attempts to continue.

"We'd do well to remember that it's Mr. Lemke who is facing charges for vandalism of Ms. Trace's store," my earlier fan, the young guy, says over the discordant chatter.

The secretary looks frazzled. "Why don't we take a break? We'll come back to discuss the matter further in ten minutes."

My excuse to leave presents itself, and I nearly run for the door.

Mayor Green catches me in the foyer while I'm searching for my keys with shaking fingers. "Ms. Trace? Are you leaving?"

"This day's been…too long. And I'm exhausted." I let my emotion show, tears swimming in my throat, if only to gain a little empathy from the man.

"I'm so sorry about your mother." He bows his head for a moment. "What you said earlier—it was brave, and had more effect than you know. Don't let Mrs. Lemke get to you. There's a small number of dissenters, and we're working with the police to make sure they can voice their opinion, but not overstep the law." He gives me a meaningful look, and I wonder if he knows about the emails. "We *are* a progressive town, and your store has a lot of supporters, believe it or not. And many more for whom it doesn't matter." He smiles and pats my arm. "Go home and take care of yourself."

I fight the chokehold of sorrow on my vocal chords. "Thank you," I manage to get out. My hand closes around my keys, and I escape into the night.

CHAPTER TWENTY-THREE
OWNING UP IS HARD TO DO

The drive home's a blur. My phone vibrates with messages, but I turn the sound off. I can't look, can't read, can't do anything until I can get some sleep. Blue's still passed out when I get home, and Lux has her door shut. Just as well, as I don't want to speak to anyone. I need to stop existing for at least twelve hours. Maybe fourteen. Amie's manning the store for me (hopefully, Mrs. Lemke and her ilk won't take me up on my offer), so I fall into oblivion.

"I put Blue in my bed," Lux greets from the couch the next morning. She's on her laptop, most likely working—or trying to, at least. I pour a mug of coffee and refill hers, then flop on the far end of the sectional.

"Can you do me a favor?"

Something in my voice must tip her off because she watches me for several moments before nodding. "What happened?"

"Look this up first, then I'll tell you. Please." I search my memory for the names of the films Lemke's wife mentioned.

"*Inside Her* and *The Woman...Beside me? Beneath me?* They're movies."

She taps at her keyboard, her gaze narrowed as she scrolls. When her eyes widen, her mouth dropping open, then snapping shut, I don't need to know what she found.

"Don't tell me. Not right now. I need to not know for a little longer." Throwing my arm over my face, I try not to see Mrs. Lemke's fervent gaze, hear the edge in her voice as she read words that broke whatever small pieces of me were still whole.

We sit there, saying nothing while I sip my coffee. Then I rehash last night, giving her a very abbreviated version of my speech.

"Wow."

"I know I've made a splash if you're speechless."

"What are you going to do?"

"Nothing. The township will decide, and it sounds like things might be fine."

"You know that's not what I meant." She types something, then whistles. "There are photos of you from the fashion show. And the 'first lust' video is up, with you and Kai kissing. That must be where she got her information. Shit." Lux snaps her laptop shut. "He never told you, am I right?"

I shake my head slowly. "No, and I never looked. I never asked, though, either. Not specifically. He told me about school, about his family, about how he got into film. I guess he skipped over that part."

Lux hangs her head, nearly as flabbergasted as I feel. "He was probably scared to tell you."

"Probably."

"That's not good enough, though, is it?"

I meet her gaze, her gray eyes bloodshot, probably a mirror of my own weary face. "Is it? When do you tell people the truth? After you're already committed? Before you say 'I love you'? What fucking excuse is there for not mentioning something he'd know would be a big deal to me?" Tears escape, and I smear them away, anger and hurt finding a temporary balance. "And the stupid thing? I know he's within spitting distance of the porn industry. I know his movies might not be porn, but let's be honest: they're sex on tape. How many times have he and I talked about where we came from and how we got better at what we do? We've even swapped stupid business decision stories. He could have told me—any time. But no—I find out from that fucking bitch who couldn't wait to spread that in public and try to humiliate me and make me into a liar." Hurt wins, though, and soon I'm burying my face in my hands, tears flowing unchecked.

Lux keeps her distance, as though sensing I don't want to be comforted. "You should hear his side, though, Zi. Maybe there's a good explanation for everything."

I look up at her, sniffling hard. "Like what? 'About the porn movies *I starred in* that I *didn't mention* even though *I knew you'd be upset?*' What's he going to say that's going to make not telling me okay? And worse yet, letting it come out in a way that damaged me and my business? How is that ever going to be okay, Lux?"

She bites her lip.

"I'm just over everything right now. All of it."

"He called me freaking out. Earlier. He was worried when you didn't respond to his texts or calls. I told him you were sleeping, but that I'd have you call him when you got up."

I suck in air, unable to fight the emotions that flow unbidden across my cheeks. "I'll call him. Fuck, I'll go see him. If I'm going to do this, I should do it in person."

So I do. With hair barely contained in a heavy ponytail and ratty jeans I've been meaning to donate to the thrift store, no makeup to cover the ravages of the last few days, I find myself on his doorstep. I drove by his office first, but his car was absent. Sure enough, he's home, and I bang on the door, then back up several paces.

"Thank God. I thought I was going to have to send out a

search party." He steps out, moving towards me, but pauses when my hand meets his chest.

"I'm here to talk." My voice is low, raw, and his brows draw together in confusion.

"Of course. Come in."

"I'd rather stay out here."

He cocks his head. "Why do I get the impression only one of us is going to be talking?"

"Because only one of us probably has anything worthwhile to say, to be honest. I attended the township meeting last night, as you know, and everything went surprisingly well until some vicious woman asked me about this." I pull out the folded printout of the article I found online. As I'd suspected, it *was* a Wikipedia entry. I hand him the wrinkled sheet and watch his expression.

His bafflement softens to understanding, and his golden eyes, the green just a faint ring around the edges, meet mine. "I'm so sorry, Zi."

When he doesn't say anything more, I snort derisively. "That's it? That's the best you've got? I'm mocked with this information, my business is put at risk, and all you can say is that you're sorry?" I drop my hand on my hip. "Unbelievable. If you had just told me, Kai. For fuck's sake. If I'd known, I wouldn't have been caught off guard. I might have walked out last night with my dignity intact. But no. I got blindsided because my boyfriend didn't mention that he started out in pornographic movies."

He stares at me, his expression flat, and his lack of response enrages me even more. "You know how I feel about porn. You've known that from day one of our relationship. I've tried to be open-minded, and I've shared my deepest fears with you. I trusted you with my goddamn soul. And it never occurred to you to tell me? Never crossed your mind that this was information I should have, if for no other reason than being honest and open with each other? What the fuck, Kai? What the actual fuck were you thinking?" As angry as I am, I can see the flood of emotions he's fighting. His desire both to explain and to comfort, perhaps even rage back at me...tempered by guilt that rolls off him in waves.

I bite my bottom lip to keep myself from saying anything more, but it doesn't work. He's trying to come up with something—I can feel it. But it's not fast enough for my ire, the hot, venomous spirit that rises high on pain, sorrow, and betrayal. "Say something. Anything, goddammit. You want to run through your anger yoga now? Do it some other time because I deserve an answer, and I'm tired. I've got a mother who just died, a grandmother who's a piece of shit, and a sister who's near catatonic with grief, not to mention a business that may or may not get to expand because of circumstances I never asked for and was never told about."

He swallows hard, then nods. "You deserve an answer. And I want to give you one. But when you're yelling at me, I have a hard time thinking straight. Can you give me a minute to come up with an answer that's worthy of you? Because I believe you deserve that too."

"No, you don't get another minute. You don't get one more second. You had what, eight weeks? You had 'I love you.' You had all the conversations that went all night where you could have told me. And you didn't. And I am not going to stand for one more person in my life who fucks with my emotions. I am over it. And I am over you."

"Zi—"

"I'm done."

I leave him standing there, his face a mask of frustration and hurt, and I race my engine on the way home, hoping the feel of power will give me a temporary reprieve from the final crack in my armor.

I sleep. Maybe for days, outside of going to work. I function when and where I have to, but when I get home, I fall into bed and hide from everything. Messages clog my voicemail, even a card left on the door, but I don't listen, read, or acknowledge them in any way. I barely recognize signals for hunger, though I do manage to get a shower somewhere in between the heavy darkness and bouts of panic.

It's several days later—three? Four?—when Lux knocks on my door. I'm not really asleep—just lying here beneath the covers, hoping the world will stop turning. I don't answer her.

"We need to talk about Blue," she says as she barges in.

A dull thud erupts in the back of my skull as I sit up and rub my eyes. The clock confirms it's Sunday afternoon. I don't recognize the sleep shirt I'm wearing, and a quick sniff assures me I should probably not wear it for another day.

"Yeah, that's Fin's t-shirt you're wearing. For some reason, you dug into my laundry for something to sleep in."

I guess I'm more out of it than I realized. "What were you saying?"

"Blue. She's barely gotten out of bed in four days, and I know she hasn't eaten. I can't even get her to acknowledge me. She's a zombie. I think there's something really wrong, Zi."

"Technically, I haven't done much more."

"Yeah, but you're aware of it—and you're going to work. Blue's not called anyone or done anything from what I can tell. And when I try to talk to her, she stares off in space. She's not just ignoring me—I don't think she's even hearing me."

I run a hand over my face, trying to wake up and clear my head. "So what are you saying?"

"I'm saying I think we need to do something. Maybe take her to the hospital. I'm not sure." Lux shrugs. "I'm not exactly the most nurturing human being in the world, but I've tried everything with her. Nothing's making a dent, and I'm getting scared."

"Let me get a shower. I'll talk to her." I nearly fall out of bed, and Lux steadies me with a hand.

"Are you going to be okay?" she asks when I'm upright.

I ponder her question. "I think so. It's..."

"A lot, I know. And for what it's worth, I'm really sorry about how things went with Kai."

"Me too."

ALLY BISHOP

I wash up, finding a fresh pair of jeans and a t-shirt that's actually mine. Blue's still in Lux's room, much like the last time I checked on her. She lies on her back, staring up at the ceiling.

"Blue? Baby?"

Her eyes blink, but her gaze remains fixed.

With tentative steps, I approach the bed as one might a feral animal. I'm worried I'll set off the screaming we witnessed at the funeral, but when I sit down, it's as though I'm not there. "Lux tells me you haven't eaten anything. You want me to make you a grilled cheese sandwich? I probably have some dates in the kitchen." For some reason, she's always loved medjool dates. "Macaroni and cheese with real milk? Not that shitty powdered dairy substitute we used to use?" I try to joke, but it doesn't matter.

I check her pulse, snap in front of her eyes, and she blinks. But there's no other response. "Is this about Mom? Mommy?" I try to think of words that might reach her, things she's said. "Do you remember the boxes she gave us? Gram mailed them—they came yesterday. Do you want to look at yours again?"

For the first time since I've known Blue, and all the crazy things she's done over the years to get attention, I worry she might have finally done the one that does the trick. The only reaction she offers as I get up to leave is a single tear that winds over her temple and bleeds into her hair.

"Let's take her in," I say when Lux pokes her head in the room. "I don't know what to do."

We operate on autopilot, gathering Blue and placing her in the car. She neither fights nor helps us, moving under our propulsion. At the emergency room, I give them my credit card, unsure if my sister even has health insurance. We go through the motions, the doctor and nurses asking questions Lux and I answer, some with certainty and others we can't possibly guess. "When was the last time she took any type of medication? Is she on any kind of birth control? Has she eaten anything that could be poisonous in the last forty-eight hours? Has she been out of the country?"

TRACING THE LINE

"You girls have had a lot going on, sounds like," the nurse comforts me. "We'll get her taken care of."

But no one has any more to offer. Hours later, after basic testing and exams have been completed, they say something about taking her to the psychiatric wing.

"What did you think was going to happen?" Lux looks at me, her eyes tired and scared, a reflection of my own.

"I don't know. I guess I just thought...that they might have something...anything for..." I feel stupid because what could they give a broken heart to mend years of pain?

So we leave our little sister, her skin nearly as white as the hospital bedding; the only color in the room is her wild shock of hair splayed across the pillow. When we reach the elevators, a high-pitched wail pierces the air, and Lux and I both run back. Nurses hold her down, her cheeks raw from claw marks, and someone calls for a sedative. I can't look away, barely able to see Blue beyond the two beefy nurses who are battling to keep her from damaging herself further. Blood seeps out of her wounds when I finally get a look at her face, and when her eyes meet mine, she screams even louder.

"Come on, Zi." Lux tugs at my arm. "We're making it worse."

But I can't leave her. Only when Lux forces me into the hallway, her firm grip inexorable, do I manage to tear myself away.

"That could be me." I speak when we're finally on the elevator, thankfully alone.

"No, it couldn't. Blue hurts with something neither you nor I took from our childhood. Whatever it is, she's got to find a way through it. There's nothing we can do."

I know she's right. I've watched Blue's slow destruction with drugs, then her recovery. She always said she'd be fine, that she had weak moments. But she's always gone back to the matriarchs of our family for approval, even though she never received any. I say as much to Lux.

"I know. I saw that too. She was definitely barking up the wrong tree."

We're quiet on the ride home, but when we flop on the couch, she flips on the television. "Buffy or Angel?"

Given how dark the last week has been, there's only one choice. "Angel." Buffy and the gang are way too upbeat with their death and destruction. Only Angel with his brooding misery will fit this chaotic mess.

TRACING THE LINE

CHAPTER TWENTY-FOUR

HARD TRUTHS

"I'm being harsh, aren't I?"

A week later, Lux and I sit over bowls of oatmeal—despite the heat, instant oatmeal is comfort food. Fin left moments before to head out for another seminar, and we're savoring a bit of quiet before we leave to visit Blue. She was admitted into the psych ward for the week, and while she's marginally better—she doesn't scream when she sees us like she did the first day—we've only been able to visit the last two days, at the doctor's insistence. Yesterday, we talked to her, and she looked at us as though trying to figure out why we were there. I'm hopeful today will be better.

"About what?"

"Kai."

We've been careful to avoid any mention of his name all week. Even Fin seemed to know the topic was off-limits, not that he'd have tried to tromp on it anyway. Men seem to have a distinct intuition around not talking about recently ended relationships.

"Do you want my honest opinion, or my sister opinion?"

I chuckle as I stir my cinnamon and apple oats. "Are they different?"

"Vastly."

"Both then." I take a bite, enjoying the tart apple and sugary goo.

"As your sister, I think you are absolutely right, and you should totally stand your ground. He's a wanker, an ass, a pissface, and should be flogged—unwillingly—until he begs for mercy."

I can't help my grin as I stare down at my hands. "I take it that's not what you think honestly."

She sighs and shrugs. "Honestly, I think he's human and didn't want to hurt you. Look, I saw the way he looked at you—the man loves you. Deeply. But loving someone and risking losing that love…" Her gaze falls on Fin's recently vacated seat on the couch. "I don't think what he did was right, but he couldn't have known how it would play out. And porn's a hot-button issue for you. Would you really have been okay if he'd told you he not only made porn films at one point, but he also starred and produced them?"

I admit—I found clips online of the films. I see why they're considered visionary. They were not like the True Lust films—these were obviously actors and some attempt at plot was made. But the sexual aspects were not aggressive or anti-female, and the storylines had thematic elements that revolved around our society's conflicts about sensuality and relationships. Are they porn? Most definitely—having seen Kai's equipment up close in person, I was mildly shocked to see a younger version of *all* of him on film. That was the only shocking element. The rest of the movies were pretty standard, perhaps even a bit staid: the women in both films had full agency in their play.

"I don't know. Now, I'd say yes, I would have been fine because I like the man he is now. But early on…I'm not sure that's the truth."

"You never gave him a chance to at least explain why he didn't tell you. Maybe that's worth listening to?"

I examine my bright green nails. We painted them last night while Fin ran out to pick up Chinese food. I feel almost guilty about enjoying simple pleasures while Blue's practically institutionalized, and she would love this color. "I'll think about it."

"I'm not condoning not telling you, Zi. You are a formidable woman, though, and damned impressive. Nothing ever seems to get in your way. It's possible you intimidated Kai a bit."

"Oh, please."

She nudges me with her foot while taking a final bite of

her oatmeal. After she chews, she continues. "I'm not kidding. You've created your own business, survived a nasty divorce, and managed to stay sane when, let's be honest, it's amazing we're not both in Blue's condition."

I wave her off, but as I dress to see Blue, I realize she might be right. Not about the "formidable, impressive" part. But Kai and I jumped in hard and fast, and there's every possibility that I didn't give off the "tell me anything; I won't judge you harshly" vibe. I can't point to one time that Kai wasn't respectful or open to anything I asked. Hell, even his own emotional issues he shared without prodding. And I've not copped to all of my family issues, even now. He only knows as little as I could share while still making sense of the wreck that is my history.

I stare at myself in the mirror. Dark smudges ring my eyes, and I've lost weight. And not the good kind you lose when you work out and feel positive about your body. My breasts are flat, my stomach saggy, and my face too narrow to be healthy. A couple of weeks of stress will do that to you. I'm not sure what anyone would even find attractive about me right now.

"Stop that," I scold myself. "You are beautiful. Own it." I narrow an eye at my reflection, then smile as big as I can manage.

Ugh.

I'm still debating my own part in the mess with Kai when we get into the hospital elevator.

"You're awfully quiet."

"Just thinking. About our conversation earlier."

"Care to share, or are you still cogitating?" Lux asks as our floor lights up.

"I'm thinking that I may have expected more than I was willing to give." I switch tracks, sort of. "Are you in the camp that we should tell our partners everything, or that it's okay to have secrets?"

Lux makes a face. "You do remember that I used to be a professional Dom, right? Do you think Fin needs to know about all my hanky-panky? Oh, girlfriend, no man—not even Fin—will ever extract those secrets. Some of the things I've done I'll take to my grave."

I raise an eyebrow in surprise. "Really? I didn't think you were embarrassed by any of that."

We get off the elevator, but she pulls me into an empty hallway across from the nurse's station. "Who said anything about being embarrassed? I'm not ashamed of anything I've done to explore my sexuality and discover my interests. But that doesn't mean Fin needs to know about them in their gory details. Just because he has less sexual experience than me—and don't be fooled, as the boy was hardly a monk before we got together—doesn't mean I have to lay down my sordid, sexy past. That's my life before him, and if he needs to know something about it, or if it's going to affect our relationship, I'll tell him. But I'll be damned if I don't get to have some things that are part of who I am that are mine alone. And you know I adore him."

I nod, considering her words and conviction. "You always manage to give me plenty to think about."

We return to the main entrance of the psych ward. "Everyone has to find what works for them, but I don't think that means you have to tell your partner every tiny piece of yourself in order to be trustworthy and lovable. Sometimes, trust means not knowing and being okay with that."

Her statement hits me like a slap, but from her expression, she's just being Lux—straightforward. I don't think she meant it as a whack over the head. So I accept her words and follow behind her. When we're admitted to see Blue, she's upright, which is an improvement over the last two times.

"Hey," she says in a small voice.

"Hey yourself." I try to hide my elation over her progress.

She's in a light blue hospital gown, the identification bracelet nearly falling off her wrist. She's gotten skinnier, if that's possible. She tucks her hair behind her ear, her eyes not knowing where to land as she won't look at either of us directly.

"How ya feeling?" Lux asks, perching on the edge of the bed.

"Better. I think." Her voice sounds strained and impossibly

soft.

I keep my distance, desperately wanting to hug her but not knowing how she'll respond. "I'm glad to see you sitting up."

"And talking." Lux eyes her closely.

Blue wraps her arms around herself, looking self-conscious and unsure. "Yeah, I'm sorry about all that."

Her apology surprises me. She's not one to offer them very often. I open my mouth to speak, but Blue holds up a hand.

"I mean it. I don't remember much of what happened—the shrink I'm seeing said I pulled out or away or something. But I didn't mean to scare you or be such a freak when things were already tough." Her green eyes meet mine, clear and tired.

"It's okay. It's not like you did it on purpose."

She lifts a frail shoulder. "Doesn't really matter. I've always been a loony. More proof that I belong here."

"That's not true. You're just going through a—"

"It's my third time, Zi. Number three." She holds up three fingers to emphasize her point. "You don't end up in a psych ward three times because you have your shit together."

"True." Lux jumps in. "But we've all been through crap and found our own ways to cope. Maybe we didn't take the same path, but that doesn't mean Zi and I haven't been certifiable a time or two. And you have choices, Blue. You have a support system if you choose to use it."

I've never seen Blue this present and serious. It's as though she's matured overnight, and I'm not sure how much to trust it...or if I'm just being suspicious. "I do. They want to commit me for a month—voluntary commitment. I'd like to do it, but I can't afford to. I worked under the table for Gram so she didn't have to pay for insurance. And don't bother making a face; I know how stupid that was."

"That woman..." I shake my head, anger rising.

"I know." Her face, usually so young and full of life, has lines that have deepened around her mouth and forehead, and Blue lifts her shoulders. "It's done. If seeing her at the funeral didn't clue me in, nothing will."

I'm stunned. How is this the same sister?

"I'll pay for the psychiatric treatment, if you promise to go and stay in for the whole month." Lux levels a hard glare at Blue. "If you pull out, I will never offer you money again. Do you understand?"

Blue's eyes widen at the offer. "It's really expensive."

"I have the money. That's not the problem. I have to know that you'll do the whole program—no quitting. I want your promise. You have school starting soon, and if you play this right, you'll only miss the first week."

"I..." Blue looks at me, her shock bleeding into some emotion I can't place. It's not one I've seen on her face before. "Okay. I'll do it."

I'm half-tempted to explore her commitment, to make sure she understands what just happened, how generous Lux is being. But something about Blue, the strange expression that I'd swear is gratefulness, halts my words. Maybe I've enabled her as much as I've helped her?

"I have treatment in a few minutes, I think."

Blue doesn't move from the bed, and I cock my head. "You want us to leave now?"

She finally admits, "I don't want you to see me when I stand up. I look terrible."

"Vanity. It's a Trace trait." Lux stands, heading towards the door. "I can totally relate."

With the first real grin I've seen on her face in probably years, Blue nods at her older sister. "At least I'm not alone."

"Can I hug you?" I ask once Lux has stepped out.

Her eyes well up as she nods quickly. She's terribly thin, and I can understand her embarrassment. Despite her annoyance at her petite size, Blue's always been very pretty and enjoys showing it off. She's a skeleton, probably less than a hundred pounds, and my heart aches for her. As her arms hang tight around my neck, I bury my nose in her hair. She's using the hospital's soap, something mildly scented with flowers. But she's still Blue, the little girl I've always tried to be both mom and sister to, and perhaps I never did either very well.

"I love you, Blue Bear. I'm glad you're doing this."

She looks more scared than proud, but a bit of fire lights her eyes again. "Me too."

TRACING THE LINE

ALLY BISHOP

CHAPTER TWENTY-FIVE

TRUST MEANS NOT KNOWING

Sometimes, trust means not knowing and being okay with that.
   Lux's words haunt me for days. I know she's saying them within the context of her relationship and her own story. But is that my problem? That I can't trust someone unless I feel like they tell me everything? I know Lux doesn't always say everything or give me the whole truth about the years we were apart. I'm not sure I want to know—she is my sister, after all. Her sexual escapades can remain untold. And hell, I've never told her all the details of my divorce. She didn't press, and it's not like I wanted to relive the embarrassing details. But Kai's omission feels like an affront to my trust in him.

But even if it is, is it insurmountable?

I want to wait until I don't miss him so much. When just the thought of his name doesn't make my heart ache with want. So that way, if I contact him, it's out of true desire to hear his side, and not weakness on my part. But let's be honest, shall we? I don't know how long that's going to take. And Kai could move on by then—who could blame him for that?

I take the wimpy way out.

"Zizi Baby! Where ya been?" Russ greets me warmly when I step inside the air-conditioned office. "You left me high and dry." He comes around his desk and hugs me.

"Wow. I didn't realize I meant that much to you." I wink at him. Russ is strangely charismatic with his crazy colored outfits and odd fashion sense. Something about his style works for him, and the unique look fits his personality. I envy him that courage to put himself out there and expect others to accept him.

"Always, baby. Always. Especially after you let me drive your car—the way to a man's heart. Well, to my heart, considering my wheel-less state." He returns to his perch, scrolling with his mouse. "You here to see the man?"

I narrow my gaze at Russ. "Are you putting me on? Or do you really not know?"

"Know what?" His dark eyes widen, guileless.

I can't always spot being fooled, but I'd bet money Russ doesn't know. "We broke up."

His expression immediately droops, crestfallen. "No way. You guys are so perfect." He turns his head, giving me a sideways glare. "Are you putting me on?"

"No, unfortunately. I actually came here to talk to him, but I wanted to make sure he hadn't..." Now that I'm saying it out loud, I feel foolish. Why didn't I just pick up the phone and call him? Oh, right, because I'm being a coward.

"You really think the boss-man would jump at the next good-looking thing that fast?" Russ sounds mildly offended. "He loves you."

I duck my head. Guilt, make yourself at home. You can just stay in that room over there—extra blankets are in the closet. "No, it's just...well, it wasn't a nice breakup. I handled it poorly, and..." I lift my shoulders, helpless. "I didn't want to show up if he was already trying to move on."

"Honey, I wondered why the man was a bit of a lump the past few weeks, but I thought it was because, well...I'm sorry about your mom."

I nod my appreciation.

"Anyway, that's what I thought it was. He hasn't said a word to anyone about you two not being 'you two' anymore." Russ sits back, linking his hands behind his head. A Dead Kennedys t-shirt peeks out behind his bright red puffy vest. "You going to break his heart again, or you going to paste it back together?"

I hear voices down the hallway, and I'd swear one of them's Kai's. Nerves leap to attention, relaxed only due to Russ's distraction. "I don't know. Hopefully we can figure that out."

He hears the commotion as well. "You want him to see

you, or are you going to hide?"

"I'll hide until they're gone? That way, I don't shock him in front of people?"

"A solid plan. Quick." He gestures to his desk, and I slip around and duck under.

Russ plasters a smile on his face as the footsteps near.

"Buddy, can you run out quick and pick up lunch? I'm starving." Kai's voice resonates like he's standing right beside me, and my heart leaps at the richness of his deep timbre. "Here—get yourself something too, right?"

"You da best," Russ answers, then leans down to grab his backpack. He winks at me. "You're up," he mouths before disappearing.

The front door opens and closes, signaling Russ's departure.

"You sure about this?"

I recognize that voice. Carice.

"I am."

"I think things could be different, Kai. I'm not the same person anymore. I've changed."

"Please don't do this." Kai sounds sad, and I wish I could see what was happening.

"You've moved on, then? Someone new?" A bit of regret mixes with resignation in her voice.

"I don't know, to be honest. I thought I had."

A long pause, then Carice speaks again. "I don't think I've ever seen you like this. You're always so confident."

"I might have screwed up pretty badly. I'm not sure she's going to get over that."

"Well, if she's worth it, she will. You're a good man, Kai. I'm glad to still have you as a business partner. And I hope we're friends."

Clothing rustles. A hug?

"We are."

The exit sounds again, and I creep from my hiding place. Kai's already left, either out the door to see Carice to her car, or back to his office. I feel mildly guilty for eavesdropping, but I'm very glad I didn't interrupt whatever that meeting was. Divorce talks?

I find Kai in his office. He stands by one of the two windows that look out on the empty lot behind the building. He's in jeans and a polo, his usual attire. I'm almost scared to let him see me. Despite Blue's seeming recovery and some distance from my mother's death, I don't look or feel myself. I'm hollow inside, and I'm scared it shows. I also purposely dressed low key—jean shorts and a tank top—so that way, this conversation can stand on its own, not on some sexual pressure we both seem to get swept away with too easily.

"Long day?"

He startles, his face surprised when he turns. We both seem a bit shocked to see the other. Sharp lines beside his eyes and mouth point to his recent weariness.

"Hi." He doesn't move from the spot.

I step into his office, shutting the door behind me. "Is this a good time?"

"I'll make it one." His gaze doesn't leave mine as I lean my hip against his desk, leaving plenty of room between us. "I didn't think I'd see you again."

"I wasn't sure you would. And that's a bad call on my part. I...acted poorly, regardless of how valid my reasons were. I'm sorry."

He walks a large circle around me, as though afraid to get too close. "I'm not sure you have anything to apologize for, Zi. You were under a hell of a lot. And I didn't make that any easier on you."

"Can we skip over the part where we go back and forth with who's at fault, at least for the moment? I'd like to hear your side. I didn't give you a chance to explain, and I held your honesty and need to gather your thoughts against you, even when I knew I wasn't being fair. Stressed or not, I hold some of the blame here too. And I'd rather get to the part where you talk and I listen because…that's the one that matters," I finish awkwardly, suddenly wishing I'd gone for slightly less casual wear. His deep blue polo sets off his suntanned skin, and those dark wash jeans fit his ass entirely too well. He looks like a dark prince, and I feel like a bit of a hag in peasant clothes. Damn him. "I mean, if you want to, you know, see if…um…" I trail off, unsure what I want to say.

"'See if' what?"

"I don't know. I made a lot of assumptions a few weeks ago because I was angry and hurt at things that had a lot more to do with my shitty family and not necessarily you. And that brought us to a screeching halt. At the time, it all made sense. But now it doesn't make as much sense. But if I'm alone in feeling that way, then I'll go."

"No. Stay." Panic widens his eyes. "I want you to stay."

"Okay." As a measure of good faith, I sit in one of the visitor chairs, pulling the seat close so I can prop my elbow on his desk.

He sinks into his leather chair, hands clasped before him. Awkward much? Yeah.

"I'm not sure where to start."

"Let's start with why you didn't feel comfortable talking to me about the movies you made before—the porn films." I'm more direct than I intended, but that's why I'm here after all. So I don't apologize.

"Um, sure." He blows out a breath. He thinks for a few moments, then looks me in the eye. "I was scared. I knew you'd been hurt, and while I don't claim to understand what that was like for you, I did see the results of it. And you seemed…free with me. You opened up, shared you desires, explored sexual fantasies that I knew you were afraid of, yet still wanted to try. Watching someone unfurl like a well-tended bloom...that's incredible, Zi. You trusted me with that, and I felt the weight of it." He stares across the room.

It occurs to me that to be with Kai, I'm going to have to be patient. He's not a guy who can phrase his inner thoughts glibly and off the cuff. As he says everything I wanted him to say and more, it breaks my heart that I didn't let him try before.

"You weren't wrong to be angry. I don't blame you at all. I had the opportunity and the openings, but I kept thinking that maybe it didn't matter. That those things were in the past, and that's where they should stay." He splays his fingers in front of him before pressing his palms together. "I'm not going to feel badly about the movies I made, Zi. They were experiments. We tried things. Ger and I were kids, and we wanted to see if we could *not* be every failed film major who ever tries to survive on his craft. Porn was an easy way in, and our movies did well, considering the genre. Not great, in large part because we cared too much about including some sort of agenda. Turns out, people want their porn intelligence-free."

I roll my eyes. "True that."

"I agreed to star in them because, well, that was one less person to pay, and I was in my early twenties. Screwing a girl that wasn't my girlfriend, and Carice was okay with that? It's like every college kid's dream." He gives me a bashful grin. "And trust me, it looks like way more fun than it was. When you have to pretend that everything's planned and perfect while still acting like you're wildly turned on? That's why they have professionals, and it's considered a serious job. In some circles," he concedes.

"When we understood how different our movies were from the rest and how that defined you as a filmmaker, Ger and I tried other things, and we hit pay dirt. We impressed someone with *Inside Her*, some guy with too much money and a strong desire to be an 'executive producer.' He gave us cash and an idea, and we wrote the script and filmed it." He points to the framed movie poster behind his desk. "*Green Beckoning* was

Fade In's first successful movie. We won an award at Cannes that year. Trust me when I say, we got really, really lucky. Very few filmmakers and screenwriters get those kinds of opportunities. It helped that Ger and I can do multiple roles—we both write screenplays, and he can do camera and sound. I'm a decent director, and I moonlighted editing corporate training films for years. Still do, when I get a freelance gig.

"Do you see what I mean when I say, in the grand scheme of our company, those movies meant very little? It's a running gag occasionally at a party—'the guys that made it with devastatingly awful porn.' Few even remember that we started out that way."

I nod slowly, digesting his words. "But you knew the risk, and you knew how much porn bothered me. Why not tell me on the off-chance I'd find out?"

We're interrupted by Russ's arrival with food. He's all business, parsing out subs to Kai and me. "I figured you might be hungry," Russ says to me before making himself scarce.

The sandwiches sit untouched. Kai looks tortured as he tries to find his momentum again. "I understand what you're saying, and I don't disagree with you—I should have told you. But I honestly didn't think it was that big a deal, and with everything else going on, I didn't know when the right time was to say it. That's not even a good excuse. But it's the only reason I have, and it's the truth."

Is that enough? I finger the cellophane wrapper of what appears to be a roast beef and provolone on rye, one of my favorites, though how Russ knew that is a mystery. *Trust means not knowing and being okay with that.* Was I? "When I was six, I burned my hand on the stove trying to make macaroni and cheese for Blue." I turn over my palm, showing him the still puckered patch of skin. It's less than an inch long, a quarter inch wide, on the fleshy ridge below my thumb. "As a result, I knocked the box of noodles and open packet of powder onto the floor. Our mother beat me for getting burned and making a mess, then made Blue eat the pasta and cheese powder raw off the floor. She apologized afterwards, and then took us out and bought us new toys. But she was always like that. The lake you took me to? She used to drop us off there for the day. We'd beg people for food, or sometimes, a family would invite us to play with them. We were always careful—we always said our mom was sick and lying down or she was sunbathing at one of the houses we'd imagined living in. It wasn't that we didn't have the money—our mother could have given us some cash—and sometimes she did. But she'd forget, or she'd be mad at us for doing something stupid that little kids do."

He stares at me, his mouth set in a tight line, but horror darkens his eyes.

"When I was twelve, I caught a man fucking Blue. She was barely eleven. He promised to buy her a game for her Game Boy if she'd give him a blow job." I drop my gaze to my hands, then force myself to look at him. "When Lux was fifteen, she was molested by the brother of our foster father. The asshole held her down and was about rape her when they were caught. They blamed Lux, and she ran away when she was seventeen, leaving me and Blue with Mama C and her asshole husband. I don't blame Lux for leaving, but I was angry at her for a long time."

I bite the inside of my cheek, trying to hold myself as emotionless as possible so I can get through this. "I'm not telling you this to make you feel bad for me. I'm telling you because these are all the things that happened—and there's so much more—that I didn't tell you because I didn't think they were important either. I'm not as strong as everybody thinks I am. Because right now, when I see Blue being institutionalized *again* and I see Lux determined to make us a family *again*, I want to kill the people that hurt us. I want my mother to be alive so I can rail at her and make her face the damage she did. I want our grandmother to pay for being such a cold bitch all of our lives and using Blue to run her diner because she knew she could, but never looking out for her." My voice trembles with rage and hurt. "Never getting her health insurance so she could pay for the goddamn mental damage this horrible fucking family caused."

His jaw grinds, but he says nothing.

I inhale, closing my eyes and fighting to find the right way to say the things I need to. "I haven't told Lux about Blue's rape because I thought she didn't need to know. I didn't want her to feel more guilt and feel less a part of our family because I kept these secrets from her. And I was wrong. I should have told her because that's part of being a family—holding each other's pain. But I do understand your reasons for not telling me." I pause, fighting emotion. "Because I'm guilty of doing the same things to the people I love."

Kai's face twitches, and I don't have to be close to him to know his muscles are clenched tight. He drops his gaze to his desk, then stands. "May I touch you?"

I push to my feet. When I nod, he crosses the distance in two steps and hauls me against him. He holds me so close, my ribs creak. He presses his cheek into my neck, breathing me in. I lay my hands on his back, reveling in the feel of him, how much I've missed the scent of his clothing and the spicy aftershave he prefers. How warm he is when I feel so empty inside and need someone to remind me I'm still alive.

When he pulls away enough to look down at me, I warn him, "Please don't say you're sorry for what happened to us. I didn't tell you to make you feel sorry for me, or my sisters—"

He kisses me, probably to shut me up, but I don't fight him. God, I've longed for this man, and the way his hands linger on my back before seeking purchase lower, as though there's time to do more, so there's no need to rush.

But his mouth pulls away too soon, and he immediately apologizes. "I shouldn't have done that."

"It's okay." I stop him from withdrawing, pressing myself against him. "As long as it's not a pity kiss."

He shakes his head, his hand cupping my cheek. As though looking deeply into my soul, his gaze never falters. After several minutes, he speaks in a hushed, low voice. "I wish none of that had happened to you, and God, I want to kill people for you, for hurting you and your sisters. No child deserves that. Ever. But I told you before—you're one of the strongest people I've ever met. Probably the strongest. And I admire you more than I can say."

"I thought you might hate me, after the way I yelled at you," I say meekly, fingering the collar of his polo.

"Never. I felt terrible. And that you found out in such an awful fashion...I could only hope that I didn't ruin things for you."

I press my forehead to his shoulder, speaking into his chest. "It's more or less blown over. Zachariah Lemke has a trial scheduled next month for vandalism and online threats. I'll have to go and testify. But several people in the community have started posting sex-positive remarks on the online message boards. It's almost as though once they all were made aware of what was happening, they came out in droves. There are still some annoyed residents, but they're much more staid than they were before." I look up, running my finger over his bottom lip. "And no one cared who I was dating, as it turned out. Or if they do, no one's saying anything."

His lips are soft, questioning as they brush over mine. I answer, yielding beneath him as his tongue slips inside. Soon, hands are headed south, and he grabs my wrists. "Wait. First, where are we?"

"Well, we were about to answer that question," I say, giving him a mildly annoyed glare.

Unsure, he gives me a crooked grin. "What's that mean, exactly?"

My inhibitions go up, but I force the words over my lips.

"It means I want to be with you."

"You're sure? Because I think you know all my secrets now, but I never want you to feel that I kept something from you."

I dart forward and peck him on the lips. "I'm sure. I trust you to tell me things if you think they'll matter to us. Maybe it's okay to have things that are private—as long as you feel as though you *could* share them with me, then...I'm okay with that. For both of us."

He loosens his grip on my wrists, but he doesn't let go. "Then we do this right. Not on my desk chair."

"We could use the desk." I lift a brow.

"No. If we're going to be back together, I want to do something for you. For us. And I'd rather not risk Russ walking in on us—my luck, he'd offer to join."

"Well, he is really cute," I tease.

His gaze turns predatory. "I don't share."

"I was kidding. Threesomes are sexy...but not for me."

He drops my hands and covers his heart with his palm. "Thank God. Because there's a lot I'd do for you, even if it wasn't my preference. But that would be testing my limits. I'm not the jealous type, but I don't think I could handle watching you with another man. Or woman, for that matter."

I can't resist snorting in wry amusement. "Oh, really, Isaac? Seeing as which I've watched both of your earlier porn films..."

"Oh God." He closes his eyes. "Okay, I'm not embarrassed about anything I've done, but I wish you hadn't seen those."

"I don't know." I nearly bite my tongue off to keep from dissolving into laughter. "You still make that sexy little grunt when you're getting close to the end. And that hip thing you do when—"

He covers my mouth with his, the kiss sloppy and silly. "Never, ever watch those again. Or mention anything about them. Please? I don't know if my manhood will survive it."

It's impossible to temper my smile, but I manage to at least lower the wattage. "I'll keep those on file, for blackmail purposes." I slip my hands into his hair, kissing him thoroughly. "So how long do I have to wait for whatever it is you want to do so we can have sex?"

He snorts. "I'll call you tonight and tell you, okay?"

"You better."

CHAPTER TWENTY-SIX

BEING OKAY

Lux nearly shrieks when I tell her about my talk with Kai. She topples me over on the couch, hugging me. "I'm so glad. That boy has it bad. And he's a good egg. I asked around."

"Does this mean you had Fiona do a background check on him?"

She settles back into her spot and shoves a spoon of yogurt in her mouth. "Mah...be," she says around the silverware.

"God save me from my overprotective sister."

"Hey, I don't want you getting hurt again."

"Fair enough." I offer a grin, secretly glad to feel so loved.

She gloats for a bit yet, enjoying her rightness about Kai. And I can't fault her. I realized my own "secrets" as the words came out of my mouth earlier with Kai. If I needed a reason to forgive him, it arrived right in time.

"Speaking of being honest with people, I need to tell you some things."

Lux nods, setting her empty snack container on the coffee table. "Shoot."

I tell her all the things that happened to Blue, to my knowledge. The rape, the details around the cutting, her suicide attempt, and all of her hospitalizations. I go over my suspicions that she may have been raped when we were older, still living with Mama C. Blue always hung out with the wrong crowd, but there was one decent guy.

"His name was Donnie. I think he hoped she'd fall for him, but Blue's never looked for commitment from anyone except people she'd never get it from. Anyway, I'm not confident what happened, but one night, Blue didn't come home. When I cornered Donnie to find out where she was, he said she went with a couple of the boys that were threatening him, and he didn't know where they went."

"You think she slept with them to spare Donnie?"

"That's my guess. She'd never tell me where she was that night. And she always seemed a little less...brave after that night. She wasn't hurt physically that I could see, and I guess you could argue that she consented if she went with them willingly, but that's still rape in my mind."

"Fuck yes, it is."

"Again, I don't know what really happened, but I know she's been lost for a long time, and I think, in some ways, I've made it worse. I always try to rescue her, even when she doesn't want me to."

Lux is quiet for a long time. She pokes around on her laptop, and I play a game on my phone.

When she finally decides to speak, she waits for me to look at her. "I understand why you didn't tell me. I wish you had, but some part of me...is kind of glad you waited until now. I'm not sure I could have handled that when I first found you. I'm not sure what kind of person that makes me, but it's the truth." Her gray eyes, usually so laconic and sparkling, have a dull pain, and I hate that I put it there.

"I'm not sure what kind of sister it makes me that I didn't trust you enough to tell you. I do trust you, Lux. But for a long time, it was me and Blue. And really, just me because Blue's broken. She's not someone I can rely on to be there."

"I know. And I wish I had been. But for whatever reason, I had to leave, and I promise not to do that again."

I shake my head and lean forward, covering her knee with my hand. "I know you won't. You don't have to apologize or make promises. We're sisters. We're not always going to agree, but we're in this together. We've both shown our loyalty in the only ways we knew how."

She nods, then covers my hand with hers. "It might take me a while to stop feeling like I need to reassure you. Maybe I do it for myself, anyway."

"That's fine. But I don't doubt you. And thank you—what

you said, about trusting meaning not knowing everything and that being okay...that hit me hard. But I'm glad you said it."

With a sharp nod, she pops off the couch and eyes her yogurt container. "I'm really tired of this healthy shit. You wanna get some ice cream?"

So that's what we do. Because we're sisters. And women. And some days, ice cream fills in the cracks like nothing else can.

Of course, some days, ice cream's a cover for something else.

Lux shoves me in the door of our dark apartment, then bolts in the other direction.

"What are you—"

Hands grab me, pulling me into a scintillating kiss. Of course, I don't have to wonder long whose delicious technique is invading my senses. As my eyes adjust, I can make out his form, as well as faint light coming from the living room. Music, some sort of soft, sexy blend, drifts to my ears, and I don't ask questions. Feeling Kai's taut body is reason enough to get lost in the moment. His very naked, taut body.

"Hi." He rubs his nose against mine.

"Hi."

"May I undress you?"

"You never have to ask." He helps me out of the sweatpant cutoffs and baggy tank I threw on to get ice cream, and then makes quick work of my underwear. His hands caress my shoulders, breasts, stomach, as though he's never touched me before. I do the same, but he knows how to distract me, and I end up sagging against the door as his mouth follows his hands.

"Come here." He guides me to the living room. Candles flicker from every recessed spot, and a thick, soft blanket has been spread across the floor.

I chuckle, appreciating the thoughtfulness. "Why start using a bed now?"

"This is a very thick, very cushioned blanket."

"Getting a bit rough on the knees, eh, Isaac?"

"I was thinking of your knees, my love." He swats my ass playfully. "But if you'd rather kneel on the carpet..."

I run my hand along his shaft, the hard length pulsing under my palm. "I may have to." He groans as I close my fist around him. "I must say, I didn't realize you had a porn-worthy cock."

He laughs, but then his breath catches as I keep up the pressure. "I don't know about that, but you gotta do what you gotta...do."

"Mm-hmm." I bend and take him in my mouth, his smooth head silken against my tongue. I find his favorite spots, unmerciful with my attention.

When he pulls me back, I don't need light to see the desire in his eyes. "Later, you may tie me down if you wish and do whatever you would like." He draws me against him, his mouth skimming my neck and shoulders. "I've missed you so much, and it's more than just sex. I've missed *you*—your intelligence and your humor. But tonight, I want you moaning with my cock inside you."

"I won't argue that." I turn, curving my back to his chest, trapping his erection between my thighs. I'm soaked, and sliding against him feels incredible. "Do you want to fuck me?"

He grabs my face so he can kiss me. Then he presses me to my hands and knees. "You didn't answer me," I say coyly. Of course, I nearly swallow my tongue when he pushes inside, sinking his whole length with one surge.

"Is that answer enough?" He withdraws, then returns, his cock spearing me in two. He slaps my ass with each thrust, until my skin burns and I want to beg him not to stop. He doesn't let up, even when my first orgasm touches off, and I'm gasping to contain it. There's no slack, no rest, and he pushes me even higher, on a seemingly unending climb to the top.

I'm about to hit another crescendo when he pulls out of me

and gently turns me to my back. He gathers my wrists above my head, placing a soft kiss on my mouth. Then he fucks me with such abandon, all I can do is wrap my legs around him and hold on. As I come, he suckles my breasts, making me buck against him even harder. When he finally finds his own release, I'm spent, but his fingers manage to send another shockwave through me.

We're a sweaty, delighted mess when we're finished, and I flop against his chest.

"I'm not sure that will ever get old."

He chuckles and tucks a lock of hair behind my ear. "I hope not. Every time you turn around, all I want is to worship your ass. And the rest of you, of course."

"Thank God someone appreciates it. I'd hate for all that ass to go to waste."

His fingers close over said derrière, squeezing my flesh appreciatively. "That would be sad. Thankfully, I'm here to make sure that doesn't happen. God, you are delicious." He massages my ample curves a bit more, then nudges me onto my side. "I love you."

I turn my cheek into his palm as he caresses my face, pressing my lips to his skin. "I love you too."

"When I thought I lost you, I—"

"You didn't." I lay my finger over his lips. "It just took me a little while to figure things out. And that's over. Let's leave it."

"Deal." He reaches above us, retrieving something from the coffee table. "I have something for you." He holds a small envelope. "This is yours."

I push up onto my elbow to open the package, and a USB drive falls into my hand.

"That is the only copy of the video you and I made. There's a sworn affidavit inside the envelope as well."

"Seriously?"

"Seriously. I know it took a lot for you to trust me enough to do this, and I wanted it done right. I edited it myself, as I promised you I would, and no one's seen it besides me. Well, in its finished form. Ger did the filming, after all."

My cheeks heat, remembering Ger...and Carla, Ben, and Samson. "Yes. Well. Thank you."

"Did you just turn shy on me?"

"Maybe a little."

He grins and brushes his lips over mine. "That's my finest work in your hands."

I lay my hand on his chest, over his heart. "No, this is."

And we spend the rest of the night proving what trust and love really mean.

CHAPTER TWENTY-SEVEN

GOLD-GILDED LININGS

One Month Later

"You haven't talked to her since when, three weeks ago?"

Lux shrugs into a black, off-the-shoulder sweater that barely skims her stomach. "She told me she wanted to finish the rest out on her own. I think she's just embarrassed."

Blue asked us not to visit, period, while she was in treatment, and I complied. Lux, however, said she was paying for it, so she was going to visit at least once. Which, according to her, went pretty well.

I lean against Lux's bedroom doorway, watching her dig through the mountain of clothing for clean pants. "You know, we have a washer and dryer. You could use it."

She ignores me, continuing her search.

"Or you could put your dirty clothes in the hamper, and I'll wash them," I say dryly.

Satisfied with her find, she shimmies into a pair of dark red skinny jeans. "I'll do wash this weekend. Or maybe when I get back since Fin's coming in tonight."

Since the likelihood of her doing laundry is up there with the return of Haley's Comet, I make a mental note to grab a few piles from her room when I gather my own wash. "We're going to be late."

"No, we're not." She makes a pout at the mirror, sliding a bright crimson lip gloss over her plush lips, then blowing me a kiss. "Let's go."

We're not late. But only because we got green lights on the way.

And I'm convinced we walked into the wrong apartment when we get there.

"Come in," Blue shouts when we knock, and when we

comply, we find a picked-up, neatly organized space. Blue's love of brightly colored sashes and scarves has transferred to elegant lamp coverings and wall designs made with strategically placed thumbtacks. Her usual piles are gone, in favor of small knickknacks that were probably hidden under the detritus. Her living room smells like cinnamon and clove, and when we venture into the kitchen, we find her pulling crusty dumplings from the oven.

Lux doesn't need to look at me to convey her shock. I can barely stop staring at Blue.

She's still painfully thin—her hipbones are visible, tiny knobs peeking over the edge of her terry cloth pants. But her hair falls in soft waves over her shoulders, her skin is clear, and she's letting her freckles show. The fact that she's been out in the sun long enough to even *have* significant freckles is telling. She wears a long-sleeve t-shirt that's been cut short—I'm the only sister whose stomach is not on display, I consider as I grumble inwardly about the unfairness of genetics and flat abs—and her face is almost...glowing.

With a quick, mitted hand, she drops the tarts on the small table, each one at a place setting. Then she turns to Lux and me, her manner suddenly shy. "Hi."

Unlike me, who's still trying to figure out if we're at the right place, Lux rushes forward and pulls Blue into a bear hug. Blue's eyes close as she lays her head on Lux's shoulder. Then Lux leans back, holding her little sister's face between her palms. "You look wonderful. And whatever you've made smells amazing. Can we eat?"

Blue chuckles, and she looks surprisingly pleased when Lux hugs her again quickly before taking a seat.

I'm suddenly the one uncomfortable, unsure how to interact with this strange new Blue. She approaches me as I struggle with my emotions. "I missed you." Her tiny arms circle my waist, and I rest my cheek against her hair. She's always felt like a child in my arms, and today is no different. But something in her stature has changed, and when she looks up at me, her eyes have a clarity and maturity I've never seen in her before. "I'm not going to break, Zi."

Her words seem to have a deeper meaning, but I ignore that for now in favor of pulling her tightly to me, emotion staining my cheeks. When she pulls away, she makes a face, and her fingers wipe at my tears. "You never wear the right mascara for shit like this." And her annoyance, the sound of Blue I remember, makes me laugh.

She smiles, then tows me behind her to the table. "Come on—I don't think Lux will wait much longer."

I take a seat between my two sisters, feeling a bit like I'm in some sort of twilight zone. "When did you get home?"

"They released me a day early, so Saturday? Four days ago?"

She'd texted me, asked me to give her a few days to acclimate before getting together. That she even messaged me was a hopeful sign. And this unusual, organized, baking Blue makes me think an alien snatched her body.

"You've been feeling pretty good, then?"

Blue breaks the crust of her dumpling, pieces of apple and gooey goodness seeping out. "Yep. And this is Gram's recipe—one of the few things she does right, I guess."

The woman could bake—that's what made her diner so popular. Gram could always make a mean pie, and her pumpkin roll was—is, I suppose—famous countywide.

"This is heaven. You made the crust yourself?" Lux asks as she pulls off crumbs while we wait for the insides of the pastries to cool.

Blue nods, pleasure written all over her. "And that's my own concoction. Gram uses Crisco, which, seriously, used to be used an engine grease. Ick. So I make it with leaf lard from the butcher down at the farmer's market."

"When did you start being so domestic?" I tease.

She cocks her head, narrowing her gaze with a coy grin. "You don't eat at the diner enough. When Gram's hands started bothering her, she couldn't hold a spatula for long. I've been making her desserts for the last year."

I stare at her in stunned silence.

Pleased with herself, she dips her fork in the steaming center of her dumping, then licks the tines clean. "You'll be happy to know, while I'm still working at Gram's, she's paying me a salary. I told her it was either that, or find a new manager. And the place is a fucking wreck since I've been gone. I also told her that she either shows me her will, leaving the diner to me as she promised, or I'm looking for another job."

Lux whistles. "Oh, to have been a fly on the wall during that conversation."

Blue shrugs, taking another taste of her pastry. "I learned a lot in the past month. I mean, I knew all of this stuff, but it's a whole different animal when you have nothing to do but think and talk about it. Sort of. It's...hard to explain."

"I'd like to hear, if you want to try," I say gently, running my fingernail over the crusted sugar before snapping off a bit of the flaky edge.

She thinks for a few moments. "It's sort of...I mean, I've gone to centers like this before, but not this one. I went to the one over in Lehigh County before, and it wasn't...I don't know. Maybe I just wasn't ready." She struggles with her words, her hands dancing across the air. "This was—I needed this. I know what you say is true, Zi. I'm not ignoring you, but I couldn't take it in before...not emotionally. Logically, I'd hear you, and believe it or not, I'd usually think you're right. But I couldn't embrace it, or put it into practice."

"Can you give us an example?" Lux asks, her expression open. "I'm not sure I understand, but I'd like to."

Blue nods—I've never seen her this willing to talk about herself—and continues. "Like the thing with Gram's diner. I knew she was using me. You were right—even if you didn't say it. I could see it in your face. And deep down, I saw through her. But I couldn't stand on it. I didn't feel like...I had a right to. But when I was with my counselor, we figured out some of why I fell apart the way I did. She thinks I have something called dissociative disorder. When I was younger and bad things happened, I would leave myself, and my mind would go somewhere else. When it was over, I would come back, but

I'd be disoriented. It's some sort of protection thing the brain does." She lifted a shoulder. "It became a habit for me, and it's stopped me from really experiencing emotions and being able to channel them appropriately. Like, when I get upset, I just want to explode. And sometimes I do. Other times, I crawl in a hole, like I did after Mommy—our mother died."

"So you've been this way since we were kids?" I ask.

"I think so. I mean, that's her theory. And she might be right. I can see it now, but I still don't entirely know how to… feel things. Like, I always look at other people, and I try to let their reactions be mine. But when I'm really upset or really excited, that doesn't work. I can't focus on anything but the intensity inside me, so then I react in a way that's out of proportion to the situation. Am I making sense?" She looks at both of us, worried.

"Perfect sense." I touch her arm.

Lux nods, toying with her fork. "How can we help?"

"You can't. I have to do this. And Gram was my first challenge—I talked with her the day after I got home. She actually handled it really well until she realized I was serious—that I wasn't just 'being Blue.' Then she fired me." Blue grins, her dimple deepening. "So I started applying at jobs as soon as we got off the phone. She hung up on me, actually. But the next day, she called back and accepted my offer. No benefits yet, but I'm working on getting them for myself."

"Can you afford them?" Not to point out the obvious, but since I pay for my own health benefits, I know how expensive they are.

She nods with hesitation. "I think so. I mean, my place isn't crazy expensive thankfully, and my car's paid off—at least, for as long as that hunk of junk keeps rolling. We'll see."

"Are you seeing a counselor now that you're out of treatment?" Lux asks, her tone careful.

"I am. I was referred to a therapist who lets you pay according to how much money you make, and I'm on medication right now. One pill for depression, and I have a prescription for anxiety, but I only have to take that when absolutely necessary.

And don't worry, my meds are monitored." She looks pointedly at me, but without malice.

"I wasn't even going to ask."

"You should. Always ask, Zi. I thought about what you said, Lux, while I was in. And you said that I have a support system, if I choose to use it. And I need that." Her eyes well with tears, and she stares down at her plate. "I hate to admit it, but I don't have that inner strength that you guys seem to have in industrial-sized containers. I was a fucking train wreck."

I hope my expression doesn't give away how familiar those words are to me. Didn't I call her that at one point?

Lux shakes her head. "You were hurting, Blue. We've all gone through that. Just because we don't show it doesn't mean it's not there below the surface."

"Well below the surface then," Blue grumbles. "I feel like I'm the only one of us that can't keep her shit together."

I chuckle. "That's because you didn't see me go off on Kai."

Her eyes widen. "What'd you do?"

With as much humor as I can inject into the otherwise painful tale, I bring her up to date on what happened after our mother's death. We giggle when I tell them about watching Kai's earlier films, and Blue reaches for her phone. "I have to see."

"You most certainly do not." I grab her hand, stilling her fingers. "He could be your brother-in-law one day. Do you really want to see his junk?"

"In all its porn-worthy glory? Fuck yeah." She smirks. "Besides, Lux has."

"No, no," Lux holds up a hand. "Once I saw who it was, I quickly turned it off. I'm no prude, and I've seen plenty of 'junk,' but I want to be able to see Kai as my brother-in-law-to-be. Not imagine what he's got going on beneath his jeans. Which, may I just point out, are often very snug when you're around, Zi. What's up with that? Is he really *that* big?"

My cheeks have gone from pink to scarlet, and I grab my napkin and shield my face. "We are not having this conversation."

Blue and Lux cackle. "Oh yes, we are," Blue says between bouts of hysterics. "I can watch the movie instead…"

I glare at her over the edge of the napkin. "Fine. He's… blessed."

Lux and Blue both raise almost identical eyebrows as they barely contain their amusement. Damn them. "Oh, that's not nearly good enough."

"What do you want? A damn diagram drawn with actual measurements?" I snap.

They look at each other, then at me. And nod at the exact same time.

"Too bad, you horny toads. Go get your own men." I point at Lux. "You have no excuses. According to you, Fin's got plenty going on."

"Oh, darling, he does. And I'll happily paint a picture for you any day of the week. That man is delectable." She licks her lips.

Blue is in stitches, nearly falling out of her chair. "Okay, okay. Enough. One of us is single, and probably unlikely to change that status any time soon. No point in discussing what I'm not having." She sighs dramatically.

"One thing at a time, Blue." Lux smiles widely at her. "I'm just glad to see you feeling more like yourself."

"Me too."

Our pastries have cooled enough to indulge, so we do, moaning over how delicious they are. Blue preens, enjoying the flattery.

When we finally leave, hours have passed. We've talked about movies, stupid things we remember from high school, and weird fashions that Lux has seen in New York that don't make much sense, honestly. But it's good. Like the days past when we'd all pile in Lux's bed to fight over a magazine. And Blue is still Blue—a bit irreverent, plenty silly, and occasionally annoyed. But the delicate connections between all three of us are forged anew, and for now, we have to see where they will lead.

Lux looks at me while I'm driving. "You're the cement that holds us all together, Zizi Baby. Without you, I'm not sure Blue and I could have found a way back."

"A way forward." I correct her. "There's no point in going in the other direction. Too much shit to worry with."

"True."

When we get home, Lux packs, and I drop her off at the rental-car lot—she needs to make some stops in New Jersey to meet with the new investors who seem to be working out. She may soon be an online dating mogul. Well, that's what I tease her about, anyway. For now, being successful enough to live the life she wants to and travel back and forth between homes are enough for her.

I, however, have a bit of "truth" that needs telling, something I wanted more than anything to tell my sisters earlier, but I didn't think that would be fair until I tell someone else.

"Hey." Kai looks up when I walk into his office. "I didn't expect to see you until tonight." He rises, automatically pulling me close and kissing me.

"I know. I was going to wait, but..."

"I can send Russ home if you really insist on trying out my desk."

I laugh, but my nerves rush to my head, making me a bit woozy. "No, that's okay. We have other flat surfaces to test out first, like your kitchen table."

"Excellent point." He gazes down at me, his brows furrowed. "What's wrong?"

"I don't know how to tell you this."

He sits on his desk corner, holding my hands. "Just tell me."

I toy with my t-shirt hem, unsure how to get the words out. Then I blurt, "I'm pregnant."

Emotions play over his expression, all tightly reigned in. The only real flaw—if you can call it that—is that I have to wait for Kai to center in on what he's feeling. While a practice I both admire and am jealous of, it does take a bit of patience.

"How do you feel about that?" he asks, his voice noncommittal.

"I don't know. This isn't planned or expected. But I was late last month, and I took a test this morning that showed positive. We have time—I don't think I'm that far along. If you don't want this, I'll—"

He kisses me, his usual method for cutting my rambling short. "Of course I want this. With you. If you're ready."

"You don't think it's a little soon?"

"Sure it is. But we're here now, and we decide what happens. I love you. I want a family with you. If our child is anything like Mia, I want at least ten." My jaw pops open, and he laughs. "Okay, eight."

"How about one? Two?"

He grins. "Good enough. Zi, I'm with you for who you are and who we are as a team. I hadn't anticipated starting a family this soon, but I'm game if you are."

"You really aren't upset? Even a little?" I rub my thumb along his knuckles, a bit surprised by his reaction.

"Not even a little."

"You're that sure about us?"

He nods, then draws me between his spread legs. "Are you not? Do you need more time?"

"No, it's not that. What if I miscarry again? I don't want you to make any grand commitments over this, and then there's nothing—"

"Did you not hear me earlier?" He presses a finger to my lips, his face warring between amusement and probably a desire to shake me. "I'm with you because of you. Not any future children we may have, not even the child this may be right now. My love for you isn't dependent on whether or not you can produce babies. Though I hope you can because I know what that would mean to you. But I'm just as happy if we adopt, make a baby in a lab, whatever."

His directness—and sincerity—goes a long way to soothe my worries. "If you're sure?"

"You know what?" He reaches behind him, closes his laptop, and pockets his keys. "We're going home. Right now." He takes my hand, leading me into the hallway. "And I'm going to show you just how sure I am, for the next," he pulls his phone out of his pocket, checking the screen, "four or five hours, and when you've lost your voice from screaming my name so loudly, I'm going to feed you, then spend the rest of the evening telling you how sure I am." He pauses as we approach Russ's desk. "And I'll spend the rest of my life doing so, if that's what it takes."

"You birds going to make some sweet love tonight? Maybe make a little Zi-Kai perhaps?" Russ calls from his desk. "Oh, wait, little Kai-Zi! Can we name your first kid that? I'm totally using that when the tabloids come calling."

My eyes widen at Russ's entirely too-close-to-home teasing.

"You better not be listening at my door again," Kai reprimands Russ, unable to keep the smile from his voice. Then he snags my car keys and tosses them to Russ. "Take that home tonight, will you?"

Russ looks way too cheerful when he waves us off.

"Does he really eavesdrop?" I ask as Kai leans me back against his car, the sunbaked metal barely noticeable next to his molten heat.

"Any assistant worth his salt does." He kisses me until I forget about Russ, about my "news," about anything other than his mouth, his scent, his skin. With a final brush of his lips, he looks down at me. "Tell me something, right now, without thinking too hard about it: do you want to do this? Do you want to dance with me?"

"I'm not much of a dancer, but this super hot guy showed me a few moves awhile back…"

He laughs and runs his knuckles down my cheek. "Should I take that as a yes?"

I lay my forehead against his. "You should take that as an 'always.'"

THE END

ALLY BISHOP

WANT MORE? HEAD OVER TO HTTP://ALLYBISHOP.COM TO SEE WHAT'S IN STORE NEXT FOR THE TRACE SISTERS!

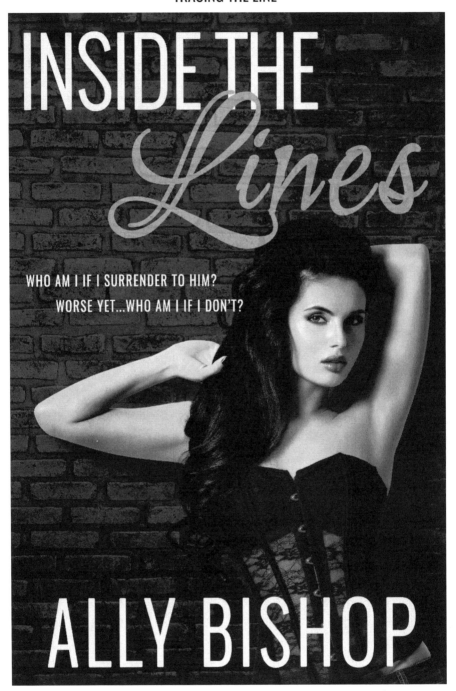

The first book in the Without a Trace series!

ALLY BISHOP

INSIDE THE LINES

Who am I if I surrender to him?
Worse yet, who am I if I don't?

What happens in love might destroy you…
Or remake you altogether.

I make a living offering men and women their ultimate fantasies…as submissives of the mysterious Mistress Hathaway.

I've never surrendered to anyone. That's not the way it works. Or rather, not the way I operate.

But when the gorgeous Fin MacKenzie shows up in my life, he throws everything out of balance.

Now I'm not sure who I am anymore, and I'm questioning everything.

What woman can turn away from a gorgeous Scotsman, especially when he sets her body on fire and her heart ablaze?

I have to stop it…us. I can't keep going like this. It will ruin everything I've worked so hard to build.

Who am I if I surrender to him?
Worse yet, who am I if I don't?

Inside the Lines take place after the prequel Crossing the Lines, so read on for a sneak peek into Lux's sexy adventures with a hot Scot…

TRACING THE LINE

CHAPTER ONE

NO NAUGHTY DEED GOES UNPUNISHED

This isn't my usual client.

Normally, they come to me. It's discreet and makes everyone's life easier. But for certain people, you make exceptions.

In the back of a sleek Lincoln Town Car, I relax into the leather as we enter the tunnel, heading for the famous Ritz Carlton. The car and driver are a courtesy of the client, and while it's not the first time I've had such treatment, I always enjoy it.

Deprived of scenery, I mentally review my gear, ensuring nothing is left to chance. Leather crop, purchased several years ago from a tack shop. Restraints in the form of scarlet cotton rope—silk ties are for movies and books. Entirely too slippery and time consuming. The usual detritus: blindfolds, clamps, rubber whips that range from noisy to pain-inducing. Sultry music, though I also brought a selection of classical entries on my iPad.

A quick check in my compact mirror assures me that the deep red lipstick I've fallen in love with provides the right contrast to my long, jet curls. My suit—pinstripe, skirted—fits my curves like a glove. Beneath, a dark leather and crimson corset meets a matching g-string, finished off with garters and stockings. Red stilettos complete the ensemble. The things I do for clients...

As we surface, I take a calming breath. There's always a bit of nerves right before an introductory scene. This client is new, and while I have a website with a photo gallery and specialties listed, each person's sexual desires are like snowflakes: while similar in appearance to others, each has their own unique intricacies.

Topping—or playing the Dom—requires you to know your bottom, or submissive. You can't push too hard or too far, as you risk injuring not only your client, but also the relationship, that's tenuous at the beginning. At the same time, if you go too light, or God forbid, too slowly, you lose future profits and referrals.

A balancing act. That's the best way to describe it. Sometimes, I wish I could be a submissive. A friend who enjoys playing the slave once told me that she loves turning inward, focusing on her own interests and pleasures, while the Dom does all the work. God, I wish I could let someone else run the show. But that's not the way it works. Or rather, not the way I operate.

Traffic in New York City is always brutal this time of day, but the driver gets a few lucky breaks. As he navigates the crowded streets, I go over my notes, replay my client's application video on my phone, and try to gauge his personality and true desires.

Creating—or recreating—someone's fantasies requires imagination and research, but it also relies on innate skills. For this client, I have a pretty good idea of what he wants.

Who am I kidding? I know exactly what he wants. Because in reality, all of my clients want the same thing.

To let go. To be in the moment. To escape life.

Sounds amazing, doesn't it? I envy them in so many ways.

The driver drops me off at the entrance. The Ritz Carlton isn't your average hotel — I probably don't have to tell you that. The lobby defines elegance, with sleek lighting, antique furniture with a modern flair, and a quiet confidence that bespeaks the well-to-do that venture here.

I visit the concierge on duty and receive an envelope from him. The elevator doors snick shut behind me, and I slip behind the crowd, falling against the back wall and closing my eyes. For once, my outfit doesn't draw hushed comments, as besides the skirt that barely covers my ass, I'm pretty low-key in a city of models and movie stars. Okay, maybe the shoes stick out a bit, too.

The elevator is empty by the time I reach the top public floor. Penthouse access requires a special passkey, and I extract mine from the envelope and slide it into the card reader. Then I wait while the elevator's silken glide ferries me to the penthouse floor.

Stepping onto the lush carpet, I have two doors to choose from. I feel a bit like Alice in Wonderland until I remember the room number the client texted me earlier today. With the Pixies' "Where Is My Mind?" forming an earworm in my brain, I knock.

A delicious man opens the door. Thick, dark hair, lightly threaded with silver, strong jaw with an aquiline nose, sultry eyes that take in the length of me. He wears an exquisitely tailored suit that cuts across his impossibly broad shoulders in a mix of elegance and power. When he smiles, even my jaded heart quivers a bit.

"Mistress Hathaway. A pleasure."

I level a gaze at him, knowing that my raven curls and gray eyes captivate my clients. "The pleasure will be mine, Charles. Naughty boys have to be punished."

As a professional Dominatrix, I follow three rules:
1. Never let them disobey you.
2. Never let them touch you.
3. Never have sex with them.

TRACING THE LINE
At least, I used to follow them...

HOW ABOUT CHAPTER 3 TOO?

**Technically, that's the end of the sneak peek, but I can't leave you hanging without letting you get a glimpse of the sexy Fin MacKenzie.
So here's Chapter 3, too, so you can meet the red-haired Scot who just might be able to handle Lux's heat...**

You are never going to believe me when I say that I work out of a dungeon space I keep on reserve, but I swear that's usually the case. But in this specific situation, I am, once again, going to the client. Tonight is a very special evening.

I arrive at the Parisienne Hotel, one of the newest hotels in Soho. This evening's client wanted something romantic and chic, and the Parisienne Hotel fits the bill, while not breaking the bank.

Everything about the hotel is European, from the creamy decor to the extravagant chandeliers that line the ceiling. I'm early, as intended, so I check-in and head for the far alcove. My stomach drops in time to the quick lift of the elevator, and I swallow hard. While I usually have a bit of nerves before a scene, this one comes with complications.

I wasn't kidding about my three rules. They've served me well. Somewhere along the way, though, I started breaking the last one. Fuck it; I'll be honest. It happened after my relationship with Evan ended. He was—and is—a sweetheart. Good looking, submissive, kind, loving, talented...the list goes on. He's what every healthy, normal woman wants in a really nice guy. It wasn't enough for me. I wanted it to be—so badly, I wanted it to be enough. But I couldn't do it. He deserved someone who loved all of him, completely. And I couldn't do that. So I let go of him. Pushed him away, really, because he'd wanted to continue dating.

Something about that experience angered me. It created a resentment that's hard to describe. So when a long-time client of mine booked me to join him in a scene with another couple, I did something I never do: I got involved sexually. It was delicious, and I had an amazing time. Limiting your sex life to only what you can create with one lover when you consistently create sexual energy for others is draining. And that experience reminded me that I had this raw need inside, and that it could be sated.

The downside: I had sex with several people. And got paid for it. I didn't like the way that part made me feel. That hasn't stopped me from doing it again and again. With only a select few clients, of course. I'm not a prostitute, for fuck's sake.

But then…what am I?

The candescence of pink light softens the room. The hazy glow turns the blood red decor into a deep maroon. This hotel made a splash because of its "red suites;" they're swanky and beautifully styled. And for this evening's pleasure, they seemed like the perfect fit. I've remade the suite's bedroom with the softer bulbs, draping scarves, red boas, and a few well-placed, cotton restraints.

Someone knocks, and I hope it's Stephen. But when I open the door, it's Ari.

"Oh, God, am I too early?" Her blue eyes go round as she takes in my cut up t-shirt that falls artfully, exposing my shoulder, and stops just shy of my wine-colored skinny jeans.

"Well, it's not quite—" I check my phone for the time but also see a missed text, which makes me frown. "What the…" Apparently, I nudged the ringer off, and with setting up and moving around, I missed the vibration of a new text. One that says Stephen can't make it. "Un-fucking-believable. You asshole."

Ari stares at me, wide-eyed. Her white-blond hair shimmers in a short, wispy cut that frames her heart-shaped face. A professional dancer, Ari has the slight build of a ballerina, but with more softness and curve.

I shake my head. "Not you, love. Come in. You're about a half hour early, so I haven't changed yet. Come in," I say again when she pauses at the door. One of the ongoing problems with Ari is her hesitance. It's taken me nearly six months to get her to this point. I'm going to kill Stephen for ruining it.

I check the text so I can read the whole thing.

Sry, dove, I'm sick. And u don't want my snot ruining a sexy scene. Found a replacement, tho. Fin. Trust me, u will luv him. xoxo.

I receive a second text as I'm standing there.

Hi. It's Fin. Stephen sent me. I'm here at the hotel. What room?

Un-fucking-believable. I text him the floor and say I'll meet him. Then I return Stephen's message: *you better die of this illness. Or I promise, you'll wish you did.*

"Ari, I'll be right back. Make yourself comfortable. Remember what we talked about. Deep breaths, center yourself—"

"Envision, and repeat mantra." Ari's light voice finishes for me. "I know." She smiles, but the corners of her mouth flicker with nerves.

Inwardly, I sigh. Then I shower her with smiling confidence and step into the hallway, closing the door snugly.

When the elevator opens, another couple gets off, wheeling luggage behind them. The doors start to shut, but then a strong hand holds them open. The man that steps off is very tall, well over six feet, and when his aquamarine eyes meet mine, he grins.

"Lux, I take it?" His deep voice holds a heavy Scottish burr. He wears jeans and a nondescript black t-shirt under a black leather jacket, and if I weren't so mad, I'd be swooning. Dear God. His shoulders and chest are broad, but not thick. He's built more like a soccer player, with wavy auburn hair with hints of chestnut. He has a crooked smile, and when I stand there staring for a moment, I get a glimpse of perfectly straight teeth and a dimple.

Holy Christ. Stephen sent me an underwear model.

"I know you. You're the guy from that ad. Th-the new Monsieur line. You're on the goddamn billboard in Times Square in bikini briefs." Monsieur is a male clothing boutique on Fashion Avenue; they've been making quite a stir with their advertising of everyday men—e.g. not celebrities or models, though you'd be hard-pressed to find one that isn't ripped—wearing their new underwear line.

His cheeks blush, which on him, is highly attractive, and I get more of that uneven grin. "Aye, well, that might've been me." He scratches the back of his neck. "Stephen said ye needed a bit of help tonight."

And with that, I remember how pissed I am. "Stephen is a goddamn asshole. Do you even know what you're doing here tonight? Did he give you the details?" If there is one thing I'm sensing, it's a distinct lack of kink. Fin looks like he should have a blonde wife, 2.5 kids, and a house with a white picket fence.

"Well, he wasna very specific with details, but he did mention that ye needed a cock." His eyes crinkle even more at his bald language, his face turning brighter pink. "Seein' as which I have one of those, I should be able to help ye." His brogue thickens with his embarrassment.

"Christ. I'm glad Stephen narrowed the whole evening down to a male organ." I glare at Fin. "Men." I turn and storm away, leaving Fin to follow. I feel like I have an enormous shadow behind me, and I realize I have to have this conversation away from the room's door, or Ari will hear it. So I turn on my heel and confront him mid-hallway.

I crane my neck to make eye contact. "Never mind. Just go home. I'm canceling this nightmare before it gets out of hand."

He lays a hand on my shoulder as I turn away, his heat searing my bare skin. "Wait, now. Look." He drops his hand and stops a beat until I meet his gaze. "I ken I'm not the charmer Stephen is, but I ken a fair bit about what he does. I think I can handle it. And he mentioned that ye were a Dominatrix, and that ye'd be runnin' things, so ye can just tell me what to do." He bites the inside of his lip. "I'll do it."

The cheer in his eyes pisses me off. "This is a joke to you. You can barely keep from laughing." I shake my head at him, my temper undoubtedly turning my own skin pink. "This is not funny. The woman on the other side of that door," I point down the hallway, "is terrified of letting herself go. She has a hard time enjoying sex because of assholes who ridiculed and abused her rather than making her feel beautiful and aroused. I will be damned if I will let you anywhere near her. Not when you think this is some kind of goddamn joke. You are—"

"Lux, I'm sorry. I wasna laughing at ye or anything about this." He steps closer, and I get a whiff of some kind of creamy, spicy cologne mixed with...him, probably. And it's delicious. "But ye have a feather here," his hand reaches towards my hair and plucks something from it. "And it wiggles, the angrier ye get."

I glare at the offending feather and snatch it from him. It's from one of the props I brought with me, and the delicate fringe crushes easily in my palm. I close my eyes and take a deep breath. If I cancel this, Ari will be heartbroken. I've fielded half a dozen texts from her already this week, thanking me for doing this and asking nervous questions. After six months of meeting with her, we're finally at the point of fulfilling her deepest fantasy. And there are worse-looking men to have in your fantasy than this one.

"You cannot, I repeat, *cannot* fuck this up. You listen to me, you do exactly what I say, and you never step a toe out of line. Am I clear?" Even to my ears, I sound like a total ass, but surprisingly, Fin only nods.

"Aye."

"You will call me Mistress Hathaway, as none of my clients know my real name."

"Of course."

"You'll strip down to your underwear when we get inside, and you will not approach the bedroom or Ari until I say so.

Got it?"

He nods, his face solemn, though I can still see the laughter in his eyes. "After ye, Mistress," he says with a small bow.

WANT MORE INSIDE THE LINES?
CLICK HERE TO GET STARTED:
HTTP://ALLYBISHOP.COM!

TRACING THE LINE

I DON'T KNOW WHAT LOVE'S SUPPOSED TO FEEL LIKE BUT ONE TASTE OF HIM, AND I HAVE TO FIND OUT

WITHOUT A TRACE SERIES

OUTSIDE THE *Lines*

ALLY BISHOP

The third book in the Without a Trace series, available at book retailers in October 2015!

ALLY BISHOP

OUTSIDE THE LINES

I don't know what love's supposed to feel like, but one taste of him, and I've got to find out.

Don't take up space.
Don't talk too loud.
Don't tell anyone.

Blue. I've always been the problem child. My name alone should have warned anyone with a half a mind that I'd be trouble. Who's named for the broken crayon nobody wants?

Professor Rhys Kennison should have seen me coming a mile away, and I should have known better than to fall for someone so far out of my league. But his touch is like fire and his taste…like the finest chocolate. What woman could resist that combination?

We're headed for disaster—after all, it's what I know best. No matter how hard I try, I can't stop destroying anyone who gets too close. And Rhys doesn't understand. How could he? When I don't even understand myself?

Outside the Lines is Book Three in the Without a Trace series and takes place after *Tracing the Line*.
Lux and Zi's little sister Blue has always been the "emotional" one, but she's trying to get it right this time. Until she meets Professor Rhys Kennison.

TRACING THE LINE

CHAPTER ONE

TAKING UP SPACE (SNEAK PEEK)

Don't take up space.

That's what I've always told myself. Not too much—a little girl like you shouldn't cry too loud, make a sound, speak your truth. Look how pretty you are—delicate as a robin's egg.

Blue.

Like the last crayon in the box. Broken in two.

I'm nothing like my sisters—Zi, big-boned, curvy, beautiful in the way her eyes see right into you and understand. Lux with her aloof perfection, always bigger boobs, better hips, prettier lips. They were all I had growing up, all I looked up to. I wanted to be Lux, with Zi's soul. Other times, when things turned shiny with pain, I wanted to be Zi—too big for someone to hold down, with Lux's street smarts and harsh logic.

Anything to be like my sisters.

Anything to be nothing like me.

My therapist says that's the wrong way to think about it. I'm me. Different from them.

But who am I if I'm not my sisters? Straggly red hair and muddy green eyes…not enough to be noticed. Never enough to be worth it.

TRACING THE LINE

Hell, blue may not have even been recognized in art for millennia, until someone noticed the sky has a shade. Look it up—I'm serious. As though the color itself couldn't be seen, so they had no word for an azure sea.

No word for me.

I'm nobody.

The girl too small to be a woman, too stupid to know any better.

Too crazy to be normal.

Blue.

And the really scary part: What if they're right?

Your mid-term grade has fallen below 60%. Please see your instructor immediately.

Your mid-term grade has fallen below 60%. Please see your instructor immediately.

Your mid-term grade has fallen below 60%. Please see your instructor immediately.

Five classes. I'm failing three of them. Introduction to Writing, Pre-Algebra, and History of Western Civilizations. The emails alerting me to my inability to pass even the most basic of classes sit in my inbox, mocking. Why not send one message? Why three? Why keep pounding home the point?

My eyes burn, emotion pushing past the dam, but I sink my teeth into my lip, tasting blood.

"What's up, Blue Bear?" My sister Lux sinks down behind me on the couch, her shoulder leaning into my back. "You look kerfuzzled."

I don't think Lux does that with anyone but me: makes up words. When I was little, she'd read me stories, and when I'd point at the pictures instead of the words, she'd run my fingers after the dark letters, pronouncing each sound so I could hear them. We'd make a game out of using those sounds in nonsense phrases. She would always laugh, a deep, raspy sound, even though she's only two years older than me. Lux always knew exactly who she was.

I shut my laptop, but when her arm circles my shoulders, I know she spotted the warnings.

"Trouble in academic paradise, Blue Bear? What's up?"

I shrug her off, standing up as though I'm going to the kitchen. "You want anything?" We're in her apartment. Well, technically, it's her and Zi's apartment, but since Zi's moved in with her new boyfriend, the place only gets used the days Lux is here. My oldest sister splits her time between here in Bakertown, a little suburb about an hour from Philly, and New York City, both for business reasons—she owns the online dating service Kinked—as well as personal—her partner Fin joins her in the city on weekends. He's at veterinary school upstate.

Zi's been pushing me to move in, largely so Lux doesn't have to maintain the rent herself. She could easily stay with Zi at her new place—or hell, she could even stay with me. Not that she would.

Don't get me wrong—the apartment offers plenty of space. Two bedrooms, lots of closets. Nice, safe neighborhood, close to everything. Unlike my little shithole.

But I don't belong. I don't feel like anything here—the walls blare too white, the carpet treads too soft, and I'm drowning in beige, tasting vanilla when only cake batter with marshmallows and sprinkles will do. I agreed, however, to try out living here for a week—five days left. And having Lux around is a plus—there's something to be said for not coming home to an empty space.

Lux being Lux, she follows me into the kitchen. I ignore her while I pour some orange juice, then change my mind and dig out some dates. Medjool are my favorite, and I'm pretty sure Zi drops some in the cupboard every few weeks.

"You want to talk about the problem? Or are you going to keep ignoring reality in hopes it goes away?" She hoists a generous hip over one of the kitchen barstools.

I should talk about this. I can practically hear my therapist whispering in my ear: she's your sister. She cares. She won't judge you.

"I'm stupid. We could talk about that."

My sister doesn't blink. "Of course. And the part where you're brilliant. Next?"

I squish the sugary fruit between my teeth, the thin, crispy skin breaking, collapsing, coating my tongue in a rubbery sweetness. The pit interrupts my mindless chewing, and I ease my tongue around the gritty cylinder, cleaning off every tiny piece. I don't know why I love dates—probably because when we were kids and people bought those dried fruit trays, no one wanted the dates. My friends said they looked like poop, and my sisters always went for the pineapples and the apple rings. I decided to like the dates, I guess. Probably so I could have something all my own that no one would ever take.

God, I'm depressing.

"I'm failing out of college, Lulu," I say lightly, using her best friend Noah's nickname for her. It doesn't fit her—she's a sexy, hard, yet wonderful, woman, ex-Dominatrix with a mouth that at times, doesn't know when to shut it. But maybe that's why the nickname works—reminds us that Lux has this beautiful spirit beneath her tough shell. "Not much else to say."

"What are your choices?"

"Jesus, you sound like my shrink."

She grins. "Maybe we're in cahoots."

I make a face, then snort. "Fin would have competition, then. Willow's gorgeous." I don't think Lux has a defined sexual status. Neither bi nor straight, I guess bisexual is as close as you'll get. She's into sexy people, regardless of body parts.

Lux twists the stunning diamond on her finger, the emerald-cut stone encased in platinum. "No, that red-haired demon has me hoodwinked, fair and permanent." Her ring should have been an engagement gift, but Fin knows better. He's buttering my marriage-resistant sister up, probably for a proposal in like, ten years or so. "Come on. Out with it. What's going on? Classes too hard? Professors who suck on ice? What?"

I pick at another date, using a fingernail to slice its soft belly, dig out the oblong nut inside. I twist the strange little stick in my fingers, the gummy remnants slowing the rotation. "They're basic classes, Lux. I'm not smart."

She doesn't say anything. What's there to discuss? You can't teach morons. She disappears to her room, then returns a few minutes later. She holds her iPad, and she taps through its contents, looking for something. When she finds the elusive file, her lips twitch with amusement, then soften. She turns the large screen towards me, spreading her fingers over the surface to enlarge the image.

"I barely finished college. I spent so much time partying, when I got to class, I couldn't make heads or tails of the lectures. Noah's final grades don't look much better than mine. When people ask about my GPA—and they rarely do—I make a joke to avoid quoting the number. One advantage to being self-employed: no one cares."

I stare at her final transcript from NYU, her business degree something I've always craved. "You almost failed."

"Yep. And if I hadn't gotten some help from teachers, signed up for tutoring, I would have spent another semester in school. Or dropped out. I'm pretty sure my professors had volunteers on standby to help me pack." Her gray eyes, clear and determined, meet mine. "Go get some help. There are all sorts of programs available to help students who are struggling. I'll go with you, if you want."

Another date finds a way into my mouth, ensuring I'm too busy chewing to answer right away. Lux is probably the smartest person I know, next to Zi. Well, secretly, I think Lux is even smarter. She's the one who got out of our shitty foster home as soon as she saw the opportunity. Unlike Zi, who stayed until I could leave. Sweet? Yes. Wise? Not when you look at what I put her through.

"I'll drive over and see what they've got." When she opens her mouth, I add, "Alone. If I have to embarrass myself, I'd rather do so in private."

"There's nothing to be embarrassed about, baby girl. We all need a little help sometimes." Her crazy-full lips quirk. "Even me. But don't tell Fin I said that."

TRACING THE LINE

Adner County Community College, also referred to "ACCC" (or "ACK!" by students), sits on the township line of Bakertown. Set in a vale at the base of mountains—no clue the names of the damn things—Bakertown remains quaint and charming in the center. Then radiates slums and rotten tomatoes as you drive towards the outskirts.

Even our slums look sort of quaint, though, if I'm honest. Hell, I live in them. Unlike other neighborhoods with homes falling apart, no heat, regular murders, my little street equals Beverly Hills. We tend towards comfy crimes like casual drug dealing and endemic domestic violence. People wonder why relationships don't interest me—gee, with influences like that, I'll skip most of the guys in a fifty mile radius, thanks.

I park, then follow the winding pathway to the math building. Since Pre-Algebra is my easiest class, technically, and my hardest class in reality, I figure I'll start there.

See, I barely passed high school, largely because I ended up on drugs when I was in my late teens. Well, mid-teens. I went to treatment (twice), tried to commit suicide, then finally got my shit together and quit hanging out with people who made access to pills easy. I've no problem staying off drugs—I've been sober for eight years or so. The spending time in my head part I find difficult to do. Energy outlets help—working a lot, touring thrift shops for things that strike my fancy, fucking strange men.

Yeah, the last part is a problem. There's no shame involved—at least, that's what I tell myself. Willow insists I need to stop attaching morality to everything. And really—I use protection, I try not to lead people on, and I avoid messy emotions. Still, watching Lux and Zi find happiness with another person makes me wonder if I need to rethink my moral standings.

Or not.

These aren't moral choices, Blue. They're choices. Actions have reactions. Consequences. I really wish Willow would get out of my head.

ALLY BISHOP

The math building must have been built by people offended by pleasant aesthetics. Squat, dark brick, and square, even the inside lacks personality. Yellowed walls, aged flooring—the kind with gold strip dividers and cracked corners—paired with pressed-wood doors and cheap finishings. God. Try a little, would ya?

I wander the hallways, looking for my professor's office. I clutch the syllabus, where his office hours declare him available to talk. But when I arrive in the vestibule of his office cluster, a single woman stands at her desk, slipping into a coat.

"May I help you?"

Her nameplate reads "Rose Fifter." "I'm looking for Dr. Meehan."

"Oh, he left for the night already. He changed his office hours last week—he should have told you in class."

I'm already small—five feet and a hundred pounds soaking wet—so feeling even smaller does nothing for my confidence. "I-I don't remember." Crap. Feel stupid much? Why yes, yes I do.

"Well, let's make an appointment," Rose says with chipper efficiency. She drops into her chair, taps her computer, then looks at me. "What do you need to see him about?"

"Tutoring. Pre-Algebra. I wanted to g-get some help." I snap my jaw closed, scared I'll stumble over another word.

"Oh, well, hang on. You don't need Dr. Meehan specifically for help." She looks over her shoulder. "Rhys, you available to take a student? I have someone here who needs help with Pre-Alg." She abbreviates the class, as though the full name isn't worthy.

In the far back corner, a single door remains open—the rest are shut tight. "Ah, yeah. Sure." The voice sounds deep, with a broad accent—British, maybe? So slight, I can't tell.

He comes to the door, tall and lanky. Not much to him, really, and he's super bookish—though his glasses follow the current trend of "frameless."

"Dr. Meehan's class or Ms. Tergan's?"

"Dr. Meehan's."

"Ah." He hesitates, as though he dreads one more appointment.

I look from Rose to this stranger with glasses and a stuck-up appearance. "I can come back another time." I start to back away.

Rose seems confused. "No, no, it's fine. Dr. Kennison has late hours tonight, and he's a sharp cookie. He's not going to do anything else besides grade papers, and I promise, he'd rather help you."

A small smile curves his lips. "True. Come on back. I don't bite."

When I reach his door, he's already crossing to his desk, gesturing to the chairs across from him. "I'm Rhys."

I take a seat, unsure how this whole thing works. "Don't I call you Professor Kennison? Dr. Kennison?"

"Only if you're in my class." He grins, but his eyes flit over my face. "Everyone else calls me Rhys."

One of my issues—the reason I ended up in in-patient treatment for the third time—is dissociative disorder. What everyone blamed on my drug use actually has more to do with my childhood. I'm told I probably pulled myself out—mentally—when bad things happened, and then returned after the ordeal was over. Because that became a coping skill for my fear, I didn't access emotions like everyone else. Which means, in addition to not handling my own emotions well, like, say, having a psychotic break when my mother died, I also don't process other people's emotions accurately all the time. Of course, that probably has something to do with being constantly worried someone's disapproving of me.

My point—I do have one: what I thought was his annoyance or ennui about my arrival, is actually shyness. At least, that's my impression. He smiles to hide it, I think. Like now, he's smiling as he digs through textbooks, but occasionally, he glances at me, then right back down.

He's sort of good-looking, but not in a traditional sense. He's half-Asian, I think, with almond-shaped eyes and black, straight hair that falls into semi-organized disarray. His cheekbones are sharp, slanted, and he has a very square jaw. Yet, he's a bit intriguing. Take off the glasses and put some trendy clothes on the guy, and he might be a looker.

Maybe.

I should probably tell him my name. "I'm Blue."

He pauses in his search. "Is that a nickname?"

If I could count the times I've been asked that... "Nope. That's my real name."

"Really? I've never known anyone named 'Blue' before."

"Congratulations."

His smile turns self-conscious. "Sorry. That's probably not the most flattering thing I could have said."

Flattering? "It's fine. I get asked a lot. Sometimes I act like a shit as a result." I offer a conciliatory smile.

If the man wasn't half-Asian, he'd be bright red, I think.

Holy shit, he likes me. Well, he likes to look at me, at least. Why, I've no clue. My face isn't half-bad, but I've been trying to avoid wearing overtly sexual clothing—part of my turning over a new leaf, I guess—so I'm in yoga pants and a thin sweater. I look like I'm twelve, seeing as which I have no ass, no hips, and barely any breasts. My hair's a ratty mess, and my pale green eyes end up washed out when I don't wear make-up, like today. But since getting checked out may be the only win I get for awhile, I won't complain.

"Let me run over to Meehan's office and grab your book. I thought I had a copy, but..." He turns in his chair, evaluating the massive bookshelf behind him. He's indexed the books by color—that's the first thing I notice. Each volume aligned beside the next, covers of multiple colors tucked in strategically. A mosaic of book spines—it's stunning.

When he leaves, I dart over, nosy at how anyone can be that anal. Don't get me wrong—since I've been working on my issues, I've gotten tired of my chaotic, messy ways. My apartment is, mostly, straightened up, and I've always kept my space clean. Mostly.

Usually.

This is impressive, though. Framed photos tuck into corners—an older man holding hands with an Asian woman, but they don't look very loving. Another offers a much younger Kennison, laughing, beers on a table before him, friends on either side, making faces. In the center of the display, he's crossing a finish line, his jersey and race badge declaring his location as the Boston Marathon. Turns out, Mr. Book-Lover doesn't have a bad body underneath the stuffy suit pants and white Oxford. On the bottom shelf, several certificates mark his education. I squint at the one, the fancy script making the letters hard to read. Does it say Deford? Wait, no, Oxford University. Damn. No slouch, this Rhys Kennison.

"Are you marveling at my OCD or my inability to get rid of a single book?"

I startle, unaware he's standing right behind me. The scent of fresh laundry, a hint of citrus cologne, and something warm envelop me for a moment. His dark gaze locks onto mine. Something burns in the depths, a heat that's almost tangible. Then he looks away, and I'm left cold inside.

"I think you're using this one, right?" He holds up a blue book, barely thick enough to be worth the $110 price tag.

"Yep." I return to my seat, unnerved by whatever transpired. Did I imagine his interest? Those emails about my grades upset me—am I displacing my needs onto someone else? Fuck. Life was so much easier when I flew off at people rather than trying to sit in my weird emotional patterns, questioning if this is what embarrassment feels like, or pride...or lust.

Forcing my mind to the task, I pull out my homework assignments, the ones I've been unable to understand no matter how hard I try. The reality: they're probably not very hard. I can't seem to figure out how the letters and numbers work together. I listen, I take notes, but everything falls into a jumble when I try to sort the concepts in my head...or on the page.

His fingers, long and precise, move with surprising grace. Tiny scars line the edges of his hands, and when he turns the pages, his palm facing up as he holds the book, more of the thin white lines, as well as thick callouses, show against his smooth skin. What's a math guy do to earn those kinds of marks?

For the next half hour, he goes over the basics we've covered in class. I finally give up sitting on the other side of the desk. Standing beside him instead, I watch, baffled as his fingers fly across the page, dropping numbers, carrying sums, and doing something to the letters to make them equal a digit. His handwriting creates perfect angles—like an architectural creation, each line exact and purposed. The problem remains that I can't understand the digits, and my frustration rises. What is wrong with me?

"Blue, is any of this making sense?" He sits back in his chair. "I feel like I'm not helping you. Tell me what stops you when you look at the equation—that second one. Where do you get stuck?"

I glare at the page, forcing my eyes to follow the hard corners and crossed sticks of language, anything to find something coherent to say. But there's nothing. I can't understand how the whole thing works, much less the pieces.

"I just..." Emotion builds, and heaviness traps my dignity as I shrivel deeper inside myself.

"Hey, it's okay. I'm not trying to frustrate you." He reaches for my arm, then catches himself. His dark eyes, gazing at me from behind rimless lenses, offer only kindness, which makes my humiliation worse. I could deal with his annoyance.

I shake my head, snagging my lip with my teeth. How do you explain when you can't even figure out what's wrong?

"It's...look, we'll go over the problems again. I don't have to be anywhere for another hour. Why don't you pull your chair over here and we'll give the first two another go?"

My breathing threatens to give me away, panic crawling up the back of my throat. I'm so tired of not comprehending, not feeling, not being enough. When I look down at him, I'd swear molten desire peeks out from behind his professional facade.

I don't think, don't consider the consequence. I silence him with my mouth. Anything to stop this growing desperation in my chest and find out what's behind that very proper exterior. He jerks back, but I follow him, my hand landing on his chest.

"What are you—"

I try again, using my tongue along his bottom lip. I don't know if he means to, or if he's stunned, but he opens his mouth beneath mine. And then we're kissing, his hands reaching for me. His chair conveniently doesn't have arms, so I straddle him easily. Warm and surprisingly appealing, he snakes an arm around my waist. I mold my body to him, enjoying the slight taste of coffee and mint. My hands sculpt his shoulders, find the hard, well-built chest from the photograph. After a few minutes, we're both breathless.

"This isn't—I mean, we shouldn't—"

I dig my hands into his silky hair. "Are you complaining?" I nudge my hips against him, discovering what I hoped to—Rhys is definitely into this. I slide my hand between us, admiring his impressive length.

His hands grasp my arms, but his eyes bear conflict. That's all I need. Drawing him into another kiss, I press harder against his arousal, my own desire spiraling. Soon his hands find my ass, guiding me into a hard friction. We pant into each other, lips almost touching as sensation takes over. He drops his mouth to my neck, and I fight the moan that bubbles up as I begin to implode.

"Fuck," I whisper as the waves buffet me into submission, and soon I'm knocked down into pure pleasure.

His hands curl over my shoulders, trapping me as he rocks his erection against my pliant cleft. The fabric between us enhances the sensation, and I grind against him. Then he groans into my neck as he comes, shaking beneath me.

Relaxation spreads over my body, and I slouch against him. His arms wrap around me, his face against my hair. He inhales deeply, as though breathing me in. I never thought of myself as sniffable. For some reason, that makes me giggle.

"I'm so sorry. I shouldn't have..." He gently moves me off him, embarrassment flooding his expression. "I, ah..." He rubs his forehead, lips pressed tight.

My (slightly) hysterical amusement makes everything funny, and I bite my lip to avoid laughing out loud. Poor guy—

getting his sexy on with a student probably equals a big no-no. He's clearly rattled, but relief saturates my nerves after the building frustrations of today. "I'll work on what you showed me," I lie. "See if I can make some sense out of the homework."

His hands rip through his hair, then clench the back of his neck. Whatever his usual behavior is, I'm guessing this situation doesn't have much protocol. "Blue, I should apologize—"

I hold up a hand. "I'm not sorry. And I won't tell anyone if you don't." I give him a grin, and the guilt in his expression darkens. Shit. I suck at this part. "Don't stress it, Professor Kennison."

With a lighter spirit than I've had in days and the heady flavor of chocolate on my lips, I head home.

Want more *Outside the Lines*?
Sign up to get the latest details on the October 2015 release, plus exclusive early-release chapters!

ACKNOWLEDGEMENTS

In some ways, this book is for anyone who's struggled with the confusion of an abusive childhood, where cruelty is often disguised with devotion. For some, though, it's an even odder mix of mental illness, neglect, and poorly executed intervention.

While romance is known as a "churn-'em-out" genre, I daresay that's inaccurate. Many of us choose to share truths and personal stories that are better served within the bounds of fiction so they can reach a larger audience. When we see pieces of ourselves in a story, we're reminded that others understand the inner dissonance that comes from complicated worlds for which we carry a legacy we never chose.

So for those of us who've been there and/or support those who have, we are not alone. Never underestimate the value of your survival—it's through doing so we have the chance to overcome, regardless of how long the journey may take.

As always, there are many people to thank in the creation of a book.

My editor Patricia D. Eddy, to whom this book is dedicated. I'm not sure how we managed to take so long to meet up, but either the stars aligned, or we're all destined for some scary karma ahead. ;) Thank you for being my rock throughout the process…and for standing with me during my battles with InDesign. I may be scared, I may be weary, but I am not broken—you will bow, Adobe. One day, you will bow.

My proofer and bestie Audrey Maddox, who puts up with my changing deadlines and bizarre hours. She's used to my crazy…and she's always up for more. Thank God for her attention-to-detail. Smooches—and I love you.

And Jane, my first reader pretty much every time, damn her. She always manages to weasel my first draft out of me—something I swore I'd never do! But she cheers me on and believes in my writing. You can't ask for a finer supporter or a more beautiful soul than this woman. Love you.

I am spoiled with incredible early readers, including Beth U., Linda S., Becky S., Amanda Y., Jeanne O., Amanda W., Kristin S., Rachel M., Kathryn D., Gina S., Fiona H., Karla H., Rachel B., and JillyG, and anyone else I missed! I am honored that y'all are willing to test out the goods and give them a pass. You rock—thank you so much. I look forward to writing many more for you.

Last, and certainly not least, are the awesome folks who support (read: put up with) the dedicated writer.

Samantha K. Williams (author S.K. Wills) always has an encouragement to offer and kindness to pass on, and I'm so blessed she's in my life.

David E. McDonald, the best roommate I could ask for, who always makes sure I have clean underwear because… DEADLINES. Laundry can wait, right?

William D. Prystauk, my phenomenal husband who often has to duck my passionate tirades, adjust to my overcommitted schedule, and sneak in kisses while I'm on ADHD-overload. More than I can promise, my love.

ALLY BISHOP, AUTHOR

When you do something effortlessly and people commend you continuously, you have found your gift.

That's what I tell people all the time. And it's true.

I get story. I always have. I started writing when I was 8 on a Smith Corona (the electronic kind — I'm not THAT old). I wrote stories in every spiral notebook I had. Eventually, I graduated to a Mac (yes, I'm one of THOSE people). I imagined new worlds, emotional conflicts, and HEAs while I waited at stoplights or wandered the grocery store. But here's the thing: I didn't just dream it up and write it down — I critiqued what I read. I knew when ideas were good, and when they stunk. I ran writing groups, judged creative contests, and eventually got two graduate degrees in writing. That's right: I love it that much.

So here I am, years later, writing kickass heroines and

devastating good guys, along with some mystery and vampires thrown in (I promise: THEY'RE COMING). And what's really cool? I do what I love. Wanna write a success story for your life: I promise you, that's it. Do what you love. And hopefully, you can make a living at it too. That's the golden ticket, Charlie.

And chocolate doesn't hurt, either…

Find me at www.allybishop.com, and feel free to email me via my website (look for the "Contact" tab). You can also discover more of my talents at Upgrade Your Story.
Thank you so much for reading *Tracing the Line*! If you have a moment, please leave a review on your favorite book websites.

Made in the USA
Middletown, DE
16 March 2016